ENIGMATIC PILOT

ENIGMATIC PILOT
A Tall Tale Too True

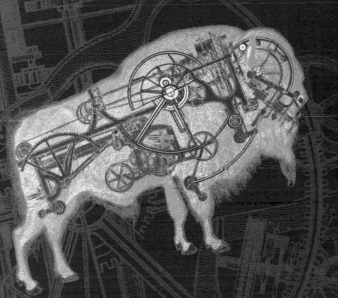

Kris Saknussemm

 BALLANTINE BOOKS · NEW YORK

A Del Rey Books Trade Paperback Original

Published in the United States by Del Rey Books, an imprint
of The Random House Publishing Group, a division of
Random House, Inc., New York.

DEL REY is a registered trademark and the Del Rey Colophon
is a trademark of Random House, Inc.

LIBRARY OF CONGRESS CATALOGING-IN-PUBLICATION DATA
Saknussemm, Kris.
Enigmatic pilot: a tall tale too true / Kris Saknussemm.
    p. cm.
ISBN 978-0-8129-7417-1
eBook ISBN 978-0-345-51902-3
1. United States—History—19th century—Fiction.   I. Title.
PS3619.A425E55 2011
813'.6—dc22   2010042113

Printed in the United States of America

www.delreybooks.com

9 8 7 6 5 4 3 2 1

Book design by Simon M. Sullivan

ENIGMATIC PILOT

A U.S. SEVENTH CAVALRY LIEUTENANT WITH THE UNGAINLY NAME of Mortingale Todd peered through his government-issue field glasses across the steep-sided flash of frothing ditchwater that on his still crude reconnaissance map had no name, and now seemed to be running much higher and faster than when he had arrived at the bank only moments before.

As a passable scout and a skilled surveyor, his attention focused first on terrain, and beyond the many thoughts that were passing through his mind—principally the threat of a Sioux arrow ripping through his gullet and the likelihood of ambush (just the concept of ambush)—he was forced to accommodate a very unsoldierish, or at least un-surveyor-like notion that the landscape he was confronting was changing before his eyes in a way that he could not quite pin down. "How odd," Todd mumbled to himself (and whenever he used the word "odd" he was made uncomfortably aware of his name and memories of childhood heckling).

Rapidly rising ground always raises questions in a mapmaker's mind, and the young point man for his division was beginning to get consciousness-raising ideas that he felt were unmanly and demonstrated the lack of internal discipline that his father, back in Turnip, Illinois, had warned most of their neighbors about.

Indeed, they brought to mind a whole tribe of concerns and speculations that he had been doing his young man's best to suppress. Most of these circled their horses around the question of what he and his unit were doing in such a beautiful but hostile place—which now seemed to him to be simultaneously dishearteningly barren and lushly blooming. What were they *really* doing?

On the surface, it appeared to be a scout mission for the United States government. Investigation of further routes for railroad development—Indian reconnaissance and possible negotiation and/or a show of military presence, if not force. He acknowledged in a loyal, simple soldier way that his outfit's brief was not limited to one specific objective. General intelligence gathering would cover everything about the Dakota or Sioux people's movements and mood (and numbers, of course), along with more information about the land itself. Better maps. More detail. Weather. Wildflowers, even. Maybe.

Of course, there was the implicit and inevitable goal of acquiring more land from the Indians, or at least more control of the land—for naturally there was not going to be any more land made. Who could do that? He accepted this underriding purpose for sending organized military forays into the frontier. To push the frontier west and, ultimately, to dissolve the barrier. This was the infest destiny of America.

But then there was the shadowy factor of the organization calling itself the Behemoth Mining Company, which young Todd did not warm to at all. Back at the fort it had been undeniable that there was some relationship in play with this body, and he could not help but wonder what the true nature of it was and how the chain of command was supposed to work. Acting on behalf of such an enterprise seemed to run counter to his understanding that he was in the employ of the U.S. Army. If the Seventh Cavalry could be dispatched to represent the interests of a private mineral consortium, what other errands were his comrades in arms running—what other fortunes were they protecting? It niggled at his Turnip-born sense of the sovereign independence of his government. It made his government feel less his.

There were also the rumors—rumors not just about gold but also about some other kind of mineral hidden in the Black Hills. He had heard one of his cohorts in the mess tent muttering about a meteorite mountain just waiting to be dug up under the buffalo wheat. Other whispers suggested that it was not a mineral at all that they were seeking information about but some living thing that had not yet been described. Todd did not like this kind of talk. He felt it was not good for morale, especially his own. Unsubstantiated scuttlebutt about some unearthly substance sought after by a mining giant or some kind of creature unknown to science were not among the reasons he had joined the military.

Much worse than these stray yarns and tomfooleries, however, were some of the other things he had heard mumbled under the canvas of the latrine, between bunks, and under saddle cinches—vague, meandering remarks about things that had been seen and experienced, things that never were and could not be. Unnatural lights and sounds. *Things.*

But what outright got his goat were the scenes and interceders that he had himself witnessed. Of what tribe, for instance, were the supposed "scouts" who had arrived so late that night at the fort? They looked like none of the native peoples he had seen in the Territory, or anywhere else for that matter. He could not help but wonder what region they were native to. And what had become of the men—some of whom, presumably, were fellow soldiers, as well as mountain men and lone trappers—who had observed the strange phenomena sufficiently directly to report it, if only in dry, desperate whispers?

And why in God's name was this area not better mapped already? From the point of view of his particular skill, this seemed the most unexplained matter of all. Cavalry divisions had been passing through for years—hired Indian trackers and raiders, outriders for the railroads, hunters working for the government, ant lines of brave and greedy settlers, prospectors, renegades, religious pilgrims, and certainly a few small teams of well-armed scientists. How else had the mining companies formed any plans? By all the rights of reason, he should have been braced in the saddle holding a much more detailed and accurate map.

Pleased initially as he was to have some sense of discovery and a chance to demonstrate his capability, it seemed outrageous to him that he had no more than what amounted to a stick-in-the-dirt scrawl that had been acquired not from a past scout mission or any approved federal expedition at all but from a saucer-eyed man he guessed had been a deserter in the War Against the South and had fled North and West to live with mountain lions and night spirits—whatever could stand his stink. That the wretched fellow had expired on the armory floor of the now distant fort at the end of some sort of epileptic fit shortly after unwrapping the sweat- and whiskey-stained excuse of the map did nothing to inspire further confidence.

No, there was something not right about all this. Something was at work in this region, between the Badlands and the Black Hills, that did not follow the pattern he had been accustomed to. Before he had crested the rise and come upon the creek, which was not where it should have been according to the map, or anything he knew about topography, he had had a creeping intuition that there was some presence in this area that posed a far more dangerous threat than any Indian war party.

Now, staring with rock-hard pupils through his binoculars into the wave of subalpine early-summer gaseous green snow grass, he knew with a solar plexus–compressing pressure that he was right. As his old chum Claudius Speerwort back in Turnip would have said, he was "shit certain."

But before we consider what it was in his binoculars that

had brought his gastrointestinal system so to the fore (and there is nothing quite as paralyzing—except perhaps a stroke, a heart attack, momentary blindness, or a pulmonary seizure, all of which he felt were impending), we need to understand that he was not just some young upstart in a stiff blue uniform a long way from the nearest outpost of encroaching civilization.

He knew a great deal about the biting scent of nitrogen in good soil. He knew how to shoe horses and maintain tack, and how to get an ox to budge and not bolt. He had shot his first pheasant with a turkey gun when he was but six, and he knew the perfect temperature for a root cellar. He had a fine eye for the constellations, and the sight of blood did not faze him. He made an excellent and not overly offensive-smelling liniment from fish guts and mallow, and he could recite no fewer than twenty verses of the King James Bible (one of which was on his tongue just then). He was decent on horseback, acceptable with a saber and a rifle, and superior at navigation, having taught himself back in Illinois. This practice, combined with his innate geometric leanings, had led to some not inconsiderable precision as a surveyor. Plus, despite his still tender age, he had savored and been scared by something of the bigger world beyond his father's farm, including more than a whiff of Lavinia Thorndike's bodice and at least a hint of the ravages of war—the War Between the States, in other words. (Was a truer name ever given a conflict?)

While too young in his crick-back father's eyes to avoid his duties on the land at the eruption of the violence, he had finally risked being nailed to their barn door like a squirrel skin and run off ragtag-drummer-boy fashion to join what had become more a river running against him than one forging south and high. It was by then a tide of blood and a tide of terror spilling back northward. What he actually saw to the south was more the flotsam-let's-go-get-some aftermath of the crisis, but it forever dispelled any youthful fantasies about the nobleness of battle. All too much of it would never leave his dreams.

He remembered a starving boy stealing an amputated limb from a surgeon's tent to gnaw. The horrors were as common as the bullet-flecked tree trunks, and no one took any notice. Some of those he watched, skulking and limping through burned-out orchards, seemed more machine than human—beast mechanisms escaped from some delirium. He could remember thinking to his young self, War is an excellent way of hiding deformities and criminal behavior. It is a harvest of madness.

Now, that may seem like an unusual thought for a young turnip-and-potato-growing lad who longed to ride horses and draw maps to have, but there you have it. War as camouflage, and a means of harnessing the energy of widespread psychic disorder. Perhaps young Todd was drawing a bigger map than he realized.

In any case, all these diversions and perversions streamed through his mind on the edge of that overly exuberant rivulet because of what he could not escape in his field glasses. Because of who or, rather, what he saw, relaxed and waiting for him as if his arrival had been long anticipated.

He was looking at a still young man of around thirty, not much older. He was not an Indian—it was hard to say his breeding—and he was mounted on a donkey, but a donkey that was twenty hands high. The man wore some kind of military costume, but unlike any Todd had seen before. It was not a Civil War uniform. Nor was it was some old Mexican uniform from the war of 1845. When he looked more closely, he saw that the emblem on the man's chest depicted a wheelbarrow with flames rising from it. On the man's head was a kind of hat made from the pelt of a skunk. Then, to Todd's astonishment, the hat stirred and the young cavalryman realized that the skunk was still alive! The man was wearing a live skunk—like a hat. And a very ceremonious headdress it appeared, too. The acid in Todd's stomach roared like the creek.

In the Man Beyond's rifle sheath was a firearm that appeared to be made of glass and in his belt, like a saber, hung a weird-shaped hunting horn, while on the pommel of his saddle perched a powerful pure white gyrfalcon.

The thing Todd found unaccountable was that the man, the skunk, the hunting bird, and the donkey all waited as blithely as could be amid a large herd of smoldering black bison, the biggest Todd had ever seen. Even standing still (and as if at attention), the massive horned and hump-shouldered animals looked more like fur-draped locomotives than even gargantuan ungulates.

Then, through the field glasses, Todd watched as the man raised his arm. The bison did not react, but the falcon flung itself into the air with a strength that Todd could feel all the way across the creek. Beating its wings ferociously, the raptor soared up over the grassland and came at him. The horse soldier was so surprised that he nearly dropped his binoculars. Faster and harder the fierce white bird came, so that Todd was compelled to reach for his Colt revolver—but then, by God, the man on the donkey waved at him!

Todd got distracted and had to duck as the falcon plucked his hat clean off his head. Unfortunately, in veering to escape the clutching talons the lieutenant slipped out of his saddle and fell on his ass, which startled his steed further and made him see red for a moment. (In fact, the falcon had nicked him.) By the time he was seated astride his spooked horse again, staunching the faint trickle of blood from his hairline, the man across the creek was holding his hat. The man then offered the cavalry officer's brim back to the beak of the bird.

This time the falcon swooped out over the creek and released the hat into the water. Todd let out a slight cry at this, for reasons he did not understand (and felt ashamed about), and watched as the hat and all that he symbolically associated with it surged off into the current.

Needless to say, Lieutenant Todd was discomposed by these events and blew a blast on his bugle to signal Sergeant Scoresby that it was time to come forward with his supporting battalion, which was poised for action about three-quarters of a mile away. Scoresby's men answered the call, but to Todd's dismay, so did the falconer. He raised the eccentric hunting horn and blew a deep, rich tone from it, more primal than symphonic—with amazing effect.

There had been no bison on Todd's side of the rushing creek before then that he had noticed—and it is very hard to overlook a huge herd of potentially deadly mammals. But there were now. More than he had ever seen, and he had by that point seen a lot. He was hurled from his horse. He felt his intestines contract and his breathing stop, and then the cowardice of gratitude—for the flood of brutes had turned in the direction of Scoresby's approach, as if on command, and begun to pound their way toward the advancing line of soldiers, who had yet to make visual contact with this fantastic scene but could no doubt hear the vibrations. Faster and harder the monsters picked up momentum, rumbling toward the hapless horsemen like an avalanche of muscle. My God! thought Todd in panic. They'll be trampled!

But Scoresby and company had turned tail and begun retreating for all they were worth—for their split-second assumption was that Todd, being closer to the rampaging herd, had already been more or less obliterated. Later, a search party would be sent out to recover his mangled body. Scoresby had a very cut-and-dried approach to decision-making, with his own survival ranking very high. He rode like the proverbial wind.

Todd, meanwhile, was too unhinged to have a strategy just then (perhaps ever again). He was relieved, of course, not to have been ground into the grass, but he was also perplexed by the lack of dust in the air in the wake of such a torrent of hooves and horns. He had, as noted, never seen such large bison. And he had never seen so many bison of any size at one time. But he had most assuredly never seen so many bison of any size disappear so fast. That concerned him—for a fleeting moment, almost as much as the dawning awareness of how alone he now was. For a man used to knowing and paid to know where he was and where others should go, he was now acutely conscious that he had no idea that he could trust anymore, save that others should not go where he was just then, and that he would have been very happy to be elsewhere—anywhere else. Even Turnip.

Nevertheless, he tried to compose himself in accordance with his military training—recalling as much the words of his scoffing, colicky father as those of his remote and safe captain. He had to meet the situation, whatever presented itself, with some semblance of dignity and astuteness. He had, after all, been chosen for this post and this particular assignment. He took stock.

No horse. Comrades scattered. And . . . and . . .

If the bison that had materialized on his side of the creek were surprisingly no longer in sight, the others across the way were still very much in position. To Todd's utter consternation, they were now sitting as if awaiting instructions. Each and every last one of them was turned to face the man with the falcon, like expectant children waiting for a storyteller to commence.

The young soldier was forced to conclude that he was in the single most awkward, irritating, and sheer shit-frightening situation he had ever been in. But he was wrong, for the next moment brought about a change of mind. A loss of mind, he feared. He had thought that the land across the water flow had been steepening, as impossible as that seemed. All too soon, however, he became convinced, because a ridge formed above and behind the man on the donkey . . . and others appeared. Not ridgelines. *Others.*

He had been prepared to see at any given moment the silhouettes of a Sioux scout party, but he was not at all prepared for the vision he was having now, still sprawled on the ground where he had fallen. The surveying and engineering training he

had, his whole Turnip-raised practical hog-and-potato background, forced him to classify the arriving visual information as
a delusion—some pathetic personal breakdown in perception
and courage. But the more he gasped openmouthed at them,
the more foreboding his surmise became: he was confronting
something—or, rather, things—that really were there. The
shock waves of this realization shot him to his feet.

Appearing on the emerging hillcrest was a spiral chain of figures arranged in a kind of military formation, he presumed—
but what kind he could not say. A severely worrying kind. There
were Indians—Sioux and other tribes he could identify. There
were also Negroes, but not dressed as any he had ever seen.
They wore bones . . . and bright colors . . . and . . . there seemed
to be some women, too. Various colors and races. He had never
seen females arrayed for battle—if that was what this was.

But there were others . . . people like he had *never* seen . . .
hairy and dressed in animal skins. They held implements in
their hands that he did not want to know about. He wanted to
know less than nothing about those who were beside them.
These could not be said to be standing, because they seemed
still to be forming, as if out of mist. They had a human form,
but it did not hold steady. There was an ungodly transparency
to them . . . and a profound blackness, too, like empty portions
of the night sky called coal sacks. While he could make out individual outlines, these seemed to oscillate and blend, so that
there was a forbidding aura of compositeness about them—like
a crowd made of fog and glass that became something else.
Something whole.

What stood grouped beyond them—this was more than his
mind could take. They were not human and never would be or
had been human. Some he might have said were creatures
from the past—beasts that he at least could imagine having
roamed the land long ago. Others he could only think were
creatures from a dream. Or a nightmare.

The one fragment of Army-trained thinking that remained

was the slack-jawed, goggle-eyed question "What kind of troops could march against *this*?"

He felt his being sag with the energy drain of it, and when he was able to blink again and hold his trembling head up, the forces across the water had receded and he was once more faced with the man from out of time, or mind, whoever or whatever he was, and his more familiar and comprehensible menagerie.

This sparked a sudden renewal of will and boldness in young Todd. Perhaps what he had seen come forth had been mere illusion. "Buck up," he said to himself—or tried to say. Yet what he heard in his mind but not in his own usual inner voice were the words *Real enough, Lieutenant. Real enough.*

The man on the donkey then produced what looked like an Indian blanket, white with a zigzag lightning pattern. This he tossed into the air, but it did not fall back to the ground. It rose and seemed to dissipate, becoming larger but diffuse. Seeing it against the sky made Todd aware again of how blue the sky was. Not a cloud on the horizon.

Now there was a cloud, for that is what appeared—and appeared to drift toward him. The blanket that had seemed to vaporize had re-formed thick and puffy, like those first little cumulus masses that are the harbingers of big thunderstorms. This sculpted single white cloud wafted over the creek until it was overhead. Over his head. Then, like a door opening, it let out a river of its own. Drenching, sopping, unstopping rain.

Todd, in spite of himself, tried to step away. He tried to run away. He did not mean to run, it just happened. He soon realized that he was weaving and darting like an idiot—trying to escape the damn targeted rain! It was appalling and reminded him of trying to avoid the missiles of rotten apples that a bully back in Turnip had smacked him with. He had not thought of that incident in years.

This was humiliation of another magnitude altogether. No matter where and how he dodged, the cloud remained immedi-

ately overhead, the pillar of single-minded precipitation sluic-
ing down. Against all his ambitions as a soldier and his deepest
aspirations as a man, at last a cloud of another kind burst inside
him and he began to cry, tears streaming down the length of his
face, mingling with the raindrops. He finally stopped stone still
and let the crying possess him. There was nothing else to do.
He realized that he had surrendered.

This had a calming effect. A translucent ribbon of prismatic
light formed before his eyes, and he pondered whether or not
he had pissed his pants. The pressure of the rain seemed to
soften in response. The downfall became gentler and gentler.

He stared out through the glistening webs of slowing water
into the rainbow obscurity before him, his heart thudding and
his throat squeezed shut, wishing fervently that he had taken
his father's advice and stayed behind the plow in Turnip, and
not ventured forth into the wild Indian lands of the frontier—
and definitely not into the more terrifying wilderness of this
other frontier that he had stumbled upon, which before his
dead-sober eyes shimmered with a dreadful surmise that he
knew he would never forget for as long as he was allowed to
live.

He glanced up and saw the cloud explode like a smoke ring.

The man—the Master—gave a nod and once more sounded
the spiral horn. The bison that had been on Todd's side of the
creek, that had charged off in the direction of Scoresby's ap-
proaching column, had all melted away. Todd realized that
he had not given them or Scoresby and company any more
thought for what seemed a very long time. But all those bulky
grazers still in view now rose with a communal murmur and approached the creek—and then entered the water in ponderous,
measured, military order.

In one enormous, sploshing, swaying, horn-to-tail double
row of meat and hide, the lines of bison heaved into the current
and formed a bridge—a bridge composed of living wildness. A

bridge of composed wildness. A bridge he knew that he was meant to cross.

And yet he could not bring himself to move. He could not. He would not.

Noting this hesitation, the young master of the realm released the falcon once more. Todd watched it gracefully bank and swerve toward him. He planted his face in resignation and his feet in hope—that it would plunge at him at full speed and end this insane ordeal. But it stalled, with perfect coordination, just above his head, like a visual echo of the tormenting rain cloud, and then came to rest upon his shoulder.

Then he saw—he fathomed—to his deepest mortification and yet inestimable delight that the bird of prey was not a bird at all. It was a device. A piece of ingeniously integrated machinery more beautiful than anything he had ever seen. Yet it seemed so very, very real. So alive.

Was it an unthinkably clever but tragic copy, or was it something else? He could not say. It was no clockwork gewgaw, however well made. He had no category handy—no technology of mind to call upon. And the more he examined it, the greater his discombobulation, adoration, and anxiety grew.

He grasped that the Master was somehow able to control the device—flying it like a kite without a string. But it did not behave like any kind of kite. It *behaved*—not just obeyed. It had presence. And then and there an entirely new category of thought and existence opened before young Todd, because he saw that the falcon was neither a fabulous machine nor quite a creature, although it seemed more like a creature than a machine.

It was an expression of the mind of the man on the other side of the creek. A direct expression that intermingled with his own. The cavalryman recognized that how he thought about the falcon changed the falcon. He could make it seem more mechanical—a trick of some arcane industry. He could also appreciate its wild, living aspect. It changed as he thought about it. It was both more a compelling creature and more a sophisticated machine than he had at first conceived—than he could conceive. Thick walls between categories and distinctions began to dissolve. And he heard a voice, very distinct but unthreatening in the air around him: *Come join me, Mr. Todd. Learn the secret of what you think of as the truth.*

He let out a jet of wet flatulence in his long johns, which seemed so hot and itchy now that he could barely stand them. Then he stepped forward. By the time he had hoisted himself and begun to crawl across the tail-whisking, flyblown bridge, which snorted and shifted beneath him but still held firm and steady, any thought of Scoresby and company, or the Army that he represented and which was in theory bound to support him, was as far away as his horse. He did not want to look in the direction of the man awaiting him in the stretch of raw meadow beyond. His focus was to hold his sphincter clapped shut and to hope the falcon claws that remained fixed to his shoulder did not strengthen their grip.

Then, in midstream, he had what he felt was the strangest series of imaginings yet. If he had seen phantoms and phantasms before, and been confused by their palpability, he now had an idea that the beasts beneath him were not there at all. They were not simply bigger and more numerous variations on the falcon; they were something else. He was wiggling on his hands and knees across thinner air than he could breathe.

The resistance of the beasts' backs altered as this idea formed. He felt himself squishing and sliding. He had to keep going.

At the slightest hint of doubt, the bridge of skins began to fade beneath him and he felt as if he were falling at first—and then rising—for instead of a bridge of bison across the creek he saw blood-damp acres of their rotting carcasses. Miles of buzzard-picked skeletons. Miles and piles. And, between the heaps of maggot-writhing tissue and sun-brittle bones, white people in alien costumes wandering oblivious, as if in a ritual. As if in a trance. Some ate food that looked like toys. Some talked to themselves or to little boxes. There were people in the little boxes, and the remnants of bison black with flies. Mounds of skulls. Crows and bones and tribes of souls—white people in bright colors and all the ground around black with dried blood. There were endless little pictures for sale, like pieces of a puzzle that no one knew how to put together. So many little pictures and little voices and little faces and little boxes filled with a noise like that of black flies. Wheels turning—wheels upon wheels driven by a hum, like the furious buzz of black flies in a box.

He had to keep going. He knew that if he did not keep his head he would fall either into the creek or into some deeper fit of madness than he was in already. He had to keep his head, and so he thought of his lost hat, imagining where it was—how far it would travel, what would become of it, what people would think. What did people think? He had to keep moving, just like his hat, which by then was very far downstream, bobbing along in the water the way it seemed to have drifted away from him in time. For time is a kind of river, it is said.

Which, to some, might well raise the question of where one goes when that river is crossed. Maybe time, if we could apprehend it, is nothing even like a river.

And perhaps Mind is not something we think with our brains that we possess and somehow are, and yet can lose in moments of calamity like a hat, but rather something both within us and beyond us, ever open to discovery . . . like a dark and shining territory . . . fertile, haunted, and filled with possibilities. Of all kinds. Of all kinds. The young dumbstruck officer kept crawling—hearing again those silent words: *Real enough, Lieutenant. Real enough.*

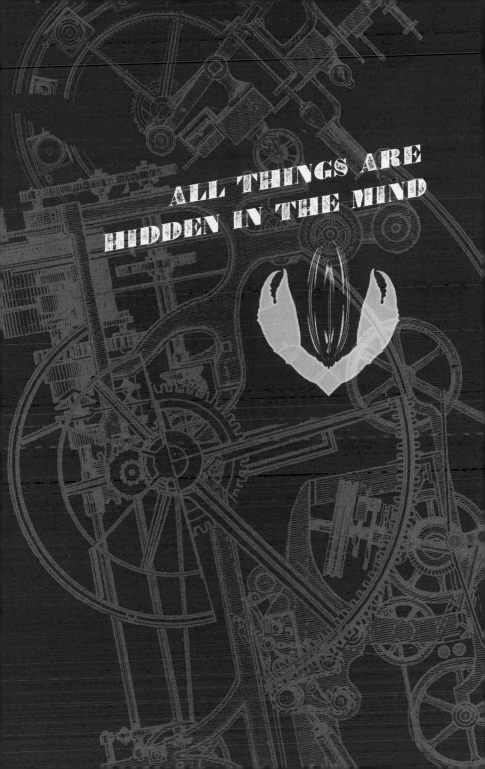

ALL THINGS ARE
HIDDEN IN THE MIND

CHAPTER 1
Time of the End

WHERE DOES THE TIME GO? THE YEAR IS 1844. KARL MARX IS IN
Paris playing indoor tennis with Friedrich Engels, who has just
authored *The Condition of the Working Class in England.* In
Iceland the last pair of great auks have been killed, while in the
booming and embattled United States the first minstrel shows
are packing in crowds in the East, as former slaves Sojourner
Truth and Frederick Douglass lecture on abolitionism, and
hosts of eastern white folk are packing up and heading west via
the Oregon and Santa Fe Trails. War looms with Mexico, the
lunatic bankrupt Charles Goodyear will receive a meaningless patent for the vulcanization of rubber, the shrewd bigot
Samuel Finley Breese Morse takes credit for inventing the telegraph, and a deluded mob murders the deluded visionary
Joseph Smith, Jr., and his brother Hyrum in a jail in Carthage,
Illinois. Many people are asking themselves, "What hath God
wrought?"

One such individual in Zanesville, Ohio, was just straggling
out of a peculiar iron sphere, about the size of three B & O
hopper cars, which sat balanced in a cradle of railroad ties
ringed at a distance of ten feet by an assemblage of timepieces
that ranged from hand-rolled, graduated beeswax candles to
sundials of various descriptions, a tribe of hourglasses, and an

assortment of borer-eaten cuckoo clocks—along with a once dignified but now gaunt and weather-faded grandfather clock that leaned into its own shadow like an old coot trying not to nod off in the middle of a story.

The bantamish man of apparently mixed breed wedged himself out of a fire grate–size hatch in the sphere and fished a pocket watch from his overalls. The watch casing was silver, but it had the dirty, worn fog of lead now. Still, the gears and springs gave out a satisfying report, as loud as the grasshoppers in the grain bin and as strong and regular as a healthy heartbeat.

"*Hephaestus,*" he heard a woman's voice insinuate.

The name mingled with the call of the clocks, which began to chime and ping and cluck, not quite at once but close, followed a silent moment later by an answering echo from inside the sphere, which caused the man's paprika-colored face to brighten for an instant. He heaved himself down to the ground, mopping his slick scalp with a handkerchief, and glanced up at the slanting August sun.

"*Hephaestus . . .*" he heard his wife, Rapture, call gently again.

The man, who was now standing in the circle of timepieces, looked scrawnier than the bulk of his cranium would have suggested. A scarecrow that had turned into a blacksmith, you might have said, and this would not have been far wrong. His name was Hephaestus Sitturd, and he was indeed skilled as a blacksmith, as well as a wood turner, cooper, tinker, and carpenter of great ingenuity (but no discipline); he was also a middling gunsmith, a dedicated fisherman, a maker of moonshine, a spinner of yarns, and a rhabdomancer (water diviner) of some repute. His white father had been the master mechanic responsible for the operation of a large cotton gin in Virginia until a religious vision prompted a change of career to Baptist preacher, a vagabond calling he set out to pursue with his son Micah Jefferson Sitturd, following the loss of the boy's mother to peritonitis. This led to various digressions as a keelboat pilot, dance-hall tenor, tent boxer, and garrulous rainmaker. Along the way he met a half-breed Shawnee woman who was related to the great Chief Tecumseh and fathered another son, to whom he gave the name Hephaestus because of one slightly clubbed foot.

This clubfooted boy was the man who now stood in the Ohio sun beside the hollow iron sphere he had forged and hammered together himself. The rainmaker minister and his half-Indian bride were long dead, and Hephaestus had been left with their crumbling ruin of rabbit-weed farm on the outskirts of Zanesville, overlooking the Licking River. Half brother Micah was believed to be a Texas Ranger who had taken a Comanche wife, but Hephaestus had not heard from him in years. His family now consisted of his wife, Rapture, and their son, Lloyd, and they were such a blessing to him that he thought of little else— save his inventions.

Unfortunately, he was afflicted with that American misconception that the world was in constant, dire need of a better mousetrap, and that he was just the man for the job. He had, in fact, invented several different kinds of rodent traps (over fifty at the time), as well as a series of wind-driven bird frighteners, an automatic fishhook, a foolproof tree straightener, a hand-operated drum-cylinder motion-picture machine (which had been dismantled by the local church matrons because he had made the tactical error of demonstrating the capability with some rather bold Parisian postcards that a man in a marmot hat had sold him in Cleveland), a flyswatter that could also be used for toasting bread, as well as a wide range of outside-the-box ideas for things like disposable dentures and the creation of a pigeon-winged federal postal system.

The mania had started innocently enough, as such things often do, when he was still a wet-behind-the-ears young boy and his father had come home wounded from fighting in Benoni Pierce's Light Horse Company at the Lakes in the War of 1812. Laid up as he was, the old man could not go fox hunting in the Moxahala Hills, which had been his great passion, and so was forced to sell his beloved hunting dogs—or would have been forced to had not the young Hephaestus hit upon the idea of using the dogs to run a drum treadmill to power the drill for gun boring. Gunsmithing became the family's primary source of income until the father died of pneumonia.

Now, years later, the sphere was by far Hephaestus's most ambitious undertaking. It had exhausted all his resources as well as his family's finances and patience. Yet he was intensely proud of it, although he knew there was still much work to be done—and so little time. Time was the problem, for the sphere was not simply a hollow iron ball. Oh, no. It was meant to be a refuge, a shelter, an ark—the Time Ark, he called it, or, in sour mash–fueled moments, the Counterchronosphere.

Although not a full practicing Christian, he had become influenced by William Miller, the numerically minded New York State farmer who had worked out that the world was soon going to end or that Christ would return, depending on your point of view. Miller, who based his theory on the biblical books of Daniel and Revelation, supported by calculations from Ezekiel and Numbers, had taken to sermonizing and lecturing at camp meetings back in 1831, and had since become a national and indeed international celebrity, with several newspapers devoted to spreading the word of imminent advent and hopeful paradise for the worthy.

Believing firmly in mathematics and partially in the Good Book—and being superstitious about his wife's name and undecided about the question of "worthiness," Hephaestus had become a default Millerite—and a very worried one at that. After all, a comet had been spotted in recent times, and just the year before a dairy farmer in Gnadenhutten had found a cow pie in the shape of the Virgin Mary. Clearly, the world was working up to something decisive. So Hephaestus had turned the bulk of his attention to the problem of how to escape time and so shield his loved ones from doomsday.

Many exceptional minds and more than a few competent engineers would have been daunted by such a challenge. But not the Sitturd patriarch. When not hobbling between the forge and the distillery shed, he pored over both engineering pamphlets and Scripture, devotional tomes and Mechanics Hall literature—anything and everything he could get his hands and mind on to help answer the eschatological call.

However, with the revised countdown on to the Lord's Return (the original Miller prediction had put it in 1843) Hephaestus was forced to admit that the technical issues were still troubling. In the evenings when he sat watching the fireflies blinking in the pea patch—his wife, Rapture, brewing some extract of wolf mint, dressing buckskins, or working at her spinning wheel; his son, Lloyd, cataloguing his trilobites or dreaming of his twin sister, Lodema, who had died at birth—doubts would overcome Hephaestus. It was when these doubts took their darkest form that the sphere grew hopelessly heavy. Gleaming in the sunshine now, it appeared to him to be cumbersome beyond all description—ridiculous—so that all his reckonings, all his research, shone back in mockery from the surface of the hot metal.

"It needs to move," a boy's voice announced. "Time is a vibration. So the Ark must vibrate in time with Time—to become transparent."

As remarkable as it may seem, the speaker was none other than his five-year-old son, Lloyd, and as the boy spoke a wishbone and paper airship wafted around the door of the barn. Powered by miniature spindlewood propellers and guided by rudder wings of dried bluegill fins, the delicate machine floated above the goat pasture, then around the barn, and finally over the peppergrass that surrounded their corncrib house, landing intact just beside the man's mangled foot. Hephaestus looked at the airship in dismay and then over at Lloyd, the craft's designer and fabricator, knowing that the ingenious trinket had been constructed in but a matter of minutes.

The child's inventive life had begun in the cradle (or so it seemed to Hephaestus). In addition to a hyper-accelerated acquisition of language skills, although small physically, the boy's manual dexterity was unnaturally adept while he was still theoretically confined to the old kindling scuttle that had been converted into his bassinet. His curiosity was inexhaustible, and by the time most children are just beginning to make sense of a rattle and how to move from all fours to wobbly legs, young Lloyd had already demonstrated an almost disturbing grasp of the principles of basic machines: the lever, the wheel, the pulley, the inclined plane, and the screw—even the mysterious utility of gears.

Inclined to wander, as well as to disassemble and reassemble anything his little hands touched, not long after his second birthday it had become necessary to remove him from the house and install him in his own dedicated section of the family barn, where Hephaestus kept his tools and maintained his blacksmith's forge.

Here the father had designed a kind of labyrinth to keep the boy's insatiable sense of experimentation occupied (and also to keep him somewhat protected from the prying eyes of visiting neighbors, whose dry, thick Zanesville tongues took to wagging whenever anything, let alone *anyone,* out of the ordinary crossed their paths). This combination of protective and distractive measures proved to have remarkable consequences.

What to other parents might have seemed a rather dangerous obstacle course of materials of various kinds (the debris of Hephaestus's own inventions, miscellaneous bits of scrap metal and lumber, spare tools, and the like) provided yet more spark to the boy's intellect and hunger for creation. To the blacksmith's astonishment, the miniature minotaur embraced the labyrinth and began turning it into a working machine of its own unique kind, so that he was soon in no sense constrained by it but using it in the prosecution of new discovery and manufacture.

"If I didn't know better," Hephaestus said to himself, "I'd say that he had somehow a very good idea of what a first-rate metal shop, carpenter's barn, and apothecary's formulary looked like."

It was not long before the supposed labyrinth become laboratory and workshop began to produce its own strange offspring—articulated puppets, for instance, brutish in appearance, perhaps, but subtle in their capabilities.

By the time Lloyd was four, he had produced a functioning aeolipile, a steam-driven monorail that ran from their house to the barn, a crude family telephone exchange, and an accurate clock that needed no winding. A rocking horse had turned into a simple bicycle, and a giant slingshot had propelled a meat safe over the river. The boy had even experimented with the use of primitive anesthetics while performing surgery on various farm animals. No wonder Hephaestus felt threatened—and the need to keep his son's innovations under wraps wherever possible. Zanesville was like that.

Lloyd Meadhorn Sitturd had hair the color of rye grass, skin the color of river sand, and green animal irises that gave the impression that they saw more than ordinary human eyes saw. There was nothing childlike about him other than his size. His vocabulary was already immense, and his mathematical ability was that of a savant. (When Judith Temby, the wife of the dry-goods-store owner once remarked, "The tree is best measured when it's down," the boy replied bluntly, "You don't know much about trigonometry, do you?")

After spending a single Saturday with Mr. Fleischer, the knife sharpener, he could speak passable German. The same was true for Norwegian and Spanish—and, even more remarkably, Chinese, as Hephaestus discovered following the boy's visit to the laundry shack down by the carriage bridge. From Hayden Zogbaum, the prodigy absorbed four full years of Latin and Greek in just four afternoons, in return for supplying the former parson with a serving of pork cheese (an Ohio delicacy made from the head, tongue, and jowls of a young pig, boiled with marjoram and caraway, poured into pudding molds, and eaten cold).

The boy's most profound aptitude lay in the area of mechanics—an innate understanding/curiosity regarding how things worked: windmills, water wheels, animals, insects, flowers. He was forever noticing and diagramming, taking things apart and putting new things together.

Though his father's inventions failed to blossom, they ensured that Lloyd was provided with tools, problems to solve, and, above all else, a pathologically optimistic climate of possibility, which was a good thing because the little schoolhouse in town had very little to offer even an intelligent child, let alone this one.

The first exposure to the sod kickers' children of Zanesville had brought instant ridicule upon him—and an undisguisable degree of contempt in his heart for their bacon-brained doltishness. Every time he got a question right, his fellow schoolchildren (some of whom were five years older) despised him more. Every time he encouraged the teacher to contemplate more interesting questions, a look of horror and fear passed over her face. It was not long before whispers and rumors about the "legend boy" began to spread throughout the town and the surrounding hamlets—and the parents became committed to their earlier wisdom of keeping the boy as sheltered from the community as possible. After all, with such a pronounced capacity for self-education, not to mention the special knowledge of his parents, would not he be much better off? Would not they all be? Small towns are notorious for their tendency to scythe down the tall blooms—and if the bloom is small and young, how much keener the edge of the blade! The problem was that such a retreat could go on just so long. Zanesville, like many, many towns across America then, was rife with reform-minded women who were intent on "education" and "civilization," without the slightest clue about what either entailed. The Sitturds knew it was but a matter of time before pressure was brought to bear to drag Lloyd once more back into the glare of the local school, however little good it would do him, and however much frustration it might bring. And they were correct in thinking that they had something to offer him within the border of their own property.

Complementing his father's anvil-and-plumb-line orientation was his mother's organic sympathy with nature. A gifted herbalist, healer, and midwife, Rapture Meadhorn was well up on biology, generally—specifically zoology, entomology, botany, and pharmacology. It was said that she knew things the Wyandot Indians had forgotten. And she was inventive in her own way, too. She had pioneered a form of acupuncture and a remedial massage technique that had worked on subjects as different as a Clydesdale mare and a Columbus socialite—not to mention cultivating some esoteric personal abilities, including, possibly, continuous orgasms and short-distance telepathy. (It was also believed that she could talk to ghosts—like Benjamin Dumm's sister, who had drowned in a tank at the tan yard.)

Rapture was the proud and voluptuous daughter of a Creole cane farmer from the Sea Islands, who had been born into slavery but had proved himself too shrewd for his plantation masters and so was freed. He left the islands and headed west, joining forces with a trapper who traded pelts in Kentucky. The trapper had a daughter who had been raised to be a "granny woman," a cross between a root doctor and a witch. The girl was as pretty as a wildflower and as randy as a river pirate, and the freedman ended up eloping with her, fleeing north to Ohio to escape the father's Hawken rifle.

Rapture's parents had both died in a cabin fire when she was fourteen, but she survived and grew up clever and curved. Although she referred to herself as a "pumpkinskin" around the family, she was in fact blessed with a creamy complexion that had but a hint of nutmeg to suggest her colorful ancestry. Her speech she could pinch into everyday white diction, but with family and friends she would lapse into the rich rhythms and eccentric phrasings of the Gullah language she had picked up from her Cumberland Island father. (If you were to speak to her, she might in private say that you had "cracked e teet.")

She eventually fell in love with the crippled but competent Hephaestus, not yet knowing about his predilection for inventing. Twins were conceived in a wild lovemaking session in the moonlight down on the Great Serpent Mound to the south, but the girl, Lodema, had died at birth, leaving them with just one child, Lloyd.

While Hephaestus struggled to earn a decent and regular living and to keep pace with his son, Rapture made money for the family with her valerian preparations, royal-jelly pills, and medicinal teas (along with two hardy crops of rich, green marijuana every year). Women from all over the river junction came to her for relief from menstrual discomfort, and more than a few men, once they'd conquered their embarrassment, sneaked out to meet her in the tent she set up down by the riverbank to enhance or resurrect their virility.

From her, young Lloyd learned how to build a cage to protect the gooseberries from the bullfinches, and more desperate arts, too, like that moment after the mallet had slammed the skull, when you had to stick the pig in the throat and catch the blood to make black pudding. He liked catching the blood.

In an era when it was not uncommon for a child to know how to pluck a squab or tap a sugar maple, Lloyd was a bright, burning candle in a class of his own. He reveled in all the intricate detail of life, sketching, with sliced sticks of charcoal made in his father's furnace, surgically precise drawings and technical determinations of the tensile strength of an orb weaver's web or some new design for a water turbine.

So all Hephaestus could do when the boy passed judgment on the progress of the Time Ark was the hardest thing of all:

consider, once again, that he might very well be right. He shifted on his clubfoot and stepped between the hourglasses. This time he heard his wife instruct him to water down the burlap walls of the earthworm farm. "C'mon," he called to Lloyd.

After seeing to the earthworms, father and son scrubbed up at the pump. They found Rapture hanging curds and whey with rennet in a muslin bag in the cool room. Waiting for them on the kitchen table was a plate of smoked trout with horseradish sauce, asparagus sprinkled with lemon juice, and a small pitcher of beer.

Rapture let the two males take a few bites before opening her mouth in a grin.

"Berry well, den . . ."

Hephaestus cleared his throat and shuffled in his chair.

"Yass?" she purred.

"All right," he confessed at last with a shrug. "I heard you. Even inside the Ark."

"T'engk Gawd, man!" Rapture declared in her spiced Gullah. "So yuh woan be sayn me peepul be fass."

"I don't know how you do it. It's some kind of witched-up ventriloquism."

"Na treken, man. Tru!"

"Magic," her husband insisted.

"Kerse tis! Kerse tis!"

"Well, I heard you all right." Hephaestus shrugged again, thinking to himself that it was sometimes surprising that he could understand his wife's more conventional style of conversation, let alone her conjure-woman mind talk. As the man of the house, it was difficult for him to accept that his son had developed a speaking form of telegraphy, while his wife, when the "sperit" moved her, could communicate without any apparent means whatsoever. Yet he loved them both dearly. Whenever Rapture grew excited, which was often, her accent and her idiomatic expressions became as thick as Spanish moss, and then he would become enraptured with her all over again. And when he thought of what Lloyd might one day accomplish—if they could survive the Second Coming—he felt profound stirrings of father-bear pride that more than offset his jealousy, most of the time.

Glancing at the boy now, Hephaestus noticed that the child had crumbled some soda bread and rolled it into a human form, but with the antlered head of a stag.

"Where did you get the idea for that?" Hephaestus asked, wiping his chin.

"In a dream," Lloyd replied, thinking of all the strange dreams that seemed to possess him. *In catacombs, creatures beyond description shrieked—living sphinxes with forked tongues and stinging tails . . . serving maidens with the heads of ibises and dogs . . . hooded cobra women . . . things with wings and scales . . . and a hulking silhouette with the legs of a camel, the barrel-chested torso of a rude galley slave, and the awful engorged head of a baboon.*

Monkish shapes in tornado-green tunics shuffled behind frail curtains of snakeskins where embalmed and dismantled bodies sprawled on stone tables. Jackal-faced children could be seen gnawing on carcasses in a cage—and in transparent jars floated lilies that looked as if they had sprouted tentacled nerves . . . frogs becoming human embryos, or almost human . . . while in slick, drained pits there lurked soft machine reptiles and enormous tube worms made of meticulous spun metal wrapped in an oozing tissue cultivated in vats.

In the hotter months the boy would flail about in his corn-shuck bed, so that Rapture took to giving him a hypnotic that she made using melatonin. While this remedy often controlled the sleeping problem, it did not alter the periods of black depression the boy could slip into, or the relationship he carried on with his dead twin sister, whom, of course, he had never known except in that blind amphibious time within Rapture's womb. He often said that his sister was right beside him, and if asked whether he could see her he would answer that he could feel her and that he could smell her. Like licorice and rain wind, he said. Rapture, who had grown up with revenants and hairball oracles, was more accepting of the boy's beliefs—but Hephaestus argued that imaginary friends were one thing, an imaginary dead sister something else.

On top of his already radically superior intelligence, the boy's mood swings and bouts of disjointed behavior did not make his socializing with other children in Zanesville any easier. That he would have some kind of seizure or burst into tears without reason, or perform some inexplicably cruel deed, made any hope for his schooling awkward and trips into town tense. Hephaestus even steered clear of other Adventists (although in truth he was worried about them learning about the Ark).

The family was just finishing their repast and Hephaestus was about to inquire further about the boy's ideas on the Ark (a discussion he hoped would lead to an opportunity to suggest the possibility, at least, of returning to school in autumn and spending more time with children his own age before this became an issue that the reform marms would raise), when their fifteen-year-old redbone, Tip (short for Tippecanoe), woke up under the porch and began howling lugubriously to announce the arrival of Philomela Ogulnick and Edna Vanderkamp, the town's two most notorious gossips and exactly the kind of women the family most dreaded seeing. Neither parent was surprised to look up and see that the lad had skedaddled.

Hephaestus had an inkling that the women were an advance party sent out by the men of Zanesville he was in debt to, while Rapture was pretty sure they were on a mission regarding Lloyd's lack of attendance in school (a tedious waste of time for him and all too often a torture of taunts and spitballs to boot). As it turned out, they were both right—and what was more, Philomela's Joe had eaten some horse chestnuts by accident and had the trots and would Rapture recommend barley water?

Of course, little Lloyd gave all this not a thought, slipping off in his mind the moment he had slipped away from the house. He went, as he always did in such situations, to his secret refuge beyond the veronica that Rapture harvested for her soporifics. The main Zanesville cemetery extended from the old Wheeling Road to Mill Run and was surrounded by chestnut trees, but this was a different, eldritch sort of place. The sprinkling of humble graves dated back only to the days of Ebenezer Zane and John McIntire, who had founded the town, but Lloyd liked to think they were much older. The tombs were marked by unnamed lichen-stricken stones but they filled him with admiration and awe, for he saw them not as stones but as doors to the world where his sister lived and played, whirling about in a singsong game until, dizzy and laughing, she would fall to the ground, looking up at the sky. That was how he pictured her— blowing dandelions to bits and tying satin ribbons between the alders and the buckeyes to give shape to the wind.

Rapture had kept Lodema's burial plot a secret to herself— an old superstition she inherited from her mother—but Lloyd identified the cove with his lost twin and had taken to grounds-keeping and decorating this secluded burial ground as a monument to her. Over the months he had made pinwheels, windmills, weather vanes, and whirligigs of all descriptions and from all materials (junk wood, scrap metal, animal bones, hunting arrows, and scavenged glass), placing them in precise arrangements, so that each blade fed off the breeze created by the others, however slight or gusty, creating a constant energy exchange that he believed would please and invigorate his sister's spirit—perhaps even, one day, call her forth to join him.

You could not have stood amid the Lilliputian wind machines and not be moved by both the ingenuity of their design and the air of devotion that drove them. This was what the boy had meant in speaking to his father about the need to vibrate at a harmonic angle to Time. Here, among the crude graves and ever-moving vanes that defined and responded to even the stillest air, Lloyd Meadhorn Sitturd felt the kind of peace that deep motion can bring.

But so deep was the meditative state he fell into that afternoon, he did not hear the figures creeping toward him until they were upon him. Jeering and stamping, and smashing his beautiful wind ghosts and carnival-colored prayer wheels! It was Grady Smeg and the Marietta Street Boys, a snotnosed gang with a fondness for decapitating geese and pelting the wood alcohol–imbibing town drunk with rotten pears. The moment they realized they had happened upon Lloyd, who was maybe half the size of any one of them, the brats knew what they were going to do—and when they were close enough to strike they charged him with a whoop of derision. Their fear and hatred of the boy was well known throughout the town and shared by more than a few adults. Not even a Jew should be able to do long division in his head, they thought. And the gift he gave to Mrs. Czeski—a butternut squash with the likeness of her own face—was unnatural. The boy was bright, people agreed, but maybe it was the light of the Devil.

Such sentiments did not fuss Lloyd much (although his parents, who were already sensitive about their mixed blood, were plenty troubled). He had never known otherwise, and most of it was just talk. Still, he was not so foolish now not to run—or, at least, to appear to run—and he led the Marietta Street tribe through a stand of poplars into an area that Hephaestus had used as a scrap yard until he found a black cat dead of snakebite. Lloyd had since turned the wasteland into a maze of chicanes and surprises.

Booth Tanner and Buddy Pitch took the first hits, tripping a crawdad wire that hurled a corn-popping basket full of fishing shot at them. A smaller but more tightly wound hairspring catapult almost plinked out Mason Griddle's left eye, while Andy Cudrup took a palm-size flywheel straight to the forehead. Then Willie Best and Oscar Trogdon stepped on partially buried potato rakes and knocked themselves silly, while Ezra Fudge planted both feet in a concealed wagon wheel and just about broke off at the ankles. The gang halted or retreated in disarray at this point—all except the hellion general, Grady Smeg, who lumbered after Lloyd with the sticking plaster from his father's strappings hanging off him.

Even with his comrades downed or deserted, Grady could not grasp that he had been led into a trap. Lloyd had covered the hole with a big swath of burlap floured with dirt and sneezeweed. Grady never suspected a thing until he landed with a thud. Everything hurt, and blood filled his mouth with a taste of iron and chagrin.

As predicted, Lloyd came home as the lengthening shadows of dusk were spreading out over the goat pen, where Hephaestus was milking the two long-eared Anglo-Nubians for the second time that day. The boy stopped by the well and washed his face, but his father could tell that something was up by the way he flustered the Indian Runner they called Cotton Mather (because the duck would often alight on the roof of the forge and "preach"). The bottle-shaped drake squawked with indignation and wobbled off to what green ooze was left of the pond. The boy marched on toward the house without pause. Such behavior worried Hephaestus more than the fits and the invisible friends. There was a scary side to the child. Normally, Lloyd was kind to all creatures, a lover of animals—but things could change, as Hephaestus had discovered to his disgust and anguish one afternoon when he interrupted the young student in the midst of a vivisection of his once favorite Flemish giant rabbit, Phineas. The sounds the creature made, its long soft ears drooping—it was something he would never forget. The boy's punishment had been to dig a regal tomb for the creature and to tend the grave every day. But Hephaestus could never get the pitiful rabbit's eyes out of his mind.

That evening they ate a pale celery soup served cool and a

spatterdock-and-spikenard salad tossed with crushed corian-
der. Not much was said. Then, just as they were washing up
and Hephaestus was thinking about getting out of working in
the garden and enjoying some parsnip wine, Lionel Smeg,
Grady's ham-fisted father, rattled into their yard in his logging
cart, old Tip crooning balefully.

"Sitturd! Yoo get that boy-a-yoors out here!" Lionel commanded.

The elder Smeg had been top bulldog in the local sport of
brawling until his love of the "Democratic comforter" had
made him too stout for such exertions, so he had taken to imbibing vinegar to reduce his flesh, and this was now ruining his
stomach.

Lloyd was already out in the settling dust, patting Tip and
staring defiantly at the blood pressure–red visitor, whose cheek
bulged with chewing tobacco.

"Somep'n's heppend to ma boy!" the man blubbered. "This
one done somep'n to 'im!"

"What?" asked Hephaestus, limping out of the house.
"Lloyd? He's only a runt compared to Grady. What do you
mean?"

Lionel's face blotched even redder at this reminder of the
physical inequity of the boys, but he stammered on, lolling the
tobacco wad around in his mouth like a second tongue.

"Thair 'as some shenanigans. Lloyd heer done somep'n dirty
to Grady. Now we kaint fine 'im."

"What's this about, Lloyd?" Hephaestus asked.

The boy looked back with his green eyes and said, without
blinking, "Grady plays with some rough boys and in some rough
places. Remember when Corky Niles almost drowned in that
sinkhole? I'd be talking to them if I were you, Mr. Smeg."

"Oh, yoo wudd, wudd yoo? Yoo little freak! Let me tell yoo
what they said—them that weernt too humped up to talk."

"That'll be enough, Smeg," snapped Hephaestus. "You don't

come to my house to insult my family. You can do your own foaling and blacksmithing—your business isn't wanted anymore."

"Zat so?" the big red-faced man snarled. "Well, wee'll see about that. Be a shame if that furnace-a-yoors was to set yoor barn on fire. Happens in summer, yoo know."

"You threaten me and my family and you'll be the one who's sorry, Smeg. I'll get my wife to put a spell on your pecker and it'll never rise again!"

Hephaestus gave a snort of laughter at the expression on Smeg's face, for he knew that Rapture's hoodoo reputation held sway over many people in town. As hard as Smeg talked, he would be worried now. You could see it in his eyes.

Lloyd's eyes, meanwhile, shone back in the deepening sunset like lightning bugs.

"All right, Sitturd. But yoo're bad business and the word's out. I reckon yoo'll lose all that high an' mighty come winter. Yoo kaint git by on what that witch cooks up firever."

"Good evening, Smeg. And don't drive those nags too hard—I can see you're about to bust an axle."

"Pshaw!" Smeg exclaimed, and spat out a stream of stringy black juice that landed on his boot before hauling himself onto the wagon and whipping the two rib-stickers out of the yard.

After Grady's father was gone, Lloyd said, "Farruh, do you think he'll try to burn down our barn?"

"Naw," Hephaestus mused. "But I reckon we should keep an eye open for trouble. He's right when he says there's folks in town who are mad with me about money."

"Because of the Ark?" Lloyd asked.

"Yep," his father said, sighing. "And the self-pulling planter . . . and the milking glove . . . and the air wheel. You don't know anything about what Smeg was saying, do you? I get the impression that you did have a run-in with them Marietta whelps."

"They chased me. I got away."

ENIGMATIC PILOT | 39

"Did they?"

"What do you mean?" asked the boy, his eyes flaring.

"I mean did you lead them into some snare of yours? That deer noose 'bout broke my good leg."

"They tripped a catapult," Lloyd answered.

Hephaestus wanted to believe that that was all there was to the story. It was enough to accept that his son even knew what a catapult was, let alone how to build and wire one.

"All right. You go lock up the hens and tend to Phineas's grave. I'm going to help your mother bring in some beans."

Hephaestus did not see that the boy headed back to the well and then off toward the no-man's-land where he had led the stooges to ambush. And he did not know how many other secrets Lloyd had on hand, from wild-turkey snares he had modified in size to deadfall netting and fermentation jars full of nasty things ready to fly up off a hidden springboard. The pit Lloyd had captured Grady in was an example of taking advantage of a natural asset. The hole was part of a seam of clay and had been excavated years before. All that had been required was to disguise it and lead the quarry there. Lloyd set down one of the well buckets to pick up a few stones along the path. A long summer twilight was settling in, full of whip-poor-wills and spoon frog chirping. But there was another sound as Lloyd approached the pit, which he had covered with a section of mite-ridden thatching. A plaintive moaning.

"Any bones broken?" he called, lifting the thatching.

"Hey!" bellowed Grady from below. "Yoo li'l weasel. Ah'll git yoo! Let me up! I mean it!"

"I'm sorry, Grady," Lloyd answered. "You need to learn a lesson. Three days should do it."

"Three days! Yoo lissen to me!"

Lloyd dropped one of the stones he had picked up along the path.

"Aw! Sheet! Damn thang hit me."

"I have plenty more," Lloyd assured him. "Now, if you want

some water—and believe me you do, then you're going to say you're sorry for what you did to my windmills."

"Sorry? Yoo goddamned mongrel!"

Another stone fell, with similar results. Then another.

"Hey! Hey! All right, Ah give. Ah'm sorry for breakin' up yer toys."

"They're not toys," Lloyd hissed. "They're *machines*. Reverence machines—and they're not for hogswill like you to touch or even see. You're going to learn that lesson over the next three days. And you'll never breathe a word, because you'll be so ashamed. Now stand back, I'm going to lower a bucket of water. I don't want you to die of thirst before the lesson's over."

The creature in the pit was very quiet now, bruised and hoarse and completely bamboozled. But the sploshing bucket came down, as promised, on a length of rope, and there followed a slurping sound of relief.

Lloyd waited for the darkening hole to go almost silent again before he unbuttoned his britches and pulled his peter out. At first the trickle of fluid provoked no reaction. Then, when it dawned on the boy imprisoned below what was happening, the yelping was louder than that caused by the stones. But there was no one else around to hear. Lloyd had made sure of that.

A New Kind of Animal

GRADY SMEG DID INDEED LEARN A LESSON, AND LLOYD WAS COR-
rect in his prediction that the bully would say nothing. The
story that went into circulation was that Grady had been angry
with his father for a licking and so had lit out on an adventure.
Then, dirty and tired of living on carp and branch water, the
dumb nut had slunk home to take his medicine, only to find
that his razor-strop father was too glad to have him back to
whip him.

Lionel Smeg never made good on his threat to burn down
the Sitturds' barn, but he did stir up a hornet's nest about the
money Hephaestus owed, and racial tensions that had long
been suppressed began to simmer. The lame inventor's creditors knew of his Millerite leanings and the talk around
Zanesville began to suggest that maybe the oddball blacksmith
was going to run up as big a bill as he could, and then he and
his brood were going to drink hemlock on the End of the World
Day (a sensational fear implanted by anti-Adventist forces
throughout the country), leaving everyone he owed high and
dry.

The autumn harvest came early, and a snake-oil salesman
showed up in a bright wagon covered in pictures of rajas and
angels. He said his name was Professor Umberto, and he had

two assistants, a squirrel monkey in a black swallowtail coat, and a fancy house woman he called Anastasia, who wore a champagne-colored ball gown. She never said a word, but strutted around playing a squeezebox and helped out with the magic tricks he did between pitches. She was especially clever at disappearing and then reappearing someplace else. Even Lloyd was impressed by that feat. He also liked the way her bosom always seemed ready to burst out of her gown.

The professor sold Indian root pills, white-eye alcohol in bottles with a picture of Saint George skewering a dragon on the side, and some expensive jars full of stuff for men that he claimed came from "the business end of a Bengal tiger." It didn't help or heal anyone for long, of course, but it made a big dent in Rapture's income. Every time Hephaestus went to town he got cold stares and dirty looks. Legal-looking notices started piling up, and a man who claimed to work for the town council came out to the property and prowled around. After that, Rapture started insisting that anyone who rode past the house was a "puhlicitor." It was humiliating and posed severe problems for the completion of the Time Ark (which, with so many people poking around, Hephaestus was forced to roll inside the forge). The mood grew darker as the days counted down.

Hephaestus had held such high hopes for the Ark based on the "magnetic properties" of the material, some of which had come from bits of what he thought were meteorites that he had unearthed. Lloyd's concept was to build a spiral track and to mount the sphere on a shaft set into a swiveling frame so that it was capable of spinning 360 degrees, driven by the force of an elaborate series of sails and windmills. While rotating thus independently in one axis, the frame, which was attached to flanged wheels that sat on the rails, would propel the entire sphere along the spiral track.

Between comments from his father regarding gyrostats and luminiferous ether (which Lloyd was disinclined to believe in), the boy produced a number of foolscap pages with fine duck-quill blueprints and infinitesimal calculations, as well as several attempts at working models—along with the pregnant speculation that "seen from the sphere, the past might lie beyond the future." But it was all to no avail. The iron of the Ark was hopelessly heavy and dense. It was all wrong. Everything.

Frustrated to the point of violence, Lloyd could not work out how to maintain a constant speed along the track, or the more difficult technical issue of how to sustain the spiral motion of the sphere without the source of power, the sails and windmills, impeding the action. He needed more and better equipment—more tools, more resources—more than what the rank barn and the dust trap of Zanesville had to offer. Ever so much more. In his young heart, he raged for precision instruments, a proper assembly space, books (books!), ideas, materials, money—and, most of all, someone to talk to, someone who truly had his wits about him. Someone of his own ilk.

Most infuriating of all, he thought he had seen the solution in a dream. Hephaestus was sympathetic in this regard. How often had he woken just before their rooster in a helpless panic at the fading vision of some grand new invention! That was what had happened to the High Speed Chicken Plucker and the Musical Millet Grinder.

Being a blacksmith who fancied himself an engineer, and a modern man of fire and steel, once he had recognized the need for power and motion Hephaestus felt that the question could be resolved with steam, and so set about collecting boilerplate and rocker arms and designing a shining piston-driven beast that looked like a cross between a grasshopper locomotive and a calliope. But the harder he worked and scratched his head, the thirstier he got for elderberry brandy and the more he realized that time was running out. Their money already had. He was trying to build the prototype for a new form of power, and day by day the hourglasses emptied themselves, the beeswax candles burned down—and one day the grandfather clock fell over in an exhausted clash of chimes, glass, and splintered wood.

But where it all came unglued once and for all was the fair to mark the reopening of the local school (which Mabel Peanut, the earnest Episcopalian school marm, dubbed "A Celebration of Progress"). The owners of the flour mill, the pottery factory, and the new tool-and-die works had all chipped in to offer a cash prize in honor of Brazilla Rice, the first brickmaker in Zanesville, to be awarded to the youngster with the best scientific exhibit—with the exception of Lloyd.

Lloyd's exclusion was phrased subtly but unmistakably, based on a condition of entry the family could not argue with: the number of days of school attendance in the past calendar year. No one was in doubt, however, about the real reason. If Lloyd was allowed to enter, there would be no contest. The other children would look ridiculous and the school itself would be revealed for the backwater log chink box of birds and mud pies that it was.

And there was another point at issue—one that no one involved, not even Lloyd, saw at the moment. Although progress was being celebrated, there was an inherent fear of it as well. Throughout all America this was true—but nowhere was that fear sharper than in a realm like Zanesville, which was neither an eastern bastion of culture and emerging convenience nor a frontier town anymore, on the edge of the wilderness. It was a crossroads town, torn between two worlds, resentful and anxious regarding them both.

The Sitturds were stung by the unfairness. The prize money seemed a small fortune to them, and any award for excellence, intelligence, and innovation had Lloyd's name on it—and the whole town knew, despite Hephaestus's efforts to keep the boy's genius hidden. Rapture insisted that they go along to the showcase, anyway, as a matter of pride. Hephaestus agreed but was still so angry and so hurt by what was happening to them that he had to take on a good load of elderberry brandy for the occasion. When it came time, they could not find Lloyd anywhere and concluded that it was perhaps just as well. Why should he want to see what to him was idiocy being celebrated?

A large crowd was on hand at the schoolhouse, some clapping, others gawking sympathetically when Sterling Riddle battled his speech impediment to present a swollen bladder worm that he had cut out of a Poland China sow all by himself. Millie Rambush introduced a charming, novel method of caring for small plants by using eggshells as flowerpots, but then went off on a tangent about where her sixth finger used to be, and how her daddy had removed it with a violin string. Hermione Witherspoon and Lucy Dalrymple had no exhibits. They had cooked rabbit pie for the judges, and as Mrs. Witherspoon pointed out, "Progress is very fine, but you can't throw out tradition." (To which Rapture telepathed to Hephaestus, *"Na, w'ich tradishun she be sayn 'bout?"*)

Caleb Holcomb was awarded the cash prize for his simple but effective idea of installing a Paint Can Hook on his Uncle Shute's ladder. However, when the applause died down something unexpected happened, which would trigger the Sitturds' end in Zanesville.

The "thingum" (to use the cogent phrase of Burgess Fluff) made its way across the floor with a telltale ticking sound and a distinctive wiggling motion. One man, the draper Herman Moody, would have reached for his pheasant gun if he had had it with him (remember, in those days some men refused to go anywhere, including church, without a firearm), but instead he was reduced to shouting, "Jehoshaphat! It's . . . it's . . . a . . . *beaver!*"

And he was right. It was a life-size, fully operational mechanical beaver. Cunningly made of corset ribbing, fencing wire, and the spokes from two umbrellas, with gears and chains cannibalized from a range of devices (including the late grandfather clock), it inched across the floor in a kind of waddling crawl and, every two steps, raised and lowered its tail. The detail was remarkable—right down to the prominent incisors, which took the form of old piano keys.

The arrival of the mechanical creature caused pandemonium to break out (which, among other results, led to Reverend Lightbody's stepping into the rabbit pie). Everyone knew who was responsible and all eyes turned to Rapture and Hephaestus, who had been taken as much by surprise as the rest of them. Lloyd was nowhere to be seen, but in the minds of many people in that room it was his presence that animated the beaver, not the gearwheels and the clicking chainworks. It was just like that little Sitturd to show up the other children, people thought. "I don't want my Andy a-goin' to school with him!" Clara Petersby hollered. "That boy is evil!" Obedict Renfrew pronounced.

Lloyd's parents slunk out of the hall. The beaver was not so fortunate. It was not quite crushed, but it was beaten into mechanical submission. Stalwart Crane, the furnace man at the kiln, had the decency to return it to the Sitturds that evening. He took off his slouch hat in respect when he knocked on their door to hand over the trashed contraption to Hephaestus. Lloyd was hiding just out of sight when the visit was paid.

"I just want you all to know," Crane said. "Not ever-body thinks like ever-body else. I reckon this is—or it was—a damn fine thing. Opened my eyes, it did. Doan you fret about them that says 'the Devil's work.' They're just green with the demon of envy. If I could make something like this, I'd set it loose, too. And the hell with the consy-kwences. This little critter gave me some new hope. I hope it duddn't bring you all more trouble. Try not to let it."

Oh, but that was easier said than done. The next morning, old Tip was found dead in the barn. Most likely it was just chance—the dog was very old and there were no signs of violence. But the timing was suggestive. Rapture saw "homens."

Had one of the infuriated townspeople taken his revenge? The intentional poisoning of animals was not an uncommon way of making a point in places like Zanesville. Lloyd wanted to do an autopsy, but Hephaestus insisted on keeping Tip's dignity and body intact. He was an old dog that had lived a good life. Maybe it was just his time to go. Besides, if anyone was to blame . . .

Despite Crane's good-intentioned support, which would not have been popular just at that moment if it had been voiced in public, Hephaestus felt inclined to reprimand his son for causing such a ruckus when they were in such heavy debt. But the compulsive inventor in him was curious about how the boy had made the creature. Lloyd shrugged, as if there were no more to it than making a daisy chain. He showed no sign of regret, and felt none, although he was angry and depressed about Tip. He retreated into his own labyrinthine section of the barn—the lamentable workshop designed to restrain him, which he had turned into a subtle machine and in which he had constructed the beaver every bit as easily as he said he had.

It was at the burial of dear Tip, with fleas still departing the carcass like the proverbial rats fleeing a sinking ship, that Lloyd conceded that immunity from Time was beyond his present capabilities and Hephaestus announced his plans to curtail work on the Ark. "Let's hope Farmer Miller got his arithmetic wrong."

When the old dog was in the ground, wrapped in his favorite blanket, Hephaestus, Rapture, and Lloyd, with the help of Pegasus, their splay-backed cream draft horse, tugged the Time Ark across the wreck of their farm and, on Lloyd's suggestion, toppled it into the pit where Grady Smeg had endured his enforced therapy.

Lloyd insisted that the moment should not be considered a defeat but a release, and so the family filled the sphere with items that had been important to them during their latest trials. Rapture added some of her root bags, Hephaestus the broken clocks and one of his old wine jugs. Lloyd laid the remains of the beaver to rest inside. It was a kind of time capsule, in the end, and it tumbled into the earth as if it were pleased to be there, free too, at last, reprieved from grand ambition.

William Miller was indeed proved wrong, as many had been before him. October 22, 1844, arrived, and with it the Great Disappointment for Millerites around the world. In November, the dark-horse candidate from Tennessee, James K. Polk, was elected to the presidency on the platform of annexing Texas for the purpose of expanding slavery. Lloyd turned six and had his first wet dream.

But the Sitturds' world kept ending. A cold Christmas came, and the family dined on their last pig and was forced to break up and burn much of their furniture to stay warm. Even Lloyd's airship got laid on the fire, much to Hephaestus's distress.

"It won't be the last one I make," Lloyd said to console him. The old man may occasionally have been miffed at the boy's precocious abilities, but he had always been proud of them, too. Or, perhaps, just in awe.

At last there came a hint of spring. For the Sitturds it brought an eviction notice for failure to pay their land tax, threats of seizure of property and chattels to repay debts—and a gut-shot Anglo-Nubian goat. There was no mistaking that sign. Perhaps Miller had been right after all, at least as far as the family was concerned.

That same week a traveling Methodist minister came to town, or at least a man who called himself a minister. He delivered no sermons. He did, however, deliver a packet that took their minds off all other matters, for its contents were exceptional in the extreme: a small knotted bag of gold, a hand-drawn map, and a letter addressed to Hephaestus from Captain Micah Jefferson Sitturd of the Texas Rangers, dated eight months earlier, from "Forever the Great Republic of Texas." It read:

Dear Brother,

I pray that this missive will promote kind thoughts towards myself. If you have heard little from me in recent years, or if the little you have heard has caused you unhappiness, it is with my regrets.

The fruits of my labors have been few and bitter, but I have at last built for myself a kind of home, a simple property of some three hundred acres that lies halfway between the western border of the Indian Territory and the settlement known as Kixworth, northeast of Amarillo.

Some would think it barren, bleak country, but it has some artesian water and soil that suits a committed agriculturalist experiment such as a hardy drought-resistant strain of cattle. I have named it Dustdevil, on account of the sudden funnels of wind that appear. I have a deed in perpetuity for this land, signed by Sam Houston himself and countersigned by Juan Herrero and the great Chief Buffalo Hump, leader of the Comanches. Of course, no title to any land can ever be secure, especially in this troubled region—and not without heirs. Hence this letter to you.

You are my only living relative, and should anything happen to me I would desire that you take possession of the property. I have found within it something of extraordinary interest but far beyond my poor powers to interpret or explain. My training has been as a soldier, not a scientist. Faced with such a riddle, I am out of my depths.

I know that you are rooted in Ohio and that perhaps you have a family now and a bright, happy life you would be hard put to abandon. But perhaps not. Perhaps something of our father's restlessness, which I seem to have inherited in disproportion, is also at work in your heart. If so, I offer you and yours a chance for a new beginning, *and the guarantee of something exceedingly curious that will stir your excellent mind. If not, then I still ask you, as my brother, to consider coming.*

It is not an easy task I set for you. It is a long and difficult route and not without danger. Yet I still ask. Come, Hephaestus. Beyond my own selfish desire to share something of this life with you before I am gone, I have a suspicion that if you were to take up residence on this property and hold it you would find that it holds more value than I can speak of here. I have enclosed what money I have to offer to help you afford the journey, or to use as you see fit. Set out as soon as you can if you are able, or forget me and carry on with your life with my blessings.

MJS

PS. You may inquire of me at the trading station in Perryton and head south to the Canadian River. A man named Bloxcomb will assist you.

CHAPTER 3

The Necessity of Adventure

HEPHAESTUS CONFIRMED THAT BOTH THE LETTER AND THE MAP were evidence of his brother's handwriting. None of the Sitturds could sleep or eat (which was just as well, because there was precious little for the pot). The proposition that the letter advanced, with its combination of familial support and an invitation to adventure, was, in their current state of finances and mind, irresistible. Still, it left them with what Rapture could not stop describing as a "big'un recishun!"

Despite their avowed intention of mulling over the matter in detail, come the next morning, by the time Rapture had prepared their daily dose of tansy bitters to keep off the ague, Micah's proposal had been embraced by the whole family with the unquestioning conviction that desperation can bring. There was no "recishun" to be made. They had to leave Zanesville. That Texas lay a long distance away, and a war with Mexico could break out any day, did not dissuade them. This was an offer and a request that could not be refused. Not in their present circumstances—and not in Hephaestus's heart, either. There was about the communication a suggestive timeliness and a hint of redemptive possibility that hooked him as cleanly as the sturgeon he used to pull from the head of the falls.

With a door of refuge open, it was their lot "ta tek 'e foot een 'e han," as Rapture put it (which was not a concept that Lloyd thought was sound from an engineering point of view). What to try to salvage was not so clear. The gold that Micah had sent was sufficient to cover only the debts they felt most honor-bound to pay, and, given the financial claims their neighbors wanted to impose upon them, removing any of their remaining possessions would technically have been stealing. None of their farm animals would make it out of Ohio except the draft horse Pegasus, and the one suitable vehicle was an old humdinger night-soil wagon that Hephaestus had traded for a pile of corn-cob coal. The wagon had been airing out among the snares and spring-loaded traps of Lloyd's minefield maze garden all winter, but it still retained a pungency that announced its history well before arrival. No matter. If embarking on a journey to a promised land (however "sabbidge" and under threat) had to be started in a cart that reeked of dung, so be it. Better to risk life, limb, and olfactory discomfort than remain in Zanesville as outcasts and debtors.

They considered rafting down the Muskingum to its inter-section with the Ohio River at Marietta and catching a steam-boat to Louisville and then St. Louis (if they could earn some money along the way). Hephaestus could get work in the cities, and with any luck they could save enough to take a steamboat along the Missouri River to somewhere like Independence and head south across the wild Indian country from there. But the Muskingum was a difficult river to navigate in spring, running high with ice melt and prone to flood, plus unsavory folk were rumored to live along its banks waiting to prey upon the flat-boats and their cargoes of grain, lumber, and livestock. The other obvious alternative was the National Road, or the Old Pike, as it was called—the original interstate—which ran through Columbus all the way to Vandalia, Illinois.

Fearing that their creditors might try to pursue them on so open a route, they opted for the more difficult but less pre-dictable plan of making for Cincinnati overland via the Great

Serpent Mound in southern Ohio, which had been a place of good luck for them in the past—the place where Lloyd and Lodema were conceived, back when nothing but love seemed to be in the air and hope grew like the sparrowgrass. Pegasus and the humdinger could get them that far, Hephaestus felt. After that, they were in God's hands.

They took blankets and oilskins and the drunkard's path quilt Rapture had made. For provisions they took a sack of cornmeal and one of flour, a small side of bacon, a bag of snow apples, one jug of wolf-mint tea, one of homemade whiskey, a bottle of taproot beer, coffee, sugar, salt, some bottled preserves, and taters. They took their old Kentucky rifle and the horse pistol that Parson Shide had used in his famous duel with the alcoholic tobacconist Daniel Christ (who later cut his own throat with a razor in his smokehouse), which Hephaestus had been paid in return for repairing a mill wheel, along with powder and shot, and what Rapture called, "de t'ings fuh mek we libbin'."

In addition to the richness of Rapture's phraseology, they took Hephaestus's blacksmith tools (except for the anvil), his main woodworking tools, an ax, some rope and drag chains, a bolt of twill plus needles and thread, and matches, candles, a lantern, Rapture's midwife bag, and Lloyd's notebook. The rest of his dreams and inventions the boy had to leave behind—but, unlike Hephaestus, he felt that he carried them with him in his mind. All these provisions they loaded on the humdinger, but Lloyd's mind was more loaded still.

Early one morning, while the mist was still rising from the pastures, like the ghosts of all their memories, they each said a silent goodbye to the family farm that was no longer theirs. One last look behind the muddy, rutted road that led either into town or into the woods and the past was gone . . . a final farewell to the animals buried on the property, the vegetable patches, and the shrouded fruit trees . . . to Lodema . . . the hidden Time Ark and its tragic treasure trove.

Even with the promise and the challenging journey ahead of them, Lloyd's mind lingered behind long after the bend that took the farm out of sight. He vowed that he would rebuild Lodema's shrine in Texas. He would one day build a city in her honor—a city of cyclones, so full of energy and life it would be. A place where only marvels were allowed.

If anyone saw the family leave, they didn't shout or wave. The whole countryside had a sleeping, dead stillness to it, so that the wheels of the humdinger and the steady clop of Pegasus's heavy hooves echoed in the mist.

By the time the sun was high enough to burn away the dewy fog, they were on the poor excuse for a post road through the rolling Appalachian foothills of southeastern Ohio, corduroy at the best of times, now sloppy and treacherous with the slow spring thaw.

Calamity after inconvenience beset them as they made their way through pastureland into thin forest and then into rugged stretches of hardwoods. Sometimes they had to chop down small trees and hitch them to the hind part of the wagon to slow their descent down hills (an endeavor that left Rapture "skaytodet"). Skirting creeks and ravines, they passed mounds and prehistoric earthworks. The trees and undergrowth were fleeting with reemerging wildlife—white-tailed deer, gray foxes, pileated woodpeckers, and hosts of woodland songbirds—but they saw few people: an Indian who vaporized into the budding trees and a mean-looking white man in dirty clothes, who looked as if he had been startled answering the call of nature. Whenever they grew tired or afraid they pulled out the letter from Micah (which Lloyd was given charge of) and savored the enticing conundrum of promise that lay ahead for them in Texas—if they could get there.

It was this hope that got them through the woods and back into farmers' fields and pumpkin patches and down to the Great Serpent Mound, which was in what is today Adams County, near the town of Locust Grove. Three times the cart had threatened to overturn. At every moment they expected trouble. But they arrived.

Still, it did not fill them with the joy and renewal they had hoped for. Both parents were shy and bumbling, recalling the passionate lovemaking that they had once known there—that had brought Lloyd into being, and Lodema almost.

Lloyd, meanwhile, went into a deep funk after their visit to the Mound, which Rapture attributed to some hypersensitive connection with his "sperit" twin. Hephaestus was of the view that constipation was the cause, and that a large dose of cod liver oil would help. In truth, both parents noticed that the boy was less fixated on Lodema—as if the connection had been broken by their removal from Zanesville. Perhaps that was a good thing, Hephaestus thought. Rapture was less sure, knowing from her own experience how helpful a relationship with ghosts could be. Lloyd kept his thoughts to himself and said not a word to allay their apprehension. In truth, he did not know himself what bothered him. It was some indefinite form of foreboding—as if they were being followed by something of much greater concern than had ever plagued them in Zanesville.

The rains came and they got bogged down for two days, only to pull free of the sucking mud and resume their journey to be struck with another violent thunderstorm and a lashing downpour that forced them to huddle on what high ground they could find while they watched their possessions get drenched. Several they were forced to leave behind. They had overpacked and did their best to keep their optimism from being ejected, along with soaked salt beef and ruined tea leaves.

Back on the road, a filthy-faced man with a spongy goiter and a woman without teeth tried to beg from them. Rapture made hardtack for them, but they continued lurking about, so that Hephaestus had to take a potshot at them with the horse pistol. By lantern light they discovered weevils in the flour.

The next day the horse pistol wasn't enough. Coming into a clearing, they were surrounded. It was more an extended back-country family than an organized gang of robbers, but robbery was what the interlopers had in mind. As outraged and aggrieved as the Sitturds felt, they were all in silent agreement that it was a blessing that the clan had no more malicious intent, for given the number of them and their pocky, lice-ridden appearance, their desires might have taken a very different and considerably nastier turn.

The leader, a gnarled salt-and-pepper-bearded git with a scar that ran from his left temple deep into his mess of grizzle, spoke in a broken-toothed accent they could barely understand, like a wild hill preacher, directing with a musket a weasel-quick boy of about sixteen and two older men with gopher teeth and eyes like toads, each armed with long, cruel skinning knives shoved in their rope belts.

With an unsettling politeness, they plundered the wagon of food and the best and most important of Hephaestus's tools as three moonfaced women in sack dresses and threadbare shawls, and another fidgety male with an eyepatch, looked on without expression down the long barrels of well-used squirrel guns, and then melted back into the woods as suddenly as they'd appeared.

When it was over, Rapture burst into tears and stamped her feet, while Lloyd's locked jaws clicked with fury. Hephaestus summed up the situation. "We're still alive. Let's keep moving. While we can."

And so they did, making do with what they had left, eating wild game they caught along the way, and pushing hard to get through the hill country.

Easter found them in Cincinnati, or Porkopolis, as it was being called—a booming new metropolis of 150,000 energetic souls, many of them German immigrants, Irish, Scots, and Poles. The family was able to find temporary lodging and employment with a man named Schloss, who made knockwurst and sculpted pigs' heads of offal and jellied marrow. Lloyd's grasp of German came in handy, and he was assigned the task of taking orders and assisting with deliveries. Rapture did laundry and cooking, while Hephaestus got work with the Cincinnati Steamship Company repairing machinery. At night they snuggled amid the pork fat and candle smoke and pored over Micah's letter, which Lloyd kept hidden in his precious bag along with his notebook.

For three weeks they lived above Schloss's meaty-smelling slop kitchen in a frame-house-and-vegetable-plot district running up from the river, where the smell of kettles full of boiling shirts mingled with the fumes of schnapps. The sounds of polka music (which was relatively new then) alternated with the lieder and the occasional hatchet fight. During that time they sold Pegasus and what was left of the humdinger to an Irish-Shawnee giant named Mulligan Hawk. Despite his fearsome appearance, he gave the impression of knowing horses and appreciating animals. Their goodbye to this, their last living friend from the farm, was less moody as a result. Old Pegasus would be looked after—perhaps much better than they would be.

The combined sale, along with a good word from the giant, yielded enough money for rough-deck keelboat passage in the company of a cable-armed Serb named Holava, who carried a bowie knife strapped to his belt that he called a "genuine Arkansas toothpick," and made his living hauling coal, nails, timber shake, and sacks of milled corn to Louisville.

Just over 110 miles of twisting river, it was. Sometimes swollen and foaming around them, other times snagged and vicious with overhang from the banks. The flow could rise three feet in the night, frothing with driftwood, fallen timber, and rubbish. And the bizarre people! Jug-swilling maniacs calling out from fortified bluffs—the last of the beaver trappers drifting like leaves in long birchbark canoes—flatboats covered in skins, writhing with children and clattering pots.

Hephaestus read, whittled, and chewed to pass the time (trying to keep ideas for new inventions from filling his mind), while Rapture would point out to Lloyd the hollyhocks and the yellow spikes of toadflax.

By the time they reached Louisville and Holava had traded in some of their Ohio cargo for a load of burley tobacco and cured meat, Lloyd had filled his notebook with elegant scribbles of ospreys with shad clutched in their talons and an idea for a huge barge to be pulled by swimming buffalo.

But the farther the family got from Zanesville the more strained their sense of family became. Hephaestus missed his tools and his inventions. Rapture missed her herbs and concoctions. Lloyd missed his secret link with his dead sister, and the ability not just to draw things but to make them. Texas seemed a world away. They reread the magical letter and hardened themselves for the next phase of their journey, each of them wondering where the elusive presentiment of deepening shadow came from—whether it came from within them or moved on larger, darker wings across America itself.

There was something in the wind that no one quite understood, and so could not talk about in any of the mélange of languages that swirled around like junk in the river.

The Sitturds were puzzles to themselves even. Were they intrepid adventurers reaching out for the bounty of a new day? Or cowardly bankrupts fleeing like frightened beasts?

It is sometimes hard to tell the pilgrim from the fugitive, just as dawn always has a hint of the gloaming. In every opportunity, there is an invitation to failure and defeat. And in every defeat there is an opportunity . . . for . . .

CHAPTER 4

River of Secrets, River of Mercy

LOUISVILLE WAS A TOWN OF EXTREMES. THE THICK SMELL OF horse piss alternated with gentle sniffs of blooming wisteria. Newly rich planters mixed sugar into their bourbon while slaves hauled tobacco and cotton crops to market, and the streets flurried with open-air stalls that sold live animals along with dried catfish, mud turtles, and skinned rabbits swarming with yellow jackets —a sight that fascinated Lloyd and disgusted Hephaestus (stirring memories of Phineas the rabbit). There was a friend left behind in Zanesville that the family never spoke of, and the blacksmith rather feared that Lloyd gave more thought to the mechanical beaver he had made than to the life he had taken.

Desperate again for funds, the family hocked most of their remaining possessions for food and lodging, and for raising enough money to cover waterline passage on a stern-wheeler called the *City of Paducah* all the way to Cairo, where the Ohio melds into the Mississippi. There they found planks and piers, mule-lined dust streets, and frame houses peering across the river to Kentucky.

Amid hanging sides of bacon and buckets of nails that smelled like dirty rain, the Sitturds negotiated passage to St. Louis on board a paddle wheeler that had been christened the

Festus in a Memphis shipyard but which its prudent new owners had renamed the *Fidèle*. The steamboat was crowded with all manner of unusual passengers, but none who intrigued Lloyd more than the man with the silver hand.

The possessor of the mechanical prosthesis was supposedly named Henri St. Ives and while he claimed to be from Vicksburg, he had the aura of those who habitually obscure their origins. It was at a card table in one of the parlors on the upper deck, surrounded by a stack of coins and greasy notes, that young Lloyd officially made his acquaintance.

The boy had been attracted to the drawing room by the smoky male voices of the players, punctuated by the ping and rustle of money and cards on the thick felt cloth. Once in position, Lloyd had refused to leave, standing so steadfast that the general conclusion around the table was that he was simpleminded.

The game was straight poker, and it was clear that St. Ives's fellow players were becoming disgruntled and a little suspicious about his run of luck. After he swept another pot, several unkind remarks were made, to which the maimed man replied, "Gentlemen, please. Good and bad fortune finds us all in its own time." He then raised his shining left mitt with a flourish and, one by one, the other men at the table grunted their acceptance and chipped in their money.

Another hand was dealt and then another, both won by St. Ives. By this time, one of the men had suffered such losses that the presentation of the artificial appendage and its suggestion of some past catastrophe was no longer sufficient to ease the tension. The man, a plump horse doctor named Fundy, lurched up, almost capsizing the table, and shouted, "I don't know how you're doing it, but I know a cheat when I see one!"

St. Ives remained impassive, save for a lightning wink at little Lloyd.

"Good sir. Here you've been allowed to play at the gentlemen's table, which, given your level of skill, is a gift. Now sit down and wager or make a dignified retreat."

A roped vein in the accuser's forehead began to throb and his skin reddened. "Retreat?"

The blustering quack then drew from his coat a tendon scalpel, which he carried for protection. The lethal nakedness of it gleamed for all to see.

St. Ives's face did not blanch, but his silver hand came alive. With a click like the lock in a drawer, from out of the index finger snapped a dagger that doubled the length of the digit—and then, with a flick of the wrist, as if he were flipping a card into a hat, St. Ives doubled the length of the blade yet again, so that he was able to slice the ribbon that held the man's pocket watch in place without stirring from his chair.

Flabbergasted, Fundy clutched his paunch as if to make sure his entrails had not spilled out across the table. St. Ives laid his cards facedown and nudged the severed timepiece forward.

"Now, my friends, if any of you feel similarly discomfited I am prepared to meet you man to man on the afterdeck to settle this affair with honor. Alternatively," he rasped—and the silver hand clicked and expanded again to reveal a set of razor-sharp claws, one from each finger—"you can learn what justice comes from molesting a helpless cripple. It's your call, gentlemen. I am at your pleasure."

This last remark was uttered through an unwholesome smile that the pudgy accuser would never forget. Faced with such an unexpected display of weaponry, the poker players decided in unison to yield the table, and when their chairs were empty the claw blades retracted and the gambler eyed the young boy.

"You think I cheated? You think me a scoundrel?"

Lloyd shook his head. "You count the cards. You calculate in your head. You have a method. It merely gives you an advantage."

"Hah! Do you know how to play the gentlemen's game, then?"

"I think I do now," the boy replied.

"How do you mean?" St. Ives puzzled.

"I watched. I listened."

"That you did, lad. I could feel your glance penetrating me like one of my own fingers. But have you ever played? Do you know the rules?"

"You just taught me. All of you . . . by how you played," Lloyd answered.

"Posh!" declared the gambler.

"Would you care to bet your winnings to find out?"

St. Ives smiled. There was something about this child, preternatural and unnerving—and yet engaging, too. "I like your manner, lad. Always up the ante."

At this point a burly steward with great muttonchop side-burns barged into the drawing room and jabbed a muscular digit into the gambler's chest.

"See here, charlatan. And don't think of taking a swipe at me with that fancy stump. I don't like your kind. Gambling is only allowed when it's honest and aboveboard."

With that the steward reached out and seized a wad of the notes that still remained on the table.

"Is that your commission for overseeing the play?" St. Ives jibed.

"That's the price a cheater pays."

"He didn't cheat," Lloyd piped up behind the man. "I was watching."

The steward withdrew his finger from St. Ives's chest and whirled around.

"What are you?" he demanded, noticing the boy for the first time. "His hired monkey? A poker table is no place for young'uns. Get along with you! Or I'll throw you to the bilge rats, you little shit."

"I don't know if the captain would be pleased to know you're taking that money," Lloyd returned without moving. "He might want some of it himself."

A spark of anger and resentment flared across the steward's face, mingled with a flush of surprise that someone so young could be both so astute and so matter-of-fact. But the boat's whistle blew just then and some other passengers waltzed by, so that he became flustered and chucked the money back on the table and stomped out.

"Well, Monkey," St. Ives said, grinning. "What a good team we make, eh? Here. Here's your share. Rightfully earned and, from the look of you, rather needed."

St. Ives swiped the notes the steward had returned to the table and stuffed them into the boy's eager hands.

"If you are the savant you appear to be, who knows what we could achieve?" the gambler mused. "As partners."

"Equal partners?" Lloyd inquired. "That's the only kind of partnership I think works."

"Right you are." St. Ives smiled. "There's wisdom in you, too."

And so their little conspiracy began.

There was a sign in the dining saloon that St. Ives enjoyed. It read, IF YOU NEED TO CARRY LARGE SUMS OF MONEY, WEAR A MONEY BELT. AVOID GAMES OF CHANCE ON RIVERBOATS. Thanks to the gambler, Lloyd made a new friend and had something to look forward to other than reading his uncle's letter yet again. He also made some much needed money. His parents were glad to have a little privacy, as their intimate life had suffered in recent times, and so let the boy wander the boat at will. Lloyd, meanwhile, was careful to keep the banknotes he accumulated for helping St. Ives hidden from his parents.

The Sitturds' stateroom was in a sorry state, six feet square with crimson moth-eaten curtains, a narrow slat bed, and a mothball-scented dresser, but it was considerably more luxurious than the bales and boxes the deck passengers were forced to share with animals ranging from horses to chickens, all sheltering among the walls of crates they arranged, and all scrambling for space as cargo and passengers came and went and the manure was scooped.

A blasted and recently repaired boiler (which had scalded a billy goat and one of the crew members) required continuous adjustments and seemed to inhale fuel, so that there were regular and lengthy interruptions to the journey to allow for wooding parties to scour the shoreline. One of the passengers, who volunteered to assist with such an expedition in order to reduce his fare, was stricken with heart failure and had to be buried in a tea chest, while another was bitten by a snake. Then a cow leaped off the deck and tried to swim home to the Illinois side, only to have the bucktoothed lad whose family owned it make the mistake of trying to swim after it. Neither the hefty milk cow nor the overbite boy was seen again.

The fine packet boats operating between St. Paul and New Orleans were famous for their excellent cuisine. This was not one of those. Salt pork, mutton, and boiled potatoes and beans were the usual fare, although wine, stout, porter, and brandy could be found in abundance. Like stage drivers, steamboat captains tried to make the most of the daylight, pulling in toward shore when darkness fell. Dead trees, snags, and sandbars, not to mention smaller craft without illumination, posed a constant threat to travel at night, although most captains would run at reduced steam if the moon or starlight allowed. The crew was a blind barrel mix of Irish, German, blacks, and those St. Ives referred to as "pure muddy." Fleets of rafts, with their cook shanties puffing out greasy odors of fried fish, could be seen en route to the sawmills. Not infrequently, what appeared to be the body of a man or a gassy inflated horse drifted by and, once, a dollhouse with a ginger cat aboard.

Travelers flowed back and forth on the gangplanks in chimney hats or swishing skirts. One afternoon the men had a shooting competition on the top deck, blasting at buzzards circling the remains of a runaway slave who had washed up on a sandbar. The weather was growing warmer and the bugs thicker, sultry nights becoming humid with whiskey and cigar smoke, perfume dabbed to wrists and crotches.

St. Ives was well acquainted with the ship's chief entertainer, a singer named Viola Mercy, a tall buxom brunette whose lavender-scented pantaloons filled Lloyd's mind with notions and cravings of a new and exquisitely painful kind. Thrice a day she performed in the dining saloon of the *Fidèle,* which was laid out around a dance-hall stage with a heavy velvet aubergine curtain. And thrice a day she would sing a song that the boy grew to love.

> *There's a place I know*
> *Where I always go*
> *There to dream of you*
> *And hope that you'll be true*
> *And someday I pray*
> *That you'll find your way*
> *Back to the secret place*
> *Within my heart.*

He became obsessed with the songstress and her exotic apparel: ostrich feathers, silk stockings, lace brassieres. How he wanted to infiltrate her private domain and experience the majesty of this dark beauty. (In truth, she kept a flask of rye in her garter belt and had done as much singing on her back as she had onstage.)

Meanwhile, St. Ives opened the boy's eyes to the larger world, relating to him the news of the day, with its cults of gangsterism becoming political forces—Tammany Hall warring with the Bowery Boys in New York, angry hordes descending on Mormons, Protestant secret societies with names like the Supreme Order of the Star-Spangled Banner murdering Catholics, abolitionists dragged through the streets, slave families broken, the women raped, the men castrated and lynched. St. Ives had dire warnings about what lay ahead, although he himself took no sides and indeed was chiefly concerned about how such turmoil might be turned to personal advantage. "In confusion there is profit, my young friend," he told Lloyd.

More to the boy's liking, however, the gambler let him examine the metal hand. The plates that formed the exterior were made of polished steel, but so well forged that they provided exceptional strength without the corresponding weight. Inside lurked the potential for a fantastic array of implements, from the throat-cutting blades that had appeared at the poker table to a choice of such accessories as cigar scissors, a lock pick, and a sewing kit—not to mention that the miniature compartments could also be used to hold coins or keys, vials of various potions (such as chloral hydrate), snuff, ink, even poison. However, St. Ives was not forthcoming with any intelligence about how he had come by it, until one evening.

It was a close night and a full moon shone down on the river, so the captain had the boiler fired. Lloyd had been encouraged out of the family's cabin to allow his parents some time alone, a practice he was growing more and more curious about. Only the thump of the paddle blades stirred the quiet, so that the occasional sounds of a baying dog or the crashing of a caving bank reached the deck, where he found the gambler smoking a cigar, staring down at the wake.

"You wonder about it, don't you, boy?" St. Ives asked, and tapped a bright ash into the water. "How I came by the hand—and how I came to lose my own."

"I do," Lloyd agreed. "There's no hiding there's a story behind it."

"Well put, lad," the gambler said, nodding. "And well spoken. Like a gentleman. I will reward your discretion. After all, we're friends, aren't we?"

"Partners," Lloyd responded.

"Indeed. Gentlemanly put again. Well. Some people would say I asked to have this done to me."

"You asked for it?"

"I said *some* people would say that," the gambler answered, and his face went glassy, as if he were now looking at something long ago. Then some hatred surged up within him, like a dead log that had been submerged in the river.

"Ten years ago, I used to be the secretary to a very rich man in the East. He valued my memory and my head for calculations. He was a fellow of extreme cleverness and cruelty—Junius Rutherford, or so he called himself then, but that was not his real name, I am sure. Owner of the Behemoth Formulary and Gun Works in Delaware. For himself he made the hand—and others like it. Said he'd lost his own in a foreign war—or with the Injuns or in a sword fight. His stories changed with his audience."

"So do yours," Lloyd pointed out.

"W-ell . . . yes . . ." stammered St. Ives. "A man must be flexible, given the unkindness of fate. But I am inclined to think that he was the cause of his own misfortune. He had the marking of an acid burn on his face as well. My belief is that one of his experiments backfired on him. He was always fiddling with new combinations of chemicals—schemes for weaponry. And other things. Weirder things. 'Better to be the head of a louse than the tail of a lion' was his motto, and if ever there were a fellow to plant the head of one creature upon another he was the one. His estate was like nothing you can imagine."

"How so?" Lloyd asked, certain that he could imagine much more than St. Ives.

"He called it the Villa of the Mysteries, and the name was apt. There were lightning rods all about, and he had hung up effigies around the grounds to keep the meddlesome townsfolk from spying. That and his dogs, a breed I had never seen before and hope never to see again. Gruesome beasts."

"Go on," Lloyd said.

"Well . . . I know this will sound like flapdoodle, but he carried a seashell around with him. Like a polished black conch. He listened to it—as people sometimes do with shells, thinking they can hear the sea. But he did it often and, stranger still, he spoke into his."

"What did he say?" Lloyd asked. "Who was he talking to?"

"I wish I knew." St. Ives sighed. "He spoke in a language I

could never understand. To whom, I have no idea. I assumed he was touched in the head. And I had good reason to think so. The estate had an artificial lake, and on the water he had a fleet of automatic model ships that reenacted the British defeat of the Spanish Armada. And there was a greenhouse full of orchids that looked like they were made of glass, but they were alive and grew. God's truth. He loved books and fine things, but most of all he prized unexplainable things."

"How do you mean, *unexplainable*?" Lloyd asked. There were not many things you could actually perceive that could not be explained, he felt. Even the way the fancy woman with the medicine show had seemed able to be in two places at once back in Zanesville. It was the things that went unnoticed that were mysterious.

"There was a collection of paintings. Flemish, I think," the gambler continued, puffing. "Milky, watery landscapes without much obvious interest—except that over time they changed."

"You mean with the light?"

"No!" the gambler exclaimed. "I mean *changed*. One day a peasant in the picture would be pitching hay, the next day a hay cart would be seen departing—a cart that had not been there before!"

Interesting, Lloyd thought.

"And Rutherford had a huge aquarium that he would swim in himself. He had a kind of vessel built—it looked like a diamond coffin—in which he could stay submerged for long periods of time. He used it to study his electric eels and those jellyfish creatures we call the Portuguese man-of-war."

Lloyd gave a low whistle. He would have liked some eels himself.

"Yes!" St. Ives shook his head. "You see, I would not have been in his service had I not found something in him to admire—and there was much to hold my interest. The trouble was I found too much to admire and ended up taking too much interest in his wife, an auburn-haired beauty with eyes like sapphires."

"You fell in love—with his wife?" Lloyd blurted, but when he spoke an image of Miss Viola rose up in his mind. A glimpse he had had of one of her corsets. It had become confused in his mind with his mystic twin.

"And she with me!" St. Ives replied. "My beautiful Celeste. Never will I experience such bliss in this life again!"

A storm of rage passed through the gambler's eyes.

"Rutherford was cruel to Celeste and ignored her—spent too much time with his compounds and machines. He was also addicted to a narcotic that he manufactured himself. A transparent liquid, tinted a faint blue—like damson plums. He called it Mantike. Every night he would inject some of the foul stuff and slip off into a meditative stupor in his library. But there were other eyes and ears about the place, and when that bastard found out about our sin he drugged me with something—whether it was the Blue Evil I do not know. I woke to find myself secured to a table in one of his infernal laboratories. And I remained awake. No drugs or sedatives after that. There he conducted a little piece of theater involving surgical instruments."

At these words the gambler's body seemed to quiver in the warm air, while Lloyd's thoughts flashed back to his rabbit Phineas. His father was wrong about him never thinking of Phineas. St. Ives spat into the river.

"But then why did he give you this?" Lloyd asked, pointing to the hand.

"Another of his hideous experiments." St. Ives chuckled. "How the nerve connections work I have no idea. But this is not the metal addition that it may appear. I *feel* the hand. It is a part of me, or I a part of it. There are other extensions and accessories that I carry, but the hand itself I cannot remove. I will die with it attached to me. Yet it will not die. And that is perhaps why he enabled me so—as an expression of his power and ingenuity. The rest he did to me was not enough. He wanted a constant, visible, and necessary reminder always before me. To make me forever dependent on his technics. Who knows? Perhaps, for all the agony he inflicted, I may have been lucky not to have been turned more fully into one of his gadgets. I might well be a mannequin whole, and not just in hand."

"I don't understand," Lloyd murmured.

"He was far, far ahead of his time, was Mr. Rutherford. His toy caravels were ingenious, but he was capable of many other feats. Oh, yes! He had designed and built a mechanical manservant. A sort of butler named Zadoc. What it was powered by I do not know, he would not reveal it—but it was not steam. A very handsome but ghastly porcelain face. Gave Celeste nightmares. But he was working on much more complex contraptions still."

"And what . . . happened . . . to him?" the boy whispered.

"I set a booby trap in his laboratory," the gambler replied with a vengeful, melancholy laugh.

"His body was never found. But pieces of another's were. My sweet Celeste. I believe she thought that I was trapped in the fire and was trying . . . to save me."

St. Ives's silver prosthesis flashed in the moonlight.

"I was questioned by the authorities, but I knew enough of his ways to make it look like an accident. And what an accident!"

"But what . . . became of Rutherford?" Lloyd asked.

"Ah! That *is* the question," the gambler said, nodding. "Well, you see, he was not a well-liked man. Almost everything he did he did in secret. He was a hard employer and a recluse who rarely ventured off the estate, and he seemed to have no close friends or immediate kin—other than my poor darling. The neighbor folk all feared him. There were stories about children in the vicinity who had gone missing. Who can say? But the members of the local constabulary were willing to take the path of least resistance. They came to believe that perhaps he had perished in the explosion, too—blown to bits, as I had hoped he would be."

"But you think differently?" Lloyd asked.

"I am certain in my soul that he is still alive!" St. Ives ejaculated. "His will left his estate to some distant relative in Louisiana—probably himself under another name. His business interests were absorbed by a consortium called the Behemoth Innovation Company, and the estate was systematically denuded of all its objets and apparatus."

"Did you investigate?" Lloyd asked meekly.

"Can you imagine me not doing so?" the gambler exclaimed, and then he drew his voice back down low. "The so-called relative now lives abroad, and I have not been able to find a trace of any news about him in any of the foreign papers—I even hired a London detective. Not a skerrick of a clue. As to the consortium, they have offices registered in several cities but there is no information about *any* of their directors. They are but shadows, as near as I can tell. And that is why I ride the riverboats, or one of the reasons— to one day learn something of his whereabouts. He would have a new name, and perhaps a new-looking face. But he is not dead! The hidden may be seeking and the missing may return. Remember that, my young friend. Beware, if you should ever cross paths with a man a few years older than I—with a hand like this, or some such invention. He would have found a way to make a better one by now, devil take him. Who knows what he has learned how to do in the years that have passed since what he did to me?"

With a vehemence Lloyd had not seen before, the gambler heaved his cigar into the river and spun on his heel, heading to his stateroom. Nothing more was said about the mutilation or the vanished designer of the mechanical hand, but the creatures and contrivances of the lost Villa exerted a pronounced fascination for Lloyd that was outweighed only by his ripening interest in Viola Mercy.

She said that she came from Maryland but, like the gambler, she seemed a child of the river and the road. Bawdy and quick-tempered, in the boy's presence she became demure. When she drank, however, in between performances, her voice deepened and her eyes burned with a lecherous yearning. One afternoon he found himself sneaking into her cabin. He had meant to steal but a glimpse, then he was sniffing her pillow—when there came the sound of hushed, lewd voices at the door!

Mortified, he leaped under the bed. The door opened and Miss Viola entered with the gambler. They drank at first, absinthe, the green liquor with the bittersweet licorice scent that St. Ives favored, preparing it with the long ornamental perforated spoon that reminded Lloyd of a decorative trowel, ceremoniously straining water poured from a carafe through a crystal chunk of sugar and then waiting and watching, and finally stirring the mix of liquor, water, and sugar until it reached a cloudy green shade he deemed right. They took a few sips, and Miss Viola shed her long dress with the plunging neckline and her bodice and something else that Lloyd couldn't see. They tumbled onto the bed and lay there together, sipping their drinks for what seemed a long time. Then they came together and started to thrash about—until St. Ives muttered something and began to fiddle with his prosthesis.

Miss Viola's cabin had once been one of the more opulent staterooms, but times had not been kind to the owners of the *Fidèle* and the chamber's former glamour had faded, so that it now possessed a peeling gaudiness along with a noisy excuse for a brass bed (which William Henry Harrison had once slept in before becoming president). It was the audible complaint of the bedsprings that allowed the boy to wriggle into a position on the floor where he could catch sight of the looking glass, in which the figures of the two adults were partially visible. There he lay, trying hard to hold his breath.

Viola Mercy's bosom was exposed, her hips arched, providing a tantalizing hint of that taboo passage that led to the secret place within her heart. The gambler still had on his once dapper but now worn britches, and his bull's blood Spanish leather boots. The sleeve of his frilled shirt drooped down from a chair. His silver hand, however, was hard at work. The dagger that had been projected from the index finger had been replaced by a device of equal length, significantly greater girth, and arguably far more ingenious utility, which St. Ives referred to as the tickler.

The "tickling" went on for a long time, with Miss Viola's rough whisper rising into what sounded like an asthmatic crisis. The boy had heard a similar sound coming from his mother from time to time, but nothing as both feral and restrained as this. Another scent filled the room, distinct but confused—like wild onions and fish eggs. Then there was a shudder that shook the bed, and Lloyd was sure that he was going to be found out. Instead, St. Ives rolled off and began dismantling his mechanical finger piece.

"Don't you fret, honey," Miss Viola said. "Most men can't do as well."

The gambler started to say something but choked on his words and reached for his clothes after draining his glass. Not long after he'd left the room, Miss Viola rose, poured water from a jug into a bowl, and bathed, humming to herself. Powder and perfume were added, and then came the slow, measured ritual of dressing. It was a delicious agony for Lloyd, who could more hear and smell than see her, and he was forced to wait, with his heart pounding, until she was at last prepared for another performance. The door clicked behind her when she departed, and still he waited until he was sure she was not about to return to make his escape.

That night, when Lloyd closed his eyes and tried to imagine his dead sister, all he could see was Miss Viola.

The next day he sneaked into the entertainer's cabin again. He couldn't help himself. This time he chose as his vantage place her steamer trunk, a great battered box that reminded him of a coffin but had the consolation of facing directly toward the bed and of being filled with costumes and under-things, all permeated by her woman scent. There, snuggled tight, he waited and watched through a tiny crack that he made by balancing the lid on his head, counting the terrible wonderful minutes. Finally, she returned—without the gam-bler. Slowly—oh, so slowly—she disrobed, poured herself a drink from a flask, then water for bathing from the jug. It was excruciating. Then she reclined on the bed—without a stitch on. She began to sing to herself, stroking her breasts and thighs with her right hand. And that was when it happened. He let the lid slip with a thump! Everything went so silent he could hear the piston rods driving in the distant engine room. He waited, then cracked the lid.

"Don't you know not to come into a lady's room without an invitation," Miss Viola scolded, and then let out a trill of con-fusing laughter.

"I—I'm s-sorry . . ." Lloyd stuttered.

"No, you're not," the dark lady replied. "Come. *Here.*"

He rose from the trunk as if from the dead, stiff, and yet in-tensely alert.

"Take off your clothes," she commanded, and with fumbling sweaty fingers he obeyed.

Perhaps the chanteuse first intended merely to teach him a lesson about spying. But as soon as she saw the boy, naked and aroused beside her bed, something happened in a secret place inside her, and she knew that for herself as much for him this was an opportunity that would never come again.

"You must never speak a word of this to anyone," she said. "Anyone."

Lloyd was not sure if he would ever be able to speak again at all.

CHAPTER 5

The Ambassadors from Mars

HEPHAESTUS AND RAPTURE WERE QUICK TO NOTE THE CHANGE IN the boy but were unable to guess the true nature of the cause. For the first time since leaving Zanesville, Lloyd seemed to have regained his inner light and his parents wondered if he might have reestablished his connection with Lodema. Not surprisingly, Lloyd declined to provide details, choosing both for his own sake and for the honor of Miss Viola to keep the matter secret.

St. Ives, in his shrewd read of personality and mood, knew that something was different about the boy, but for reasons of his own did not inquire further. Instead, he slipped back inside his armor of pseudoaristocratic condescension, yielding only upon his farewell.

"Remember our lessons, Monkey," he said with a world-weary smile.

The boy had been quick to learn the art of card counting and odds estimation, as well as many of the psychological subtleties of gambling.

"I will," promised Lloyd, and for a moment he longed to disappear with his damaged friend—off into the teeming world in search of money and risk, dark fragrant women, and the grotesque riddles of Junius Rutherford.

Miss Viola gave him a quick, chaste kiss on the cheek in public, and a very long, slow kiss somewhere else in the privacy of her cabin before whisking off to find another drinking partner, lover, audience—whatever it was that she was searching for.

St. Louis had come a long way since the French fur trappers drifted by in birchbark canoes to barter with the Peoria Indians. And it had come a long way even faster since the first steamboat arrived from Louisville on July 27, 1817. Many Negroes still spoke French and signs of the Spanish colonial period were everywhere to be found, but the city's aura of European empire had been transformed into the energy and friction of a thriving outpost of western expansion. This was a border town now, a crossroads dividing North and South, East and West. Fifty steamboats provided packet service to exotic destinations such as Keokuk, Galena, and Davenport to the north, Louisville, Cincinnati, and Pittsburgh to the east, and Memphis, Vicksburg, New Orleans, and Mobile to the south—while the passage along the Missouri (where the Sitturds hoped to go) opened the way west to Independence, Westport, St. Joseph, Omaha, Council Bluffs, and beyond.

The city had boomed from a bluff-town harborside of around seventeen thousand people to almost four times that number, although the German Revolution and the Irish Potato Famine would soon swell the ranks to make it the largest center west of Pittsburgh.

Rapture had never imagined so many "parrysawls." Hephaestus counted the number of taverns and public houses. Lloyd took in the grim, overburdened Negroes and the quizzical Indians, the street Arabs, imbeciles, and ringworm hillbillies—offset by lily-white gentlemen and ladies rattling around in lacquer-black carriages with shining wheels.

It was here that the infamous Dred Scott lawsuit would soon begin, igniting the Civil War, many would say, while still burning torturously in the collective memory was the case of Francis McIntosh, a free mulatto steamboat steward who had been chained to a tree and roasted alive in a slow fire in retaliation for stabbing a sheriff's deputy—as well as that of the antislavery newspaper editor Elijah P. Lovejoy, who was shot to death and trampled in nearby Alton, Illinois, a year later (still later to be the birthplace of a boy named Miles Davis).

While Lloyd had been busy learning his bold new lessons from St. Ives and Miss Viola, Hephaestus and Rapture had been engrossed in Micah's map and in planning the next stage of their journey to Texas. Their decision was to take a boat up the Missouri River to Independence, the southernmost of the supply towns on the route to the Pacific Coast. From there it looked like a long, strange trip across Kansas and what was then the Indian Territory—and would later become the state of Oklahoma—to reach what they hoped they would find in Texas: a new home.

Unfortunately, the riverboats for the Missouri journey were crowded—always crowded now—with such a miscellany of humanity that could scarcely be believed. One would have thought that America was coming apart at the seams, or mutating to form some crazed new creature.

Once again, money was tight. What provisions they'd been able to salvage from their earlier adventures were running low. "Life is a casting off," Hephaestus reminded his family (which prompted a jab in the ribs from Rapture). Young Lloyd took this opportunity to introduce the money he had made with St. Ives, pretending that he had found it along one of the bustling streets. His parents were too overjoyed to ask any questions.

Hephaestus reckoned that with this windfall they were able to afford passage on the *Spirit of Independence*, newly overhauled and freshly painted. But they had to wait for three days. Ever worried about conserving money and knowing that they now had a stateroom to look forward to, the family sought temporary shelter in the loft of a mice-infested stable behind a glue renderer's.

It was in a thronging market square below on their second day that they were surprised to see a wagon decorated with rajas and angels—and who should be beside it but Professor Umberto, the traveling medicine showman and magician who had passed through Zanesville. The spruiker was now calling himself Lemuel Z. Bricklin, "Master of Teratology, Clairvoyance, and Prestidigitation."

Lloyd wanted to say hello, his parents believing that the sight of the colorful wagon had brought back a fond memory of Zanesville. The truth was that their old town held but one happy recollection for the boy, and that had to do with his ghost sister's memorial. The reason he was interested in the professor was that he wanted to catch sight of the man's fine-figured assistant, Anastasia. His experience with Miss Viola had opened up a new kind of precocious craving within him. And the earlier magic had intrigued him.

Rapture, still miffed about the downturn in business she had experienced owing to the professor's arrival in Ohio, found herself "haa'dly 'kin" to say howdy to him in St. Louis and went off to round up ingredients to conjure a little "tas'e 'e mout" for the family's supper, reminding Hephaestus to keep an eye on the boy and for them both to stay out of trouble. Of course, Lloyd gave his father the slip.

The square was jammed with people buying fresh pig snouts or honeycomb tripe, and Hephaestus became so absorbed that he did not feel a passing thief's practiced hand snake into his pocket and dexterously extract the money that was intended for their boat fare.

Lloyd, meanwhile, made a beeline for the medicine-show wagon, which had a tent set up behind it. The professor, a springy man with a waxed mustache and a receding hairline hidden under a leghorn hat, had just produced a fat Red Eagle cigar from a pocket in his coat when Lloyd strode up.

"What happened to your monkey?" the boy wanted to know.

"Why?" queried the professor, lighting the cigar with a crack of his fingers. "Would you like to apply for the position?"

"That was good." Lloyd grinned, mimicking the finger snap.

"Prestidigitation, my boy. Legerdemain. I do three shows a day and you're welcome to see one, if you would be so kind as to bring along your parents or guardians as paying customers. The Bible says blessed are they who pay in cash."

"No, it doesn't," Lloyd objected.

"Mine does," the showman replied, tipping his hat to a woman with a rustling bustle who shuffled by. "But never fear, the instance of instantaneous combustion you have just witnessed was a complimentary sample—gratis, without obligation; in other words, free of charge. Now, if you'll excuse me."

"You didn't say what happened to the monkey," Lloyd pointed out, reaching for the man's coat sleeve as he tried to turn away toward the tent.

"No," agreed the professor, wheeling back and chomping on his cigar. "I have neglected to fulfill your request for further intelligence and so have left you in a state of sustained bewonderment and speculation. And there you shall remain. I have work to do." Once again he made a move toward the tent pitched beside the wagon, nodding at a man with a thimble hat who ambled past with a frown of suspicion on his face.

"Is he dead?" Lloyd asked, refusing to budge.

"As a matter of fact, poor little Vladimir was consumed by some sort of cave lion during our recent sojourn in Kentucky," the professor announced, glaring down at the boy. "Most distressing. Now, if you'll excuse me!"

"Did you shoot the cave lion?" Lloyd inquired.

"Go home, young lad!" The professor waved. "I must prepare. Magic doesn't just happen!"

"I thought that was exactly what it did," Lloyd replied. "That's why it's magic."

"Touché," the showman retorted, appearing to bow, but

really examining the boy's sorry excuse for footwear, which confirmed his initial impression. "But if I were truly a master of the art," he continued, "then I would wave the wand of this cigar and *you* would disappear—back to wherever it was you came from."

"Zanesville," Lloyd supplied. "Ohio. I saw you there."

"Aha," the professor returned, his eyes following a blooming lass with a rose-hips complexion, who giggled behind a handkerchief as she passed. "Where on earth did you say your parents were?"

"I have neglected to fulfill your request for further intelligence regarding that," Lloyd answered.

"Touché again, my effervescent little friend. But circumstances beyond my control, otherwise known as life, require that I spin gold from straw, separate wheat from chaff—in a word, earn my daily bread. Now *please,* leave me to my fate as I bid you goodbye and good luck with your own." He gave the boy a hearty pat on the head, the universal sign of condescension in adults toward children—and one that he felt certain this particular child could not fail to comprehend.

"And what about the pretty lady?" the boy asked. "Did a cave lion get her, too?"

"Boy! I am going to perform some magic on you yet if you don't move on!" This time the showman took a decisive step away, prepared to fend off the lad with an elbow if necessary.

"Do you still sell the powder made from tiger penis?" Lloyd asked.

This inquiry caught the professor by surprise, and was made at too loud a volume for his liking. He glanced around, thinking, *Damn this boy.* What he said aloud was "Shush, please! Here, my friend. Come now. Take this delightful toy as a token of my exasperation and carry on."

The medicine man produced from inside his coat a sheet of heavy paper neatly folded into the shape of a bird, which he uncreased, and adjusted, and then lofted into the air. The flat wings carried the construction several feet toward a scowling lady who was hawking carrots.

"Now, go and collect that novelty and it is yours to have, without payment or condition, save that you leave me to the tasks at hand!"

Lloyd scoffed at this offer but went and retrieved the paper bird—and then whistled at the showman, who, in spite of himself, spun around.

Lloyd then tilted both wings upward and sent it soaring over the head of the carrot woman, where it caught an updraft and sailed well out of the market.

"Inclined wings produce more lift and also more stability," he called out to the showman, whose eyebrows had arched in surprise. "Now, what about the tiger powder?"

"Please, my young friend!" the showman entreated with nervous gesticulations, buffaloed at last. "Just come in here and let me give you something to take your mind off all these questions."

Lloyd's eyes adjusted to the change in light. The tent was much larger than it had looked from outside, and set out like a room in a house, except that over in one corner was another tentlike structure, like the sort of cloth-screened cubicle one might find in a doctor's surgery. Worn Turkish carpets had been laid down, with satiny pillows strewn about, creating an ambience that was both cozy and exotic, although a distinct mix of odors permeated the enclosure: a chamber pot, perspiration, lice soap. Lloyd felt at home.

This impression was strengthened by the presence of two women. The first Lloyd recognized as the beautiful Anastasia he had been wondering about (who in truth was as worn as the carpets, but still richly patterned). She was seated on a camp meeting chair mending clothes, dressed in a forget-me-not blue frock that showed off her figure in a manner that he found quite compelling. His enthusiasm intensified when his eyes took in the other woman, who was standing a few feet off to the left—on her head. She was dressed in tight-fitting mannish garb that accentuated her curved shape. Lloyd was soon unable to hide the prominence of his enthusiasm.

Amazed but sympathetic to his condition, the professor gestured broadly. "Ladies, meet a persistent new friend. Your name, young sir . . . ?"

"L-loyd," the boy stammered, transfixed by the gymnastic calm of the other woman, who in his mind's eye he had transposed into a conventional standing position and realized that she was the spitting image of Anastasia. So that was how the trick was done, Lloyd thought.

"Young Lloyd hails from Zanesville, where he made something of our acquaintance during one of our past peregrinations," the showman explained, and took more notice of the boy's fatigued clothing and unscrubbed state. Here was another child of misfortune trying to find his way. Rather like the son the professor had lost long ago, only more touched by the sun. Anastasia looked up from her sewing and smiled. The woman, whom Lloyd took to be her twin, or at least her sister, waved one of her feet.

"Hello," Lloyd tried, but the two women just repeated these gestures as before.

"Ah," the Professor said, shaking his head. "Don't be offended. I'm saddened to say that both my lovely ladies have been deprived of speech, a diabolical punishment that was conferred upon them as children by a mad father."

"Anastasia can't talk?" Lloyd asked.

"Mrs. Mulrooney," the professor corrected. "Or Lady Mulrooney, as I prefer to think of her. For Mulrooney is the surname I was born with. The other monikers and personae I use are but stage machinations to heighten and enhance the mystique necessary to build confidence and create an atmosphere of possibility, credibility, and awe."

"And she . . . is your wife?" Lloyd asked, digging his right hand into the pocket of his dirty knee pants.

"Yes, son. In a word, we are matrimonially united, conjoined, and conspicuously complementary."

"And who is the other woman?"

"Technically speaking, she is my wife's sister—twin sister—and how beneficent and expeditious it has proven to have two female assistants who look virtually identical! I mean from a stage-magic point of view. But privately, confidentially, and just between you and us, she too, is a partner in the adventure of my life that combines entertainment and enlightenment to provide illumination and enjoyment for all those who experience it!"

"You mean you have two wives?" the boy asked. Now, there was a goal worth aspiring to, Lloyd thought.

Mulrooney blinked at this, for he realized that he had just let his staunch guard completely down and offered far more detail regarding his personal affairs than he had ever intended to with anyone, let alone a strange boy.

I must be slipping, the showman mused. Apart from the somewhat darker skin tone and the green eyes, the lad did remind him very much of his lost son—perhaps that was why.

"Well, now, sonny boy," he humbugged, trying to regain mastery of the situation. "Let's not put delicate matters quite so baldly, eh? I think if we are discoursing privately and confidentially, in a manner of speaking, one could answer in the affirmative, while conceding that the arrangement is not to everyone's taste. In some regrettable cases it is not at all celebrated with the level of tolerance and understanding we would like, so we do not normally make a habit of announcing the status of our little family outside our little family. Coming from a place like Zanesville, I'm sure you understand. I would therefore appreciate your respecting that fact and this rare confidence—and, for reasons inexplicable, I have sufficient faith in my assessment of your character to believe you will."

"And neither of them can talk?"

"No," Mulrooney assented, concerned about how much

harm he had done. "But their wits are as sharp as any, and I could not ask for better companionship. Besides . . ." He grinned. "There is something to be said for women who can't answer back."

This attempt at levity drew an immediate response from the two mute sisters. Mrs. Mulrooney the seamstress launched a ball of woolen socks, while Mrs. Mulrooney the gymnast whipped off a shoe. Both missiles struck their target full in the face.

"Bah! Ladies!" the professor complained. "You see what I mean? You have no reason to feel any pity for these two, young lad. They are more than able to look out for themselves! It is I who am outnumbered."

Mrs. Mulrooney No. 1 licked an end of thread and darted it through a needle with a grin of vindication, while Mrs. Mulrooney No. 2 clapped her feet.

"And now," said the professor. "Won't you repay our candor and tell us your story? It's plain you have one. Else you would not be so far from Zanesville."

Just then a sound came from behind the cloth partition in the corner. The showman and his two wives showed no sign of acknowledgment. Perhaps a child was sick behind there, Lloyd thought, although the idea of having two wives still occupied him. Two wives this side of the curtain seemed to increase the possibilities of what lay behind. He tried to focus on the professor's query.

Ordinarily he would not have satisfied such a request with much detail, but as a result of his time with St. Ives he was growing more secure in his ability to gauge people's character and, as the professor had trusted him with a confidence, so he related as best he could his family's trek from Ohio and their hopes of beginning a new life in Texas (save for the mystery that his uncle had referred to in his letter and the nature of his relationship with Miss Viola).

The professor and his two mute wives were both entertained

and reassured by the boy's account. "We are all strangers and pilgrims," the showman summed up when Lloyd was done. "I wish you well on your journey to Texas. We are headed north for the heat of summer and then back south when autumn comes."

It was at this point, just as Lloyd was thinking that it was time for him to get back to his father and how he hoped the professor would give him a bottle of the tiger powder, that another sound came from behind the screen partition—a very odd sound that was soon followed by odder noises still.

"What was that?" Lloyd asked when he could no longer resist.

"What?" answered the showman coyly.

"That. *That!*"

"Hmm. Yes . . ." the showman was forced to acknowledge now as the sounds grew odder and louder. "They're awake."

"*They?*" the boy repeated. "Who are they?"

Mulrooney's face fell as if he had put his foot in his mouth again.

"The Ambassadors from Mars. The strangest strangers and pilgrims you will ever see," he said at last. "But, my boy, you must *swear* not to tell a soul, because it's not my intention to exhibit them yet."

"Exhibit them?"

"Well, my commitment is not to exploit them but to help them maximize those features that offer such singular advantages if understood properly and positioned effectively. As their sponsor, I am obliged to insure that such an arrangement is practicable and sustainable—in a word, sufficiently profitable to cover the costs of their maintenance."

"May I see . . . them?"

Knowing that the child, with curiosity now aroused, would not be likely to give in and go, the professor reluctantly motioned for him to approach the cubicle. This boy has got under my skin in the damnedest way, Mulrooney thought to himself, as he pulled back the swath of drape to reveal a sight that made even Lloyd's mouth drop open.

The figures were dressed in clothes that conjured up images of Washington and Jefferson at the signing of the Declaration of Independence.

"I call 'em Urim and Thummim," the professor announced. "Or the Ambassadors from Mars. Don't know what they call themselves."

The creatures who now stood before Lloyd were remarkable individuals by anyone's standards. Short but not exactly dwarfs, they were obviously brothers—both microcephalics, or pinheads. They were Negroid, perhaps, but pale-skinned, with highly distorted features and an animalish clicking-grunting type of language.

"Why do you call them the Ambassadors from Mars?" Lloyd asked.

"I don't plan to outside the smaller burgs," replied the professor. "Wouldn't do a'tall to get the tar bubbling."

"You mean to fool folks," the boy chided.

"My young friend, let me say this about that. As a rule, people *like* to be fooled. If you mean inspired, surprised, delighted—made to wonder and to wish for things. If I can make the world bigger and brighter for a moment for some boot stone or put even a tintype star in the eye of some leather-skinned lass, where's the crime in that? But when you say fool, you not only make it sound cheap, you make it sound easy—and t'aint always so. You can't fool or enlighten all the people all the time, son. That's why it's so very important to be clear about who you are trying to fool or enlighten at any given time."

"But they're not from Mars, are they?" the boy continued (which stirred the Ambassadors into a fit of clicking and grunting).

"No," agreed the professor, twisting his mustache. "They're from Indiana, far as I know. That's where I found 'em, at any rate. But their story is just as hard to swallow, in its own way.

The free niggers looking after them swore on the Bible that these two were dropped out of a tornado."

"A tornado?" Lloyd puzzled.

Mulrooney held his hand over his heart. "Urim and Thummim came down out of the storm unharmed about two years ago, they said. No hint of where they started from or who their real family was. The niggers took it as a sign from the Almighty and took 'em in, but they kept 'em hidden in their barn for fear of someone doing 'em harm."

"So you bought them?" Lloyd asked, thinking back to how he had been hidden away in the family barn.

"The nigger and his wife were damn grateful when I proposed taking the boys off their hands. But now, when you see the lads in the sumptuous duds designed by the Ladies Mulrooney, prognosticating and pontificating in their mumbo-jumbo, who can but conclude that they are emissaries and apostles from some distant kingdom of celestial grandeur far beyond our ken?"

This assertion prompted more clicking and grunting from the Ambassadors, and the showman observed how closely the boy was listening.

"You look like you understand them."

"I think I could, with a little time," Lloyd replied.

"Balderdash! You can't tell me there's anything to their doggerel. Or if there is, only they know it!"

"No," Lloyd answered. "I think it's a real language—a spoken one, anyway."

"Oh, they write, too—if you can call it that," the professor remarked.

"Could I see?" Lloyd cried, unable to hide his interest.

"My boy, you're as curious a specimen as they are in your own way," the professor replied. He went to a trunk, which made Lloyd wince with the recollection of Miss Viola, and produced a large handful of paper scraps all covered with a tiny but precise cuneiform-like writing. Holding the dense lines of unknown symbols together was a repeated icon that resembled the spiral shape of a tornado.

"Now don't be telling me you can read this!" the professor scoffed.

"Well, not yet," Lloyd agreed. "But maybe . . ."

"Son, all the clever men in the world would be a long while in unraveling the secret of this doodling. And it may well be that there is no secret—that they've just scribbled and scrawled to please themselves and what looks good is good enough."

Lloyd noticed a wooden matchbox, or what he first thought was a wooden matchbox, edging out from under the Ambassadors' bed. It was in fact triangular in shape, rather like a hand-size metronome, and when he picked it up he was surprised by the almost total lack of weight. Its surface, which had the smoothness and hardness of metal, not wood, had been covered, but here the writing had been engraved. The weird ciphers flowed in their swimming lines, but the lines took on a larger shape of the cyclonic spiral.

"Could I have this?" the boy asked. "I want to study it."

Urim and Thummim exchanged determined clicks and grunts.

Lloyd nodded at them, and they seemed to nod back.

"I take it they approve," the professor said. "That's how I'll take it, anyway. You may keep the box, young Lloyd, as a souvenir to reward your sagacity and a memento of the amazements you have seen. Learn its secret if you can."

The boy tucked the talismanic object into his shirt. Then he said goodbye to the professor and his unexpected family, not knowing how much trouble lay ahead for his own.

"What an unusual lad," the professor said when Lloyd had departed. He was unable to recall what he had intended to lure the boy's thoughts away from the tiger powder with when he invited him inside the tent.

The Ambassadors clicked and burbled.

CHAPTER 6

A Lust for Learning

LLOYD WAS A LONG TIME TRACKING DOWN HIS FATHER AND mother, because Hephaestus, when he discovered that he had lost the money, began combing the market, hoping against hope that it might just have fallen out of his pocket. Beside himself with anger about the loss, the reformed inventor limped out of the square and into a district of warehouses and then down a brickbat alley where he was waylaid by some toughs and might well have been beaten to a pulp had not one of them had a gimpy foot himself, and so called off the assault out of sympathy.

Meanwhile, Rapture found that haggling for bargains amid the produce merchants was exhausting work (and they sometimes found that talking to her was not so easy, either, even though she put on her whitest accent).

When Hephaestus and Lloyd were not at the agreed meeting point, she too went searching the adjacent streets and, following the commotion of a carriage accident, got lost for a time amid the dust heaps and sale yards, where it was lucky she did not get jumped. Or worse. While she could pass for white most of the time in Ohio, St. Louis was a more sensitive, volatile environment. She sensed that, but concerns about her menfolk made her bolder than she should have been.

So it was well after the professor had gathered a crowd and performed his magic show with the help of Mrs. Mulrooneys 1 and 2 (who were, of course, thought by the spectators to be the same woman) that the Sitturd family was finally reunited. And the mood was not pleasant when Hephaestus confessed what had happened to the money—or, rather, what he did not know had happened.

"How could you?" snapped Lloyd, thinking back to how hard he had to work and scheme to make it and, even worse, how honorably the rogue St. Ives had treated him, always dividing the money on equal terms. He was so put out and let down, in a way, he wished the gambler had been his father. However wounded he might have been, he was at least a man with backbone and cunning—and style—and knowledge of the world. Lloyd knew from having prowled the market himself just what had happened—and he knew that it would have been a very sorry sneak thief to have attempted such with St. Ives.

"I—I'm sorry," Hephaestus whimpered. For the first time, Lloyd felt a cold and pure disdain for his father, which was made even worse, for it brought with it a premonitory fear of further dissolution and foolishness. I am too young to be made to lead this family, Lloyd thought. But what other choice is there if this is to happen?

They took shelter in the rodent-busy stable, with the smell of the glue boiler mingling with the smoky red grease lamps down in the street, and the collard greens and charred pigs' feet rising up from the shacks and shantyboats.

It was a miserable night despite the butter beans and cinnamon that Rapture managed to serve, along with a slice of smoked fatback, a loaf of day-old flatiron bread, followed by a variation on apple pandowdy and quick mud coffee.

The mice were so insistent—and when they weren't running wild across the rafters and the floor the rats in the walls and the birds in the roof sounded even louder—and Hephaestus was so disgusted with himself for losing Lloyd's money that no one much enjoyed their food. Rapture tried to console her husband by reminding him that Lloyd had found the wad of notes, which meant it had been lost by someone else and so was "bad luck 'n' kemin home." Lloyd kept his mouth shut at this, although a part of him longed to tell them both the truth. He wanted the praise he was due for his resourcefulness and knack. There was more Zanesville in his parents than he liked.

But the important fact was that they could no longer afford their stateroom on the *Spirit of Independence*. A new life with Micah seemed farther away than when they were in Ohio. They were stranded and disheartened, and just before they tried to go to sleep Hephaestus started blubbering. It was not an easily stomached sight, and filled Rapture with fear. Lloyd felt his disdain turning to shame. Suddenly, the family was outright foundering—and a long way from home.

"Listen, Hephaestus," he said in a dark, calm voice, the first time he had ever called his father by his first name. "You have to pull yourself together. Tomorrow I will go out and bring some *more* money in. I don't know how yet, but I will. But you can't be a machine that breaks down now. You're supposed to be the father in this family."

There was an almost chilling sobriety to the boy's words that shook both parents—perhaps because they each suspected that the money that had been lost had not been found. In any case, the next morning while the sun was still low, at the tender age of six, Lloyd Meadhorn Sitturd went to seek employment with the one person he knew in the river city.

"A job?" Mulrooney sighed. "My boy, you overestimate the financial fertility of my little enterprise. I regret to disinform you of this misconception, but last night, despite significant audience attention, the like of which any entertainer in any city of substance would be pleased to inspire, I ate fish-head soup. This morning I dined on oatmeal and brine. Please accept my apology for having to deny your request."

"Why don't you exhibit the Ambassadors?" Lloyd asked.

"They are not yet ready," came the answer.

"Then why don't you let them go?"

"Where?" the showman countered, and Lloyd saw that beneath the apparent flabbiness of his character Mulrooney was a victim of his own soft heart.

"But I can do things!" Lloyd insisted. "Things that will stir the crowd."

"Such as?" the showman queried.

"What about long division—in my head?" Lloyd demanded.

"*Long* division? All right." The showman smiled sadly. "What's 648,065 divided by 17?"

The boy thought for a moment and then replied, "38,121.47."

"That answer sounds as plausible as any," Mulrooney admitted.

"It's the right answer!" Lloyd cried. "You can check it!"

"Bravo. But this is a magic show. Bewonderment and mystification."

"What about calculating the number of beans in a big jar?"

"My boy, the best place to hide a buffalo is in a buffalo herd, and the best way to figure the number of beans in a jar is to be the one who put them there. That's what my business is all about. That's why it's vital to think there is only one woman and not twins. But these little tricks of the intellect lack the necessary appeal for public performance."

"But I have to earn some money!" the boy cried.

The shrillness of this outburst unsettled Mulrooney. There were people trawling the riversides who would be very interested in a child his age. Despite his apparent self-sufficiency, if the boy became desperate enough he could fall prey to some very undesirable folk.

"All right," Mulrooney consented, racking his brain. "Let me think. Does your family know about your intentions?"

"N-no," Lloyd admitted. "Not yet."

"And I assume they would not approve if they did. So we know where we stand. All right, then. What about this? I believe we could fabricate . . . a mentalist attraction. In a word, mind reading. Hmm? We will ask questions of the audience and have you secured in such a way as not to hear. Then I shall ask you questions and you will tell everyone what it was the person said."

"How will I know that?" Lloyd inquired.

"Because of the order of the questions that I ask you and certain key words I will use. We will have a code. With your quick head, we will fool and enlighten many. The rest will be amused. Then you can do some calculating feats and we can sell some special mind-strengthening tonic, for sharper wits and clearer thoughts."

"Do you have some of that?" the boy asked.

"My little friend, I have but three tonics to sell, and they all have the main ingredient in common. The secret to tonic is not how it's made but how it's sold and therefore what it's called. I will pay you one-third the price of every bottle of tonic we sell. I'm afraid I can do no better than that."

"Thank you!" Lloyd smiled, imagining, in his naïve enthusiasm, the residents of St. Louis lining up for miles.

"Come back this afternoon and I will have written some patter for you to memorize and we will rehearse the code. But be warned, young Lloyd, show business is a difficult business. So keep your mind clear and your wits about you, or we may both find ourselves in a situation that no tonic can cure."

Lloyd ran back to the stables and the showman slipped into the tent, where his wives were debating in their personal sign language and the Ambassadors from Mars were clicking wildly. "Well," Mulrooney told himself. "At least the boy will be safer with me than roaming the streets."

Lloyd returned that afternoon as ordered. In but an hour he mastered the speech the showman had composed and a host of variations, all the intricacies of the mind-reading code, and some simple ways of integrating his calculating and spelling abilities—along with various musical improvisations on the mouth organ, squeezebox, and an old dimpled bugle that the showman had kept from his own boyhood. Lloyd had not had much direct exposure to music; he had been too busy with his inventions. But he quickly, intuitively grasped the system of music, and if his instrumental technique was raw that actually worked in his favor as far as performance theatrics went—or so Mulrooney thought. On the squeezebox, he became an imp of melody with astounding rapidity. "Damn me if that boy couldn't be a musical genius if he turned his mind to it," Mulrooney told his wives.

Then Lloyd had to decant a large cask of transparent liquid that gave off fumes that brought tears to his eyes into a series of little bottles with corks in the end. The magical-memory and mind-strengthening tonic was 140-proof alcohol laced with juniper and spearmint and could not have been more effective at clouding memory, although Mulrooney dubbed it LUCID! (He was particular about the exclamation mark.)

While working to fill the bottles, Lloyd listened to Urim and Thummim, and the more certain he became that, as freakish as they were, there was something about their language that was beautiful and subtle.

The showman retained his reservations about putting the boy "up on the stump," and if Mabel Peanut, Lloyd's sometime teacher back in Zanesville, could have seen him in St. Louis, performing on the medicine-show wagon, she would have felt confirmed in all her predictions about the family's errant ways. But for Lloyd the experience of being THE MIRACLE MIND READER & MYSTIFYING CHILD OF VISION was as invigorating as a whiff of ozone or the taste of sarsaparilla—a brazen vindication of his special abilities, all the things, or at least some of them, that he had had to cloak or to be ashamed of back home. It chuffed his pride to be able to help his family, when he felt that, for all his singular gifts, he had caused them distress in the past.

Yet it also piqued his native rebelliousness and his no longer secret contempt for his parents, try to hide it deep down in his heart though he did. The stinking hobnailed boot was on the other foot now. They were of necessity grateful for his earnings, and gratitude is a double-minded emotion that can snake in many directions.

The *Spirit of Independence* may have departed without the Sitturds, and Texas may have slipped farther out of their grasp, but the youngest family member at least began traveling all around—from Spanish Lake and the Missouri Bottoms to the other side of the river on the smoking ferries, wherever Mulrooney thought they could draw a crowd.

From the self-named Professor of Teratology, Lloyd learned a plethora of new words (such as "plethora," "pinguid," "paludal," and "uliginous"), not to mention the more utilitarian skills of how to make change, short change—upsell, distract, hoodwink, and hornswoggle a crowd into being an attentive audience. And a great success the arrangement was, at least at first. For a couple of golden weeks, the showman began to have Barnum-like aspirations. With a little luck, maybe he could get the boy to travel with them to Chicago. The Ambassadors would eventually be incorporated into the act, and with the proceeds he would begin to build himself an empire of novelties—a true touring odditorium featuring headhunters from lost islands and living skeletons, with scientific displays to delight and inspire all ages!

After the second successful performance, Lloyd invited his parents along to watch him work. He was proud of himself. Meanwhile, Rapture had humbled herself and found employment as a scrubwoman for a fetid old wharf doctor who sold laudanum and performed abortions on the sly. She was upset to learn of Lloyd's exploits, but grateful that her son had risen to the occasion.

However, the boy's new career did not sit at all well with Hephaestus. Lloyd's dressing down of him had yanked him out of his blither for a day or so, but without any inventions to occupy his mind, with Micah and Texas now seemingly out of reach, and with a growing sense of impotence as the head of the household, and no house to hold, the former blacksmith soon began to wallow in drink, exaggerating his limp for the purposes of begging, so that he could afford a cheap charcoal-flavored mash that a freedman named Little Jack Redhorse made.

When not moping and sulking in the loft of the stable, where they were forced to remain, he took to panhandling near the main market—and if fortunate in his takings he went in search of companionship and diversion, which he ended up finding at a place called the Mississippi Rose, an apparent chop shop and taproom that was in fact a seedy house of blue lights (a favorite among the preachers and the civic leaders). In addition to five floury white floozies and a very popular quadroon named Black Cherry, the entertainments ranged from cards and billiards to wagers on rat-catching dogs or bouts of barefisted boxing if two Irishmen could be found.

The proprietor was known as Chicken Germain, a Melungeon woman built like a cart horse with straight black hair and steel-blue eyes. She loved fried food and men, especially well-endowed men—and especially well-endowed men who also had some physical deformity. The first night Hephaestus managed to sneak in the door, Chicken was about to have him evicted when she noticed his limp. An hour later she noticed that he was anything but limp, chicken bones and gaudy silk stockings strewn on the floor beside her carved oak bed upstairs.

Despite his age, Lloyd was in his own way tortured by the temptations of desire into which Miss Viola had initiated him. There were not many avenues for sexual fulfillment for a boy of his age—particularly one who was new to town and without spending money, because, unlike Hephaestus, all the money he made he turned over to his mother.

From a street waif named Scooper he heard about a teenage half-breed called Pawnee Mary, who would let you do her if you gave her chewing tobacco. There was also a beefy bucket head named Betty, who would get down on all fours behind the feed-lot if you gave her a pig ear to chew on. But the Christian Union rode Betty out of town on a rail (which some local wags claimed she enjoyed), while Pawnee Mary was found floating facedown in the river. Young Lloyd grew ever more restless for company and release, and might well have wandered down a short, dark path himself had his yearning for female affection not found another outlet.

One night after he had fled the stable, where enough rancor was brewing between his parents to set the horses snorting in their stalls below, he happened upon a Lyceum-like institution that called itself the Illumination Society. The establishment was filled with horn-rimmed fusspots arguing about a magic-lantern lecture on the life history of the bee. Was it too bold? Too suggestive? The opinions were hot on both sides of the de-bate, and no one noticed Lloyd slip into the adjacent library. He was starving for intellectual stimulation in the same way that he craved sex.

In the hushed, stuffy book room he found copies of Shake-speare and Horace. But when he went to look beyond one of the rows, in the darker part of the room, he pulled out a heavy volume on the history of the Punic Wars and found on the shelf behind it another book tucked away, as if in secret. In the dim light, he strained his eyes to take in the contents. The pages were filled with illustrated pictures of men and women. Naked men and women posed in positions that he hadn't even thought of! His heart leaped. Page by forbidden page, the pictures lubri-cated his imagination. Fortunately, the members of the Illumi-nation Society were now immersed in an earnest discussion regarding dues and the privileges of officeholders. Oh, how he longed to steal that book—so crammed with fantasies and flesh! But it was too large for him to slip under his shirt. He no-ticed a small card glued inside the front cover. It read RARE BOOKS & MAPS, and was followed by a St. Louis address—on

Fifth Street, not far away. His whole body quivered at the prospect! Perhaps there were more such books to be found there.

The next afternoon, following a show where sales of LUCID! hit a record high, Lloyd went searching for the shop (with the express intention of locating and stealing a forbidden text). The address in question was a very narrow shop front, not much wider than the single door, with just one small window. The pane was so caked with mud and crusted insects that it was impossible to gain any idea of what type of business was conducted inside, but the moment Lloyd was inside the door he knew that he had found what he had been searching for. The shop was much deeper than he expected, laid out in a series of small plaster-peeling rooms and alcoves built off one long hall lined by a tatty Oriental carpet. On the wall behind the door hung a Dutch map of some section of the coast of Africa, and on the floor below lay a transparent celestial sphere and a page from an illuminated manuscript depicting a sleeping peasant being inspected by a family of hedgehogs. The place was silent but for the buzzing of a bluebottle butting the inside of the clouded glass. As there was no one about, Lloyd peered into the first room. More maps covered the wall—or pieces of maps— some framed, some torn and decomposing. Piles of books lay everywhere.

He found amid the mouse dirt and cobwebs a fat vellum volume concerning the history of military fortifications. In the neighboring alcove he found the travels of Hakluyt and the *Wildflowers of the Southern Alps,* which had several blood-smeared mosquitoes smushed between its pages. At last, however, on top of a crooked chimney pile of texts, he came upon an edition of Nicolaus Steno's famous anatomical work on the ovaries of sharks, which gave him hope that he might have hit on a heap of biological or medical texts. Perhaps somewhere near the bottom was hidden the documentation of some forensically vivid mating ritual or a diagram of the female organs. He became so engrossed in this possibility that he was not even aware of the hint of witch hazel insinuating itself through the haze of cracked book paste and Graeco-Latino-English terminology—until the man's stealthy approach was announced with a phlegmy clearing of the throat. Lloyd tipped over a pillar of crumbling books and stared up in panic, choking on the dust.

The man who confronted him now was but a smidgen over five feet tall, with tufts of wild hair and bushy eyebrows giving way to a domed forehead. His hands were soft and effeminate-looking, yet there was about his frame a contrasting hint of martial energy and force of character, which was undermined by a noticeable hump on his back. The man's attire consisted of a neat but worn dark twill suit with a faint powdering of dust, an expensive-looking white shirt and a silver pocket watch suspended from his waistcoat by an oily chain. On the thick hooked nose above a bristle of gray mustache propped a pair of round wire spectacles, and when he opened his mouth to speak Lloyd spotted a calcium stain on his front tooth.

"This is not a lending library, young man. These books are for sale. Get along."

He pivoted to leave, but Lloyd piped up.

"But it looks like there are a lot of books that no one wants to buy! Wouldn't it be better if some were read?"

"You know nothing," the man croaked. "I do a brisk trade with bibliophiles from all over the country and indeed the world. From here to Boston, London, and Antwerp. There is a buyer for every book under this roof. You do not look like a buyer to me. Please go."

"Couldn't I just sit in one of the rooms and read?" Lloyd begged. "I won't disturb any of the . . . buyers."

This plea grated on the humpy man's nerves, for he slapped his hands together and stuttered, "H-how . . . how did you come to find me?"

Lloyd fidgeted again, not wanting to recount how he had

learned of the shop and certainly not what he had hoped to find.

"I . . . I was just . . . walking past," he muttered.

The man slapped his hands together again and said, "Then you may kindly just walk out. Books such as these are not for children."

"Don't you think that education is a good thing?" Lloyd asked stubbornly.

"Allein die Dosis macht dass ein Ding kein Gift ist," the book-man said, sighing. "Good day."

"I know what you said," Lloyd replied.

"Yes, but you are not leaving as I asked. Will I have to call a constable?"

"No, I mean what you said in German."

"Bully for you. And now I am addressing you in Latin. *"Nemo me impune lacessit."*

"Why would I want to harm you?" Lloyd puzzled.

"What?" the dainty humped man started. "You know Latin, too?"

"Yes," Lloyd answered. "Of course."

The proprietor gave a sniff of disbelief and strode over to the nearest shelf and whisked out a volume of Catullus's poetry. "All right," he said, handing the open book to Lloyd and pointing. "Tell me what this says."

Lloyd glanced down at the selected page and read, *"Odi et amo. Quare id faciam, fortasse requiris. Nescio, sed fieri sentio et excrucior.* It means 'I hate and love. You may ask why I do so. I do not know, but I feel it and am in torment.' "

"Hmm." The man smiled, showing his calcium stain. "And what did I say before in German?"

" 'Only the dose insures the thing will not be a poison.' "

"Correct!" snapped the bookseller. "And in reference to education you may already have had too much—at least of a certain kind."

"I hardly ever go to school," Lloyd corrected. "But I *am* quick."

"Perhaps," the man said, flexing his hump. "But you are slow to leave. I believe you were sent by one of the local dilettantes to goad and annoy me."

"I wasn't sent by anyone!" Lloyd insisted. "I'm here on my own."

There was something about the emphatic way the boy uttered this last remark, combined with his unexpected erudition, that made the bookseller change his attitude, for he brushed some of the dust from his suit and said, "All right, my learned young friend. Since you are so committed, you may remain here and read. I close at four, and you are not to wander outside this room. Understood?"

"Thank you!" Lloyd beamed. "Thank you. But . . . is there any key to how the books are organized?"

The humped man stroked his mustache.

"The key is right here," he said, pointing to his shining forehead. "I know where every book is in the entire shop. Does my young sir have special interests?"

"I am interested in science. And magic," Lloyd answered. "And . . . secrets."

"I . . . see," the bookseller said, arching his woolly eyebrows.

The humped man disappeared into the next room and Lloyd heard him foraging among the piles. He returned with an armload of Euclid's *Elements* and a book concerning Hooke's microscopy and an alchemical folio titled "Tract on the Tincture and Oil of Antimony," by Roger Bacon.

"Feast your mind on these. But mark what I say about staying in this room."

So saying, the man spun around and retreated back into the gloom of maps and tomes, taking the delicate astringency of the witch hazel with him. To the boy's surprise, other people did enter the shop. Those that he glimpsed passing by in the hall did not look much like buyers to him, but as they did not take any notice of him he paid them little mind and burrowed deeper into his reading. Once he heard the bookseller speaking in French in low tones to someone in the back. At five minutes to four, the humped man reappeared carrying a heavy set of keys.

"What is your name, young scholar?" the man asked.

Lloyd told him his name and swallowed a clump of dust and phlegm.

"My name is Wolfgang Schelling," the bookseller informed him. "I must say, you look more likely to pinch an apple than to go to the trouble of finding a book to read. But perhaps I don't know very much about boys. I was never allowed to be one myself, and I have no children of my own. In any case, it's time for you to go wherever you call home. Would you like to come back here again to study?"

"More than anything," Lloyd cried, and this was almost true.

"All right," Schelling purred. "Here are the rules. You are not to rummage about. Ever. I will select the books or find ones of interest for you. Do your parents or family know you came here? Does anyone know?"

"No," Lloyd answered.

"Then let's keep it that way. Trouble is easy to find these days, and I have no need of it. If I find that you have told anyone about your visits here, your privileges will be terminated. Always come in by the back door, which I will show you now, and you must always leave whenever I tell you to. And I do not want to hear anything about your life and problems—your family or the lack thereof. I will not tolerate either disrespect or private confidences. Understood?"

"Y-yes," Lloyd answered.

"You may come tomorrow at either ten or one but not in between, and you must be punctual."

"Yes, sir," Lloyd said, nodding. "And may I bring my notebook?"

"You may. Buy you must not leave pencil shavings or do anything untidy," Schelling replied—a remark that struck Lloyd as amusing, given the thick fur of dust that haunted the shop.

"And to resolve any unpleasant curiosity you may have, the hump on my back is a benign growth that is too close to my spine to be removed. No surgeon has the skill to remove it without endangering my life. So you need not stifle any impertinent questions on that score. Now follow me, and do not return except at the times I have indicated. Oh, and do consider bathing. You reek of fried catfish and the honey bucket."

Lloyd flinched at this remark but picked himself up off the floor and followed the bookseller down the long hallway to the back door. Outside was an alleyway jammed with crates and excelsior, but he knew the way back to the stable and sprinted down the jagged cobblestones, leaving the humpbacked man watching him from the doorway. Once the boy was gone, Schelling returned to the room he had been reading in and took a mental inventory. The bookseller noticed that a treatise on the Greek Archytas of Tarentum's mechanical pigeon, the first model airplane, was missing. Then, on the back of an old newspaper advertising a slave auction, he spotted something that made his bespectacled eyes bug out. Using but a hardened clump of street mud, the boy had managed to scrawl a rather fine imitation of one of Hooke's microscopic drawings.

"I wonder . . ." Schelling murmured.

CHAPTER 7

Wild Science

THE SITTURDS' MORALE COLLAPSED IN ST. LOUIS. THEIR WORLD always seemed to be ending. Rapture felt degraded and confused by the "w'ich en w'y talk" of the metropolis. She had lost her ability for "sperit voicen" and seemed fatigued at heart. Hephaestus teetered into the gutter. Where up to this point the trials of travel had brought them together in their quest to reach Texas and learn the secret of the "salvation" letter, now all the distractions and pressures of the city and their changing roles seemed to bring them undone. Each in a private way was homesick for their old life, as much as that had seemed a burden in the past. Each felt somehow to blame, especially Hephaestus.

The lame patriarch's dalliance with Chicken Germain had been his first betrayal of marital fidelity and had been instantly apprehended by his wife the moment he staggered back to the stable. In Rapture's mind there was an unbridgeable difference between chugalugging moonshine and doing the jellyroll with an "oagly" cathouse madam who consumed fried chicken by the plateful. The root witch in her was quick to take retaliatory action, concocting a noxious salve and applying it to Hephaestus's manhood when he fell asleep. The next morning he experienced the kind of profound contrition that only a severe mix of pain and embarrassment can elicit. Since then his condition had improved but had not cleared, and his mood remained sullen and dejected. He was angry with himself for what he had done, angry with his wife for what she had done to him, and angry with Lloyd for keeping his head and becoming the family breadwinner. It was not right, and undermined what fragile dignity he had left.

Lloyd's answer to this tension was to throw himself with full force into his work on the medicine show and into his secret studies at Wolfgang Schelling's bookshop. While back in Zanesville Mabel Peanut and Irma Grimm battled to teach their students the multiplication tables, Lloyd considered the implications of a pendulum being perfectly isochronous when describing a cycloidal arc. In one sitting, he consumed and appeared to understand a complex dissertation on celestial mechanics. Even the densest algebraic equations were soon rendered in exact visual form on a graph. In Schelling's experience, for sheer power of processing and retention the boy had no equal.

The book and map seller nourished the lad's hunger for learning with the *Poetics* of Aristotle and the metaphysics of Kant, but Lloyd much preferred the researches of Gauss and Coulomb into magnetic induction and resistance. While other bright boys his age would have delved into the adventures of Sinbad or the Swamp Fox, Lloyd opted for the scientific treatises of Swedenborg. His weakness lay in the area of magic, and Schelling's shop was more than able to accommodate these diversions with dusty grimoires, Books of the Dead, and volumes devoted to alchemy and divination.

Hour by hour Schelling imagined that he could see the boy's mind changing shape to accommodate the new learning and, despite his best efforts to remain remote and uninvolved, when the usual look of forlorn acknowledgment swept across the prodigy's face one afternoon at closing time the humped scholar found himself providing take-home reading—which

Lloyd began to indulge in by candlelight when his feuding parents had finally dropped off to sleep.

The first work he devoured was on thaumaturgy, the engineering of ingenious machines for the purposes of theatrical or religious magic. It included the triumphant contrivances of Hero and Vitruvius, and John Dee's panic-causing stage effect of a mechanical flying beetle in Aristophanes' *Peace*. The second book was about Sir Joseph Banks, Captain Cook's botanist and science officer, who smuggled into his cabin a woman, dressed as a boy, to be his "assistant." It cheered Lloyd to learn that a man of science could also be a man of lust, and when the book described Banks as a "voyager, monster-hunter, and amoroso," he decided that that was what he would dedicate his life to becoming.

Apart from a dog-eared Japanese pillow book, he did not find many books to titillate his erotic senses, but he did find descriptions and drawings of the mechanical iron hand designed by Götz von Berlichingen in 1505—the Little Writer, the ingenious automaton conceived by Pierre Jacquet-Droz and his son, in the 1760s, as well as Vaucanson's miraculous mechanical digesting duck.

Lloyd rather felt his beaver was not altogether an inferior creation, but he resolved to become ever more ambitious. In response, he filched some items from a dustbin and a jeweler's workshop and one afternoon presented his host and patron with a foot-high clockwork mannequin modeled on Andrew

Jackson and armed with a whittled dowel flintlock that fired a mung bean. After that, the bookseller began showering the youngster with more than books. From the nether reaches of the dusty warren came horseshoe magnets, lengths of coiled copper and chemical solutions, lenses and grinding tools, professional carving implements, and a miscellany of objects to further entice the boy's imagination. Lloyd responded with a dollhouse incorporating hidden passages and optical illusions, and a miniature paddle wheeler with a high-pressure steam engine that, in proportionate terms, produced twice the power using less than half the normal fuel. An ear trumpet attached to a night watchman's knuckle-duster and some homemade gunpowder became a handheld cannon capable of projecting a load of ball bearings. (Lloyd field-tested it against the Rovers and the Mud Puppies, two warring gangs of urchins, who were less visible on the streets thereafter.)

When he set to work on improving the primary battery cell developed by J. F. Daniell, Schelling's eyebrows stayed raised. Most significant of all, Lloyd proved that what the book merchant had taken to be a toy was at minimum a very sophisticated toy. It was a hand-size locomotive that appeared to be made of glass, which Schelling said had come from Austria. Lloyd recalled the story St. Ives had told him about the crystal orchids of Junius Rutherford, and performed a series of experiments. He revealed that the object responded to the energy of the sun and posited that the glass was really some form of disguised plant material. Schelling was careful to put the locomotive under lock and key after that, and he began to consider that it might be wise to do the same with Lloyd. Such a development prompted the bookseller to relax his rule about private confidences, and he began soliciting information about Lloyd's family and their plans. He was pleased that the boy was as forthcoming as he was.

The problem Schelling perceived was that the lad's interests flitted from subject to subject—one minute daguerreotypes, the next ideas for an internal-combustion engine. Of far greater concern, however, was an incipient sadism that the book merchant found despicable.

Deciding that Lloyd's education required something other than scientific literature and handbooks of magic, the humped man provided an illustrated volume on Greek mythology. On the way back to the stable after closing, Lloyd trapped a wharf rat, which he named Theseus. The next day he built a maze for the rat to explore, but when the rodent failed to extricate itself Lloyd attached one of his battery wires and proceeded to torture it with electricity. Schelling was left to perform a merciful extermination. The next day when the bookseller inquired what the child was clutching in a damp handkerchief, Lloyd replied, "A cat's brain."

Schelling was forced to admit that his protégé's moral intelligence lagged far behind his mental aptitude. When he quizzed the boy to describe what his special field of interest was, Lloyd muttered, "Wild science."

"What do you mean by that?" the bookman queried.

"The life of machines," Lloyd said with a shrug. "The machinery of life."

Schelling was taken aback to learn that a further inventory of the subjects that exuded fascination for the prodigy included ghosts, dreams, and the female anatomy. When asked what he would most like to accomplish, given his prodigious gifts, Lloyd replied, without a hint of irony or self-consciousness, "Design a female playmate who will remain forever young, communicate with the dead, formulate a detailed map of the mind, and perhaps travel to other worlds."

Fortunately, Lloyd had to use the privy in the back lane, so Schelling was left to splutter to himself. Then he sneaked a peek at the boy's notes. In the beleaguered two-penny Buffalo book, he found an amalgam of symbols, numbers, and marginalia—from mathematical calculations and sketches depicting various mechanical actions to a chain of hierograms that made him gawk. These emblems spiraled through a series of schematic drawings that merged existing and imaginary machines with animals and insects, along with humans and mythological beasts in graphic sexual poses. Lloyd returned and picked up his work just where he had left off without noticing the disturbed look on Schelling's face.

While his education under the bookseller's patronage progressed at the speed of thought, out on the medicine-show circuit the brisk sales of LUCID! were beginning to fall off. From long experience, Mulrooney sensed that the "hole was pretty well fished out" and the solution was to move on, upriver to Hannibal, Quincy, Rock Island, maybe even St. Paul. Of course, Lloyd could not go. The Sitturds' way led west and south, yet the boy's share of tonic sales was still nowhere near enough to pay for all three fares on the Missouri.

Mulrooney encouraged the prodigy to improvise more flamboyant expressions of his talents with an "enterprise point of view" in mind. Lloyd answered with theatrical exhibitions of magnetism, mirrors, and various volatile chemicals, which stimulated both consternation and raucous applause but did not lead to further sales. However, when he unveiled a flock of soaring toys and wind flyers public interest took a decided turn. These were simpler than the ones he had made in Zanesville but more elegant in their efficiency and less labor-intensive to produce. They had the added benefit of being disposable, which encouraged repeat purchases. They achieved an instant local vogue. Children and grown-ups alike were smitten by the sleek white arrows and bird-shaped creations. Prices varied, depending on the size and the materials, but the sudden popularity of the flying toys brought the Sitturds momentarily back together again, as Lloyd, Rapture, and the repentant Hephaestus were forced to work side by side in order to keep pace with demand as clubs and competitions sprouted wings. Yet even this success was not enough to satisfy Lloyd. His inclinations and impatience spurred him on to new heights.

The next phase started with a caged dove, a lamb, and a rooster. While gathering his things to leave Schelling's book-shop one afternoon, Lloyd stumbled upon a volume on the history of ballooning, which began with the story of the Frenchman Pilâtre de Rozier launching the first animals in a balloon of paper and fabric, then making a solo ascent himself a few months after—followed later by a true free flight in a balloon designed by the famous Montgolfier brothers in 1783.

In the early hours of the next day, Lloyd launched his own straw fire–fueled balloon made of butcher paper and hat wire, sending aloft one of the stable mice he had nabbed. He watched with pride as it disappeared in the vicinity of the Nicholson grocery store. (Unbeknownst to the boy, the balloon bounded about in the framing of a rooftop water tank before crashing near the Wheaton drugstore, to the mystification of a clerk named Balthus Tubb, who would go to his grave puzzling over the singed vermin that fell from the sky and hit him in the head.)

Reading how kites had been used in ancient China to elevate fireworks for military purposes set off fireworks of its own inside the boy's mind. With funding from Mulrooney, Lloyd began constructing, demonstrating, and selling kites as big as himself along the levee as part of the medicine show's new pro-gram. The sight of the creations trembling on their tethers over the river brought whistles from the packet steamers and cheers from the freight-loaded flatboats. The size of the kites grew, and so did their efficiency. When the Fourth of July came, Lloyd incorporated his emerging capabilities into a pyrotechnic display along the riverbank. Mulrooney handled the ticket sales and was delighted at the takings. Schelling was circulating in the crowd that night, too, but he was far from delighted.

The next day at closing time, the humpbacked bibliophile buttonholed the wunderkind and said, "My boy, I have some-one who would like to make your acquaintance. Someone I think it would be very strategic for you to meet. She is known as Mother Tongue. She is elderly and eccentric, but if favorably disposed toward you—and I believe she will be—she could become an invaluable . . . sponsor."

"Why?" Lloyd asked.

"Because of your unique abilities. And because she is eccentric. I would like you to meet me at the old ferry landing at midnight tonight."

"Midnight?" Lloyd cried. "What will I tell my mother and father?" Although he protested, he was beginning to think that he did not owe his parents any explanation for his actions anymore.

"You must not tell them. You must wait until they are asleep and slip out."

"But why so late—and where does this Mother Tongue live?"

"I can only say that she is eccentric, as I have told you. But she *is* worth meeting. Trust me," the bookseller replied, and the lump on his back twitched.

"All right," Lloyd agreed, and turned to head home, thinking all the while that his own fortunes seemed to rise in proportion to the fall in his parents'. It stung him, though, how they were forever undermining his elation, flinging filaments if not cables of guilt and responsibility at him, needing him yet holding him back. But from what? Perhaps the answer to that question was about to take more than a dream's shape.

CHAPTER 8

Midnight Is a Door

LLOYD ARRIVED AT THE OLD FERRY LANDING DEAD ON THE AP-
pointed time. A full moon reflected off the wharf and the chim-
neys of the docked boats, giving the Mississippi a sickly silver
sheen. Schelling was waiting for him. Two stevedore-muscled
black men were on board a cramped, decrepit steam launch
with him—one at the helm, one standing guard. Despite the
warm summer night, the boy shivered.

Stoked with cottonwood and cypress, the boiler of the dilap-
idated boat powered the craft out into the current. The telltale
silhouette of a yawl rowed off south beyond them, and a beaming coal barge loomed out toward the Illinois side. Beyond that,
no one appeared to be on the water except for them and the
moonlight.

Schelling handed Lloyd a strip of dark muslin. "Please blindfold yourself."

"Why?" Lloyd asked, the hair rising on the back of his neck.

"You will see," Schelling replied. "Trust me."

Lloyd flopped down on a crate and wrapped the cloth around
his head as he was instructed. This was not at all what he had
expected, but the familiar sounds of the boat surging through
the river filled him with a confused sense of resignation and anticipation. Surely this man meant him well.

He listened hard, trying to picture their progress away from St. Louis. The hiss of the gauge cock. The low rumble of the mud valves. At first he was sure they were headed upriver, and then they turned, and perhaps again. Twice Schelling raised him up and spun him around, as if to further disorient him. Not a word was spoken between the humpback and his dark-skinned crew. On and on the boat plowed. Then drifted.

At last it became clear that they were docking. There were all the sounds of pulling into a wharf: the change in the rhythm of the machinery . . . backwash . . . scrambling of hands and legs . . . ropes heaved. Lloyd was lifted onto some sort of pier (by one of the Negroes, he surmised) and pushed gently but forcibly into a seated position. After several minutes, he heard the clip-clop of a horse's hooves and the clump of a wagon. He was hoisted again in one graceful maneuver and set down in what felt like a dogcart. He could tell that Schelling was beside him by the scent of the witch hazel. Reins jingled. The cart rattled off on a rutted, hard-packed road.

They rode for perhaps twenty minutes. When the blindfold at last came off, and Lloyd's eyes had got used to seeing again, he saw that they had come to a dismal clearing back off from the river, set on a cliff. A forbidding wall of pines ringed the lumpy open ground, which was studded with shapes that brought to mind his chapel cove back in Zanesville.

"What is this place?" he asked.

"A slave cemetery," Schelling answered. "At least, it appears to be."

He stepped down out of the dogcart and helped the boy to the ground. With his eyes growing more alert, Lloyd saw that the moonlight rained down across a field of primitive graves—rock markers, splintered wooden crosses, and iron bars. The eerie call of a screech owl echoed through the trees.

"Why are we here?" the boy asked, feeling a ghostly presence rising like mist from the stumps and stones.

The antiquarian did not respond but instead looked around

the perimeter of pines, listening hard. Then he lit a lucifer match and held it above his head. In the still, soft air it glowed white-gold for a few seconds before he shook it out. A moment later, a flicker of light answered back from the cliff side and a whip-poor-will called from a tangle of rosemary to the west.

"All right," Schelling decided, and directed the boy toward a grave marked by a slab of granite that in the glare of the moon Lloyd saw had gouged into its surface the words HIC JACET. With unexpected agility and strength, Schelling bent down and heaved the slab to one side, revealing a sturdy wooden ladder descending into the blackness beneath the burial ground.

Lloyd was alarmed at this discovery, but intrigued.

"Wait a moment," Schelling commanded, and disappeared down the ladder.

Lloyd heard another match crack and saw a faint flare from below. There was the clunk of a chain, then a lock clicking, and a door being pried open. Schelling's head reappeared out of the ground. "Come," he whispered.

Pale light streamed to meet them now, and Lloyd followed the man down ten rungs into what he took to be a crypt but which smelled like some kind of root cellar. As soon as he stepped off the ladder and had his feet planted, he saw that this "cellar" opened up into what looked like a gallery of natural catacombs, only the first of which was lit by a lantern. The air was cool but surprisingly dry. As his eyes became adjusted to the shadows, Lloyd saw that the chambers stretching into the distance were filled with paintings and statues, row upon row of shelves lined with leather-bound books, stuffed animals, skeletons, weapons, scientific instruments, and unidentified machines.

"High ground," Schelling announced. "Part of a cave system that the river can't reach. It has been used for many purposes in the past, but now it serves as our hiding place."

"Who are you hiding from? And what . . . is . . . all this?" Lloyd asked.

"It's but a Main Street museum of anatomy compared to what it was," Schelling answered somberly.

"Where . . . where did all the things come from?"

"Europe, Egypt, Syria, Palestine, Mesopotamia. Massachusetts. All over the world."

"Are they yours?" the boy asked.

"I am the custodian and cataloguer, but the collection belongs to the Spirosians. Mother Tongue will explain. Are you ready to meet her?"

"I . . . guess . . . so," Lloyd answered. Up to now he had supposed Mother Tongue to be some senile member of the Illumination Society. What if she was something else?

Schelling lit a hurricane lantern and steered him past a Chippendale cabinet on which perched a dented conquistador's helmet. A curve in the rock wall brought them to a flight of steps hacked into the clay stone. The humped man motioned for the boy to follow.

The stairs led down to a landing that was flooded with the light from a golden candelabrum that took the shape of a tall, full tree. On each branch burned a thick green candle, and between the spitting and dripping of the wax Lloyd heard the gentle lap of water below. Outside the aura of the tapers, the cave ceiling opened up like a tunnel that had been blasted to make way for a train, and then narrowed to a tight stricture on the other side of a large obsidian-dark pool. Floating in the water before him was a small ornate steamboat stained with moss and algae. All its windows were dark except one. A black man dressed as a coachwhip stood beside a gangplank that led from the landing to the riverboat, holding an oil lamp.

"Mother Tongue is expecting you," Schelling told him. "Blazon will be your escort. I will wait for you here."

Lloyd was gripped with such a blend of apprehension and excitement that he could barely move, but move he did, into the black man's lamplight and over the gangplank, half thinking that the weird boat would evaporate the moment he stepped

foot on board. It did not, but it looked as if it might well sink—
or had sunk and been raised from the depths of the river. In the
stillness of the cave, Lloyd imagined that he could hear the very
nails aching in the swollen planks.

The man called Blazon remained stone-silent but led him
straight to the central parlor on the main deck where the
lamp shone. Then, just as he was opening the weather-beaten
wooden door, the most miraculous thing Lloyd had ever seen in
his life happened. Everything around him burst alight, so suddenly that he thought the boat was in flames. He let out a giant
gasp, which seemed to please Blazon. The boat was not on fire
but shimmering with tiny prisms that looked as if they were
made of isinglass and filled with lightning. By what means the
prisms came to life Lloyd could only guess, but as instantly as
they had ignited they expired and he found himself blinking
hard. He heard Blazon close the door behind him, then his own
heartbeat.

A single glass oil lamp with extended wick stood on a walnut
table beside an old cane plantation chair and a ladder-back
rocking chair made of pine. Seated in the cane monstrosity was
the oldest woman Lloyd had ever seen. Her hair was pure white
and thick. Her face, which was the color of blancmange, was
fantastically wrinkled, yet she sat upright without a hint of
palsy, dressed in a cool-looking long white dress, like a southern
lady about to serve tea. The only other piece of furniture in the
room was a weary haircloth sofa on which a mangy coonhound
was fast asleep.

"Come," the old woman called to him, indicating the ladder-
back.

"The lights . . ." Lloyd said, but he couldn't complete his
question.

He found himself meandering toward the rocking chair as if
in a trance and, once seated, was startled when one of the run-
ners pressed down on the tail of a cat—but not like any cat he
had ever encountered. It was hairless. Sleek of body, its skin

was rose-pink, becoming the color of pencil lead on its paws, with a face that reminded Lloyd of a mask, and remarkable slitted eyes that were as green as his own.

"Curiosity!" the old woman commanded, and the cat leaped into her lap. "You are always putting yourself in harm's way."

Lloyd tried to ease himself back into the chair, glad that the hound hadn't stirred. When he managed to settle, he was again shaken by the old woman's eyes. He had noticed from across the room that she wore no spectacles, which had surprised him, given her obvious age, but he was surprised still further to find her now looking straight at him with eyes as green as the cat's—and his, too. As green as absinthe, but clear.

The room was silent but for the purring of the feline and what he imagined to be the trip-hammer of his heart. He wanted to know about the lights . . . what he was doing there. He tried to remain still. The old coonhound slept on.

At first the woman's green eyes stabbed at him like darning needles, but gradually the intensity of her scrutiny eased. There was no decaying odor of ravaged flesh or incontinence about her, as he had experienced with the older Zanesville biddies; rather, a clean simple scent of lemon verbena. Despite the alien surroundings and the circumstances that had brought him there, he began to feel reassured. Until the ancient lady spoke.

"You've already been with a woman, haven't you? A grown woman."

"How did you know that?" Lloyd cried. "Can you read minds?"

"I've heard that you can," the woman answered, and her face assumed an inscrutable smile. "Can you guess how old I am?"

"Eighty?" Lloyd tried, afraid that he might offend her.

"Fiddlesticks!" She laughed.

"One hundred, then."

"Oh, I'm every bit of that." She sighed. "Every bit and then some."

"I think you're the oldest person I've ever seen," Lloyd admitted.

The old coon dog dozed.

"I am. And I don't know how much longer I have. So let me cut off the gristle and get to the meat. There's nothing wrong with your discovery of your manhood, even if you are still a child. The first experience of the flesh is a great challenge for everyone, but it is a special trial for males and you have passed yours. That may bode well. You are destined to run well before yourself in many ways. Now, before I tell you the things you were brought here to hear I will let you ask me one question. What would you like to know about—the lights?"

Lloyd pondered for a moment, feeling for the woman's intent.

"I think you'll tell me about the lights," he replied at last. "What I'd like to know is how you get this boat through such a narrow passage."

The woman gave the cat a long, deep stroke.

"The boat never leaves this grotto. Nor do I. It wouldn't be safe for me to move about anymore."

She clutched the hairless animal tighter and lowered her voice.

"And I don't mean to frighten you, Lloyd, but there may come a time, sooner than you think, when it won't be safe for you to move about so freely, either."

Lloyd shifted in his chair, unable to turn his gaze from the woman's eyes, which reached out and embraced him, her words filling the sparsely furnished room like the shadows that closed in around the lamp.

CHAPTER 9

The Hunger for Secrets

"DID I SCARE YOU, LLOYD?" MOTHER TONGUE ASKED AFTER A moment of silence. "Or is your hunger for secrets so great that you are immune to fear?"

Lloyd tried to feel in his mind, reaching inside and then outward into the shadows for some sense of his dead sister's protective presence. Why was there a museum under a graveyard and a riverboat stuck inside a cliff? How did the darkness suddenly burst into light? A wave of fatigue washed over him and he longed to snuggle with the dog on the rough couch.

"We'll see," he answered at last, not wanting to show that he was scared—and scared because he did not know why. "Who are the Spirosians?"

Mother Tongue gave another one of her odd smiles.

"The movement dates back to very olden times in Europe and the Middle East, but it draws its strength from even longer ago, in ancient Greece and Egypt. It is based on the thought of one exemplary man, Spiro of Lemnos. Some stories tell that he was a hermaphrodite—both a male and a female. But that may be just a legend. We do know that he was a Phoenician by birth—sometimes called a son of Atlantis, the original philosopher-scientist. But he was also a practitioner of what some might describe as magic. A man of unique genius. The superior of Thales, Pythagoras, and Archimedes, and greater than all those who followed—Leonardo, Copernicus, Galileo, Newton. He saw more deeply into the mysteries of life than anyone else before or since. In fact, his ideas were so far ahead of his time that he was constantly in danger of persecution, imprisonment, and death. So he concealed his discoveries and teachings in a secret language—hierograms embedded in beautiful, intricate puzzles that he called Enigmas. No one knows how he came by this language or the design for these puzzles, but there is a myth that this knowledge was given to him by the gods. Others believe he stole it."

"What sort of things did he know?" Lloyd inquired.

"The intimate dependencies of energy and matter—hidden correspondences. The lights you witnessed? They are his conception. A form of electrical power harnessed two thousand years before Benjamin Franklin experimented with his kite and key."

"Two thousand years ago!" Lloyd coughed.

"The world is not always what you think it is, and history is most certainly not what you have been told," Mother Tongue replied.

"What else did he do?" Lloyd asked, thinking back to St. Ives's story of Junius Rutherford.

"He grasped the most complex relationships between numbers, music, and the stars. He looked deep into the idiosyncrasies of other creatures, the chemistry of healing, and the nature of disease. Most important, his thought embraced the relationship of language to life and the shape of the mind. He was a geometer, dreamer, and diviner—a maker of medicines and occult machines. One legend says he could even raise and animate the dead."

"That sounds like an awful lot for one man to know," Lloyd said, whistling.

"Yes!" agreed Mother Tongue. "That was his most insightful idea of all. The necessity of camouflage to survive. The need to appear to be many men instead of one, and the need to *become* many men—and women, too—in order to make his ideas live."

"How do you know that he was just one man?"

Mother Tongue stroked the cat. The coon dog never moved.

"The same has been asked of many," she answered. "There is a view that all the great figures of inspiration—Socrates, Moses, Jesus, Muhammad, Buddha, Zoroaster—do not represent individual historical figures but, rather, are code names for composite characters uniting the thoughts and visions of many people. There is no way to prove or disprove the actual life of Spiro now, for he chose always to hide in the shadows, and so his reputation and his achievements have been relegated to the shadows of history. But upon this skeleton of shadows most of what we know of as the modern world has developed.

"He traveled widely—to Rome and the deserts of Arabia. Jerusalem, Baghdad, Alexandria, and deep into Europe—India and China, too. His knowledge he passed on to carefully chosen pupils who were sworn to secrecy. Magicians, physicians, alchemists, philosophers, architects, engineers, and artists. To each of them he gave a piece of the master puzzle, one fragment of what he called the Great Enigma."

"Why?"

"So no one individual or even generation ended up knowing the master goal—they only knew the pieces they had been entrusted with and the implications that flowed from them. This protected the Great Enigma, for if one person or school failed, for whatever reason, to pass on or build on their knowledge, there was always the hope that others would survive and continue the work."

"What happened to him?" Lloyd asked, leaning forward. "When did he die?"

"In one sense, he never did," Mother Tongue replied. "Because we are talking about him now and still coming to terms with his thought and deeds. But in the sense you mean, what happened to the one man is lost in the puzzle that he created. What happened to the many men and women that he became—that is much better known. Because, you see, it was inevitable that the pieces of the puzzle would seek each other out and try to form the Whole."

"How do you mean?" Lloyd asked, and was surprised when the ancient woman gestured toward the wall of the cabin behind her. He could have sworn that the wall was bare before, but now it showed a map of the world that seemed to glow and swirl like the marvelous lights that had illuminated the crusted boat upon his arrival.

Mother Tongue cleared her throat, as if savoring the taste of her phlegm.

"From the sands of Egypt to what is now Italy and France, Holland, Germany, and the forests of Northern Europe, England and Ireland, all the way to the Orient, the lineage of the students of Spiro's teachings coalesced to form a confederacy with the grand design of unifying magic, religion, and science to lead mankind to the fulfillment of the destiny he foresaw. Many of the greatest minds and prime movers of Western culture were later Spiro's followers, bound to secrecy by the oath of the Order. Paracelsus, Nicholas of Cusa, Raleigh, Bacon, Van Leeuwenhoek, Pascal, Lavoisier—and countless others who remain unknown. The names and contributions are so entangled in history that it is impossible to separate the individuals and the strands. Cosmographers and mapmakers joined the Order. Noblemen and divines. Caliphs and rajas. The Spirosians infiltrated the Catholic Church, the Jewish merchant-finance networks, and the cabalistic enclaves—even the dynasties of distant China. They directed emperors and later formed the major craft guilds. They sponsored secret expeditions of discovery.

"Through oblique channels, it was Spiro's thought that lit the fire that fueled the Renaissance and allowed the birth of science, and later inspired the Spirosians to take key steps that led to both the French and American revolutions. From the

Great Pyramids to Trafalgar Square, Mecca to Monticello, his influence has been felt. But secrecy and subterfuge was of necessity always the rule. From the first fog-enshrouded moment of inception, the leaders followed Spiro's practice of concealment and distraction, creating or sponsoring most of all the major secret societies that have ever been heard of, in order to cloak their own investigations and innovations. Many you might not have heard of yet. The Assassins, Knights Templar, Freemasons, Rosicrucians, and the Illuminati—all these had members who believed in the reality of their confederacies without ever knowing the true nature of their origins."

"But why?" Lloyd queried, glancing again at the sleeping dog.

"To confuse enemies by creating figureheads and decoys," the ancient answered. "The attraction and fear of cabals is so ingrained in human society, the Spirosians always sought to use this stratagem as the primary defense and principal tool of direction—misdirection. Spiro taught that it is through the study and practice of illusion that we learn the art and science of the truth, and this philosophy has proved immensely effective. Yet it was always a point of vulnerability, and through this point a splinter was driven that changed the history of the movement and, indeed, the world."

"A splinter?" Lloyd asked. The curious map was now gone from the wall.

"A schism developed. Another sect or school of thought took shape and broke away. They called themselves the Vardogers, a Scandinavian term for a 'psychic double,' but their true name is the Order of the Claws & Candle, which comes from the practice of canny northern priests of old, who attached candles to the backs of crabs, releasing them in graveyards to simulate the spirits of the dead to impress the credulous.

"They believed that mastering the Great Enigma was a task they alone could be trusted with. They retreated so far into their own secrecy that their ingenuity began to fester. They grew to love the interplay of hidden forces and came to believe that the masses must be manipulated like the figures in a vast marionette opera. They turned their composite mind to engines and methods of war and domination, strange new vessels of transport and division—and ever more ingenious techniques for influencing the will. Those of us alive today are just beginning to see how far back in time this labyrinthine campaign began to be waged."

"Wait a minute," Lloyd grunted, leaning back in the rocker. "From what you say—if you are to be believed—the Spirosians have been busybodying themselves all over for a very long time. What makes your view right?"

Mother Tongue's green eyes gleamed.

"It is true that the movement has always sought to steer the secret course of world events—the dissemination of ideas and the prosperity that ensues. But the difference between the progress of humanity at large and the enrichment of a clandestine élite at the expense of whole peoples is as profound as they come."

"But hasn't the movement always been clandestine—and élite?"

"Yes!" snapped the old woman, and heaved the cat to the floor. "The means have been similar in some respects, but the end is entirely different! The candle of the Vardogers' knowledge is very bright, but the crab of their might has very long claws. They are not averse to intimidation, betrayal, and murder. And now the key battlefield is here!"

"In St. Louis?" Lloyd squawked.

"In America—which has long been the jewel of contention in the holy war of dreams and ideas, yes! This nation was founded on just such conflict. But this area in particular has now become a cauldron. It is a focal point for the ravenous plans for expansion and development—the struggle over land and railroads, the erosion of the Indian's ways—and for the spread of the hideous practice of slavery. You are well aware of the slave pens scattered throughout the city that are operated by the auctioneering companies. There is one on Olive Street, and another on Fifth Street that specializes in the sale of children. Children, Lloyd. Younger than you! Your own family walks a razor's edge."

The hairless cat leaped back into Mother Tongue's lap. The coon dog never flinched. Lloyd set the pine ladder-back rocking like a clock pendulum.

"If this time and place is so important, then why is a woman in charge?"

Mother Tongue's eyes flamed and then she smiled again, wrinkling every cleft and furrow in the pudding of her face.

"Spoken like a true little boy. The simple answer is that we are losing the war, Lloyd. I hold the position of authority that I do now out of desperation. We have recently lost a valuable colleague in the South, who was supposedly teaching slaves how to read the Bible. For that, he was ostracized. When it was discovered that he was really teaching them mathematics, he was hanged. Our leadership is embattled, our fund of knowledge is in tatters. The lights you saw—we know how to turn them on and off, but the man who was beginning to understand their secrets is dead. Others throughout the world who might understand them we dare not approach, because they are under close enemy surveillance or we are in doubt about their affiliation."

"I'm sorry to hear that," Lloyd said, yawning. "But my family sleeps in a smelly stable. And I still don't understand what this all has to do with me."

"My boy"—Mother Tongue smiled, her bright green eyes flaring—"the great mission of the Spirosians has been subverted. Our work has been sabotaged and our membership has been preyed upon. Operatives in Europe and abroad have been deposed. Others have defected—won over by greed or fear. Or delusion. We know that deadly new weapons are being made in Germany—and right here in America, in Connecticut and Rhode Island, Mobile and Charleston. Meanwhile, marauders, slave speculators, and any number of professional rascals and rabble-rousers are pouring into Missouri daily. There is trouble brewing in Kansas and Texas. Impending war with Mexico. And still the monster of slavery grows. Our abolitionist agents are all under threat—those that have avoided outright assassination. One day soon, I will be gone. Wolfgang, too. The rest, scattered through the nation and overseas, will go the same way. We need new blood, Lloyd. We want you to join us—to become ordained. We want you to leave your family and the path you are pursuing to be given tuition in ways of thought worthy of your emerging genius. Your friend the showman talks of 'marvels.' I am offering you the chance to change America and the world!"

For an instant there was a mad glitter in the old woman's green eyes that did scare Lloyd, but the words blurted out of his mouth anyway.

"You want me to . . . leave . . . my family?" As much as he had sometimes dreamed of this, it was something he could never do.

The cat uncoiled in the old woman's lap and began to bathe itself with its tongue. The dog dozed on indifferently on the sofa.

"I know that in your heart you are still very young, Lloyd, even though you take much responsibility for earning the family money." The old woman sighed, regaining her composure and evenness of tone. "Your loyalty is admirable. It takes desperate times and dark challenges to make the dissolution of yet another family acceptable. Believe me, I do not make the proposition lightly. But there are such things as casualties of war."

"I'm not at war with anyone," Lloyd responded, and then paused. "Unless, of course, you won't let me go."

"You will go back to your family tonight with my blessing, child—and under the best protection that I can provide. Wolfgang tells me you have plans to go to Texas, to meet your uncle. A very risky undertaking. Well, we can provide that money now, for your parents to depart—in as much style and safety as can be arranged. Or if they wish, but I do not advise this, they can remain here in St. Louis under guard. This, I believe, is much less safe. But we need your help, Lloyd."

"My help?" he yelped. "I thought you were going to help *me*!"

"And so we will! We will help each other. For years we have been awaiting someone of true vision—a mind as bright as that of the first Enigmatist. We believe you are that person, Lloyd. Wolfgang has recounted to me your feats and abilities. With the education that we can provide you, who knows what you can achieve?"

"You would give me books . . . and instruments? Tools?" He thought back to the drafty barn in Zanesville—his yearning for resources worthy of his ambitions.

"And time, Lloyd. Everything you need. A personal key to a library the superior of any you will find in America. You will be given access to the notes and private papers of those of genius from the past. Letters of introduction, and arranged meetings with those living luminaries whom we can trust. You will be tutored in physics, mechanics, optics, acoustics, ballistics, magnetism, electricity, mathematics, chemistry, medicine— whatever you chose."

The boy's eyes brightened at this prospect, and then his face sagged.

"But my family needs me."

"A bigger family needs you," Mother Tongue retorted. "And you know in your heart you need the opportunities we can offer. I can see that you are starving, Lloyd. Not just for beef-steak and fresh vegetables, but for knowledge. For power."

"But I can't leave my parents. Not now!" he moaned. "If we can get to Texas, everything will be all right. I know it. We al-most have enough money. Just a little more work. Just—"

"A few more days or weeks working as a talking monkey on a medicine-show wagon?"

"I do a lot more than that!"

"Indeed you do. As the showman knows too well. Are you re-munerated in proportion?"

"He's my friend!" Lloyd wailed, turning to see if he had woken the dog.

"I say again, your loyalty is admirable," the elegant crone re-joined. "It gives us all confidence in our belief in you. But what of the other matter—your experience with women? Tell me, have you met any suitable females since arriving in St. Louis?"

"N-no," Lloyd stammered.

"Would you like to?" Mother Tongue wheedled. "Sex and the cravings of the body are nothing to be ashamed of—even in one so very young."

Lloyd squirmed in the rocker. He could not hide the fact that he liked what Mother Tongue was saying, but he did not like the way she spoke. There was something in her voice that made him think of a trapdoor.

"What you can learn of books and science you can also learn of love." The old woman smiled. "Wouldn't you like that? To one day become not only a master of ideas and technology but an adept in the erotic arts?"

Lloyd was aroused by this prospect but repulsed by the wrin-kled old woman's offer. It was not something anyone else would say to a boy his age, he knew. And the thought of leaving his parents to themselves at such a tense juncture filled him with guilt and despair. They had already lost his sister, their home, perhaps their happiness together—how could he leave them, too? He stared at the coon dog, which still had not stirred.

"It's late," Mother Tongue acknowledged. "And you must be getting back to your mother and father—at least for now. I did not intend for you to decide on such a weighty matter tonight. But I want you to consider one other reason that you would be well advised to accept our invitation."

At this she lowered her voice and raised her withered hands.

"The Vardogers are able to project and cultivate fear. They are equally skilled at orchestrating a mob brawl, mining a bridge, or breaking a mind. They have many much more subtle arts, I am afraid. Investigations into forbidden realms. We know they have taken notice of you, Lloyd. One of their agents has been seen observing your performances with the showman. Do you not think that very soon they will seek you out with an offer of their own? But will it be an offer? Or will it be an edict? What if instead of asking you to leave your parents they take your parents from you? What will you do then? No one goes far who travels alone."

The old woman's voice had taken on such a dramatic tone that Lloyd instinctively slipped from the rocker onto the sofa. But when he went to pat the hound he found that it was as stiff as a statue, sculpted into a position of peaceful repose. He could have sworn he had heard it snoring, like his father.

"He . . . he's dead!" Lloyd recoiled. "You've—"

"Old Lazarus is sleeping very soundly, but he keeps me company," the old lady answered, and blew out the lamp. "Now reach out your hands to me. I have something to give you. A token of my faith in you. And a sign of our trust in your judgment and discretion."

Lloyd clambered to his feet in the dark, unnerved by the stuffed dog.

"Take my hands, child," Mother Tongue whispered.

He heard a sound that he guessed was the cat lighting on the floor as the old woman rose. Bracing himself for the feel of her soft white talons, he thrust his own hands forward. Into his moist palms plopped two warm spheres as his fists tightened. Polished jewels, he imagined—fabulous treasures from some far corner of the world.

"Good night, Lloyd," Mother Tongue said. "For now."

Lloyd stuffed the jewels into his pocket and stumbled toward the door. Blazon was waiting outside with a flickering lamp. Without comment or question, he led the boy back the way they had come, where Schelling greeted him with a brusque presentation of his calcium-stained tooth. The grotto and the passageways seemed to be much darker now. Why not turn on the marvelous lights? The humpback refused to be engaged on this or any point, and so the boy had to mind every step as they climbed back up to the cemetery. Once they were free of the tomb, the blindfold was reinstated and Lloyd was encouraged back into the dogcart. Their voyage was repeated in reverse without any words being exchanged, Lloyd's head swirling with questions and worries—and hopes—until, lulled by the legato rhythm of the boat, he slipped into a hypnagogic drowse. When he came to himself again, the boat was docking back at the ferry landing and the air smelled very late—or very early. One of the powerful black men set him down on the pier, and Wolfgang Schelling removed the blindfold.

"All right, Lloyd," he said. "Hurry home. I will see you in the afternoon. But be careful. Not everyone means you as well as we do."

These words echoed in the boy's mind as he raced back toward the stable, wondering if his parents would be awake and waiting for him—and what he was going to say if they were. The streets were dark but for the lights of a shuttered tavern. No one else appeared to be around. Still, there was a sinister sense of watchfulness about the lanes and it wasn't until he was all the way back to the familiar smell of the glue renderer's and the stable door that he felt calm again. Gratefully, his parents were both sound asleep—Hephaestus hog-breathing with drink, Rapture sighing low, sometimes saying something the boy could not understand (which was not that unusual at any time).

At the rear of the stable, Lloyd sneaked off with one of his father's hoarded matches and scraped it hard to make enough light to examine the prize that Mother Tongue had entrusted him with. He expected gemstones plucked from some harvested diadem, but he gasped and almost dropped the match and set the rank-smelling barn on fire when he saw that what she had given him was two brilliant green glass eyes.

What did it mean?

Was the ancient woman really blind, or was this just some trick? After he recovered from his shock, Lloyd extinguished the match, but the two orbs seemed to continue glowing, as if his recognition had triggered some covert luminosity within them. Or is it in my mind? he wondered.

In either case, as he fondled them—and peered into them in the pale light of morning—they seemed to take on a deeper presence. One globe he imagined gazed back at the moments that had brought him and his family to this crossroads, each of the scenes and encounters since leaving their home suspended like prehistoric insects in amber. The other sphere was a lens that he fancied looked into the future, a lightning-lit horizon of messenger possibility and foreshadowings . . . frozen pictures melting alive . . . unknown faces beginning to form.

Cupping them in his palms, Lloyd sensed an occult quality of heat and energy about them. What if these really were Mother Tongue's eyes? he pondered. Maybe she *is* blind—and yet through some arcane mechanism the spheres allowed her to see. A kind of sight, anyway, delivered by a spectral science he didn't comprehend . . . but might . . . in time.

Something deep within him felt a magnetic summons toward these enigmas—via Mother Tongue and her minions or not. "The door of my destiny is opening," he whispered to the slowly graying dawn.

THE HIGH COST OF BEWONDERMENT

CHAPTER 1
Rara Avis

AFTER HIS PERPLEXING MEETING WITH MOTHER TONGUE, LLOYD found it hard to rouse himself in the morning. Through a haze of threats and twisted images, his consciousness was brought back to St. Louis and the stable by the piggish noises of conjugal struggle. While the manufacture of the flying toys had brought his parents together in the matter of practical survival, their intimate life had not recovered since the Chicken Germain–root salve treatment, and Hephaestus's libido had been bottled to bursting. Up to this point both parents had been discreet regarding Lloyd's awareness of their lovemaking, but the urgency of the need and the systemic erosion of his dignity provoked Hephaestus to risk skin discomfort and to break with all decorum in a loud, and to Lloyd's ears, exceedingly boorish way. Lloyd could not tell how much his mother resisted at first, but in the end she succumbed and seemed almost to enjoy it. Perhaps her need was too great to ignore as well.

Lloyd was smart enough to know that, in the matter of sex at least, there was much that he yet had to learn. Still, it sickened him to hear them, for in one guttural exclamation from the other side of a pile of mice-warm hay he realized that this was how *he* had come to be. At least in part. Maybe the circumstances had been different—the place, the mood, the smells and tastes—but at the heart it was this same bestial dance-brawl. "There should be a better way to be born," Lloyd said to himself, even as his own desire was shamefully aroused at the sounds of his parents. Then he clutched himself to fulfillment.

He pulled up his pants and dragged from his pocket the two glass eyes. The more he examined them, the more they seemed to examine him. Disconcerted and afraid, he thrust them back into the depths of the bag, far down into the wads of soiled clothes where he had hidden the box adorned by the Ambassadors from Mars and his uncle's letter. Then he stowed the bag well under the hay.

None of the Sitturds had anything to say while they breakfasted on stale rolls and can-brewed coffee. Chastened by post-coital remorse, Hephaestus and Rapture did not press Lloyd for any information on how he had slept and gave no indication they knew that he had disappeared in the night.

Meanwhile Lloyd's brain, once free of his own sexual obsession, began whirring with worries and considerations about the Spirosians and the Vardogers. Could the things that Mother Tongue had told him be true? A war in time between two great secret societies—the real powers behind all other secret societies—the hidden orchestrators of history now brought into lethal conflict over the issues of slavery and expansion, the destiny of America?

He had seen the lights; he could not get around that. Some unthinkable harnessing of electrical energy. And the library beneath the burial ground, the riverboat festooned with moss—he had seen these things with his own eyes. Still, he could not believe that he had been told the truth. Something in a secret place inside him rebelled at the choice he had been given, and the feel of the stuffed dog on the couch returned to make his skin crawl. He was certain that he had heard it breathe.

He bolted from the stable still swallowing a lump of bread, wondering if once he had gone his parents might continue their passionate battle, or if his mother would go off to her laundry

and nursing duties while his father returned to his aimless dis-
integration. It appeared to him that as his capabilities increased theirs diminished, so that even his mother had become
his child now. His work was how the family fed itself. And if the
family was somehow feeding upon itself, he felt that it was not
his fault. St. Louis was the poison. The dance-hall lights. The
necessity of money. All the hopeless and hope-mad people wandering through. The one solution he could see lay in getting
back on the road to Texas, back to their dream. Then his father
might wake and his mother would remember her old, quick joy.
He ran to meet Mulrooney, who was camped on a dry-grass
common to the west.

The Ambassadors and the Ladies Mulrooney were all sick
from rancid milk. The tent stank of their sufferings and
hummed with flies. Regrettably, a competition between the two
largest of the flying clubs that had formed was scheduled for
noon along the riverbank. Given the gastrointestinal crisis that
had seized Mulrooney, the showman did not feel fit or able to
attend, so Lloyd was left to gather all the soaring toys he could
carry on the back of one of the wagon's horses and make his
way there all by himself. The obligation of rewarding the faithful and the opportunity to make some much needed sales was
too important. But it did nothing to allay his fears. He had
never faced the wall of faces on his own before. Never all alone.
He realized that Mother Tongue had been right in a way: he
was Mulrooney's monkey. He had always had the showman to
lean on, to back him up. Now it would just be him, a little boy
from a small town—a boy with a big brain and bigger dreams,
from a small-minded town, now confronted by what seemed a
huge city and the inherent hostility of strangers.

The sky was achingly clear, and a gathering had already
formed by the time he reached the bank where the competition was to be held. At his arrival, a cheer went up and people rushed toward him. They all wanted to greet the "little
genius"—the boy who made the paper birds and gliding gadgets,

a hundred or so of which now lay on the grass in the summer sun.

The onslaught of adulation puffed up Lloyd's spirits (and ego). Maybe St. Louis wasn't such an evil place after all. Perhaps fame and fortune could yet be his. That would save his family. Surely. Yes, there were cruelties and injustices. Vigilance committees, bushwhackings, and intimidation. Freed blacks could be falsely arrested and sold back into slavery, and some of the antislave voices were nonetheless anti-Negro, advocating the establishment of a whites-only territory. But right in front of him were people lined up to see him and shake his hand— many, if not most of them, good people (a few of them the same good people who had looked on as Francis McIntosh fried).

With newfound confidence Lloyd scanned the throng, trying to pinpoint some presence that was hostile—one of the Claws & Candle spies that Mother Tongue had warned him about. Was it the man with thinning hair who was still wearing his leather blacksmith's apron, the same kind his father used to wear back in Ohio when he was working—when he did work? What about the striped-vest barber or any of a number of mulatto traders, Spanish boatmen, or French fortune hunters? Perhaps one of the high-toned ladies hiding behind their fans. He tore the crowd apart face by face. But they were all watching him, and none of them appeared hostile. Yet they all could become so, he knew. He had already learned how fast the tastes of the horde could change—how insatiable they were for novelty, for innovation, and for failure. Whether or not the Spirosians and the Vardogers were real, he understood that the cries of ovation he received were but catcalls in reverse. The words of Mother Tongue came back to him: "No one goes far who travels alone."

Alone now with his cargo of toys for sale, he felt the painful wisdom of her words. Then he glanced back up at the soothing blue emptiness overhead. That was something important that she had overlooked. There were places one could *only* go alone.

That was the difference between the assembled mass on the riverbank and himself, Lloyd realized. The same problem as in Zanesville. What no one else could grasp, or what they could but dream about, he could *do*. It put his relationship with his family at risk. It put his life at risk, yet what would he be if he did not reach out? How could he lift them up—how could he save his father from himself—if he did not reach further, higher? Fear of the crowd? Yes, but what of the fear of the future?

In that fleeting instant before he was forced, all by himself, to welcome the masses and to officiate at the start of the competition—to hawk his wares like a common street vendor, to represent the interests of not one but two misfit families—he saw the sky opening before him like a welcome beyond anything that Mother Tongue and Schelling could offer. It was his destiny to ascend still higher. He would rise up into the sun above the river and all that it represented. Above the flatboats and the barge lines. Above the steeples and the columns, the plush townhouses and the claptrap cottages. He would soar above every dock walloper and carriage hack—so high that every merchant and magnate would see him, not just these few folk scattered here. There might yet come a time to travel in time, as his broken father had dreamed of. But for now, what people would pay to see was a kind of travel they could understand. Memories of Zanesville and the beaver came back to him. The trick—and perhaps it was a trick that the Vardogers, if they were real, had mastered—was how to scare people in the right way. Bewonderment. For what is fear but the other side of the nickel of surprise?

The competition was a tremendous success. The club that called itself Wings Over Walnut Street managed a narrow (but very popular) victory over *The St. Louis Dispatch*–sponsored Harriers. Young Lloyd was interviewed for the first time. The questions came fast and furious about where he got his ideas and where he lived and went to school—answers that he fudged as best he could. He was able to sell almost all the soarers he had brought, and he was repeatedly asked what new treats of whimsy he had in store. When the crowd broke up and people resumed their humdrum lives again, he was riding on air. From the tawdry trickery of a medicine show he had created a genuine phenomenon. Then and there, he made a decision about the patronage of Mother Tongue.

After returning the horse and giving a cursory report to Mulrooney (who had been reduced to squatting upon a makeshift thunderbox in abdominal agony), Lloyd kept his appointment at the bookshop, sleepy though he was. Schelling was there as usual, primly dressed under a veneer of dust. The humped man was reserved in his remarks, but Lloyd sensed that he was trying to sound him out for clues to his response to Mother Tongue's interview. The boy focused on his reading with renewed intensity. Schelling masked his curiosity as best he could and let the boy study until the normal time without interrogation—something he was soon to regret.

CHAPTER 2

Ascension and Deception

WHEN LLOYD LEFT THE BOOKSHOP, HE WAS FOLLOWED. THE MAN wore a black flat hat and was dressed like a Friend or Quaker in a dark single-breasted collarless coat without buttons. Two perspiring Negroes emerged from a furniture store trundling a sideboard, and Lloyd used their cover to slip behind a butcher's wagon. He waited until the man tailing him was just pulling even before darting out and snatching the big black hat. The man uttered an oath, but Lloyd was too quick for him. With a flick of his wrist, he sent the flat hat flying under an ambling oxcart, where it became flatter still, and then shot off back down the street the way he had come, his little legs working like steam pistons. Once around the corner, he ducked down the glassblower's lane and then back around to the glue renderer's over a tomcat fence. He did not spot the man in the buttonless coat again, although the more he thought about it, the more he realized that it was possible that the figure had been female.

That night, at Lloyd's uncompromising insistence, the Sitturds decamped from the stable and took refuge in a boiled linseed oil–smelling mission house operated by the Temperance Society (where, to Rapture's relief, Hephaestus was forced to swear off his drinking and men and women were not allowed to sleep together). The next morning, on the way to see the showman, Lloyd learned that a fire had broken out in their former abode. Only one of the bony nags that had been stabled there (and was not long for the gluepot anyway) had died in the conflagration. No one else was injured. "Trust your intuition," St. Ives had advised him.

Maybe it was just a coincidence, Lloyd thought. The building was a tinderbox just waiting for a spark. But maybe not. Mother Tongue had warned him that he was being watched, and he knew for himself that he had been followed. Of course, it was possible, he reasoned, that the spy in the buttonless coat worked for Mother Tongue and Schelling, whoever they really were. In any case, arson—if that was what was involved—was a big step up from being tailed. The safe thing to do was lie low until the family had enough money to leave town. Lloyd had made up his mind that he was not going to accept Mother Tongue's proposal. Nor, if he could help it, was he going to fall into the hands of the Vardogers—supposing that they were real and were really after him. He was going to go his own way.

He never returned to Schelling's bookshop, and the next morning he told the still weak but recovering Mulrooney that he intended to take a break from the soaring toys in preparation for an entirely new kind of venture that would be noteworthy and lucrative beyond any of their previous ambitions. This latter note cheered and "bewondered" Mulrooney, but the "unfortunate intelligence" that the boy would not be present to stimulate further sales in the flying gizmos when the local interest was running "so heartwarmingly hot" provoked boisterous resistance.

Lloyd took pains to point out that a little time off, and the resulting suspense this would create, would be good for business. Besides, he needed time to perfect his new innovation and, as the showman knew so well, magic did not just happen.

Mulrooney plunged into the dumps over Lloyd's news, believing that the lad, in an attempt (probably encouraged by his parents) to show that he was wise to the ways of show business, was holding out for a larger share of the takings. The old sales-man sensed that he had reached the *terminus ad quem* of their commercial relationship and began making mental prepara-tions to depart the city before the summer heat became any more oppressive (which did not seem possible). For the mo-ment, however, he did not feel safe buttoning his pants all the way. Lloyd said goodbye without further comment or any ques-tions about the condition of the wives or the Ambassadors. It was clear to Mulrooney that the boy had some pet scheme of great pitch and moment in mind, but his curiosity was tem-porarily overmastered by digestive discomfort.

Life in the mission house brought the Sitturds to serious grief. For Lloyd there was a constant threat from the inmates, many having bounced between the jail and the insane asylum. For Rapture there were endless smiles to fake, chamber pots to clean, and boils to lance. But Hephaestus suffered the worst in the Cold Water Army. While he craved succulent hams glazed with brown sugar and sweet fat orange-peel muffins, he was served sinewy gruel and biscuits as hard as musketballs—then told to wash the dishes. Lloyd would spare him no pocket money from his accumulating savings, and Rapture refused to sneak into the pews with him after lights-out to spoon and nuz-zle. The gimpy blacksmith found himself brooding over the providential letter from his brother—and dreaming of his forge in Zanesville, of toad-sticking and fishing in the Licking River with a jug of his elderberry wine beside him. There was no place for him in St. Louis—no place for him in the family any-more. He had sold what tools he had left from their earlier mis-adventures. Little Jack Redhorse's mash was pestering his kidneys and giving him the shakes. Now all the prayer-meeting hubbub and the sudden interruption of his escalating alcohol consumption drove him into a hallucinatory frenzy, so that Brother Dowling was forced to threaten him with ejection from the refuge. Then he was gone. Just like that, one morning.

Rapture, who felt that all her "speritual" links and secret

skills had run dry (in the same way that Lloyd's mystic connection with his ghost sister had been severed), returned from a foot-swollen day of drudgery for the sawbones who patted her rear end to find that her husband was not curled in his sweaty cot in the men's dormitory and in fact had not been seen since what passed for breakfast (which often did not pass for several days). How I hate my father sometimes, Lloyd thought. If only I did not love him.

Rapture cried herself to sleep that night, missing the garden back in Zanesville, her herbs and remedies, the cooking, the animals, the life they used to have. Lloyd took the news in apparent stride, keeping his hurt and worry to himself. He dared not tell her about the Spirosians or the Vardogers, and if his father was bent upon his own destruction he saw nothing that he could do at the moment save what he was trying to do—one final show that would be remembered forever in St. Louis. One grand performance that could rescue her.

From the platform of his modest celebrity, he would leap into the rarefied blue of legend and newfound wealth. Statesmen, speculators, and the captains of industry would woo him. He would save his mother and father, and they would not need to go to Texas to live off his uncle's charity. They could stay in St. Louis. They would eat French cheeses and broiled chicken. They would have a Negro footman and drawers full of patent medicine and ready-made clothes, a snooker table and brass spittoons, and decanters of absinthe, the Green Fairy that St. Ives drank. One day he would track the gambler down and invite him back to work for him. The rooms of their white-pillared mansion would be lined with books, telescopes, armillary spheres, and oil paintings of naked women with breasts like rolling waves. It would be "up tuh de notch," as his mother would say. If the Spirosians and the Vardogers wanted his loyalty, then let there be a bidding war—not a war of nerves but one that he could win, with negotiations out in the open, and with buckwheat griddle cakes, sirloins, and giant influence machines into the bargain.

When Hephaestus did not return the next morning, Rapture grew even more morose, but Lloyd assumed that he had sought refuge with the mud and root dwellers of the shantytown below the docks. It was true that there were razor fights and fisticuffs down there, but there was also boiled crawfish and banjo tunes, so perhaps the old man was not so crazy after all. In any case, Lloyd had bigger birds to fly, and he turned all the strength of his being toward his goal.

Via a circuitous route to throw off any pursuit, he went each day out to a rolling stretch of open land to the northwest of the city and began experimenting. Long before 1894, when Lawrence Hargrave was lifted from the ground by a chain of his cellular kites, or 1903, when Samuel Franklin Cody crossed the English Channel on a vessel towed by kites, the young genius from Zanesville was contemplating the logistics of his own ascension. It was what Mulrooney would have described as a "hurculanean task," for his imagination sought to integrate balloon, kite, and glider design to create an aerial display that would leave the people of St. Louis aghast.

He recognized that the issues involved in powered flight could not be solved in his present circumstances. The development of an internal-combustion engine both effective and light enough to drive an aerocraft would require tools, time, access to a machine shop, money, and fuel that he did not have. His idea was not to try to invent something new from scratch but to perfect what he already knew about. For background and inspiration, he had taken from Schelling's shop *The Notebooks of Leonardo da Vinci,* with his drawings of the famous ornithopter, *The History of Ballooning,* and the book of Chinese kites (a slender seventeenth-century Dutch text on using kites to lift fireworks that he had referred to before), George Pocock's sketches of his carriage-pulling kite system, a book on bird anatomy, the best physics manual he could find—and the published works to date of Sir George Cayley, the English aeronautical pioneer who had identified the separate properties of lift, thrust, and drag.

From initial experiments with kites, Lloyd read that Cayley had moved on to gliders (a progression that would lead to the first recorded manned flight from the top of a dale in Brompton, England, with his terrified and soon-to-resign coachman as the pilot guinea pig). Eight years before the English baronet, the so-called father of aviation, would achieve this first fragile success, young Lloyd Sitturd, on the outskirts of slave-era St. Louis, was on the verge of another order of breakthrough all his own.

He began by building models, trying to understand and outline the precise sequence of events involved and therefore the technical problems he would need to overcome, in the exact order that he would confront them—collecting the materials he needed for assembly from his different roundabout journey each day to what he called the Field of Endeavor. The summer heat rose like his hopes, and Hephaestus still did not return to the mission house.

One night he found his mother talking to herself via a string sack of onions that she often consulted with in the cool room. He knew that she despised the "sweetmout" rot doctor she worked for, and that coming back to the gristly "bittle" of the long-plank church dinners was too close a reminder of things she had witnessed during the day. She had to "tie up me mout," as she put it, around the other women, and the "she-she talk affer praisemeetin' " always left her silent in a grim, hurricane a-comin' Gullah way. The onion sack at least provided some consolation.

"Dey, dey," she mumbled. "He naw be attackid. Naw capse. Jes gone 'way."

Lloyd could see that she was "bex vexed," and he did his best to console her. To help her " 'traight'n." The last thing he needed just then was for her to slip her chain, too.

Where had that image come from? St. Louis was getting to
them. More of the ominous words of Mother Tongue came
back to him. He tried to hold Rapture's hand, something he
rarely did and had not done for quite some time.

"Saw a blackbu'd attuh brekwus widda bruk-up wing," she
said with a sigh.

"That's just superstition," he said.

"Eb'nso. Fell down a chimbly. Buckruh seen it, too."

"But that doesn't *mean* anything. Birds sometimes fall out of
the sky. It wouldn't be anything to fly if it was easy," he said, trying to soothe her. "Even for birds."

"Seen a plateye affer!" she hissed, by which she meant an ap-
parition.

"Murruh, you can't go around thinking you see ghosts all the
time," he told her, but he thought that his voice seemed to lack
conviction. The ghost of his lost sister, Lodema, had been very
real to him back in Zanesville. And now he was coming to think
of ghosts in a new way yet again, as that familiar ghost slipped
further into the past. The trouble was, it was in a ghostly way—
not fully formed, just out of clear sight. Yet present somehow.
Active. Intent.

"He be haa'dhead. A hebby cumplain. Bit Ah's sponsubble."

"No more than I am," Lloyd replied solemnly. He knew that
his father resented his talents, even as he so very much appre-
ciated them. The old man was like a crib-sucking mule you
forgave for doing damage. But the boy did not like to see his
mother ornery and blue at the same time. And he did not think
it was wise for her to lapse so completely into her native dialect,
even if she was addressing a sack of onions. The walls in St.
Louis had ears. Strange things were afoot.

"Here," he said, reaching down to the floor. "Here's your
hengkitchuh."

His accent was authentic and sharp. She bristled at it.

"Ain't gwine crya!"

He made a move to embrace her, but she shoved him away.

"Git 'way, l'il swellup!"

That hit Lloyd in the lights. He would rather have fallen from a rooftop.

But his own tar boiled up inside and he struck at her, landing his child-boy blow just about where she had given birth to him.

Rapture gave out a dreadful wheeze but still retained her "tan' up." Then they both gave into hugging and crying—softly—for fear of the church matrons in their Balmoral skirts and their shush-shush disapproval of anything vaguely human.

"It's going to be all right," Lloyd heard himself saying. "It will. I will make it all right."

They kissed, for the first time in a very long while, and he slunk off to the chaos of the dormitory to prepare for another night of alley-cat scavenging.

Like his mother, Lloyd wanted to believe that Hephaestus was passing the jug and sopping gravy maybe two miles below, but he could not escape the possibility that an accident had befallen him. Of course, even if this was the case, it did not mean that the followers of the Claws & Candle were involved. His father was, after all, more than capable of doing himself harm. And there were always the knife houses to consider—floating brothel-saloons based in firetrap launches and decommissioned steamboats that renegade whites ran or that freed blacks were able to negotiate, smoke-filled mobile roach pits where men of all colors gambled on barrels and dance girls would put their legs up to knock over the whiskey. Then the razors would come out. There were rumors that a gargantuan woman named Indian Sweet ran one of the most popular and violent boats on the river. After his father's foray with Chicken Germain—and given his weakness for sour mash, blackened fish, and raucous music—Lloyd could imagine all too clearly his sire facedown in the Mississippi as the morning sun rose.

It was then that he would take from their hiding place Mother Tongue's terrible green eyes. He could not return them.

He could not discard them. Some moments he thought that he should just accept her offer of help and be done with his family—perhaps that was the way to really save them. The problem was that he did not believe he could trust the old witch—or Schelling, either, for that matter. Mother Tongue might give him gifts of education and money, but then he would be forever beholden to her and her hidden officers. Once initiated into either the Spirosians or the Vardogers (assuming there was any true difference between them), he knew that he could never leave.

Rapture became more and more distraught, muttering to herself and to the onions, which sometimes sprouted long green shoots, and which in his troubled dreams Lloyd imagined stretching out to strangle her. He did not like to see how carefully and methodically she washed her hands and arms in the tin basin after returning from work each night. Where else did she wash so diligently when no one was looking?

And so he redoubled his efforts, skulking in the small hours through the factory lanes, the holding pens, and the residential enclaves, searching for abandoned items amid the ash-hopper-sleeping-porch-outhouse-junk-lot backstage of St. Louis. What he did not find in these places he went looking for down on the docks at night—sneaking out of the male dormitory, with its bedlam of tubercular coughs and alcoholic dementia. Throughout the day he read, sketched, pondered, and paced. Then he began making and breaking, dismantling and reconfiguring—sewing, pasting, running, chucking, checking, measuring, and reassessing—driven to the brink of madness by his dream of flight and his yen for female flesh.

On his nocturnal hunting expeditions he witnessed things that opened dark new doors in his longing: a white woman in a rose arbor behind one of the well-to-do houses, kneeling down to her black houseboy, whose pants she lowered. Through another window he chanced to see a wattle-chinned oldster disrobe and allow a bare-breasted harlot in creased trousers and pointed boots to insert a bridle bit in his mouth and flail his wobbling buttocks with a riding crop. These visions fired his fantasies and made him all the more desperate to take to the sky.

Not only had his knowledge of physics and mechanics deepened; his understanding of people was sharper and subtler. He knew that he could not fulfill a project of the scope and magnitude he had in mind without the help of others. Yet he could not afford to fall into the clutches of either of the twilight leagues that Mother Tongue had told him about. As he could not avoid experimenting, or the need to gather equipment and materials, he had to run the constant risk of being seen—whether by some hired whisperer or by a trained agent and perhaps assassin (who would no doubt be skilled in the arts of camouflage and deception). Was it the peanut peddler? The ink-and-parchment lawyer, or the coffeehouse Romeo? It could even have been one of the slatternly wash girls or the Negro boys in their tow-linen shirts. Sometimes Lloyd thought that the notion that he was surrounded by emissaries of a powerful occult order would drive him around the bend. Yet his intuition remained keen. If the ghost of his dead twin was not as present to him anymore, he retained his sensitivity to what passed below the surface of daily life, and his time on the medicine-show wagon had made him a wiser judge of character than he would otherwise have been. It was this skill that allowed him to see the possibilities presented by the timely emergence of the figure of H. S. Brookmire—what his mother would have called a "spishus" arrival.

But desperation is both the mother and the father of invention and, for better or for worse, Lloyd saw no way around trusting in the man's assistance. Not if his dream was to be realized. What had Mother Tongue said? His intention was to travel right far.

CHAPTER 3

On Glory's Fragile Wings

HANSEL SNOWDEN BROOKMIRE HAILED FROM THE EASTERN MILL town of Manchester, and offered Lloyd two crucial benefits: he was eager to make a name for himself and, while not especially clever himself, he knew what cleverness smelled like. Just twenty-five at the time, he was in St. Louis visiting his older sister, Rudalena Cosgrove, who had come into significant assets following the death of her much older husband, Jarvis—a fortune large enough for Rudalena's father to excuse his only son from his managerial duties at their New Hampshire textile mill and dispatch the fledgling to Missouri to provide guidance and ballast in the dispensation and investment of the widow's capital.

Brookmire thus arrived in the river city with both a mandate and a line of credit commensurate with his ambition, and not an idea in his head of what to do next. He did, however, think he knew a good thing when he saw one, and two weeks into his stay the best or at least the most surprising thing he had seen was little Lloyd's flying toys and the fascination they induced.

The meeting, or rather collision, occurred as the important meetings in life often do, seemingly by chance, following Lloyd's return from the Field of Endeavor, scuffed and bruised from his first serious fall and smarting with worry that, now that his researches and his test work had moved beyond the model stage, he was sure to be seen and that word would get out and some vicious circle would close around him. Brookmire, who had witnessed the child in action down on the riverbank, took the force of the Market Street meeting as an omen. Not having noticed the boy's banged-up state prior to impact, he at first believed himself to be the cause of the injuries. Lloyd quickly ascertained that if the man were an agent of conspiracy, then he was not one to worry about, and so let Brookmire buy him a treat from a chocolate shop. A fateful discussion ensued.

Lloyd needed a backer. Brookmire needed an investment. Along with canals and railroads, the nation was being laced with telegraph wires as fast as men could string them. New inventions were being introduced at dizzying speed. When the easterner learned what Lloyd had in mind for the next phase of his career, he was openmouthed. But intrigued in spite of himself. A notional, confidential agreement was reached later that afternoon in a laneway beside a pharmacy, the streaked windows full of foot powder and bottles of witch hazel, which reminded Lloyd of Schelling.

Brookmire was the sole other person who knew of Lloyd's audacious project. No doubt he must have had his share of misgivings. But as the only son of a domineering father he had experienced how detrimental external meddling can be. He had seen for himself examples of Lloyd's perspicacity and his ability to work a crowd, and the idea of investing in new technology thrilled him. If there were risks—and the sum total of his investment strategy was the greater the risk, the greater the return—he had the funds to cover them. Besides, he argued, "The boy is taking the real risk."

And the risks were great. Accounts of kite fighting can be found in the Sanskrit religious writings of the *Veda* and the epic *Ramayana,* but the young Zanesvillean's battle was not with another solitary opponent, it was with himself and the ever-present factors of money, time, and the physical forces of the world. Just as his father had become obsessed with the Time Ark, so Lloyd became fixated on his daring quest of conquering St. Louis by air. A sufficiently bewondering spectacle, and maybe his family could be salvaged—and he could be free. There would be marmalade and venison—and real scientific equipment.

Brookmire could do little or nothing about minimizing the physical risks of flight, but he worked minor miracles when it came to the problems of money and privacy. Without question, he purchased (as Lloyd requested) lumber, wire, fishing nets, ropes, cable, bellows, baskets, sailcloth, and muslin. He arranged for the use of a large high-ceilinged warehouse suitable for the boy's very specific needs, and he secured the services of a rust-blooming steam barge owned by a burned-face roughneck named Lucky Cahill, who had earned his nickname by virtue of having survived two furnace explosions caused by his driving his boats too hard.

Brookmire had no idea what Lloyd meant when he jabbered on about "cambered airfoils," but he kept the boy's belly stoked with ham hocks and grits, corn Johnny and green tomato sauce. He knew how to grease a palm—and how to find the sort of people who did not ask awkward questions when he did. The talk around town was all about Texas becoming a state and an impending war with Mexico, but Lloyd did not pay it any mind. For four sweltering weeks he battled on in a delirious state of detachment and absorption, all his talents and attention channeled with manic verve into the silkworm-and-catgut task he had set himself.

His father had not returned, he suspected that his mother had at last succumbed to the advances of the laudanum-addled doctor she mopped up after, and his old friend Mulrooney had been laid low with a fever picked up in the pestilential marshes where he had insisted on camping, following the clan's bout of dysentery. All hope of reaching Texas, or some shining tomorrow that would restore the health and happiness of his family, hung in the balance of his great design, Lloyd felt. But every day brought new engineering conundrums. Altitude, balance, directional control. Discovery, failure, damage. Repair, breakthrough, breakdown. Then a tantalizing hint of success, only to be confronted with some horrendous new challenge.

His plan divided into three stages. First, the manufacture of a small but potent balloon that would serve to lift a man-size kite. Sufficient initial propulsion and additional lift would be provided by the forward momentum of the barge to which it would remain attached. Once equilibrium at maximum altitude had been achieved, the kite platform would be cut loose for a brief moment of spectacular display. Then the third stage of the project would be deployed—a fixed wing glider. This would be the all-important steerable component in the mix.

It was a complex affair, but broken down into sections he felt he could get his mind around. A balloon he had already manufactured; it was just a matter of scale. The problem lay in producing sufficient hydrogen, a painstaking process involving exposing iron filings to acid. But a balloon of itself lacked the requisite novelty to provoke "bewonderment." The people of St. Louis had seen balloons before. So the second element was demanded. In his mind, Lloyd saw a diaphanous skeletal structure that would create a theatrical focal point and a sense of awe, and here again he felt confident. His work with kites had proved tremendously successful. (While it is considered an accomplishment for a kite to fly at angles of up to 70 degrees, he had achieved efficiency close to 110 degrees, moving to the kind of tetrahedral design that Alexander Graham Bell would later introduce—and then beyond.)

It was the peculiar hierograms of the Martian diplomats that gave him the critical idea. Using woven strands of cane and millinery wire, he pieced together an enclosed scaffold in the most exact shape of their repeating tornado icon that he could, then he set it loose in a whirlwind of dust in one of the city's weed lots. The woven spiral, which in his concentration and ex-

ENIGMATIC PILOT | 155

citement he had forgotten to secure, rose so fast that he could barely watch it. He made a larger model, and this time remembered to keep a lead attached. Because Lloyd had integrated panels made of umbrella cloth and handkerchiefs, the structure was able to support a terrified young pig that he pinched to a height of almost a hundred feet. More work, he had no doubt, would produce a still stronger and more effective model, and once the physics were right he knew that it would be a simple matter to enhance the dramatic grandeur through the use of color, reflective materials, and improvised noisemakers. "I am going to build an enormous kite in the shape of the Ambassadors' favorite symbol," he said to himself.

The most difficult part was the critical third element—a working glider. For hours he labored, hallucinating a storm of theoretical insects and birds. Ever shifting between the strength of structure and the responsiveness of form, his designs evolved with a life of their own, as step by heartbreaking misstep he taught himself about flight.

He introduced a slight reflex curve at the trailing edge of the wings. Into the body of the glider he fabricated a rudder and an elevator rigged through a universal joint. Then he fitted a moving weight to adjust the center of gravity and improved stability by setting the wings at a dihedral angle. He rose and fell and swung on ropes. Every frantic hour brought a crash and then a jet of hope . . . some radiant insight . . . some fresh despair.

He so covered himself in bruises that Rapture tongue-lashed Brother Dowling and the prune of the Baptist school marm, who she assumed had been too vigorous in punishing the boy for missing the sorry excuse for "class" that consisted of nothing but rote memorizing of Bible verses and some half-wit figuring. As if the Wizard of Zanesville would sit still in a stifling prayer room to count on a slate with the dim little dumpling Hiram Pennyweight, an orphan with a knob on his forehead the size of a duck egg, and Cecilia Tosh, who had lost her leg in a wagon accident and smelled like boiling hoof jelly! Lloyd would rather have faced the strap, and often did. But, despite the enthusiasm of these whippings, they were nothing to what he put himself through when he sneaked out to conduct his trials.

One night a man with a harelip and huge meat-slab hands ambushed him in an alley on the way home. Living in fear of the Vardogers, Lloyd fell victim to this more predictable predator, who brained the boy with a barrel stave and, stinking of dog-piss ale, stripped his britches down.

The pain was excruciating, but even worse was the bestial grunting of his assailant, who left him swollen and bleeding in a pile of ox excrement. Never a tear did the young innovator shed. Not one. He took each thrust straight into his heart and darkened his being around it like a toad trapped in a hot iron box. One day, he vowed, he would find that creature again, and then he would perform some fiery experiment of justice—but in the meantime he had a mission to fly. He renewed his exertions with the cold-blooded certainty of desperation.

Success continued to elude him until one afternoon a waft of wind came up over the water and tickled a wreck of spiderweb, which chanced to break free just as he was watching. Lloyd noted how the transparent netting caught the zephyr, like the sail of a boat, and lofted it away out of sight. A breeze stirred in his mind.

Up to that moment he'd been concentrating on evolving the technology of the kite into a full-size glider, taking what the tethered kite could teach and turning it into something more maneuverable, more protective and sustainable in its flight, a giant version of his popular whimsies. In the glider, Lloyd could see great potential—almost limitless. Falling reluctantly away into the dissolution of sleep, he would glimpse wondrous engined machines propelling hundreds of people through the air at speeds beyond belief—gorgeous riverboats of the sky, able to master space and distance as his father had hoped the Ark would transcend time. Travel to other worlds, yes!

But in structure there is also weakness. This subtle paradox now struck Lloyd with irresistible force. Perhaps the most beautiful machines are the ones that are least visible.

Abandoning spars, frame, or any form of rigid bracing, he designed and stitched together himself an ingenious parafoil made from the two types of material that held the most fascination for him: a couple of large American flags and enough women's underwear to have dressed both a whorehouse and a church social. While porcelain-skinned matrons dozed on their goose down in the drowse of horsefly afternoons, Lloyd worked an ivory sailor's needle, fashioning a perforated chamber that would theoretically fill with air when the fabric was fully unfurled and aloft. More veined than ribbed, with slender but strong strands of twined fishing line that he stole from a boathouse—feeding into steering toggles of thick hair ribbon—his new creation traded the toughness of a wood-and-bone enlargement of his soarers for the tuftiness of web and thistle. A second principle of his life had been sewn together in the process: in the face of failure, always become more ambitious and daring.

The breakthrough with the parafoil allowed him to focus more attention on the manufacture of the balloon and the kite components, and Brookmire, understanding these elements better, was able to throw the full weight of his support into their fabrication to a high standard, given the amount of time and materials available. The mill owner's son recruited a family of free Negroes and an old Indian weaver woman without teeth but with nimbleness to spare, and was enthralled by Lloyd's supervisory skills and native authority. The boy knew what he wanted, and he was a stern taskmaster when it came to getting it.

There was still no word from Hephaestus, but Lloyd had heard nothing to quench his hope that his father was still alive and surviving better than he would at the mission house, which had just about sapped his mother dry. He labored on, heaving himself into every stitch and crease of the parafoil, so that whenever he did fall into a doze he felt himself airborne. Airborn.

The giant kite assembly was finished and stress-tested by the boy in the abandoned warehouse. Lloyd hadn't seen Schelling in weeks and was curious about how much he knew about his activities, if anything. He thought it unlikely that the humpback and Mother Tongue would just let him go. Perhaps they were simply waiting, wondering what he was up to.

He had no way of knowing that his former mentor did indeed know something of his whereabouts—just not the magnitude of his ambition. The bookman would later blame himself for what transpired—or what he felt he allowed to transpire—but there were many things on his mind. Dark forces were gathering strength in Missouri. At night the bloodhounds of the "nigger catchers" bayed in the woods, and men and women from faraway places stepped off the riverboats each day and disappeared but were not gone.

Lloyd was only subconsciously aware of this undercurrent, because the full strength of his intellect was directed to his aeronautical researches. At last, with balloon and kite elements resolved, it came time to formally trial his parawing out on the river, behind the barge, under the cover of night. Of course there were dangers, and of course there were a few glitches at first, but nothing he could not handle. The cells of the fabric wings filled with air, and within two trials he rose to the full tension length of the line, albeit very wet.

And what a feeling! In his dreams he saw future creations, combining the lightness of cloth and the capacity to change shape with the strength of reinforced structure and the thrust of unthinkable motors. He would think them! After his display over St. Louis, he would turn his mind to engines and generators. Beyond steam, electricity, and magnetism, there were miracles on the horizon of his imagination. Mirror-bright machines with the maneuverability of dragonflies. Vast airborne opera houses. Enormous bullets with men in them. He no longer cared about Texas and his uncle. He longed to get to the future. To plant a flag and stake his claim. Pathfinder. Priest of Invention. Impresario.

The searing heat of September found him ready to step beyond theory and trial. He could not rehearse the complete performance; there were not enough materials or secrecy to go around. He felt that he had mastered the physics and engineering problems as completely as he could without open and comprehensive testing, which he could not afford or risk. His butcher paper and Buffalo-book notes were full of coefficients of drag and the effects of air pressure on airspeed, calculations about wingspan and weight-to-lift ratios—a miniature history of the mathematics of flight strained through a sieve. If only he had more time. If only he had better equipment. If only he could come out and work in the open. But he did not, could not, and a natural tendency toward arrogance settled him on what he had accomplished. It would do. It had to.

So he turned his mind away from the science of his creation to its aesthetics, with particular attention to the stimulation of bewonderment. For this he looked to Mulrooney, master of tinsel angels and two-headed cats. The professor and his mute wives were still battling the marsh fever but had managed to relocate nearer the fresher air of the river. Urim and Thummim remained hardy in health where the fever was concerned but incomprehensible as ever in terms of speech.

While Lloyd had been tackling the ancient dream of human flight with some success, Mulrooney had made no headway whatsoever in cracking the brothers' private code, and the two preterhuman charges seemed as remote from the world as when the boy had first met them. They had, however, been busy in their own right, although Mulrooney could make nothing of their written efforts. Since Lloyd had last seen them, they had filled up every scrap of paper and smoothed-out rag that they had been given with more of their queer hierograms. The tent was now littered with their work. In addition to the repetition of the singular tornado icon, their row upon column of insectoid deliberations mingled regimented dots and curls like imaginary musical notes and unknown mathematical symbols with the filigreed suggestions of animal forms and crystalline shapes that brought to mind the snowflake images that float across one's eyes when staring.

Lloyd was struck by the fact that, with the exception of his graphs and diagrams, the brothers' esoterica bore an inescapable resemblance to his own figurings and formulas—to the extent that if some ordinary person compared his Buffalo-book pages with the sheaves and remnants here, they might well have assumed that the teratoids had been working on the same problem in parallel, but from an encrypted perspective. To his further puzzlement, he could not avoid the impression that if gazed at without close scrutiny the goblins' ciphers took on an overall pattern—a hypnotic labyrinthine spiral. It took an act of will to force himself away from contemplation and back to the reason for his visit.

Mulrooney was beside himself with curiosity about the boy's request, but believing in Lloyd's assurances that his plan was almost fulfilled and would soon create significant new business opportunities for them both, the showman was willing to supply what goods he could: strips of painted cloth, jars of colored sand, and bits of broken mirror—all sorts of things he had magpied from his "peregrinations" to fascinate children and lend an enchanted air to his performances. To these Lloyd would add some of his own improvisations back at the warehouse.

An ominous rumble of thunder rolled over the encampment, followed by a flash of light and the intoxicating bite of ozone, which always reminded Lloyd of Lodema. A storm was moving in and, given the hothouse air and the voraciousness of the midges and mosquitoes, a dump of rain was seen as a relief. Lloyd considered it a good omen. He wanted the air fresh and clear for the morrow, with a good wind. Not gusty but steady.

The first pregnant drops of rain hit the roof of the tent and the wagon, and Lloyd hastened to gather up his booty. He did not want to get caught in the downpour. Before he departed, he gave the Ladies Mulrooney each a kiss on the cheek and told the professor to be at the courthouse on Fourth Street no later than noon the next day.

"I wish you would let me in on your little secret, my boy," the showman lamented. "After all, we are partners. Aren't we?"

Lloyd had grown adept at his management of both information and personnel. He thought of Brookmire's intensifying questions, and how the easterner was probably pacing back at the warehouse awaiting the final preparations.

"Trust me," Lloyd said. "Remember what you have taught me."

"That's what I'm afraid of!" the showman confessed.

"Fear is the price of surprise," Lloyd answered.

The professor twisted the ends of his mustache at this remark, trying to think if he had said it or if the boy had out-Mulrooneyed him.

"I'll be at the appointed rendezvous—with bells on," the showman confirmed. "How will I find you?"

"That won't be a problem." Lloyd smiled and then was gone, picking his way through the trees as fast as he could, eyes ever on the alert for confrontation, the warm big drops of rain sticking to his back like flies.

In spite of the boy's nonchalance, the professor had the nagging suspicion that he would never see his protégé again, and it pained him to think that he was in some way responsible. Little did he know that the boy would be back again later that night.

In the interim, Lloyd had a hectic schedule. He had to return to the mission house and see his mother before lights-out, then slip out of the dormitory, as usual—go meet Brookmire at the vacant warehouse, beautify his creation with Mulrooney's baubles, make his final inspection, and then return to the showman's camp amid the storm to perform what would be the most troublesome part of the entire scheme. He had left this crucial element to the last minute because he had no choice. If he had put forward an open request to Mulrooney, he knew the showman would have outright refused.

Once his delicate errand was completed, he would then have to get himself and his unlikely accomplices over the river to where Cahill's barge was moored and across to Illinois, where they would lie in wait for the morning light. Meanwhile, Brookmire and the covert team he had employed would transport the balloon, the kite assembly, and the parawing glider. If the storm did not pass, all these preparations would be for naught. It would be the busiest night of his life, and a day of reckoning whichever way the wind blew. "So much to do," he mourned. "And so little time."

It was the familiar complaint of his father back in his inventing days, Lloyd realized, and the thought of his missing father and the concern over his whereabouts wavered before him like a ghost. "But I can't think about that now!" he told himself. There were theatrical effects that needed to be applied, checks and counterchecks to be performed. His mother would be fretful and despondent. Brookmire would be wound as tight as a cheap watch. The Vardogers could be laying for him—or some villain like before. And always the specter of Schelling and Mother Tongue's emissaries haunted him. Even if they meant well, they could derail everything. But there was no turning back now. He had to hurry and be very careful. He darted through the gathering storm unaware of the greater storm that was mounting.

Back at Mulrooney's, the showman battened down the wagon and the tent. The horses were jumpy, and so were the brothers. Not even a foot rub from his wives could dispel the professor's apprehensions, so he had a nip of LUCID!, then a vial. Then one more. His silent wives laid him to rest in a rumpled state and extinguished their candles. White barbs of lightning tore the sky and precipitation plummeted, pounding down on their tent so hard it almost drowned out the sound of his snoring.

Yet as deeply as he had fallen asleep, some inner alarm woke Mulrooney. He was still groggy with liquor, but an old traveling man's instinct had sounded in his dreams and forced him, thick-tongued and sweaty, to his feet. He stepped over his slumbering women and lit a lantern. Outside, the storm had calmed, but the ground around their camp was alive with web-footed rain. No one seemed to be lurking, although the mud was as rich with footprints as Urim and Thummim's pages were with enigmatic emblems. That thought triggered a sudden horror. He flung back inside the tent and poked the lantern toward the brothers' modesty screen. It was a very long moment later when Mulrooney accepted what he found. The pygmies from Indiana were gone.

Dumbstruck, the professor staggered out and hunkered down on a log in the slowing rain. The clothes his wives had made for them were still there. He could not imagine what had happened. The coincidence of Lloyd's earlier visit crossed his mind but could take no clear form that would explain his wards' abrupt removal. Soaked to the bone and sobering fast, he kept thinking of the whirlwind from which they had supposedly emerged.

What if something in the storm had returned for them? It was improbable. But so were they. He had always been so assiduous in keeping them hidden from prying eyes—never an easy task. Perhaps they had *not* been captured like runaway slaves by blood-money ruffians. Perhaps they were *not* wet, lost, and afraid, having been stolen away—or having, in their foolishness, fled to some mooncalf idea of freedom—but home and safe, retrieved by the weather-stricken night and taken back to the secret place of the thunder? It was not much to hold on to, but Mulrooney tried. The rain dripped from the branches around him like tears.

CHAPTER 4

The Price of Surprise

THE MORNING DAWNED CLEANER AND CRISPER THAN ANY IN months. (For Mulrooney, the feeling was foreboding and re-called the day that the unfortunate Vladimir had gone missing.)

There was a rustling of ledger pages and the tapping of morning cigar ash at the City Hotel—and more than a few wa-gers laid over breakfast at Planter's House, which consisted of arrowroot biscuits, coddled eggs, fresh trotters, and a serving of wild pigeon—the aromas of black tea or chicory-laced coffee cutting through the stale fumes of pipe smoke and brandy that had followed the coq au vin and bordeaux the night before.

It was the morning of a major sale. The auction house of Bladon, McCafferty & Co. of Chestnut Street was putting up on the block one hundred of the sturdiest Negro field hands valued generally at a whisker over a thousand dollars each—seventy-five older adult males, forty-eight females, and a litter of children that one squire from Kentucky likened to "French-prattling young crows."

The event, as usual, was to take place on the steps of the proud domed courthouse on Fourth Street at noon. Typically, the public did not take much overt notice of these occasions, there being studious attention from those informed profession-als either bidding or methodically recording the prices submitted by their peers. These seasoned agriculturalists and their entourages had serious business in mind and had come more than a few miles to do it. So the amateurs kept to the fringe.

Slave auctions represented significant investments in new capital equipment—gambles taken on increased productivity. An air of sober deliberation and dispassionate judgment was the rule, and for the most part an auction was no more undignified and violent than a sale of horses or cattle and easier on the nose, since the prize specimens had often been treated to a bath and an improved diet to inspire higher prices. "Beef for muscle, fresh fruit for the teeth and breath, and cod liver oil to put a shine on their hides" was the recommended short-term practice advocated by the trading houses.

No, the systematic brutality of these events was more in the mind, the soul, and heart than in the flesh. But since Negroes were not credited with having minds or souls, any explicit cruelty was considered an unfortunate by-product of what needed doing. Mating a stallion or wringing a chicken's neck—life was filled with raw necessities, and people were much less squeamish then.

Naturally there were whips and guns on hand, but they were primarily ceremonial and symbolic. And of course the goods to be traded appeared in shackles (the young bucks, at any rate), but that was just common sense and economic prudence: the traders were not immune to the high spirits that some slaves felt at the thought of being separated from their wives and children. Better to secure the chains than to have to raise the whip or, worse still, fire the gun. In fact, there were few fatalities at the auctions—a testament to the efficiency that had been achieved through decades of practice.

And not all the slaves stood defiantly flaring their nostrils and rattling their manacles, dreaming of escape, either. Many of them welcomed the change that new ownership would bring. For some it was a chance to find a new life and the faint hope of security, or to be nearer a loved one who had earlier been prised away and sold downriver. For an attractive female who had been forced to service in unspeakable ways a Missouri master, a plantation owner in the Delta, who was less Christian but perhaps more decent, held some distinct appeal.

The upshot was, every auction was a crossroads. Money, emotions, human dignity, and the very destiny of America were all at stake. So it was no surprise that very often a fringe of loitering onlookers would form into an attempted crowd at a distance that allowed them the benefits of aspect without appearing too suspect.

The gathering that tried to take shape on the day in question was unusually large, and all the more faceless and amorphous for its size and prurient interest. Recalling the catastrophe years later in his privately printed memoir, Brookmire would speculate that it was the very size of the assembled host that so diffused the memory of what transpired (a suggestive observation, given the days of instantaneous mass communication that have followed). Perhaps the more witnesses, the less reliable their testimony—until by extension it becomes possible to deny that there was anything to witness at all. This phenomenon may go a long way toward accounting for why such abrupt and incoherent reportage was provided by the local media. Of the major regional newspapers, including *The Bulletin, The Boatman, The Advocate,* the Catholic weekly *Shepherd of the Valley,* and *The Missouri Republican,* only *The Star* contained any more than a passing reference to what resulted, and it was the sole mouthpiece to attempt a description, let alone an explanation, of the cause.

Here another overlooked law of human nature and mass perception may have come into play. The more unexpected and unprecedented an occurrence, the more likely it is to slip into the realm of legend, which may be interpreted as a communal way of forgetting what actually happened.

Both of these factors were at work in St. Louis. And, as Lloyd would come to see, other hidden influences were at work as well. Had he not been advised that a war was being waged by secret alliances masked in the shadows of history and camouflaged in the chaos of the hour? Had not Schelling warned him that the capabilities involved were formidable in their reach?

If events could be orchestrated, could not their perception be manipulated, perhaps even eradicated? Personal reports and newspaper accounts of the lynching and burning of Francis McIntosh had diverged wildly and more than a few residents had clean forgotten their involvement, so in the end it was not surprising that those citizens of St. Louis who were watching on the day could not agree and many did not want to admit what they saw sailing toward the city—not on the river but in the sky. Though it came out of the heavens, it looked as if it came from hell. Or perhaps Chicago, Mulrooney thought as he watched from the crowd in astonishment, his good heart pounding and perspiration beading under his leghorn hat.

As Lloyd had predicted, if it had been just a balloon that drifted over the city people would have known how to respond. But it was ever so much more than a balloon that detached and exploded like a slow-falling star over the esplanade. What emerged was nothing like anything anyone had ever seen before. Imagine a swirled cage made of fishing net, bone-dry cane and broom straw, twined wig hair, umbrella spokes and wax, rippling with a patchwork of bandages and bed linen—with a puff of silken sail atop. The rising power of the balloon had lifted the surreal structure into the freshening breeze, where it was then driven forward by all the boiler-bursting speed that Lucky Cahill spurred his smoking steam barge to provide since lugging it out of its secluded mooring on the Illinois side.

Young Lloyd had named his creation the *Miss Viola*. Atop the domed roof of the courthouse, Hansel Snowden Brookmire squinted through a spyglass when he spotted it. Fragments of American flag crackled in the wind, mirrors glinted, feathers rained like snow—and a voice called out of the blue, "All Hail the Ambassadors from Mars!"

The voice was Lloyd's, projected through a huge knitting mill cone used for winding yarn, but there were other voices that might have been heard—namely, the hysterical cluckings of Urim and Thummim. Lloyd's initial plan had been to dress Mulrooney's charges in stovepipe hats and swallowtail coats, as befitting their introduction to St. Louis society and the earth at large. But he had been unable to acquire togs in their size and so had been forced to improvise again, arriving at a solution that he felt was economical and more appropriate given their supposed otherworldly origin (not to mention the wind!). The brothers were now dressed in toga-like gowns made of ladies' undergarments and equipped with tiny gold wands the boy had foraged out of a rubbish bin. Trembling hundreds of feet in the air inside a bird-delicate cell of spiral-arranged bladders stitched with bass line, linen, and scavenged wharfery—and now, hovering free of the barge with no balloon to support them—the twins were literally at the end of their tether.

It was pure adrenaline that kept Lloyd from taking more notice of their consternation—that and the sheer novelty of the view. The sight of the people and the horse carriages, the packing crates and the ship pipes, pony carts and rooftops! He could not believe that he was seeing it all just as he had imagined. He had done what he set out to do—to rise above the hordes and sweep all attention skyward! For a moment, it seemed to him that he owned the town. And the river. Everything he could see.

When he did acknowledge the Martians' expostulations, he was upset to find that he was becoming less effective in calming them. When he had appeared in the dark of the storm the night before to lead them away from Mulrooney's camp, they had showed an instinctive sense of trust that encouraged him. Up to the precise moment of their departure in the soaking confusion (he disliked the thought of its being *kidnapping*), he had harbored a concern that his plan violated the trust of his old business associate. That it also put at grave risk the lives of the two teratological brothers was just now beginning to dawn upon the boy, for in his mania he had discounted all risk to himself as well.

Once aloft, any fear had left him, and with it all reasonable consideration of malfunction. Ironically, the very moment when his father was more absent from his thoughts than at any time in his short life, Lloyd was more in harmony with Hephaestus's blindered faith in the magic of invention than ever before. Airborne above 1845 St. Louis on the day of a major slave auction, he was not only his father's son; he felt the uncanny sense of his sister's spirit for the first time since leaving Ohio. He was going to rescue his mother from drudgery and humiliation. He was going to lead them all forth to meat, wine, and fresh linen.

This invigorating delusion did not last very long. Urim and Thummim became more agitated as the craft wisped over the humming port like a crazed eclipse heading toward the city buildings and the scene in progress on the courthouse steps. Lloyd rode in a harness that he had fashioned from pilfered horse tack attached to the great plume of flag-and-underwear canopy that fanned out above and behind the miraculous kite cage. His intention was to pass over the courthouse dome and heave a fine fishnet rigging line down as an anchor that Brookmire would attach, and then to cut himself and the parafoil loose and ride the wind line down and around to make a spectacular landing amid the auction. Then he and Brookmire would wind down the weird-shaped giant box kite and introduce the brothers to the stunned populace. It would be the perfect theatrical occasion to launch their show-business career. As mortified as Mulrooney might feel at their disappearance (and did), he would be speechless with delight and gratitude when the crowd roared. And the fact that the entire performance would overshadow a slave auction was an inspired twist that Lloyd could not resist. The whole deranged caper sparkled in his mind.

Mulrooney would forgive him the fright he had caused and

grasp the commercial opportunities the stunt would create. Although not everyone (fortunately enough!) would believe that Urim and Thummim came from the Red Planet, their singular appearance and bizarre mode of arrival would cause a sensation. Mulrooney's future as a famous showman would be assured. Lloyd himself would be hailed as a god of invention and adventure. There would be no more broadcloth and boiled-leek broth. He would have a Villa of Wonders and roast duck, and every night a lascivious lady would come to him. His father would have a workshop again, and his mother a garden, roots, herbs, sweet-smelling leaves, and healing teas always brewing.

The possibility that even if the aeronautics went off without a hitch—which was hardly likely, given the many unknown and unforeseeable factors involved—the appearance out of the sky of such outlandish-looking individuals as Urim and Thummim, and the disruption of a significant slave auction, might instigate something more like a riot rather than endless rounds of applause did not occur to the boy with anything like the clarity it should have. He was blind to everything but his own ambition and his desperate craving for adulation—the sanctuary of money and freedom he hoped would descend upon him as soon as he descended into the thoroughfares of the city. This was his moment, his chance to reverse the fortunes of his family and establish a place for himself in the history of transport, science, and entertainment. The world.

Then a sudden rogue gust rose up as they crossed through the hotter air of the cityscape. The thermal blast destabilized the *Miss Viola* after its smooth drift over the cooler water. Lloyd's parawing ripped free and swept him up to breaking point above the kite nest, the perforated panels bloated with air. Mulrooney's stomach leaped up into his throat at what he saw next. Brookmire nearly fell from his perch.

The spiral kite cell caught the updraft and surged up to graze Lloyd's swinging legs and then veered off back toward the Mississippi, the Ambassadors clicking and squealing like hysterical animals in a drowning cage. The tether that Lloyd held to the kite now threatened to drag him out of control and he was forced to let go, releasing the deformed brothers to the mercy of the sky. Meanwhile, he was rising higher than he had intended, the figures below seething like ants before a rainstorm. The power of the wind billowed out his homemade wings and filled his belly with the butterflies that a normal person would have felt long before. His whole being was alive, and terrified at the volatile elements now determining his fate. The kite was but a speck in the air. He felt the world slipping away. Then he remembered that he could steer. He had to steer—for his life. And yet even now—ruptured from the *Miss Viola,* with the Ambassadors from Mars doomed to some terrible crash in heavy timber—he felt the psychological as well as the physical force of the wind lifting him, calling him upward. . . .

Years before Sir George Cayley's hapless coachman was compelled to make his historic glider flight (which inspired him to defecate in his trousers and resign his post). Long before Lawrence Hargrave and Alexander Graham Bell experimented with their kites and Otto Lilienthal broke his neck. Before Samuel Pierpont Langley catapulted his Aerodromes—and before the bicycle-repairing Wright brothers from another small town in Ohio took their fifty-nine-second flight into history over the dunes of Kitty Hawk—Lloyd Meadhorn Sitturd was flying, fulfilling the dreams of the Egyptians, Assyrians, Chinese, Indians, Norse, and Greeks. Not falling. He was riding the wind in a winged vehicle that, while neither heavier than air nor machine-powered, possessed a capacity for maneuverability that would not be achieved by others for another fifty years.

But herein lay the great shortcoming of his undertaking. Wilbur Wright's critical insight was that the secret of controlled flight lay as much in the skills of the pilot as in the capabilities of the craft. It was not enough for the machine to have the ability to maneuver; it was essential for the pilot to

172 | KRIS SAKNUSSEMM

have the experience to utilize this potential. Without control, the solutions of lift and propulsion were meaningless. Despite the feverish pace at which he had been working, Lloyd had not had time to align his personal skill with the potential of his creation. Faced now, at approximately three hundred feet, with the combined circumstances of the failure of one half of his enterprise (the loss of the *Miss Viola* and its cargo of the Ambassadors) and the success of his own means of aviation he was forced to apply all that he had learned about the wind with perilous immediacy.

He pulled the left steering toggle and swung left, sailing faster down and forward, whistling over the steeples and the carriage-colliding laneways to the horror and amazement of Mulrooney, Hansel Snowden Brookmire, and the people of St. Louis. Flaring slowed his driving speed and restored lift, while his body trembled in the risers. The thought of the helpless brothers breaking every bone in their bodies stabbed him with remorse and doubt. He whooshed around a smokestacked section of town, heading back toward the courthouse, but in banking the toggle tore and a puff of air stalled the edge of the parafoil.

Where the wing had been filled like a lung, it now gasped and he jostled in the rigging. The sunlight burned into his retinas. He heard a cry come up from the streets beneath him and the whinnying of crazed horses. The turbulence batted at him like a spinning leaf—his nerves were frayed like the ribbons he clung to.

He tried to readjust, flying at half brakes, one toggle up, one down. But in swerving around to make the courthouse and the confusion of Fourth Street, where he was to have made his epochal landing, he overcompensated and then had to brake full—which battered the wing chute more. One of the main leads streaming down to the risers broke—the toggle did not respond. He felt the heat waves rising up from the bricks below— the smell of horse manure and the din of human panic.

Ground rush hit him—the mess of scattering street traffic engulfing his field of vision, all the glory gone, leaving stomach-churning, muscle-bracing expectations of obliteration upon impact! He yanked the toggles, beginning to plummet, regaining control too late, and swooping down like a raptor to strike a fleeing rodent in a field of dry corn.

While this private drama had been playing out in the air, a rather more public debacle had been unraveling below. Representatives of Bladon, McCafferty & Co. had led their assembled offering clanking and shuffling like a parade of the damned from the auction house's pen on Chestnut Street to the courthouse steps, where a pompous man in a frilled shirt and a broad-brimmed hat read out the particulars of the sale and clarified the terms of purchase in stentorian tones. The planter aristocracy was well represented, decked out in top hats and European-tailored finery. Some had come from as far away as the black-loam bottomlands of Mississippi and Alabama, or the sugar kingdoms of Louisiana. The merchandise stood glistening and grim in the brassy sun. Errant schoolboys gapped and stretched. Idlers spat tobacco juice; skinny dogs panted under drays. Hoop-skirted women with complexions like clotted cream dabbed their throats with eau de cologne as barrel-chested saloonkeepers emerged blinking in the glare, hooking their thumbs into their braces.

Down on Fourth Street, a hatchet-faced plantation foreman watched from the saddle of a bay gelding while his tight-lipped overseer stood gripping a musket on top of the courthouse stairs. Another man in a baggy black suit, with a head as bald as a fire bell under a black silk hat, leaned over a weathered pinewood podium that had been wrestled out of a wagon, while two hulking guardsmen strolled the lines of slaves—some slumped with weariness and despair, others standing erect, both male and female, radiating the strength they had earned by long work in bright light and all weather.

The two hard-bitten white minders had hairy arms as thick

as the limbs of hod carriers and skin not much lighter than the individuals up for sale. Their square-toed boots were flecked with the pale green-gold of dried dung, and faded red or threadbare white bandannas poked up under their chins as if to hide some growth. Everything as usual.

Until the *Miss Viola* appeared.

The outré vessel came across the river and the sky like some narcotic vision of the future. The sausage casing–like balloon, which had provided the initial elevation, detached and expired in what from ground level Lloyd would have considered a disappointing poof relative to the incendiary excitement he had intended. (The problem was that he could not use any true ordnance for fear of incinerating the Ambassadors and himself.) But to those who were unprepared it was fireworks enough. The river-slapping force of the barge, stoked to boiler-blowing overload, hauled the beautiful abomination forward, where it was set free in a dense shower of glitter, sparks, and feathers.

It was right about then that Mule Christian glanced up from his row of chained fellow slaves and came to the conclusion that this was the sign from God that he had been waiting for. There was no other way to interpret it. This was a message from the Almighty. And he knew in his heart just what the message was.

Mule was what white plantation owners of the day would have described as a "big field nigger"—and big he was, in every way. Worth fourteen hundred dollars in St. Louis. More in Memphis or New Orleans. Six feet five inches tall and as muscled as a well-bred fighting dog. He had the mind of a child but a clear head, except when it came to his religious visions. Somewhere in the past his people had come from the Bight of Benin, that gouge in Africa that extends from Cape Verde to the Congo River. They had given him a name that sounded like Mulu, but all that was a cloudy memory. Mule he became to everyone he met in the cruel New World. An earlier owner had been known as Christianson, but it was thought that his American surname owed more to the fervent faith he had adopted. In any case, Mule Christian knew what he must do. The moment he gazed up at the terrible blue sky, he knew.

"Heee comin'!" the giant boomed in his work-gang baritone. "Heee comin' to sabe us all! Lord beee praised—heee comin'!"

This remark, uttered as loudly as it was, at the precise moment that it was, by someone not expected to speak at all—and by someone of Mule's impressive physical stature—had a profound effect. The tall-hatted white dandies in polished boots moved toward their carriages. Several of the auction items sought to plunge to the ground in fear and supplication, which, chained as they were, caused havoc among the rows. Others, in a state of understandable panic, tried to bolt. They had no clear thought of trying to escape. They had no clear thought at all—and, pulling in different directions, manacled together, they created a gibbering tangle of prostrate and floundering black flesh.

For the whites in official control, this was problem enough to loose a tide of anxieties that translated into physical force—which served only to intensify the confusion and the fear. There were also their own concerns to deal with. What had emerged out of the blue was odd enough to make even the most tough-minded of them drop their jaws and entertain the flickering conclusion that Mule Christian may well have hit the nail on the head (which had been a part of Lloyd's intention from the start).

The uncertainty flashed like flint in a caved-in mine and triggered a series of incidents of localized violence that turned into streetwide turmoil. Whips cracked, horses bucked, a carriage turned over, at least one firearm was discharged—to no effect, except to heighten the hubbub. And Mule Christian managed to break free. How he did it no one in the confusion saw, but while the overseers were busy trying to regain order and the loiterers were scattering like mice—the drunks and larrikins rolling over themselves in stupefaction—Mule Christian broke free of his chains and stood tall on the steps of the courthouse staring at the sky, waiting for the salvation that he knew was coming.

Brookmire had had all his attention riveted at the end of his spyglass, staring at first with pride, then shock, and then abject devastation. Something in the course of events in the sky convinced him that things had not only gone very wrong, they were about to get much worse, and a finely tuned instinct for self-preservation sent him scurrying down from the courthouse.

There were too many other things to take interest in: ululating slaves, shouting foremen, barking dogs, wagon smashups, and the risk of being trampled—and above all else, above them all and closing fast, a magical marionette of an angry bird boy descending to wreak vengeance or enact some revelation.

The truth, however, is that if Brookmire had managed to maintain his poise and position he might have become aware that he was being scrutinized himself—from two different rooftops and two very different points of view. He would have observed that when the commotion began other men who had not been seen before appeared below and began taking charge. It was one of these men, moving with practiced skill, who hustled Mulrooney into an alley, where he woke up hours later lying in a masonry wheelbarrow with a taste in his mouth like copper wire.

By the time Lloyd overshot the courthouse and made his attempt to bring himself around to land, there were not that many people left on Fourth Street to see it. A subtle but relentless force had been unleashed to quash the slave upheaval and coerce the potential witnesses from the scene. Only Mule Christian seemed immune to these efforts. Whip leather slashed across his shoulders, but this just served to encourage him into the middle of the street, where he braced, with outstretched arms, forming a tiny post-noon shadow in the thoroughfare, as Lloyd whisked down and toward him.

Lloyd tried to swerve, which spoiled the stalling power he tried to call on—his vision blurred, his reflexes jangled. He had a faint greenish flash of his sister's face—she who had never had a living face. A rush of doom and shame whooshed through him, and his wind-filled wings ripped away as he tumbled headlong into the dark man who stood before him with open arms.

Even if Brookmire had still been at his station and watching then, he would have found it impossible to say for sure what happened next. For a few seconds, an ancient cart nag stood draped with the remnants of Lloyd's parawing. Cudgels thudded. A broad-brimmed hat lay mashed in the street. And toppled at the foot of the stairs was the auction podium, a ledger book trodden on the ground beside it. But no one saw what happened to the boy or his flying harness. Mule Christian, the most expensive field nigger on sale, had seen a miracle coming for him out of the sky, and he had stepped forth to embrace it.

CHAPTER 5

Fleeing from Grace

PERHAPS IT WAS A KIND OF BLESSING THAT MULE FOUND. HE WAS certainly released from bondage. There was no pain. His neck snapped on impact. In giving his life, he cushioned Lloyd's fall and the little giant from Zanesville rose out of the wreckage of the giant black man in the hot Missouri sun, like some part of Mule Christian that had lain hidden all the hard years of his life.

Lloyd managed to gain his feet for a moment and then crashed for true. The brick façades, the courthouse dome, Mulrooney, Brookmire, thoughts of his mother, his father, and his ghost sister—all swirled into a spiral that seemed to take him with it, and he remembered nothing more at all until the agitated face of Schelling yawned down into his like a pit that had learned the art of looking back.

Smelling salts were applied, hands groped and tugged at him, voices were raised and then stifled into whispers, stars—or things like stars—seemed to whiz past his head. He glimpsed his mother—or glimpsed her smell—his senses muddled. Then there was cold water and warm candlelight. He remembered one man with a face like a snapping turtle and a tall, thin white man cradling him into a passageway of dirt behind two shuttered buildings . . . the aroma of pumpernickel bread.

Every so often he regained enough coherence to imagine that he was still flying, higher and higher up to heaven to meet his dead sister, who waited in the dandelions at God's feet, flying a kite with his face painted on it. Then the face on the kite would change. It would be his father, bright and ebullient as he once was ages ago back in Ohio. Then the image would change again, into the mangled bodies of Urim and Thummim. Someone stuck a rag down his throat to keep him from biting his tongue. Fragments of memory haunted him: the sight of Mulrooney's hat in the crowd . . . skiffs along the esplanade . . . the mirror burn of Brookmire's spyglass.

It was nightfall by the time Lloyd regained full consciousness. He was out on the water, in a larger version of the kind of boat that Schelling had used to take him to meet Mother Tongue. A tallow candle beamed out of a battered lantern hanging on the side of the pilothouse. His mother was there, looking perplexed and horrified, chattering and sobbing over him in her gumbo accent, any fussy white pretense stripped away. To his profound shock and relief, his sack of personal things lay beside him on the deck, tied up tight just the way he had left it stuffed inside his excuse for a shuck pillow back at the mission house. He longed to claw it open to see if Mother Tongue's eyes and the Ambassadors' box, and the precious letter from his uncle, were safe in hiding. Everything came back.

His body ached, from his skull to the legs that had slammed into Mule Christian. The slightest movement brought back sickening waves of falling. Along with Schelling, there were two large black men, but not the same men he had met before. His stomach felt like a mess of cogwheels and syrup. He wanted to throw up, but nothing came out of his gullet. The dark, thick air was hot and still, and smelled of wood smoke and river muck.

The joyous power of the wind came back to fill his smarting bones. He saw the city laid out beneath him . . . the ineffable experience of flight . . . then the shadows rose up to snatch him—the accusing face of the showman—and at last he did vomit, over the side of the boat, his bile mingling with the Mississippi as the launch chugged upriver.

Silently, his mother sidled over and put her arm around his shoulder. He realized that he was wearing some other boy's clothes. Whose? And what had become of Brookmire? Rapture crooned sad nonsense words in his ear, as she had done when he was wee. Why did everything go so wrong for them? Was he cursed? Would there ever be a home full of peace and belonging? Schelling scowled at him. The boat churned on.

They were headed north to the junction of the Missouri River, hugging the shore. In about two hours, they had melded into this other flow and arrived at their apparent destination, a clutter of what in the dark looked like drying sheds and some sort of chandler's warehouse at the end of a sagging pier. The boat docked and up on the bank a hound moaned. A hard-looking white woman in a plain black frock appeared, carrying a bear rifle. With her was what Lloyd first thought was a boy, perhaps the boy whose clothes he was wearing. The lad hoisted at arm's length the kind of lamp Lloyd had seen dangling on the bows of the fishing boats, but when the couple got closer Lloyd saw that he was in fact a midget—with a tight dried-apple face that rose up out of dirty flannel like the head of someone who had drowned. The pair spoke not a word.

"Where are you taking us?" Lloyd asked Schelling.

The humpback cast a glance at him, like a chunk of gristle to a mutt.

"You will stay here the rest of the night, then be on your way tomorrow."

"Where?" the boy queried. He tried to reckon the number of days since he had last seen his old patron, but the midget's face distracted him.

"Where you were heading before you created such trouble."

Lloyd flinched at this remark but grabbed at his satchel and hugged it to his chest. Schelling gestured them off the boat and accompanied them down the rickety gangplank. The midget and the rifle woman led them up a cut-clay path through a tangle of unlit buildings. They passed a chicken coop, coming to a windowless chinkwall cabin. A drainage trench ran around the place like a moat they had to step over—and when they did, a towering but emaciated deerhound ambled out of the shadows, assuming horselike proportions up against the midget. One of the black men who had been with them on the boat was left outside on guard.

Inside, the floor was packed dirt and the only light came from the hearth, where a spunk of resiny pine was smoldering and popping. The cloistered air was oppressive with mosquitoes. Lloyd's eyes shot around the room. A pewter jug and a stack of scratched tin plates stood on a turned-leg table with two milking stools beside it. Another chair was a rocker like the one he had sat in during his interview with Mother Tongue and, next to it, a pathetic-looking child-size wheelchair. In the corner rose a jailhouse bunk with a patchwork comforter laid over each bundle of ticking. A polished cherry-handled dueling pistol lay on the bottom bunk.

Schelling spoke to the woman and the midget in some language that sounded to Lloyd like German but was not. A cold leg of poached chicken, corn pone, and some black-eyed peas were served to him and Rapture, along with a lopsided bottle of birch beer to share. He felt as ravenous as the insects and as dry as the air. When he had finished gnawing his bone, Schelling ordered him toward the bunk. Carefully, the boy laid the dueling pistol on the hardened mud floor, which had been swept smooth by a stiff broom and strong arms.

Lloyd lay back on the ticking but kept his eyes on Schelling and his ears open, the mosquitoes whining around his head. The humped man whispered to Rapture for quite some time as the woman and the midget crouched in their respective chairs, staring hypnotically into the fireplace as if they were all by themselves. At last the bookseller reached into a pocket and produced a sheaf of paper money. The notes he pressed into Rapture's hand. Lloyd caught a hint of the calcium-stained tooth, and then his old patron's face marbled over into blankness once again.

Soon after, Schelling left without saying anything more to Lloyd. The beer had softened and slowed the boy's thinking, and the whirring of the skeeters and the hissing of the sap in the lump of pine eased his alertness away from its moorings and out into the current of slumber. Only once did he stir— some upsetting dream about the midget watching him in his sleep—but fatigue and despair got the better of him again, and it was not until the light of a sullen morning spilled through the open doorway that he woke up properly.

His mother squatted on one of the milking stools, and beside her, hunched over the table, was what might have been a scarecrow that had been plucked out of the river and left to dry on a line. Schelling glowered at the boy.

"Here is your father," he announced acidly. "Or what is left of him. Very soon now a steamer will put in. You are all going to be on it. Do you understand?"

"Where are we going?" Lloyd mumbled, rubbing away the crust of sleep.

"Far away, I hope," Schelling said, shrugging. "And never to return. Don't you remember you were going to Texas—before you took to trying to fly? Or did your brains get scrambled when you crushed that poor fellow?"

Rapture squirmed at this remark, but the huddled figure beside her did not respond. The woman and the midget were nowhere to be seen. Despite Lloyd's native self-possession, he felt that he might cry. He climbed to his feet instead, too curious about the derelict plopped on the stool.

"Keep to your cabin as much as you are able," the bookseller commanded. "Use the money I have given you and pay the bursar direct. Talk to as few people as you can, and tell no one your plans. You are a little boy, after all, Lloyd. A dangerous, selfish,

ENIGMATIC PILOT | 183

foolish little boy. In spite of your genius, your stupidity is matched only by mine for watching over you and not taking action before you did. I thought I was protecting you. Already it seems the better question is who will protect the world *from* you. I leave you to your destiny, just as you leave me to clean up your mess."

Rapture sat speechless, propping up the figure that Schelling had called his father—rousty with chiggers and alcoholic delirium (a condition that Mother Tongue's lieutenant treated with an injection from a horse needle). The skeletonized tramp slumped with the shot as a riverboat whistle tooted in the distance.

"He will rest for a while now," Schelling rasped, his hump twitching. "I recommend that you restrain him—and keep his head turned. Plenty of water and time can get him through this. Now go. And be gone."

Moving toward the gray light, Lloyd could see a paddle steamer pulling into the ramshackle wharf, where a man in a buckboard loaded with sacks of flour waited. The air was greasy-warm and smelled like dead fish.

He tried to imagine where Mulrooney was at that moment, but he could not bring the showman into focus. What would Brookmire tell his father? And what of the Ambassadors?

The steamboat let out another whistle that reminded him of the screech owl in the slave cemetery the night that Schelling had taken him to meet Mother Tongue—a cry from out of the stillness, between the land of the living and the brilliant darkness of the dead.

UNITED WE ESCAPE

CHAPTER 1

Awakening West

IT WAS NOT THE SLURPING OF THE PADDLE-WHEEL WOOD WHACK-
ing the water that first penetrated his consciousness. It was
another softer, nearer sound. After all the horrors and the
tremors—the weevils burrowing into his flesh and the clam-
sweat-salt-dry-throat retching and gulping of buggy water—he
now heard a persistent nibbling rasp just above his head. At
first he thought he was back in the stable in St. Louis, but
the stench of the urine-soaked hay and the wafts from the
glue renderer's were different. Instead, he smelled the odor of
damp hemp and warping lumber, with traces of vinegar and
gunpowder—and somewhere the scent of a woman's underthings.
He blinked, trying to focus—to both remember and forget.

Gradually, Hephaestus Sitturd came to accept that he was
lying in the dingy waterline cabin of a steamboat, going where
he could not yet fix in his brain. The noise he had been hearing
was an industrious little mouse, pecking at something in a
hammerhead-size hole just above a bent-slat rail that ran across
the wall behind the rope-hinged excuse for a bed. The creature's nose poked out at him once or twice, sniffing for news of
danger or sustenance. After the insidious roaches and the rats,
and the other beady-eyed nameless things that had tormented
him in his delirium, the affront of this actual rodent might have

seemed a cruel reality to awaken to, but it struck the stretched-
thin blacksmith instead as innocent and reassuring. Despite
the wagon wreck he had made of his life, he was still in the
world—and not alone. There were others struggling just as pre-
cariously as he. He held out his right hand and the mouse's
nose twitched at the lip of the hole, then withdrew in a scurry
of tiny-clawed feet.

Hephaestus recognized that, humble though they were, his
surrounds were much more gracious and hygienic than where
he had been previously, even though he could not summon a
precise image of what that had entailed. He noted the presence
of his son's and his wife's things. They had been huddling on
the floor, it appeared, while he had occupied the narrow bunk.
Inching back the sheet of nubbled muslin, he saw that he was
naked. One of his shins sported a livid bruise, which brought to
mind a baby bluebird he had found at the door of the forge
back in Zanesville one spring. A boil on his left thigh had been
lanced and dressed, and a purulent sore on the ankle of his
deformed foot was sealed and calming beneath a dab of lano-
lin. His arms were flaky and pocked, but his body did not stink.
Rapture, he guessed, had managed to bathe him in his trials.
He thought that he could recall her firm hands pouring over
him like tepid water.

His ribs stuck out like the skeleton of an abandoned boat; he
seemed to remember blacking out with an old boot full of
mash. The beard he had managed to accumulate more than
grow had been trimmed, and the lump of pig iron that had been
his gut had managed to relax back into sausage skin and digestive juice. He felt right hungry. For pickled eggs and black loaf
bread, a stuffed squab or a nice piece of charred fish.

He would have given himself over to an imagined banquet
had he not become aware of another kind of longing rising up
between his legs. The insistent appendage was as thick as a
scrubbed yam and as stiff as one of his old farrier implements,
but with a peeled, raw quality that reminded him of a flayed

squirrel. He stared at it. A tear formed in the glass of his rifle eye, one pinched branch-water pearl of thankfulness and disbelief. It was in this condition that Rapture discovered her husband. Lost forever for safekeeping and now returned, home to his fugitive family, sheltering in a mouse hole of their own and steaming west. West!

She jetted out a whisper that might have been "Mussiful Gawd" but which sounded as hopeful to Hephaestus as a kettle just beginning to purr on a flame. A rough swish of linsey-woolsey and his tight stone tear became a river to soak her bosom when she stepped over the piled garments on the floor to first embrace and then slip astride him.

After a while the kettle began to rattle, and at last whistled, then stilled to a riffling sob. Wherever it was they were right then, Hephaestus knew that he was indeed home—returned from the haunted wilderness of himself to the vagrant sanctuary of their lives together. Whatever scraps they would have to scrounge and whatever risks and rapids they had yet to run, he knew that he would remain, and remain himself. Hurt but healing.

Many tears were shed then by both husband and wife. Tears of anger and tears of gratitude. When the last cascade had run dry, the grief and celebration still seemed to seep from the pores of their two hushed forms, like the last residual drops of alcohol that had poisoned Hephaestus and the desperate, shamed memories of what Rapture had had to do to survive in St. Louis—and all that she had done to keep her mate alive and her family from foundering irrevocably since their departure under weird and watchful eyes.

Jolted to the core by the half-fathomed report of her son's undertakings—fearing news every day of her husband's drowned and bloated corpse wheeled to greet her on a donkey cart by some hogshead Samaritan with a hand out for compensatory silver, and then to be confronted with the miraculous abomination of Hephaestus's rum-keg carcass still breathing—she had been hard pressed to keep her wits about her. So much had happened to unhinge her. The dandy with the humped back and his dark henchmen. The midget and the woman with the hairy mole. That fetid cabin with its guns and torches, and the signals to unseen overseers—they swirled in her thoughts like backwash around a towhead.

Leaving the Mississippi, they had not left their tribulations behind. Far from it. For what seemed like the worst part of her whole life, Rapture had been forced to nurse her sodden, mumbling husband at close quarters with no relief. Bullboats, canoes, Mackinaws, and keelboats were all used on the Missouri, which was notorious for its obstacles and its obstreperous nature, but the vagaries of the spring and autumn high water, along with increased demand for goods and transit west had favored the rise of the steamboat, which flourished.

Now, in between the dry of summer and the heavy fall rains, the going was particularly difficult and muddy, even for a boat with iron muscle. Three times they had been forced to halt, once for an entire day, because of treacherous snags and sandbars. Then a wild downpour after a thunderstorm unleashed a flash torrent that dredged up keel-killing logs and the debris of old wrecks, making progress slower still. A "wood hawk," one of the local shore dwellers hired to help the fueling parties find timber to feed the ravenous boilers, had turned out to be in cahoots with a ruffian gang who tried to board the steamboat and were repelled by gunfire, which left a crew member wounded and two of the villains dead. A fast boat at the time could have reached Independence in eight days. They had already been gone five and were not even as far as Jefferson City.

Hephaestus had been racked with fever and visions while all this was happening. Meanwhile, Lloyd had remained locked in a catatonic state of retreat and denial. In all the years, Rapture had never seen her son so remote, so enclosed. She had managed, because she had had no choice, to accept that he had endeavored, by some means that remained mysterious to her, to attempt to fly. In a dirt-floor cabin, from a man with a lump on his back the size of a feather pillow, she had gathered in some uncomprehending way that her son had been the perpetrator of a deliberate and unnatural spectacle that had cost at least one wretched slave his life and had permanently jeopardized their safety in St. Louis and perhaps all America.

But these bizarre intelligences had not shed any light that she could see by. With the demonic, muffled counterpoint of Hephaestus's ravings, they had just served to make the voyage they were committed to now seem more amphibious and ghostly, until she began to doubt her own sanity, and the pain in her feminine heart began to strain her resilient will to live. The tears and the lovemaking released her. It was Lloyd's return to the cabin that wrenched the couple back to reality and the tenuous situation they found themselves in once more.

"He better now," Rapture announced, trying to adjust her dress and bodice back into place.

"I see that," the boy sniffed, his eyes as green and hard as old Chinese jade.

Hephaestus craned his neck, fearing for an instant that he had been under some dire spell longer than he imagined, so much older and cynical did his young son seem.

Lloyd wore a knitted skullcap that Schelling had stuck on his head to make him less recognizable, with an orphanage long shirt over short cotton sack pants and rough leather shoes. The blacksmith's mind flitted back to the horror in the eyes of Phineas, the vivisected rabbit. At last he found his voice.

"I'm sorry, Lloyd," he said. "I've—I've made a mess of things. I don't know what came over me."

"I do," the boy returned, but despite the blankness of his tone his father spied a flicker of something warmer and human in the cold green eyes.

"It won't ever happen again," the scrawny blacksmith vowed with a clearer voice. "Now, tell me what has happened and we will make a plan. A new plan."

Rapture's eyes darted to her son, and then and there she decided an issue that had been weighing on her soul since boarding the boat. They would say nothing about Lloyd's misadventures in St. Louis. There was nothing she could say that she understood herself anyway. Maybe the black times behind them would drift into obscurity like some washed-away raft they passed in the night. There was at least no use in troubling her troubled husband with uncertain details now. Now was the time for simple known things, and for coming together.

She was relieved when Lloyd assumed an Indian squat on the floor amid their few belongings and remained still but far more attentive than she had seen him in days, as she recounted in broad, general terms her conclusion that getting them out of St. Louis and back on their way to Texas and whatever lay ahead for them was their best course, and so had brought about their departure. Lloyd's face betrayed no emotion as she steered around the prickly matters, hoping that her husband's clouded memory would stay clouded. The money they had now, she said, she had stolen from one of her employers—a desperate act that she was not proud of but which seemed necessary given Hephaestus's fragile condition. His discovery and retrieval were credited to a free Negro who frequented the fish market in town, who had found him passed out in a shack downriver. The senior Sitturd seemed too exhausted from his ordeal and too ashamed to inquire further. Like his wife, all he found himself caring about and able to face up to was where they were at the moment, and where they were going.

In truth, their current position had to be deemed a significant improvement over the near-end of the world in St. Louis. They had lower-deck cabin passage paid to Independence, Missouri, on board a side-wheeler called the *Defiance*, built in Louisville fifteen years before and overhauled one too many times. Just under two hundred feet long, with a thirty-five-foot beam and a cargo capacity of five hundred tons and carrying six hundred, it was a "floating palace" that had been forced to earn its keep. In its heyday the *Defiance* had transported explorers, soldiers, fur trappers, mountain men, and missionaries, but more recently it had given passage to settlers and would-be western travelers, some laden already with overloaded wagons and visions of vast expanses of free land to turn into farms. Its cargo manifest was as miscellaneous as its passengers: Hudson's Bay blankets, indigo cloth, frock coats, flannel shirts, Marseilles vests, and fancy calico shirts; Indian trading trinkets (like wampum moons and medals featuring a representation of John Jacob Astor on one side and peace and friendship on the reverse), horse bells, yellow bullet buttons, gun worms, awls, padlocks, oval firesteels, black-barley corn heads, octagon brass barrel pistols, hunter's clay pipes, tinned rivets, iron kettles, refined borax, powder horns, oakum, pitch, pilot bread and Havana sugar; violin bows and Manila rope, emery paper, twist tobacco, sealskin trunks and sealing wax, rattail files and trap chains, sturgeon twine and silver gorgets; ladies' Moroccan heel pumps and men's thick brogans, ivory combs and silk handkerchiefs, bags of shot and pounds of chalk-white beads; butcher knives and boxes of thimbles, ground ginger, Seidlitz powders and lucifer matches; cod fish and pepper sauce, lime juice, Lexington mustard, bacon, rosin, foolscap paper, salted mackerel, and barrels of molasses (and, for Fort Atkinson and Fort Benson, plenty of alcohol and gunpowder).

The Sitturds' fellow passengers included such a motley assortment of failures, fanatics, coarse-shirt dirt growers, and the odd silk-hatted scoundrel, they had been able to go relatively unnoticed so far, and God willing might yet arrive at their destination without drawing unwanted attention, despite the endless delays. They had a dwindling but sufficient number of provisions that Schelling had supplied, and with Hephaestus regaining clarity, and more money in their pockets than they had had in a long while, there at least appeared to be cause for some little optimism. There was also before them again the prospect of Micah's legacy of Dustdevil, a tarnished star that had renewed in luster.

"We have a whole new life ahead of us now," Hephaestus announced, as if he had just found the money that had been stolen by the pickpocket back in St. Louis.

"Hopen net wus'den 'ebbeh," Rapture remarked.

"Now, don't be thinkin' like that, Murruh," the revived souse insisted. "Who knows but that the jerkiest part of the road is well behind and that maybe a treasure awaits us. The treasure of a fresh start, if nothing else—which seems mighty valuable to me."

"No moa saa'bints en slabes," his wife answered, as if that would be good enough for her.

No, thought Lloyd. No more servants and slaves—at least not the way she meant. He thought again of the wretched thing he had done on Fourth Street. Did anyone know what lay ahead for them? A trap? Prosperity? Safety? Damnation?

His mind once more moved to the uncle he had never met, the man they hoped to find still alive . . . the cryptic words of his letter, which had set their rickety wheels in motion. So many enigmas—and that made him think once more of Mother Tongue, hiding like a spider, feeling for the trembling in her web. Was she another shape the darkness took—or an angel of deliverance, a guide to the labyrinth? He had no answers, and so he said to his parents, "Well, it will be good to have a home again—that's ours. If we get there."

The Missouri is now and was then a wilder river than the Mississippi, requiring more alertness from its captains and crews, especially since the *Defiance* was a tawdrier vessel than her competitor cousins. Like a dusky maiden lurking on the edge of a debutante's ball, her attempt at Gothic finery was too soiled by hard circumstance to afford much grandeur anymore. And perhaps she heard, in the escapements and the jeering bells of the stern-wheelers that were beginning to gain prominence, that her days were numbered. In any case, her piston rods were well greased and her heavy heart thumped in time to the deeper rhythm of pioneer expectation, as if there was something animate and fulfilled in her to be again heading west.

The Sitturds were once more embarked on a journey, and so had rediscovered their place together. Even Lloyd could not ignore the change in mood since seeing his father's remorseful but lucid eyes greet him across the cabin. Like sleepers awakened from a communal nightmare, they reunited now with a common will. And if it was a delicate task getting the sobered drunkard out of the bunk and dressed again, and then to limp—a stealthy expedition up into the open air, lingering in the shadow of the pilothouse on the hurricane deck with the escape pipes belching—they all rose to the challenge.

It was just on sunset, and they were halfway on their voyage west to the frontier-fueled outposts of western Missouri. A fresh autumn breeze strengthened as the blood sun sank. A lone chicken hawk circled beneath high smoke-signal clouds, and the artery of muddy green river lapped up to the ravaged base of rampart sand cliffs that flowed and smeared out like time itself into the starved suggestion of lonely prairie beauty that lay beyond the shoreline chains of surging settlement. Voices echoed in the speaking tube, but the family from Zanesville was listening farther away. Rapture was trying to hear the spirits of her lost parents, the ghost music of places she knew that she would never see again. Hephaestus was trying not to hear the demons of backsliding degradation and oblivion, and to catch some whisper on the wind of his brother and the promise of what awaited them in Texas. Young Lloyd, who no longer looked young—at least not the way a child should look—was listening for pursuit, still reeling from his attempt to mate with the sky: the terrible inviting softness of death, the fatalities he had caused. Somewhere, out there in the distance, or perhaps as close as on board the same boat, were forces that he barely understood, if at all. But the piles of cloud above the river gave no sign of collusion with anything other than the setting sun and the strident smashing of the wooden wheel in the current.

It was this pervasive sense of doubt that had kept the boy sharp enough to stay free of the clutches of a deep depression from which he might not have recovered—a survival instinct channeled through the fine filaments of his heightened intellect, which kept him linked to the world despite an anguish and a regret that made his father's look paltry. The voices of the past—Zanesville bullies tormenting him, St. Ives and Miss Viola, the professor, Schelling, Mother Tongue, Brookmire, the black man beneath the courthouse crying out to heaven, and the insane chatter of the doomed Martian Ambassadors—they were all stilled in the splash of the steam-driven wheel and the new look of longing in his father's eyes.

Lloyd reasoned that he must maintain not just his mother's pretense about what had caused them to leave St. Louis but the much larger and more complex fantasy of a world without the Spirosians and the Vardogers. "I cannot tell them about what I do not understand myself," he admonished himself. "They have lost innocence enough, better to keep these other, longer shadows to myself." And so he did.

Both adults experienced a wave of reassurance in the few remarks their son offered before they all slipped back down to their cabin for refreshment and rest. They chose to forgo the dining saloon (as much to avoid what passed for the "boiled meat" as to avoid questions). There was still a span of river to survive, not to mention the so-called Indian Frontier, which at that moment in history extended from the Lake of the Woods in the north to Galveston Bay in the south (and, of course, was being pushed inexorably west).

All the known routes to the Pacific were alive with white settlers. The great thrust of migration along the Oregon Trail had commenced in earnest, making mad boomtowns of places like Council Bluffs and Omaha. The Potato Famine in Ireland and the war with Mexico were about to send more shock waves rippling out through the long grass. Then the insanity of the gold rush. Once peaceful relationships with tribes of Indians across the continent had already strained to the point of bloodshed and were building in intensity, just as the tensions over slavery and the great ideological and cultural differences between the North and the South were mounting to what would end up being a sprawling red mountain of corpses in the years to come.

Farmers, freed slaves, miners, Mormons, and families like theirs came spilling domesticated animals and heirlooms in the hope of finding some semblance of home, disrupting cycles of wild game and dispossessing native tribes on a scale and at a speed unseen on the planet before. The newspaper editor John O' Sullivan was about to coin the phrase "manifest destiny." It insinuated itself into even the Sitturds' cloistered cabin, and began to make Lloyd restless.

Rapture and Hephaestus, quite content to have some moments alone, allowed the boy to slip out after darkness fell. He had made a habit of this late at night, when his mother collapsed in discomposed sleep on the floor beside the tortured patriarch, always on the lookout for some stranger who might know more about them than he would like. Gorging on the sustenance of rediscovered intimacy, his parents allowed him to exit on the last stroke of the eleventh bell, imagining that he would slink around the boat like their cabin-mate mouse.

It was in fact a very different plan the boy had in mind now that his father had arisen from his stupor. But this plan was to be subverted, and it was a little after yet another midnight when Lloyd found out that there was indeed a stranger worth knowing about on board the *Defiance*. Someone stealthier than any mouse.

CHAPTER 2

A Different Kind of Darkness

THE WIND HAD DIED DOWN, BUT THERE WERE NO STARS OR MOON-light visible, for a low ceiling of cloud had fallen over the river, warming the air and dulling all sounds. Almost all the other passengers, save a few men playing poker on top of a barrel in what they called the poop-deck salon, had taken to their cabins. The burly crew, who were not resting fitfully below, huddled around lanterns, sucking on pungent cigars.

The Sitturds' fellow travelers were a furtive lot in Lloyd's view, a ragtag of prayer-sayers, blue-sky believers, runaway thieves, and would-be saints mixed up like nails and raisins in a jar. On nights before, he had heard the men playing. He had smelled their smoke and cheap whiskey, and caught the occasional loud oath or imprecation giving way to murmured bluffing and wagering. More than once he had felt the pang of memory, pondering where St. Ives and Miss Viola were—itching to be able to join the game and clean the shaving brush–bearded simpletons out of every pot. The thought of having to live in hiding even for the duration of their river journey sickened him, the stupid skullcap pulled down tight on his head like a badge of shame. And what about the future? Would he and therefore his family always be looking over their shoulders, shuttered up in claustrophobic spaces while the bright, teeming world grew faster and ever more luminous outside?

Old mud-rut routes and plank toll roads were giving way to macadamized causeways. Lloyd knew that the world would one day soon be speaking the firefly language of the telegraph (like the kind he had designed back home). Mechanical marvels would rumble over the earth and city-size balloons might rise like new suns. He wanted a part of it—to lead it, to steer the future. To soar above the flour mills and the distilleries like a lord of innovation. To him, it seemed that they had only appeared to leave Zanesville. The truth was it had followed them—or, rather, he had managed against all intention to re-create it.

The roof of heavy dry cloud weighed down upon him. His mind kept zooming back to the night he had met Mother Tongue in the grotto beneath the graveyard—the miraculous lights that had illuminated the cavern. If he had accepted her offer, everything might be different. Even if she had exaggerated in her story about the Spirosians and the Vardogers, he was convinced now that she was telling some species of truth. He could have had a rich, sparkling education. He could have shared in deep matters and worked with others more like himself to solve complex riddles. There would have been fresh meat and vegetables, scientific instruments—and the acquaintance of women, not girls but grown, knowing women like Viola Mercy. For the life of him, he could not recall what had blinded him to the epic opportunity he had been offered.

He saw not a single star or night bird. Only blank, cheerless clouds reflecting back the blur of lights from the foredeck and the pilothouse, and the intermittent flickers from the shacks and settlements along the shore. The dimness he glimpsed all around was surpassed only by what he felt inside. What did it matter if they did reach Texas, as unlikely as that still seemed? There would be no books or microscopes or dynamos there. (Note: the term "dynamo" had yet to be coined at that point;

Lloyd's term for such a device was an "electrogene.") His desire was not to plow fields for cotton or wheat but to harvest the treasures of magnetic fields. To master lightning. He had no yen to raise snap beans and hogs like a high-ranking beast of burden. He yearned to penetrate the mysteries of minerals and numbers—and the secret machinery of the mind. To invent new forms of power—new vehicles, new hybrids of intelligent light.

What he foresaw for them in Texas was dust and wind and poverty, the perpetual seclusion of guilt and disgrace. "This is no way to live," he told the thick Territory night. And yet, as he expressed this verdict, he saw that perhaps for his parents things could be different. If it was true that he was the principal cause of their troubles—and there was a strong argument that this was the case—then would not his parents' lives, now that Hephaestus had recovered from his alcoholic debauchery, be happier without him? Of course they would grieve, he acknowledged, but ultimately they would worry less. The sorrow would pass, and then they would be free. Perhaps they would have another child in time, a child less likely to cause heartache and destruction. A child less gifted but not damned—or, at least, not dogged by shadows and perverse ambitions.

The more he dwelled on this notion the more it formed in his mind. Another bitter bite of shock for his father and mother, yes, but then release, maybe forever. Besides, since the old man was back among the living Lloyd had no place at the head of the family. His childhood had been lost in the scent of Miss Viola's thighs and in the glare of the sun when he fell to earth, and he had killed at least one other human being and perhaps two innocent monsters, and caused who knows what hardships and dismay for the professor and Brookmire, not to mention Schelling and his clandestine tribe. The solution to all the conundrums facing him seemed amazingly simple when he examined it in the faint light of the empty deck. He found himself climbing up onto the rail, staring down at the dark flow that

surged around the shape of the *Defiance* just as the blood
coursed through the vessels in his throbbing, cap-hidden head.
All it would take was a little weight, and he would disappear
without a trace.

Speak to me, Lodema, cried out Lloyd in his mind, reaching
out with all his will to feel the spirit of his dead twin. *Give me
a sign.*

"You best get down," a voice behind him said, and the surprise almost sent him plunging into the black water. Instead, he
tumbled back onto the deck, eyes wild, heart racing, all the old
fears rekindled and the thought of jumping jettisoned utterly.
"Who are you?" he rasped, but he might well have asked where.

"No damn fool like you," the voice answered, and it seemed
to Lloyd that the night itself was addressing him. The pitch and
tone were female, but unlike any he could remember.

"I'm not a fool," he answered, raising himself up cautiously.

"Could've foxed me," the voice replied, and still Lloyd could
not pick out a face or body in the gloom. Could this be some
magical science of the Spirosians or their foes, or was he imagining it?

"Come out and let me see you," he said, and was struck
dumb when a hand patted his shoulder in response.

He whirled about, but it took several seconds for his eyes
to adjust and comprehend the new information that had presented itself so dangerously close beside him. Ever since the
alley in St. Louis, he had prided himself on his alertness. Now,
here someone had crept up within knifing distance—and a girl
at that! She had emerged from under a roll of oilcloth behind
one of the distress boats lashed to the rail. She was dressed in
dark clothes, like a boy, and was as far as he could tell several
years older than he—taller, anyway. She wore a skiff boy's cap
and kept both hands in front of her. Lloyd blinked, half expecting her to fade back into the murk, but her figure held firm, like
a phantom reluctantly fleshed.

"Come," she whispered, and seized his elbow. "Out of sight."

To his further astonishment, Lloyd yielded to her touch. She pulled him down one of the crew-ways to a step rail that led toward the cargo hold. He had peeped down that way the day before but had grown skittish when one of the crew members, a snaggle-toothed moron they called Clapper burped at him. Inside a tiny storeroom with an ax mounted on the wall, a bald man dozed on his hands at a knotwood table that played host to a tin cup and a spitting candle in a blackout box. The Night Girl shuffled Lloyd softly past and into the jumbled shadows of another chamber. A stack of firewood and some smoked meats hanging in nets met his eyes—a gaff pole, crates, kegs. With impressive certainty, the girl steered him through the maze to a trunk against a bulkhead, and then eased the trunk back without making a sound. She lifted a plank and motioned to him to step down into a hole.

Through the taut working wood Lloyd could feel the thrum and clunk of the engine, chugging at reduced speed now at night—and he imagined that he could also feel the vibrations of the other passengers, tossing in their sleep or making love, fending off creditors in dreams, savage beasts or Indian war parties that awaited them in the wilderness beyond. He had visions of stepping down into some iron cage to be trapped, and yet he did as his strange guide directed and was relieved beyond measure when she followed him, the bare skin of her hands brushing against him when they were settled in the inky confinement just below. Shades of the false-bottomed graveyard, Lloyd thought.

They crouched on the floor, facing each other in total darkness, and he heard the plank slid back into place. A moment later, the mysterious girl lit a small storm lantern that sat between them. The light flared up as if inside a cave.

"Smuggler's hold," the girl muttered. "Doan nobody know we're here, so talk low."

There was something about her voice or, rather, her way of speaking that perplexed Lloyd. He let his eyes suck in the surroundings, which were so near there was not much to see. A rough bedroll and a sack of food that smelled like cold mutton and boiled potato—their refuge was no more than a large mouse hole. Then the girl pulled off her cap and he let out a stifled sigh.

She was a Negro with milk-coffee skin and eyes that shone like the color of honeycomb in the lantern reflection. Her hair was not kinky, puffed, or nappy like that of other dark girls he had seen but straight and tinged a rich cinnamon shade, clipped as though she had taken a pair of pinking shears to her head without a mirror. She smelled a little—or perhaps it was the mutton—but her teeth were clean and white, her nose sleek and narrow. He guessed her age to be about twelve, although it was hard to tell. Thirteen, maybe. He knew that she was taller than he, but there was a womanly cast to her face despite the hardened scowl she affected and the boyish clothes she wore—a rough cotton tow shirt under a mussel-blue fisherman's jacket and loose britches that looked as if they were stitched out of some old curtain. The garments smelled of smoke and sweat, and the moist, greasy air of the boat. Her feet were bare, the soles as pale as butter.

"Why you gwain jump?" she demanded, and then cleared her throat.

Lloyd tried to think, but all he could do was stare at her.

"You crazy or you in trouble?"

The way she said this was different. Her speech seemed to shift between dialects.

"You can talk. I heard you. Whatchyou lookin' at?"

Lloyd had never felt so lost for words.

"What's your name?"

This question was delivered with a steeled self-assurance.

"Are you scared?"

She sounded almost solicitous now, with the tone of fine breeding. He could imagine a wealthy white girl fondling the family cat, yet inches away from him was a Negro filly in sooty boy's garb with grown-up eyes and a soft, full mouth. He tried to look away but could not bring himself to do it.

"Worried 'bout bein' with a nigger?" she challenged, and her whole bearing seemed to change again.

"Who . . . are . . . you?" Lloyd managed at last, and felt reassured to be able to speak.

"Wailll . . ." she smirked. "Dey calls me Shoofly." She flashed her white teeth in a mocking way and then, in sharp finishing-school diction, added, "But I call myself Hattie. As in Henrietta LaCroix. That's my proper name."

Her posture and tone had shifted again, becoming haughty and cool, educated even. He could not control his gaze. The brassy glint of her high cheekbones, the buttermilk soles of her feet—everything confused him, and the thought of leaping into the river was as lost as something he had thrown overboard.

"That's . . . a fine . . . name," he gurgled, realizing to his mortification that he was becoming aroused between his legs.

The girl gave a slight snort and rolled her filbert-shaped eyes. "I don't need the likes of you to tell me that," she said, as her hands whisked out faster than he could move and zipped the skullcap from his head.

His hair was dirty and matted and, as good as it always felt to take off the cap, he felt naked now and was all the more embarrassed about his incipient erection. What made matters worse was that he had the sudden impression that the girl was drawing some disdainful conclusion about him. He had sensed this attitude from Negroes and mulattoes a few times before, and now the way she regarded him he could almost look back through her eyes, like a reversible lens, to each of those incidents, silent little moments of conspiratorial reckoning—sometimes condescending, other times rudely compassionate, and always happening at the speed of a glance. In her weird honeycomb eyes, he knew that he looked like trash.

"You're beautiful," he choked at last, and was instantly sorry he had said it.

The girl made a mute pucker with her lips and her face flared like copper under a flame, but she did not move.

"Like niggers, huh?" She squinted, putting on her poor, shiftless voice again.

Lloyd could feel some violence coiling up inside her. She might have pulled a water moccasin out of her breast—or a blade—but he made no move to protect himself.

"Rub my feet," she commanded.

"W-what?" he stammered.

"Rub my feet, boy," she repeated, with a face like a fist, and in one fluid motion she brought her legs up over the lantern and into his lap, so that if she had extended her toes they would have pressed against his straining hardness.

Lloyd gulped and took the right foot in his fingers—and, without being able to take his eyes from hers, he began to stroke and caress the arch and ball, feeling the coarse skin soften with the oil of his palm. The girl blew out the lantern.

His parents did not know where he was. No one on board knew where he was. He did not know whom he was with. She might have been mad, for all he knew—and must have been mad in some way to be hiding down there in that hole, stalking the boat alone late at night, with no family or traveling companions. A girl her age. And a Negro—or half Negro. Yet, plunked down now in complete darkness with her, massaging the calloused flesh of her foot, he was flooded with an unknown calmness. He kept his hands at their task, trying not to breathe.

What seemed like a very long time passed, and at last the girl said, "It's different in the dark. Some folks is afraid of it. I ain't—I'm not. Are you?"

"Sometimes," Lloyd managed. "But not . . . now . . ."

"Call me Hattie. What I call you?"

"L-loyd."

"All right, then. Lloyd. Were you really going to jump?"

Lloyd could no longer picture her firmly in his mind. Just her eyes. He felt as if he were caressing the darkness itself. Her tone was sultry and soothing, but the words were young and white. Southern. Mixed up. Like someone in a dream.

"I don't know," he answered.

"Someone's affer you," Hattie said, again sounding black.

"How do you know that?"

"I can feel it. I can smell it."

"I thought that was mutton."

The girl gave a light grunt.

"Well, you don't have to tell me about it, if'n you don't want to. Got troubles enough of my own."

"Are you . . . running away?"

"Yep," she answered. "I surely am. Folks affer me for sure."

"Are you . . . a . . . slave?"

The softening foot withdrew, then thrust forward deeper into his hands.

"Not anymore," the girl replied, her voice whitening once more.

"You don't act like . . ." Lloyd's cracking voice trailed off.

"Thass 'cause I ain't!" Hattie hissed. "Not for true. I'm from downriver—the Mississippi. Long way. Been sneakin' on boats and layin' low and trampin' for more than two moons. Covered a lot of ground. Gwain to keep movin'."

"So . . . you escaped? Were you on a farm?"

"*Plantation.* Big one. With a big white house and los of niggers."

The last word stalled in the air like a belch.

"W-where?" Lloyd asked, squeezing the other foot.

"They calls it—call it—the Corners. Arkansas, Mississippi, and Louise-y-anna. Down on the line there. Grand place back off the river a few mile."

"Why—did you run away? Was the master mean?"

The girl's right hand whipped out like a frightened bat and cuffed his face in the dark.

"The mastah was my papa!"

Lloyd's cheek smarted from the blow, but he did not stop working his fingers into her other foot, which seemed to him to have taken on a life of its own, like some cave animal he was cuddling. He thought back to the professor's monkey, Vladimir, and Mother Tongue's odd cat.

"I was born in the cabin, as they say. But he allas treated me special. *Right*. Gave me learning. On the sly. Told me one day I'd go to school. Europe. One day . . . I'd be a lady. Fine dresses. Books. Music."

"Then why . . . did you run away?" Lloyd gasped, confused about why his companion in the dark had thrown away the same sorts of chances that he had.

"His wife hated me! She knew the truth. She saw I waddn't like the other niggers. She hated my mother, but she hated me more. When I's younger, it was just mean. But when I got a figure—and she found out I could read and write and do sums— she became a devil. Thought it was a sin that I should know about paintings and novels. Wouldn't raise a hand to me long as Mama was alive. But when Mama died last year—I reckon she was poisoned! Then the old thing laid for me."

Lloyd swallowed hard.

"She sent me up to Memphis to be sold away. It was her daddy had the land first. She was older 'n Papa. He married her back when she was still a little pretty. But she got crooked and sick—and evil inside. Lay up in her white bed all day dabbing her throat with cologne and whining for the nigger girls to fan her and shoo the flies. Story was she lost a baby. Wouldn't let Papa come to her bed after that. So . . . he came . . . to my mother."

"Why didn't your father . . . protect you?"

"He tried." Hattie sighed, with a mixture of fatigue and sadness that made Lloyd lighten his touch. "But men are weak. They're all . . . slaves."

This last assertion made Lloyd wince, but he kept rubbing the foot, subconsciously easing it against his erection. This girl was like no one he had ever imagined. Shining machines and flying over rivers and cities did not seem so wondrous as before.

"Papa's heart was broken when Mama died," the girl continued, as if she were reconsidering the events as she recounted them.

"He sounds . . . like a sad man," Lloyd offered, feeling stupid. He kept imagining her eyes in the dark.

"He was a brave man and a wise man, and a good man," Hattie insisted. "Let all the niggers read the Bible—and more. Got 'em learning arithmetic—and the stars. The neighbor white folks hated him for that."

"He must miss you now."

"He's dead," Hattie said, and must have reached in the sack for a hunk of mutton, because Lloyd could hear her jaws click. "Hung hisself."

"He did?" the boy wheezed, thinking back to his own actions on the deck.

"Died in shame," the girl continued. "Man named Barlow— plantation owner nearby—challenged him to a duel. Said he was a nigger lover and a traitor to the South! Papa strung himself up the night before. His old wife had her way after that. Her and the overseer."

Lloyd did not know what to say. It reminded him of the story Mother Tongue had told him. Perhaps the man had not hanged himself. But it was not his place to speak now.

"Give me your hands."

"What?" Lloyd whispered, feeling his stomach turn.

"Give me your damn hands," Hattie hissed.

He loosened his grasp of her feet and stretched out his hands. There was a rustle of fabric and then he touched warm skin. Girlish breasts beginning to form. A fragile hint of womanly fullness. And ripeness. His own skin tingled. But her flesh was ridged and welted. The body before him leaned into his grope, filling his fingers with a different kind of darkness. Lloyd could feel the girl's breath, mutton-scented, on his face, while his intrigued, frightened hands were allowed to roam over her bare skin.

Where there should have been nipples there were lumpy crosses of scars. His fingertips explored small slices and pocks and bumps that reminded him of the Ambassadors' secret hierograms. The girl's entire chest and belly rippled with markings that seemed to radiate an angry heat.

"They . . . did . . . *this* . . . to you?"

"Not all at once, mind," Hattie whispered. "They took their sweet time. Her and Riddick."

Lloyd recollected the tone of St. Ives's voice when he told of his maiming at the hands of the diabolical Rutherford. The odor of the mutton was starting to make him nauseated. Or maybe it was the scarring.

"And that's not all they did," Hattie hissed—and Lloyd caught the faintest hint of a sob in her voice. He pulled his hands back.

"I'll never have chillum—children. And . . . I'll never have pleasure. With a man. Understand? I reckon you old enough to know what I mean. That's what the old hag wanted. Then she sold me off. Up Memphis way. That's when I run off. First chance I had. Only chance I thought I'd get. "

Lloyd could think of nothing to say. His hands had retracted from the girl's wounded skin, and yet had been drawn to the feel of her, as if through some perverse attraction. His stomach growled—still his erection stiffened. The space they were in seemed to contract around them, as if somewhere deep within he retained the memory of what it had been like to be so close to his twin sister, Lodema, back in the mother darkness.

"So. *Lloyd?*" Hattie inquired after a long moment's silence. "Why you wanna end your life? 'Cause you a mongrel colored boy in disguise?"

"What?"

"I see through you. Niggers will. Smart ones, anywise. I knew it the first time I saw you sneakin' around with the Judas face."

Lloyd remained still, listening through the coffin-creaking walls.

"You gots woes and worries? You gots scars, too?" Hattie badgered. "Hmm? Let me feel 'em!"

"I killed a man," he answered at last. "Maybe three. Back in St. Louis."

"You lie!" Hattie scoffed and jabbed her feet into his belly. "How a li'l skunk like you do that?"

"You wouldn't believe me if I told you," Lloyd replied. "But I did. Just as sure as I'm sitting here."

"White men? Or niggers?"

"I killed a . . . slave . . ." Lloyd answered, not sure what to say about the Ambassadors from Mars.

"Well, then. That ain't so bad," Hattie said, sounding younger and blacker again. "Less'n he was somebody else's. And I reckon he was—way y'all look. I seen your mama slinkin' round, too. She white, I eat your stinky hat. But she pretty and smart. Plays good."

This calling attention to his mother's ancestry, and therefore his own, did not sit well with Lloyd, although he was relieved that she did not seem to know about his father. He had come to believe that the family had overcome or managed to obscure their mixed blood, and that their problems lay on another level. But seen now through the eyes of this blighted creature before him—in the dark, torn between tribes and destinies like two girls separated at birth by a knife and then sewn back up in a single body—he felt again the stirrings of the monstrous within himself. Had not the professor once joked that he was as anomalous as the Martian brothers in his own way? He may not have scars on his skin like this half-educated, half-slave girl, but what if someone were to feel deeper?

His head and heart were inundated—the hosanna-shouting

Mule Christian below the courthouse, the chatter of the freak-ish twins borne away into the sky. Every detail of the infernal incident came rushing back upon him like the rising of the ground. And before he could master himself he burst into tears.

"Boy, stop that!" Hattie demanded. "You gots nuthin' to cry over. You want me to strike a light and show you what these scars of mine *look* like?"

Lloyd choked on his words. "I . . . I was done, too," he gasped. "In St. Louis . . . this ugly man . . . in an alley one night."

The girl paused at this announcement. This sounded to her like a much more believable claim than the murders the boy had mentioned before. But she wanted to be clear before pro-jecting any sympathy.

"He take down your pants?"

"Ripped them down," Lloyd sobbed. "Then he slammed my head down into a dung cart . . . and . . . and . . . he did me. Hard as he could."

Hattie LaCroix remained silent and still, waiting for him to catch his breath. She knew there was more to come.

"He said . . . he said . . . I felt just like a little . . . *pig!*" Lloyd wailed at last, and even though his voice never broke above a whisper, the admission broke him wide open.

Had that horror and humiliation been what had driven him to take to the sky? He had dreamed up the flight before the rape, but there in the dark intimacy of the hold, with this fellow fugitive, it struck him that maybe there was more to the grand design of his disastrous undertaking—the insistence on fulfill-ing it—than he had seen before. He knew the man had a hare-lip, but it was the meat-slab hands he remembered. The terrible, grunting skewering—so different from his afternoon with Miss Viola . . . so different . . .

More like some hideous revenge . . . of . . . Phineas . . .

The floodgates were open now, and when she saw that she could not command the boy's tears away she set aside the unlit lantern and moved, so that her legs were twined around him. His body fell against hers, his wet, sputtering face pressing against her still exposed bosom—half boy's, half girl's and raked like a battlefield—hot tears soaking her like an Indian-summer rain across shallow graves. His breathing heaved as she clutched him closer, at first to quiet him and then out of some deeper need of her own.

He smelled like other children she had cradled in dirt-floor cabins and dogwood arbors, like the Persian rugs she had helped Sarah beat with a stick broom out on the fine green, rolling lawn. He smelled like her desperate, chicken-stealing tramp-night stowaway antics. He smelled like life—dreadful, sinful, tragic, precious—and she held him and held him. The baby she would never have, the white child she would never be.

"Shush, boy," she whispered in his ear, embracing him, though the tears soaked her more than him. And still he cried. She suspected that he was not one to cry much—too proud, just like herself. So he would be full of it, like a tent roof too heavy with rain to tip. He was full of a lot of things, she sensed.

Boy though he was, she felt the manhood bursting out of him. It was surprising in one his age, but she had become accustomed to surprises. She stripped down his britches, as the garments had been rent from her in the past, taking hold of his privacy as if reaching for a chunk of meat. Maybe a different kind of darkness would cure his grief. Boys, like men, were like that.

Yes, he was young. Very young. But what did that matter when there were people hunting her?

She had done it before with a boy named Samuel and another named Tee, with a white man named Johnson and another called Cooley. She had always done what she had had to do. And she had survived what had been done to her. In a corncrib and a canebrake. In a shell-pink high-ceilinged bedroom, razor-stropped to an iron cot with the queer scents of magnolia and quinine oozing in.

Lloyd was too jangled to resist. Even as his precocious lust sprang forth, he gave in—let her lead. Hattie used him like a rag to staunch a hemorrhage. Hers—and his, too. She always imagined blood streaming from between her legs now. She would wake in a cold sweat at the memory of it. Not like the blood of the moon, the blood of the garden. No, like the blood of the living dead. She could take no pleasure and extract no seed that would take fruit—still, she would take something. And maybe in doing so now she would give something back.

They merged into each other's wounds with an urgency that made them both quake.

CHAPTER 3

No One Sees the Thunder

THE SUDDEN CHANGE IN LLOYD'S DEMEANOR RAPTURE ATTRIB-
uted to the return of her husband's sobriety and health. Even
the bung foot seemed to bother Hephaestus less now, and he
took to exercising in their tiny cabin and accepted with grace
the restrictions on his open appearance throughout the boat in
daylight. Lloyd, meanwhile, had lost his sullen casing of detachment and seemed positively cheerful. To Rapture, it was a
blessing. Perhaps the past was behind them.

The *Defiance* plowed on westward, and Lloyd sneaked out of
the cabin every single chance he could, which allowed his parents to rebuild their romantic bridges as well as to talk about
the next stage in their journey. Of course, Rapture worried
about her son when he was out of sight. Not understanding the
nature of the crisis that had forced their removal from St.
Louis, she retained anxieties both about what the boy would
get up to and who might be taking an interest in him. However,
the thought that her only child, who was still only a child, was
often, at the very same moment that she was in the arms of her
recovering husband, languishing and coming to life in the arms
of a half-breed girl (much as she had been at the same age) in
the world hidden between decks of the riverboat never once
crossed her mind.

That he satisfied himself with his hand and took great satisfaction from the practice, she knew well and discreetly ignored. Her own upbringing had been free and earthy in matters of the body, and the enjoyment of sex fit into her view of the world just as a belief in haints or the protective and restorative powers of lynx spice and fennel. But the thought that her son was not a virgin, and was in fact engaged in the most torrid romping that Hattie's stowaway status would allow, would have come as a shock, and Lloyd was careful to spare her and his fragile father.

Lloyd Meadhorn Sitturd, the willful prodigy and fallen angel, had found something he had known only in his imagination while lying among the wind machines of his shrine to his lost sister back in Zanesville. It was an energizing, redemptive peace that seemed to flood his entire being.

There would have been countless other things that might have occupied his mind, such as the performance of the steam engines or the physics of the current. There was plenty of river traffic to note and wildlife to observe along the shore: deer, wolves, bison, elk, and the now extinct Carolina parrots. There was a joint-skinny German on board, whose sagging flesh told a story of hardship and deprivation, who nonetheless would ascend to the hurricane deck at twilight and play a mournful silver cornet—in thanks, he said, for coming to America. And there were always stories to hear among his fellow passengers—tales of taxes and lost farms, of grubbing out trees and burying sick children, whispered fears of Indians and blizzards, and of fortunes to be made in trading whiskey, salt, tobacco, and beeswax.

But Hattie LaCroix, bastard mulatto woman-child, was all he could think of. The smell of her on his hands, the sounds she made, the things she said, the tears that she gave him, were like rain from a higher sky. They watered and nourished him out of his arrogance and guilt, his self-pity and his clumsy boot-encased boyness. He always felt naked with her, even when they sneaked out late to smoke her corncob pipe, dressed and wrapped in a stolen horse blanket, beside the distress boats up on deck, where on that first murky night he had contemplated leaping into the river and she had saved him.

She *had* saved him. The slightest scent of her skin or breath of her voice would set off a tremor inside him, but a tremor that seemed to make him stronger. Back with his parents, chattering about the road ahead to Texas or lying on his slender dog shuck on the floor of their cabin, the memory of something she had said, or the whiff of her body that still clung to him, could make him dizzy. Whenever he closed his eyes, he saw her scars burning in his mind, a diabolical language of pain, but a beautiful secret language, too, of survival—the kind of deeper language he felt underlay the world, which he one day hoped to read as easily as algebraic equations or sheet music.

He understood in some storm-lit, intuitive way that she represented a kind of psychic union of the females whose lives or spirits had touched his most profoundly: Lodema, his mother, and Viola Mercy. But the girl was too much her own person, too much her own parents, guardian, and deliverer to be compared with anyone else. Sometimes he thought of her as the gift from his phantom sister, charmed out of his mixed-blood refugee life to give him gumption—more precious than anything Mother Tongue or Schelling had promised. No dusty scientific secret or antique treasure but a contraband friend and soul mate.

Lloyd spent every possible moment he could with the runaway girl. When he was not with her, he was thinking about her. Fixated on her. Hattie was a gift. A sacred, unexpected gift. A mercy. The miseries and sins of St. Louis were all washed away in her presence. She took his mind off the suffering of the past and the uncertainties of the future. He wanted the time with her to extend—for the boat never to reach its destination, but for them to be stealthy, secret, and together always. In all ways.

For her part, she waited with pining impatience for his arrival (although she would never have admitted this and tried hard to suppress any perceptible exuberance at all when he appeared in the dark or in the lull of the afternoon, when the other passengers were fat and sweaty with drowse. It was getting cooler now, though, and oftentimes when they got naked together they needed to hold each other all the tighter so as not to ripple with gooseflesh.

Then they got teeth-chattering cold, when Lloyd let Hattie talk him into something that would have seemed insane to anyone who had not gone sailing three hundred feet into the air, in what amounted to a membrane of handmade spiderweb above a teeming city. She coaxed him into joining her in dangling from one of the towropes down into the river. They did it fully clothed; Hattie referred to it as "doin' laundry," and made it sound practical, but Lloyd suspected it was pure adventure that thrilled her, and that it was a kind of challenge to him. He smuggled along another set of his ragged clothes, in case by some wild chance they managed to survive.

They did it at night, when the boat was barely moving. Still, the risks were great. It was a long way even from the service deck down to the water, and of course it seemed infinitely farther coming back up the rope, especially shivering with wet, slippery hands.

"You think you strong enough to make it?" she asked.

"You bet I am!" he snapped back. Good Lord, he thought. She is more boy than I am, and more woman than girl. He could not let himself be shown up by her, even if she was older. But there was something about her that inspired confidence, and made this daredevil rite seem not just possible but casual. Fun. And perhaps something more serious, too. Strengthening. Lloyd had never known such a quality of leadership in a female before. "She would make a good soldier," he told himself. "A captain of midnight raids. Or . . . a spy."

But all the confidence she projected did not take away from the threat of falling off the rope into the current, which was too swift to swim against. It did not keep the floating logs away, or make it any easier to be quiet so as not to alert the crew. Hattie was, after all, a stowaway and a fugitive slave. She had, as she said, "folks affer her for sure." The river was colder than he had ever known the water to be back in Ohio. It seemed to move with a serpentine force, and there was always the chance that there still were some snakes in it—and to see a snake swimming, as he often had from the decks on their travels, is a disturbing thing. (Of course, *not* to see one swimming, when you are in the water, too, can be fatal.)

The clasping, gasping, reddened hand-over-hand, leg-and-foot-shimmying drag back up the heavy hemp braid—freezing with even just a light breeze on soaked clothes and skin—was the hardest thing Lloyd remembered ever doing.

It was made no easier when one of the crew appeared in silhouette above them, smoking a cheroot, which forced them to pause in their ascent, just about the time Lloyd felt that his arms would explode or drop off. The pain and strain were excruciating, but there was cloud cover above and a fine mist rising off the water, as if the river really were a kind of monstrous snake and the vapor was the skin it was shedding.

As exhausting as it was, it somehow filled him with an electric zest, because he was not clutching onto the rope in the dark alone. Hattie was just below him, and he knew that she was exerting extra effort to help keep him braced. He knew that she would not have hesitated a second to leap into the current if he had slipped. He was not sure what he would have done if she had fallen, as deep as his feelings ran. She had more than courage. She had a mastery of herself that made her a captain of split-second decisions.

At last the infernal idler finished his smoke and abandoned the deck to them, where they scrambled up and over, dripping, shaking with the wet, the cold, the struggle—and the grand achievement of clandestine triumph. Then they crept back as quietly as they could, given the drenched garments, to Hattie's hideaway, where with almost ritual devotion they undressed each other by stubbed candlelight.

It was then, with the bracing sensation of ducking down into the fast black water still fresh and vivid in his very bones, that Lloyd realized that Hattie had "bactize" him, as his mother would have said.

What was more, she had enacted with him—virtually holding his hand, certainly holding his heart—a ceremonial variation of the blind, desperate act he had been contemplating the night she had intervened. She had made the darkness visible and livable. He was cured of that attraction forever.

He held her and held her and held her. They melded together for warmth, and the heat of their longing softened their chafed palms. Mother Tongue had teased him with the promise of learning the art of love. But, in all the world, Lloyd doubted if he could have found a better teacher—one more generous or less ashamed.

Sexually maimed though she was, Hattie had not lost her young, powerful libido. It had diffused across her whole body. The blossom may have been cut, but her deeper bloom had not perished. Her skin had a hunger to be touched, and her scars an incandescent need for acceptance and blessing. She found in Lloyd the eye and tender hand witness she had hoped for, without even knowing it.

She was both rough and gentle with him—giving and greedy. She let herself open her broken wings to his mingling, teaching him how to use his penis; it was in the end a tool, just as it is often called. She understood the driving male pleasure, and shared an injured version of the penetrative desire herself. There was the two-becoming-one delight that no mutilation could revoke. But she showed him there was more. Oh, so much more.

There was tongue and breath, kneading and brushing. There were eyelashes and whispers, and the simple ecstasy of mutual grooming. Instead of rutting, panting, and spurting hot wet seed, Lloyd learned some of the secrets of temptation—of fondling, kissing, the exquisite anticipation of a feather down a belly. And he learned the profound wholeness of a shared silence.

It was like being back in the womb again, in a way, he thought. But a new kind of guiltless womb made by consensual, collusive imaginations—two people giving birth to themselves through the vulnerability, faith, and vigor of true nakedness. For all the talk of conspiracies back in St. Louis, this was the one conspiracy he was certain that he wanted to join.

That night, after they had returned from out of the river—after they had mated and consecrated each other with hushed entwinement—Hattie said to him softly, "Roll over."

Lloyd winced at this, bristling with fear and embarrassment. Some intuition born of their intimacy warned him of what she was thinking. Yet he could not resist her direction, although he asked in a quavering voice, "What are you going to do?" Knowing already.

She moved the candle closer and produced from behind a crate a tin stew pan full of soapsuds, water, and a flannel rag. "You seen how I was hurt," she said. "That all's had time to heal. I want to see if you all right. You likely didn't say nuthin'."

To his amazement, he found himself turning over onto his stomach, as she brought the candle closer still. He flashed back to Mother Tongue's story about the Vardogers, the Order of the Claws & Candle. That was the thing about candles—about all sources of light, heat, and hope, he realized. Some have caring fingers . . . some have seeking claws. The desire to help and heal . . . the call to crush or to possess. The two sides of the coin of bewonderment: inspiration or terror.

Hattie's hands were both firm and respectful. She washed him there, the part of our bodies we are all most sensitive about. She dried him, and then brought the candle in close enough for him to feel the urgent caress of the flame.

In truth, he had often bled when relieving himself since the incident in the alley, and the feedbag-and-gut-clog diet had not helped. But the pain had eased. He felt very exposed for her to have bathed him that way, though—to examine him. But who better to do it?

"You all right," she pronounced at last. Then she said, "You gwain be all right, too. Lotta boys had that done to 'em, they'd neva be good inside again. You got nuthin' to be 'shamed of—hear? You let the pain go, all right? You keep yo' anger. But you let the pain go."

"How . . . how do I do that?" Lloyd asked, his voice muffled, as he lay facedown on the strewn hole floor.

Hattie said, "Reach behine you and pull your cheeks apart."

He did. To his intense bewonderment, she kissed him there—with the fullness of her soft mouth.

"You be all right," she said, blowing on his lower back, so that he squirmed. "And doan ever let that hurt you inside anymore. No shame."

For the second time that night, she had worked a kind of magic—the type you can feel and smell. Lloyd trembled beneath her body, as she enveloped him, the heat of her scars and her tenacity melting into him, just as the wax dripped from the shaft of the candle into its cup-lipped dish.

But despite this depth of animal affection, physical intimacy was not all they shared—by a great measure. They were, after all, still very young—even Hattie. They both savored pickles and would pilfer them from the oily jars in the storeroom, feeding them to each other. They stole squab nuts and beef jerky, a sumptuous wheel of fragrant cheese—and a smoked chicken, too. Then they would dine down in the murk of Hattie's cubbyhole, pretending they were a lordly couple in some fancy stateroom or a luxurious private railway carriage, rattling through the snowcapped mountains of Europe.

Both of them had at least glimpsed books with brilliant illustrations of the Alps and the lakes of Italy and Switzerland,

Paris, Rome, the temples of Greece. Those visions seemed so remote from their circumstances, to openly conjure them would have seemed plain cruel with anyone else. But they had each other, and they somehow gave each other permission to dream aloud—perhaps the greatest intimacy of all.

"I think I should like to be . . . the first lady prime minister of England," Hattie announced at one point, with her mouth full of plundered pork crisp and what passed for quince paste (and later passed as gas, which set them both snorting). She had put on her best, crispest "elegant" white accent for this confession, and it set Lloyd chortling, trying to stifle his hilarity—with his own mouth full of what he hoped was smoked side ham. For someone whose thoughts had stretched into abstruse realms far beyond his years, he had done precious little laughing. It was like balm for his inner being. But it did not stop him from ribbing her.

"I don't . . . think . . . that they'll let you be . . . prime minister," he asserted at last, almost hiccupping.

" 'Cause I's a girl?" Hattie retorted, chucking his cheek.

"Because . . . because . . . you're not English!" Lloyd replied, which made them both collapse into the delicious foolishness of shared hysterics.

They both seemed to want dogs—several of them—so the hounds could keep one another company. They wanted dogs, books, art. Hattie stressed the importance of music, Lloyd the essentiality of science.

Hattie wanted horses, too—she had never been allowed to ride. Lloyd insisted that new forms of transportation were already taking shape (and he recalled the bizarre locomotive, seemingly made of glass, that Schelling had shown him).

She named him Li'l Skunk. It was not easy for her to express affection, in spite of her passionate nature, so the nickname conveyed more than it appeared. She had first thought of Li'l Pig, to help Lloyd own the evil that had preyed on him and to turn it around—to transform shame into a badge of honor, which was how she felt about her scars and welts. But she knew instinctively that those words rubbed too close to the wound. He would have to make his treaty with them himself now. She had shown him the way.

She chose Li'l Skunk instead, because he was both black and white, because a skunk protects itself through ingenuity rather than physical strength and aggression, and because it gave concise expression to her joshing about his body odor. She meant, in part, that he already had a man smell about him, even though he was still so young.

Rather than taking offense, Lloyd found any comment about his scent amusing, because he was pretty certain that if either of them was more odiferous it was she. Both in a womanly way and because he had the refuge of an official cabin with a washtub, while she was stranded down in her hiding place.

He dubbed her the Brown Recluse, a moniker that at first puzzled and almost pipped her temper. "Why you call me that? A spider? And a dangerous spider, too."

"There's something of the spider in all females," he replied. "And a spider is the first thing I remember, other than my dead sister. It used to come down to visit me on an invisible thread in the kindling scuttle I slept in as a baby. She taught me about time and light, and how to make something out of thin air. But brown recluses don't spin webs—they hunt on their own, just like you. And in case you didn't know, you *are* dangerous," he told her. "You are *very* dangerous. You aren't afraid of things you should fear and that others would. You're clever and brave, and you have the control to strike when you have the advantage but the sense to conceal yourself, as a rule. You would go about your business without disrupting anyone, yet you have poison enough if the need arises."

Hattie had to smile at this. Presented thus, the title seemed more a badge of honor than she could have imagined. It was like a promotion in life rank—a reflection from out of the depths of a very subtle mirror of all that she valued and hoped to be seen as—to be.

How often we forget, or are forced to overlook because of lack, that the true fire of connection between hearts and souls is fundamental. Are you seen by the adored as less than you are at your best, or as all that you could be? That is the one sure measure of the health of any adoration. Both of them grasped in the other what was unique, what shone, what was to be prized, and that is rare at any age.

So it became graceful and relaxed to share other secrets, and commonplaces as well. Hattie told Lloyd more about the persecutions she had endured, the horrors she had felt, along with just the day-to-day fowl-plucking, slop-bucket, and weed-pulling life of the Corners. She painted a bright, detailed picture of working, loving, hating, surviving life on a major plantation, and filled in many gaps in his understanding.

She explained that because there was always some movement or migration of slaves due to sales or exchanges between owners, news and gossip about other plantations spread. They were each run in their own ways, yet most of the same larger principles applied. There were pecking orders, an assignment of tasks and a deployment of resources that remained relatively constant. Conditions and treatment might be very different, but there were protocols and codes of action that never varied.

As she spoke, Lloyd realized that what she was providing in her descriptions was both an internal and an exploded view of a very intricate machine. An organic machine, yes, but to him the concept of a machine *was* organic. Without knowing, she brought forth into illumination the idea of the self-assembling, self-consuming, self-sustaining complex system in his mind.

It suddenly struck him, for instance, that the definition of a complex machine was one that was five-dimensional—time defining the fourth, psychology the fifth. Mind transcended time, the same way that language tried to, and could indeed transcend space.

He thought back to Mother Tongue's remarks about Spiro of Lemnos, the Enigmatist who had glimpsed more deeply than all others into the mesh of things—all that was hidden in plain sight.

It also came to him for the first time that if the complicated workings of something like a plantation—a machine both built by humans and including them as critical components—could be understood as a machine, working within a network of other similar machines to form a bigger, still more complicated machine, then there were two contrary but very pregnant implications.

First, the notion of mechanism, as in the mechanistic philosophy he had become acquainted with in Schelling's bookshop—as in a reductionist strategy—was categorically deficient, if not totally wrong. Second, the far more interesting idea that such a thing even as multifaceted as a plantation could be rendered diagrammatically, as could any machine. It was just a question of what the hierogram looked like. Then he said to himself, "I meant diagram."

Even as she spoke, his mind raced. The problem with the traditional mechanists, he grasped, was that they merely broke processes and subassemblies down. There was no integration. Therefore no creation. Everything their method touched died in their hands. Their wholes were always less than the sum of their parts. That had been his problem with the parafoil system in St. Louis. It was not a lack of time and quality materials. It was not just hubris and pilot error. He had not had the model clear enough in his mind, because it was the wrong model. It was only a model.

Without realizing, Hattie taught him—or helped him teach himself—more than all that he had learned up to that moment. She was like the frizzen that fires a flintlock, for a consideration began to take form in his mind: when you really understand something—even a very complex process or system (and what is not complex, if you give it deep enough attention?)—then you can picture it whole. And the picture somehow *is* the whole.

The hierograms of the Martian Ambassadors streamed through his mind, and it occurred to him to ask, What if their inscrutable emblems were not symbols representing sounds, ideas, and things as other languages do but, rather, intense distillations of relationships between concepts, so that figuratively speaking, if you could step to the other side of them in your mind they would be prismatic ways of seeing certain kinds of complexity whole and clear?

He was wise enough to leave off this spiral train of thought for the moment, but it released him to tell Hattie about the mutant brothers and the ravaging remorse at what he had done.

At first she was very skeptical about his claims of flying, but he spoke so matter-of-factly of how he had gone about it that her doubt wavered. There was no gainsaying his guilt over the deformed twins—and, like her descriptions of plantation life, she heard in his words the unmistakable accuracy of the authentic.

She chided him about what he had done, and yet when he made mention of them having apparently, at least, fallen out of a tornado, she posed another surprising question. "How you know they wasn't taken back?"

"How do you mean?" Lloyd asked, eager, of course, to find any mitigating circumstance.

"Mebbe, you didn't do ever-thing. You was just the way it happened. The way you talk about 'em, they wasn't from here."

"No," Lloyd agreed. "They were from Indiana."

"I doan mean that, fool! I mean from somewheres else."

"Like Mars? I don't think so."

"Mebbe, more places to be from than you think."

Lloyd heard the wisdom in that.

"Some kines of knowin' just doan answer ever question. My Papa, he had a sayin':

I seen what the sun, the moon
And the lightning do
But no one sees the thunder
Till they learn how to

Indeed, thought Lloyd.

Learning to see the thunder is what he should have told Schelling when asked his greatest aspiration.

CHAPTER 4

Fetish

Lloyd put together for Hattie a simple yet very functional all-purpose tool kit that she could keep rolled in a pinched oilskin furnace apron, with separate corn-sack pockets for each item, which he stitched himself with a heavy bagger's needle that he had kept from St. Louis, while his parents were preparing food. (His experience with the kites had taught him a great deal, and he had the artificial hand of St. Ives in mind.)

The kit included a general lock pick that he had sharpened out of harvested wire, a jimmy made from some window flashing, a miniature hammer he had fabricated from a hickory-barrel hove and one of the large bolts from the boat rigging, a carving knife and whetstone, along with a flint and striker from the cabin crew's quarters, an adjustable wrench he had nipped from the engine room, some lady's sewing implements that had been left about, a small hatchet that had dropped below the boilers, a magnifying lens he made from some plucked spectacles, and an assortment of bandages and a bottle of iodine wrapped in cotton wool so that it would not break, which he had nicked from a doctor's bag.

From this same bag he took a vial of laudanum and added to the kit the one bottle of LUCID! that survived from his medicine-show career, in case she became injured and needed pain relief. What he did not find in the bag was an item that he felt was important, and so he made one himself from one of the extra steam valves in the engineer's room—a stethoscope.

"What's this for?" Hattie asked, when he proudly laid out his offerings.

"That's for listening to sounds," he said. "To hearts—and to the other side of walls, if you have to. I didn't have time to make a good one. But you'll hear better than you would on your own. And this, this is for making sounds—music—if you're alone and need to make noise, instead of shushing all the time. To cheer yourself up."

The final inclusion was a crude bunch of short, tensioned metal rods screwed into the base of a burgled clock with a hollowed-out hole for a resonator, which Lloyd, in what remained of his innocence, believed at that point he had invented. It was in fact a very old kind of musical instrument—what today we would call a kalimba, or African thumb piano—like a Jew's harp but with a much wider range of tones. He had at least adjusted the rods in the precise order to create a true musical scale, and the simple strumming of these vibrating keys produced a quiet yet pleasing sound.

To his surprise and delight, she played a plaintive yet charming melody on it. She had seen and heard many such instruments in the secrecy of plantation cabins, and was herself surprised that Lloyd knew what one was.

As to the whole of the gift—for it was a whole—she did not know what to say. Not since her father had anyone given her anything but a belting or a form of torture, and even her father had not given her things he had made himself. And so many things! Each with a sense and a purpose, but with flexibility—the whole being greater than the sum of its parts. She admired the things stolen as much as the items made, because she intuited that everything would have been made specially if there had been time and materials at hand. The important thing was the totality of the package, and she had the wit to appreciate that.

"Is there anything you can't make if you set your mind to it?" she asked. "I means—mean—if you had the time?"

"I can't make more time to be with you," Lloyd answered. "Not just yet."

Her kiss then was something that would sustain him through many trials to come, because it was not a lewd or debauched kiss as Miss Viola's had been. It was as innocent as his desire to help her, to give what he could. But it was filled with the fire of passion—and of something so often missing in all romance, whatever the ages: true partnership.

Therein was the great problem. The Sitturds' way, once arrived in Independence, lay back south, into unknown territory, but almost certainly greater risk for a runaway slave girl—even one who knew that through any two points in space there is one line, and that it was Wordsworth who had suggested the shooting of the albatross in Coleridge's "The Rime of the Ancient Mariner." (That she could also bend the note of a white-bean fart and have at least the semblance of an orgasm through the sensitive indulgence of a tongue kiss were other talents that won Lloyd's deepest admiration.)

What might have been a joy thus became a torture for the young Ohioan. Once more he felt that the blessing of travel and adventure, discovering intimacies with strangers, was a cruel and unusual punishment.

For Hattie, as hard as her heart had become, she too felt the pang of inevitable separation. Lolling with him in the dark of her smelly hidey-hole—or risking all and venturing out at night into the open air of the top deck to smoke some stray leaf—she knew that her life would never be the same if this boy-man were taken from her. She had never had the luxury of not being cunning—of letting down her guard or saying anything she did not really mean. She had lived her whole life with at least "one eye open," but with Lloyd she relaxed for the first time, drawing energy for what she knew would be more strenuous times ahead.

"You could . . . come with us," Lloyd whispered in the dark of her smuggler's coffin, which was permeated now by the aroma of the sharp cheddar they had plundered from the boat's larder.

Hattie gave his scrotum a gentle grope. The pain inside was greater than he had ever known. Even the sins and crimes of St. Louis, when he had sailed above the row houses and cobblestones to fall through his own shadow, seemed to have been rinsed from his conscience.

"Then what will you do?" he asked, when she remained silent. "What will you *really* do?"

"I'll make my way," Hattie answered. "Just like I tole you. I'm headed west. Where I can be free. I'm going to California. And I'm going to be rich."

"You're thirteen," Lloyd reminded her. "You're a runaway slave, and you've got—"

"My markings? Boy, it's these markings of mine that are going to make me rich. You may be smart when it comes to numbers and ideas, but you've still got a world to learn about folks. Especially white folks—and especially menfolks. You take a good, Christian white man, never laid a hand on his wife—he get with a colored girl and he's another creature. The thing I got in my favor is that I *am* another creature. That's the gift the old bitch gave to me. She didn't mean to, but she did."

"So you'll be a whore?" Lloyd groaned.

"I may be a queen!" Hattie snapped. "I'll do what I need to do. What you have to do to get by isn't who you are, Lloyd. You remember that—and remember I tole you. You say I act and talk white sometimes. That don't make me white. I got no intention of lowering myself, believe you me. I'm goin' to learn French. And I'm goin' to play the harpsichord, and I'm goin' to have me some silk dresses, buttercup-yellow and watermelon-pink, and I'm goin' to make sure other black folks learn how to read—and know the names of the stars and how to measure a circle without thinkin' they have to walk around it."

"What about me?" Lloyd asked.

The forlorn, honest tone in the boy's voice reeled Hattie back from her dream. She felt her vulnerability full force once more, and yet she saw what she had sensed the very first moment she had met Lloyd: that here was someone lonelier than she, lonelier than she would ever be. A creature so different, not by markings or skin color, or anything anyone could definitely see, but by who he was inside. He could not just run away to find a better part of the world to live in; he would have to invent his own world if he was to survive. He might have to invent many worlds—so many that he might end up forgetting which were his creations.

"You'll be something nobody's ever thought of, Lloyd," she answered.

"But I want to be with you!" he wailed, and she had to stifle his plea with her warm hand.

"Shush. Don't you be ruinin' things now. You gotta buck up and be strong. That's what bein' a man is. I'd want to be with you, too, if life would let me—but it won't, so there's no use cryin'."

As she said this, the Zanesville prodigy saw that the older girl was working very hard to restrain her tears. She has enough to cry about, he thought to himself. No need for me to make her sadder still.

It was the first time in his life that Lloyd Meadhorn Sitturd had ever had such a sentiment about another person, and the novelty of it took him by surprise. He reached out and embraced her, with a firmness and a tenderness that made even the resourceful runaway tremble inside.

"One day I'll come find you," Lloyd said, and to Hattie these words hung in the tight, cramped air like a melody on the thumb piano. There was nothing more to be said on the subject

of the future and their different destinies, for those words, uttered with complete calm and conviction, had done what every
inspired melody does: condense a welter of emotions into an
unconflicted clarity that one can instantly recall and call upon.
Like a hierogram.

Those words gave Hattie the courage to seek a deeper hiding
place when the *Defiance* landed at last at Independence. To
Lloyd, she had given her abused body and something of her
hidden soul while in transit together. In parting, she gave him
her most prized possession—a token of the love she felt but
could express only in deed. It was a tiny ivory skull, carved with
gorgeous simple precision, with a hint of a smile. The size of a
marble, it nonetheless contained an undeniable radiance. It
had been given to her by her mother a few weeks before her
death. The girl was told that the icon came from Africa and had
been passed through many hands to reach her.

"Mama called it a fetish," she told Lloyd. "She says it's good
luck agin enemies. It means Death smiles on you."

Clutching the talisman in his own hand, Lloyd had no doubt
that it held some unusual power, for it seemed to retain the vi-
tality of all those who had held it before, and the suggestion of
the smile imbued it with an eerie optimism, however grim its
appearance.

The moment he cupped it, he was charged with a realization
that had been waiting for him since birth. He, too, had black
blood in his veins. Though it sometimes may have taken a light-
skinned Negro to spot it, and this had often been to his advantage, he saw the truth, whole and clear. He remembered every
taunt from the Zanesville hooligans he had ever heard. Every
sidewise glance from the children in St. Louis. He was not a
mongrel, for the Europeans he had encountered in the family
travels were as mongrel a bunch as you could imagine. He was
part white, part Indian, and part black, and each of those
breeds carried its own unique burden and heritage, especially
in the America of those times. Something in him connected

back to Africa—to the dark magic and turmoil of that faraway continent. He felt the literal truth of this course through him when he gripped the skull. This was a piece of his own puzzle handed back. It daunted and augmented him all at once, and he placed it with extreme, gentle care deep in his little knapsack next to the box with the hierograms of the Martian Ambassadors, his uncle's letter and map, and the always watching glass eyes of Mother Tongue.

Before Hattie, he had not had the wherewithal to look upon the Ambassadors' box since leaving St. Louis. Now, nurtured by the girl's devotion, he could and did examine the container again—and saw in the intricate alien characters that it displayed a message for his life that he knew he must do everything in his power to understand. So Hattie's gift, no bigger than a berry, served both to free him from his horror of losing her and as a seed. He cried when it dawned on him that he must say goodbye to her. But when the tears were gone he felt refreshed and full of her spirit, as if she had given not only her body to him but all that she had—all that she was. And so, he gave her a gift to remember him by, to watch over her and link her to him.

"Is this a jewel?" Hattie asked when Lloyd put one of Mother Tongue's eyes in her hands.

"It's a species of jewel, I believe—and a very great mystery," he answered. "A very powerful, very old white woman who helps the slaves gave it to me. It's a match of this," he told her, holding up the mate.

"They're eyes!" Hattie cried. "Made eyes!"

"Yes, but who they were made by is the thing. The old woman, who is a kind of witch, you'd say—before she took them out she could see with them, I swear. And I've thought I've seen things in them, too. There's some sort of magic to them, just like there is to your fetish. I want you to keep this, then we will each have one."

Hattie had no doubt about the sincerity of the gesture, and

was warmed inside to have something of Lloyd and his past to take with her. There was indeed something touched about the sphere, a talisman to match her skull. She cupped it lovingly in her hand, then hid it away inside her clothes.

The steam whistle blew.

"Do we say goodbye?" Lloyd asked.

"Not folks like us," Hattie replied.

Lloyd did not look for her when the family stepped off the gangplank at their destination, for he knew that she would not be seen, but that she was moving forward with a will stronger than any river current could ever be.

But God he missed her. The Brown Recluse.

CHAPTER 5

Reliable Omens

INDEPENDENCE, MISSOURI, IS A PLACE RICH IN HISTORY. IT BEGAN as a fort when Osage Indians would come to trade furs and pause at the window of Agent George Shipley's house to listen to his daughter play the piano. A little log courthouse was later built, which doubled as a pig pen and became so infested with fleas that it was necessary to invite sheep inside while the court was in session, to give the bloodsuckers something else to feed on. In the 1830s, the Mormons settled here and for a time prospered, only to be tarred and feathered and eventually burned out. Much, much later, Harry S. Truman would go to high school here, the man whose middle initial stood for nothing—"Mr. Citizen," who became a judge without ever having been a lawyer, the first and the last United States president to run a failing men's clothing store, and the man famous for his belief that "the buck stops here." (He apparently gave the two most important military orders in the history of Western civilization, carried through on August 6th and 9th of 1945.)

What the Sitturds found when they landed was, of course, a very different scene. As the family disembarked, there were a few raised eyebrows about Hephaestus's appearance, but there was so much activity in this western Missouri "jumping off place" (where many folk, indeed, looked as though they had hurled themselves off the precipice of reason and restraint) that no one in the family, including Lloyd, worried much about who might be watching them just then. There was too much happening.

It was midafternoon and saddles and harnesses poured off the *Defiance* in piles. Goats, mules, horses, and oxen raised a thick cloud along the long dock road running alongside the mule-drawn railroad link leading to the actual town. Barrels rolled, crates trundled, dry hides flopped. While huge numbers of western emigrants bound for Oregon to the north or Santa Fe to the south had departed months earlier in the year (the moment sufficient spring grass had grown to feed their animals), still others had poured in since, intending to hunker down for winter and either trade their stores or accumulate more for a prompt decampment come the first thaw the next year. It took six months in those days to make the two-thousand-mile trek to Oregon, and planning and provisioning for such an expedition was no small matter, given the number of thieves and scalawags always eager to prey on the unwise.

What was more, another cholera scare had encouraged still more pilgrims and strangers to seek shelter in Independence. While the disease did all too often wreak genuine devastation along the western routes, as well as up and down the Mississippi, it was not an uncommon practice among unscrupulous promoters and shopkeepers to spread rumors about such outbreaks in other settlements, because towns like Independence vied with the likes of St. Joseph, Omaha, and Council Bluffs for trade money. Recently, the nearby haven of Westport had been chosen, and now there was an epidemic of fantastic reports that "folks there is droppin' like horsetail flies." This panic precipitated a shift in an already itinerant population and put still more pressure on scarce accommodation and inflationary-priced supplies. The result was a cacophonous hammering and banging, as new and often ill-made buildings were erected as if by indefatigable insects, and the hawking of wares in loud voices for absurd sums.

The first steamboat to venture up the Missouri had stopped here in 1819. Now it seemed that nothing would stop for long, and any signs of the famous personages who had passed through, like Lewis and Clark and Sacagawea, or John James Audubon, were lost in a carpentered frenzy of plank, tank, and chicken dirt. Hephaestus had never seen so many blacksmith sheds or wagons that needed repairing. There looked to be a mule for every man and at least a bottle of whiskey (which was perhaps not a good ratio in a locale where each adult white male more than likely also carried a loaded firearm).

Smitten with sorrow about Hattie, Lloyd dragged his feet forward, his eyes blinking at the populace that swirled around them, every bit as turbid as the river had been. Wary-looking Spaniards, their faces shadowed by broad hats, cooked over both open fires and buried ovens. Smells of corn bread, charred rabbit, pulled pork, and bubbling beans surrounded them, as if they had concocted a fortress of aromas to defend against the pipe smoke, forge fires, and manure. Travel-weary Baptist women as stiff as split-oak rails peered out from under sweat-stained blueberry bonnets, stirring great boiling kettles of laundry with fence pickets. Negroes lounged under sagging awnings, eyes peeled raw for trouble, and more Indians than Lloyd had ever imagined lurked and bartered or tethered shaggy ponies to flagpoles and barber poles and poles that held up signs saying not to tie up horses there.

There were Foxes and Sauks, some with shaved heads and painted faces. Others with visages that looked vaguely Mexican wandered in and out of the shops wrapped in old blankets, muttering. Germans mingled with Scots decked out in plaid pantaloons and hobnailed boots. Methodist-looking ducks paraded about. Children's faces peeped out from the covers of the heavy French carts called mule killers. A grizzled loner leading a buffalo horse on a rope shared a water trough with a busty Mexican lady beneath a battered parasol astride a white donkey, just like a man. And everything was for sale—from a rotgut alcohol whose origins lay in homemade sorghum to apple butter, corn pones, and fresh brown eggs in hickory-bark baskets.

If you had the money you could buy women's dresses colored with walnut dye, men's shirts that felt as tough as chair seats woven from slippery elm, or telescopes, knives, shovels, and guns. A barrel of salt, a beaded necklace, a young hog, or an oxen yoke—everything had its price. And there was always someone happy to yell out the amount if you were in any doubt.

Desperate to keep his mind from thoughts of his beloved Hattie, whom he felt sure was safe but probably scared for her life on board the *Defiance,* Lloyd scanned the throng. There were so many strange- and dangerous-looking folk, it would have been impossible to pick out any potential threat of the kind he was concerned with. He took it for granted that any emissary of the Vardogers would be invisible in such a tangle, and so he just let his eyes feast on the scene for color and detail, trying to distract himself from the grief of his lost love, and the fear for her safety on the lonely, risky road that lay before her.

Despite the swagger and suspicion of the loiterers or the boisterous perspiring of the workers, amid all the hagglers, speculators, and adventurers that had gathered there were many glimpses of innocence and normal life—an unleavened boy in a jerkin rolling a hoop, or a little half-naked dark girl fondling a hen. The Indians, though sometimes fierce at first glance, were by and large intent upon their own business and carried themselves with an impressive lack of self-consciousness. Lloyd thought of King Billy back in Zanesville, the supposed hundred-year-old Wyandot Indian, who lived by himself in the woods—one of the few citizens of that world that he cared for. And he thought of his own Indian heritage, which the family never spoke of.

After the Sitturds had managed to haul themselves and their few belongings up the congested road from the wharf and through the knot of the main street to a point of refuge between two of the larger stores, Lloyd found his eyes drawn to a group of people, some of whom wore bloodred cloths wrapped around their heads. "Who are they?" he asked his father.

"I don't know," the lame blacksmith replied, itching to get his hands back on some tools, while Rapture feared it was one of the bottles he craved. "Maybe they had a wagon accident."

Of course, the people in question were not really the victims of some common mishap. Not exactly, anyway. They were the first Quists the family had ever seen.

The Quists, as may be recalled, were another divergent nineteenth-century religious sect afflicted with the same kind of persecution the Mormons faced. They took their name from the visionary Kendrick Quist, an illiterate young horse gelder from Nineveh, Indiana (later famous as the home of Hungarian mammoth squashes).

While returning home from a job at a neighboring farm, Kendrick stumbled upon what he called "the Headstones of the Seven Elders." These so-called Headstones were in fact thinly sliced sections of petrified tree stump and not much bigger than a child's writing slate. Nevertheless, Kendrick Quist was instructed in a dream to refer to them as Headstones, and he was informed that they had been set down long ago using a special tool made from the beak of the ivory-billed woodpecker. The day following this dream, Kendrick was kicked in the head by a stallion intent on remaining a stallion and went into a kind of delirium in which he was able to translate the inscriptions to a visiting cousin from the Virginia Tidewater named Buford Tertweilder, before expiring. Buford, who back home had been a failure as a clammer, cobbler, and tobacco farmer, became somewhat more successful in Indiana as the Quists' first prophet.

Like the Book of Mormon, the Book of Buford, or the Quistology (the correct name was a matter of ongoing debate), was a blend of fiery Old Testament prophecy and adventurous but unverifiable American history regarding a group of obscure Irish Vikings, who were in fact one of the lost tribes of Israel, and who had made it to America in a longboat inscribed with sea serpents, Celtic crosses, and Stars of David well before Columbus was born. They had then set out on a holy mission of discovery deep into the interior. They arrived in Indiana (which, you would have to admit, defines "the interior"), and it was here that their leader carved and left behind the inscriptions for Kendrick Quist to find centuries later.

Although the young horse gelder shuffled off his mortal coil, in addition to the kernel of a new religion he left behind the bloody bandage that had been wrapped around his head, and many of the Quists chose to wear a ceremonial red turbanlike wrapping in his honor. Unfortunately, such head garb often called unwanted attention to them and had increased their harassment at the hands of small-minded local officials and authorities of the more established churches.

Not long after Governor Boggs of Missouri had set forth his famous Extermination Order of 1838, which drove the Mormons to Nauvoo, Illinois (where all too soon vigilante gangs lit torches and knotted nooses and sent them on their continuing pilgrimage west to Utah), similar edicts were issued against the Quists. In 1840, they were expelled from the Hoosier State and established a community at Pumpkin Creek, Illinois. A year later, Buford Tertweilder was skinned alive in what became known as the Pumpkin Creek Massacre, and leadership of the flock passed to one Increase McGitney, a lapsed Presbyterian minister who had led a heroic but inadvertent one-man charge against the marauders when his head got wedged inside a butter churn in the barn where he was hiding. In a frenzy of what was really claustrophobic terror but looked very much like a God-inspired hunger for revenge, he shot out of the milking barn and bolted straight through a clothesline, picking up a white bedsheet on the way. Along with his improvised helmet and flailing arms, the flowing white fabric created the impression in the cowardly dogs that had besieged the Quists that a heavenly demonic warrior had risen up against them.

McGitney took this new image of himself to heart and transformed himself into a brave and demanding patriarch. "Increase Charged!" became the catch cry of the Quists, and the feat did indeed temporarily stave off eradication of the faithful. But the onslaught against them continued, and their leader did not help matters by making the morally admirable but politically lamentable decision of decrying the government policy of relocating Indians, welcoming them into the Pumpkin Creek community and seeking their advice as farmers, hunters, and fishers—as well as the unforgivable stance of opposing slavery and encouraging free and equal intermarriage with Negroes (in Increase's case, several).

The effect of this obstinacy was that barns and temples were burned, woodpeckers were ritually slaughtered, and more than a few members were impaled on stakes or hysterically kicked to death by angry mobs who feared the new faith might have a sufficiently oblique and inclusive appeal to unite fringe Christians, Jews, Indians, blacks, and the always superstitious and rabble-rousing Irish, who were arriving in ever-growing numbers. The threat of Illinois becoming a quasi-renegade Christian-Zionist-Indian-Hoodoo-Druid state had forced the second Quist diaspora. Sadly for them, Missouri, as it had for the Mormons, had proved even more hostile, and so they were forced to flee farther west. Just like the Chickasaws, Choctaws, Cherokees, and Seminoles, and other tribes and nations too numerous to mention—along with thousands of West Africans and, of course, the Latter-Day Saints. (Here was another displaced people on the move, trying to sow the seeds of their own survival in a whirlwind of ideology, emerging technology, and the culturally sanctioned greed known as eminent domain.)

"I like those things they wear around their heads," Lloyd remarked.

"You stay clear a-dem," Rapture cautioned, noting the number of Negroes and Indians shouldered up beside the wild-eyed white people. In her mind, the last thing they needed, other than for Hephaestus to go off on a drinking binge, was to fall in with a rebel congregation of colored misfits and crazy folk. What they needed now was to lie low—to find a place to stay and plan their supply-gathering and transportation needs for the journey across the wilds of Kansas, a lawless outland of harsh weather, savage animals, desperate people, and mysterious unknowns.

Lloyd took the opposite view. He saw the presence of blacks and Indians in the ranks of the head-wrapped and plain-dressed whites as a good sign. After all, were not they, the Sitturds, refugees from Zanesville, just as much a mixed bag? Having shared those secret moments with Hattie, he felt different about his breeding now, and he was becoming aware that there are kinships and affinities within us all that we may never know or understand, but which attempt to reveal themselves in the people we gravitate toward and the paths our lives take. Rapture, however, stood firm on the matter and focused the family's attention on getting fed and finding someplace to stay.

For refreshment they settled on thin flour tortillas, which they bought from a stumpy old man who worked from a stone fire and a foldup table among the Spaniards. To everyone's satisfaction, Rapture handled the whole transaction without saying a word, and Hephaestus wondered if her mind talk was working again. Accommodation did not look as if it would be so easy to find. All that passed for the local hotels and rooming houses were crammed with human body heat. German families clung to their wagons, Irish to their carts. Blacks pitched makeshift tents, Indians threw up hide-framed shelters. Some stray men just overturned crates. The excuse for the town hoosegow was full and foul, as were the grim attempts at houses of worship. Everywhere one looked, there was more canvas than lumber and more people and animals than either.

While sawmills up and down the river had been busy, the rumor mills had been frantic. In addition to tales of the latest cholera scare, there were stories going around of far stranger outbreaks. Some Kansas Indians up from the South had appeared with bizarre deformities they insisted were due to bad medicine in the water. A small hamlet south of Kansas City had been struck overnight with what appeared to be some kind of religious mania. The Sitturds listened to an earnest mail rider recount scenes of communitywide speaking in tongues and nervous spasms. Children whispered about ghostly forms that were abroad in the night, and from the German that Lloyd understood he was able to pick up hushed mentions of a "monster" that had been sighted out on the prairie. He chose not to pass this intelligence on to his parents. There was enough to worry about as it was, and from the look of the sky and the smell in the air a weather change was coming on fast.

It was in the midst of these mounting anxieties that an incident occurred which punctuated the tension with special force. At first, it seemed to be a perfectly normal affair, given the surroundings. One of the Spaniards had a dog, a large, threatening thing with a mottled coat. Its ribs were visible, but it had a big, powerful head and shoulders, and what were obviously strong, bone-crushing jaws. The cur stood guard by one of the cooking ovens, drooling and sharp-eyed for any scraps it might be offered. Out of the crowd between the wagons there appeared a much smaller black dog, short-legged and ragged of coat.

The scent of the food wafted. The two dogs' eyes locked. No one spoke up to claim ownership of the smaller mutt. The Spaniard's dog gave a low warning growl. Then the two dogs were at each other's throats. All the people in the vicinity stepped back, except a man who said that he was Australian. He stepped forward and proposed taking bets. Several of the men watching were about to take him up on this idea when the dust around the dogfight swirled up in a furious blast and a yelping rose out of the haze.

Everyone assumed the Spaniard's dog had drawn blood, but then the beasts went silent. The dust settled, and to everyone's surprise and horror the bigger dog had gone limp and hung from the teeth of the little one. Several of the men were about to express their regret at not having a wager down, when to their further amazement and disgust the small black dog began to eat the other. There was nothing rabid about it—the stunted canine acted with methodical, almost serene ferocity. The mouths of the onlookers, most of whom had seen and even bet on many dogfights in their time, dropped open.

The Spaniard leveled a hunting rifle at the mass of bloody fur and shining fangs. The victorious critter stared back at him with composed and utter disregard. Lloyd, along with several others, was in a position to see the expression in the creature's eyes and he felt cold inside as a result. The Spaniard shot the dog in the head. He then took the rifle and walloped the mongrel's rib cage and smashed its skull. When his temper had been vented, he wiped the rifle butt on the fur of what remained of his dead animal, then picked it up by its hind legs and took it off to bury it. The carcass of the murderous black thing was left in the dust for the flies. No one said a word, and it was a long minute before the crowd that had formed began to disperse. In the distance, down the dock road, Lloyd heard the whistle of the *Defiance,* on its way upstream, laden with new passengers and cargo, and a fresh stockpile of fears and dreams about the future. His heart ached for Hattie. He had never known such a sensation of longing, and it almost swamped him with its force and poignancy.

While all this had been happening, a huge white cumulous blob of shaving lather had transformed into a darkening thunderhead just beyond the town. There was that heady, sweet, dangerous smell of heavy rain in the air, and within the half hour the sky opened up and bucketloads began falling. What a scrambling mess of jostling, lunging, scurrying labor followed. Cooking fires were extinguished, kids were swept into or under wagons, people hopped and hobbled for awnings and doorways, horses and mules bucked and snorted, poultry squawked and darted. All the hammering ceased and workmen hustled down ladders. The deluge struck with genesis force, shimmering over the roofs and canvases like a collapsed wall. Umbrellas and tents strained and tore. Wagons lurched. Oxen lumbered. Indians, Negroes, settlers, and vagabonds were all caught in the same storm, lashing down on dry timber and dust, livestock and hardware.

The downpour did not last long, but it turned the town into a slippery, squishy, tinkling bog of wagon wheel–sucking mud and overflowing gutters. Anyone who had managed to reach one of the protected plank boardwalks or covered porches braced himself there, ready to defend his refuge. The Sitturd clan had headed for the open door of one of the stables, but even so had got soaked. Like their place of residence back in St. Louis, the building was alive with mice. Water dripped down through holes in the shingled roof. The smell of damp hay, leather, and dung greeted them. Worse still, the shadows within showed signs that several other families had already had the same idea, and the stableman, a fellow with a barrel body and arms as thick as the rafters, did not look pleased.

The Zanesvilleans took the hint and inched back out into the mire of the streets. Lloyd could not help himself and went over to inspect the remains of the black dog. He found that the corpse was already badly decomposed. It was not the violence of the Spaniard's desecration that was responsible, though; it was more like some accelerated internal process. Lloyd's native curiosity gnawed at him, just as the black dog had ground down its teeth into the other. Despite all that they had to think of— all that lay behind and ahead of them, and the immediate difficulties they faced—he would very much have liked to save the remains of the dog to examine, but he had a feeling, which he could not explain or account for, that within but a short while there would be nothing left of the body to study, perhaps not even bones. Rapture kept the family moving.

At one of the many blacksmith sheds, Hephaestus introduced himself as a member of the trade. Although he had not regained his old strength, and it had been quite a while since he had swung a hammer or used a bellows, he showed himself adept enough to be offered employment starting the next morning. The shed owner and chief smithy was a blunt, compressed anvil of a man named Bevis Petrie. He and his wife and four children occupied the back quarters of the shed and so could not assist with the Sitturds' accommodation needs, but he did feel charitably disposed enough toward them to recommend that they head to the other end of town and find a man named Othimiel Clutter, who happened to be his brother-in-law and one of the town's numerous undertakers and coffinmakers.

Rapture, with a tradition of complicated relationships with the afterlife on both sides of her ancestors, was not pleased about this suggestion. But, with the autumn dark about to fall and with it the chance of more rain, she bit her lip and kept her peace. "De dead is jes like us," she told herself. "Jes got to treat him wid rispect."

So through the muck the family moved—or, rather, slithered. Several disputes if not outright brawls were in various stages of eruption in the streets and doorways. The saloons were busy, cooking fires had been relit, barn cats licked themselves on roof ledges, and everywhere the flow of runoff water gurgled and spilled, searching for the lowest point. The clouds cleared and a prairie-fire sky lit up the west, as if all the country that lay beyond were burning, which might have seemed menacing and more than a little apt, were it not that a red sky in the evening is a reliable omen of good weather the next day.

The Sitturds trudged through the mud, recalling the miseries of Zanesville. At last they came to a dripping, peeling storefront with a selection of crude pine caskets lined up against a covered porch like skiffs that had been washed up out of the river.

Othimiel Clutter and his wife, Egalantine, turned out to be one of those childless middle-aged couples who seem to have been middle-aged their entire lives and yet had grown alike during the course of their marriage, so that they were now hardly distinguishable, moving, speaking, and even thinking as one. Neither showed the slightest ability to express a complete sentiment without the assistance of the other—and, once voiced, every utterance needed to be echoed several times, just as the casket lids Othimiel sawed and nailed all needed sanding and a knock to be called done. He was forever tapping on the lids of the things in a way that made Rapture most uncomfortable (because she could not help thinking that soon they might be tapping back).

Nevertheless, the Clutters agreed to let the Sitturds "camp out" with them for a fee, once they were assured that the Ohioans were bound and determined to depart before the winter set in. Each member of the family was restless to get moving as soon as possible, a change of season or no.

Of course, it was obvious where the Sitturds were supposed to sleep—not just with the coffins but *in* them, there being no other space available. (Lloyd took particular note of the smaller-size coffins, of which there was an abundance.) Othimiel, perhaps more devoted to his surname than he should have been, had got a little ahead of himself in his production over the summer. The town had been spared some of the scourges of dysentery, fever, and cholera that many had been prepared for, and the more violent, criminal deaths had been handled without proper ceremony. Besides, given their location near the river, some bodies just disappeared, he and his wife managed to point out (each contributing a word to the finished sentence), which set Lloyd thinking again both of Hattie and of the body of the fierce black dog that had seemed to fall apart before his eyes.

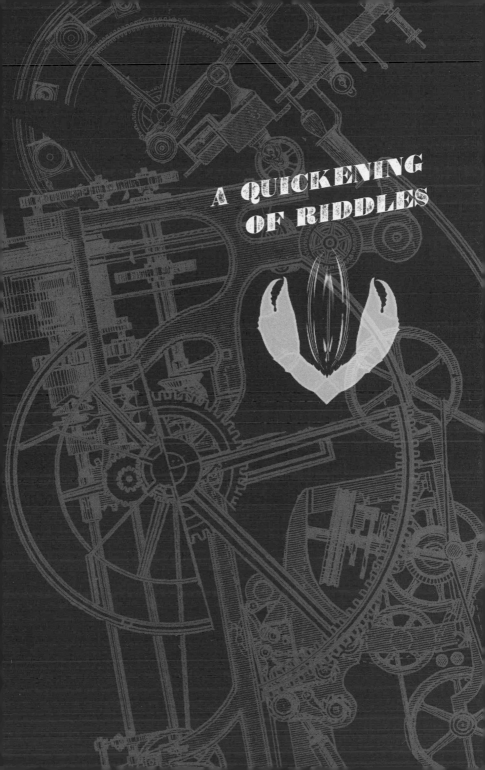

A QUICKENING OF RIDDLES

CHAPTER 1

Strange Languages

HEPHAESTUS AND RAPTURE PROPOSED A PAYMENT TO THE CLUT-
ters that they felt they could afford for the time period they
thought they would require (which the reformed inventor and
drunkard optimistically estimated as a week). Once the older
couple had nailed, sanded, and knocked these negotiations into
an agreement that they could echo and be sure of, they took a
handful of the green coffee Egalantine had browned in their
oven in the back room, ground it in a mill, and boiled it up with
some tin-tasting water and they all shared a bitter but celebra-
tory cup.

Without children and but the coffinmaking and undertaking
trappings and each other to keep them company, the Clutters
seemed somewhat deprived of stimulus, and so quite delighted
(in their own tapping, echoing, uncertain way) to have some
live bodies under the same roof. How else would they have
learned, for instance, that it was at all noteworthy that the two
rooms that passed for their living quarters behind the shop
were as crowded with music boxes as their official business
space was with coffins?

The boxes were in themselves quite beautiful to look at, the
size of snuffboxes and made of a variety of woods: burl walnut
and elm, rosewood and bird's-eye maple, while others had lids

inlaid with tortoiseshell. Fascinated by anything mechanical, Lloyd asked if he could inspect them and found them to be disappointingly simple devices comprising a metal barrel of about three inches with a shiny-toothed steel comb inside. He understood the mechanics and the musical principles at a glance.

All the music boxes played the same tune for a little less than a minute, a rather pedestrian arrangement of the French children's song "Au Clair de la Lune," which was nonetheless quite engaging and ended with a gentle, invigorating flourish. Rapture, in particular, was taken with the contraptions, and after some sanding and tapping the Clutters were able to present her with one as a gift. But this just raised another question in the Zanesvilleans' minds.

Given that small lovely boxes that could make music were ever so much more interesting than plain pine boxes big enough to house the dead, and given that the Clutters had so many of them, why did they not contemplate another kind of business, or at least a separate enterprise? It was clear from their humble standard of living that some extra money would come in handy. Surely, even out here on the frontier of Missouri, there would have been at least some demand for items that were so visually appealing, so charming to listen to, and so portable. Rapture put the question directly, as she always did.

"Dissuh hice de chune. Hoa comen ees doan graff de goodfashin? Fsuttin exwantidge!"

The result was such a commotion of gapping, filling, sanding, and knocking, it became uncomfortably apparent that a nerve had been touched. Finally, after another round of coffee and more half-finished sentences than the Sitturds had ever not heard, the truth at last came out.

Outside, the brick-kiln sun had set and pale watery stars had appeared, glinting down in rutted puddles of rain in the street before the whole of the story was thoroughly sanded, tapped, and echoed—but the gist was that a settler from the East had left the boxes with them a year before. He said he had found them in a crate floating in the river, stuck up under some tree roots five miles below. He had the idea of selling them himself, he said, but had left them with the Clutters for the time being in payment for their assistance regarding his dead little boy. He had never returned.

"So you made his child a coffin and he left you with all these?" Hephaestus queried.

After still more sanding and tapping, Mr. Clutter and Mrs. Clutter managed to convey that it was not a coffin that had been required. The man, whose name they had never learned, had asked for his child to be embalmed and he had taken the body with him. This admission led to yet another digression, this time regarding the broader spectrum of funereal services the Clutters felt it necessary to provide, and concluded with Othimiel Clutter producing a brace of jars that contained the embalmed cats he had practiced on (and, ostensibly, succeeded with).

Lloyd was excited by the embalmed cats and, coming so soon after the investigation of the innards of the music boxes, they threw him into a fit of inquiry that removed him for the moment from all other thoughts and doubts, except, of course, Hattie.

He rose from the slat floor where he had been sitting and began examining the room. That was when he found a music box that was different from all the others. Mr. and Mrs. Clutter were still gapping and filling about the cats they had come by— or, rather, how innocently they had come by them—when the boy's attention fixated upon one of the music boxes, which was not housed in a wooden box but made of a sleek, almost wet-looking metal. It was a margin larger than the rest, but what caught his eye was the design on the lid. Neither inlaid nor etched, there was nonetheless the image of a candle—with the suggestion of a flame rising above it. A pair of crab claws extended from the candle. Lloyd felt the breath sucked out of him.

He had never seen such an emblem before, but he recognized it instantly as the mark of the Vardogers—and quite intriguing it was to look at, too. Whoever had designed it had suppressed any presence of the crab's body, choosing instead to arm the candle with crustacean claws, a bold and striking abstraction.

While all the other boxes opened with a quiet but definite click that would set the music playing, the box with the Vardogers' emblem remained steadfastly shut, no matter how much pressure Lloyd applied.

"Don't fuss yourself, son," Mr. Clutter said, shaking his head. "It twon't ever open. We've tried."

Lloyd turned the box over to examine its underside and discovered a row of precisely etched letters that were so small even he had to ask for a magnifying lens, to read the words YOU MUST SAY SOMETHING THE BOX UNDERSTANDS.

"It is curious," Hephaestus agreed, noticing the intensity of Lloyd's consideration.

"Witched!" Rapture decreed.

Lloyd, on the other hand, held the box up close to his mouth and said as clearly as he could the word "Something." To the sheer dumbfoundment of the adults in the room, the smooth metal lid clicked open to reveal not a bright barrel cylinder and sharp-toothed comb, or even the more intricate componentry of a musical clock. Instead, what met their eyes was a detailed, miniaturized orchestra. It was impossible to tell what the figures were made of because they were so small, but a heartbeat after the lid had opened by whatever unseen mechanism, the exquisitely tiny artificial musicians began to play—and the music rose to fill the room with a volume and a depth of presence that exceeded all the other music boxes put together. It began like the fugue from Mozart's *Magic Flute* overture, but then evolved into a kind of marching rhythm, and then gradually shifted once more into a bell-like tune or a blend of tunes like nothing the Zanesvilleans had ever heard before. The effect was hypnotic. Transporting. And also disturbing.

Lloyd noticed that he was no longer marveling at the exactitude of the mechanical innovation inside the box but drifting in his mind. Fabulous, half-formed scenes and visions came into his head, like his dreams of old. He could not say what he was seeing, but it made him feel woozy. With an exertion of will, he slapped down the lid and the music died. The expressions on the other faces worried him. They were each dazed in their own way and somewhat hostile, as if he had cut short their fun. There was an oppressive closeness to the atmosphere in the room, which was so pronounced that Egalantine Clutter went so far as to open a window all on her own initiative to dispel it. Hephaestus seemed to have slowed and turned a bit surly, as if someone had waved a draft of pungent-smelling rum under his nose and then pulled it away. But Lloyd could see that his mother had regained her alertness, and was agitated, as if the coffee was just kicking in. He felt convinced that they had experienced something unwholesome.

As pleasing as the box was to look at, as satisfying as it was to fondle, and as badly as he wanted to speak to it and have the lid open, to have the microscopic orchestra perform again, he sensed a presence that was not benign. Beguiling, perhaps, but not benign. His own curiosity and need were so great, it turned around on itself and stared back at him.

Then he noticed the clock on the Clutters' crowded mantelpiece and the breakout of sweat on his hands made him drop the box. Unless by some infernal magic the music had tampered with the operation of the clock, more than half an hour had passed since he had spoken the password and opened the lid. The other music boxes with straightforward mechanical means had played for forty-five seconds or less. No one had noticed the time that had passed.

"How did you know how to do that?" Othimiel Clutter demanded, when at last the spell had lifted.

"It was easy," Lloyd answered. "What you were reading as one sentence is really two, so the direction could not have been clearer. Those are often the most difficult riddles to solve—the ones you mistakenly make for yourself."

This observation, coming from one so young, provoked much discussion among the childless Clutters and the other two adults, although, of course, Rapture and Hephaestus were long inured to Lloyd's perspicacity. While the older folk nattered on about what seemed transparent to him, Lloyd was more interested in the fact that, despite the amazing mechanico-musical phenomenon they had witnessed, no one now seemed at all eager for him to open the box again, not even himself anymore, Lloyd realized, which he could not account for logically but only in terms of the disquieting intuition he had had before. It seemed like such an elaborate folly to be listened to but once. Already the sense of the music was slipping away. Only a faint memory remained, like a dream.

The prolonged distraction had upset the Clutters' normal dining schedule. On this evening, with "guests" in attendance, Egalantine insisted on laying out "a spread." Said spread consisted of a large plate of cold small meats (which, of course, was a rather sensitive choice, given the surrounding jars of embalmed cats and the coffins), an exceedingly odd-textured goat cheese, hunks of shack-smoked bullhead, and a mound of jellied offal, which bore an unappealing resemblance to trifle. Unexpectedly, all the food on the platter soon disappeared, and Lloyd remarked on how hungry everyone seemed, eating with an almost mechanical urgency, verging on trance. He missed his mother's fresh corn bread, but he, too, hoed in.

Seeing that the spread had been enjoyed (engulfed was more like it), Egalantine set about reheating a cast-iron pot of mutton-and-vegetable stew. This was how the dish was described at any rate, but the aroma that rose from the coals of the hearth, where the pot sat farting like a petulant mud pool, strongly suggested something else (for instance, the renderer back in St. Louis). Indeed, the atmosphere that filled the room was such that Rapture even wondered if the Clutters might not be inclined to create their own customers. Amid chunks of parsnips and what looked to be some highly suspect carrots were bits of bonelike knuckles and a film of what might have been a long-soaked doily but which Mrs. Clutter insisted had recently been red cabbage. A bowl of wax beans with a fine fungal fuzz brushed off at the last minute rounded off the repast. This, too, was consumed. We must be very hungry, Hephaestus told himself. We must be foolish proud, thought Rapture, hoping they would not become ill. What if this all has something to do with that music box, Lloyd puzzled?

Normality of interaction returned come cleanup time and the Clutters resumed their eccentric stop-start mode of conversation. Once some order had been restored to the kitchen area and the cooking fire damped down to embers, the Sitturds were shown to their grim beds in the main shop (with visions of the embalmed cats curled in their jars and the music boxes lined on shelves in the other room). General comments were made regarding plans for provisioning the next day and reassurances given that their stay would not be long, and that they would do all in their power not to disrupt the Clutters' day-to-day lives and business. Then the candles were extinguished and the Zanesville refugees were left to themselves, each in a coffin packed with old mothball-smelling bedding.

Lloyd found it hard to sleep. Thoughts of Hattie filled his mind, and even without a lid on it was impossible to forget where he was lying. His restlessness set him floating back down a dark river of memories . . . to the trunk in Miss Viola's cabin . . . to the trapdoor graveyard that Schelling had led him to the night that he met Mother Tongue . . . to the box of the Martian Ambassadors . . . and the secret hold where he had hidden in Hattie's arms, making the love a child his age should not have understood. Then there were thoughts of the man who had brought the music boxes—his embalmed child—and the box with the Vardogers' symbol, which seemed to contain an unnaturally suggestive music embedded in the workings of the miniature metal orchestra. It was a lot for him to think about. Just missing Hattie was enough.

Rapture had similar problems getting adjusted, but after a couple of dozy nightmares that startled her sheer exhaustion took hold and she collapsed into a deep slumber, grateful not to have been seized by stomach cramps. Hephaestus, who in his time on the bottle had grown accustomed to blacking out and waking up in unusual places, gave himself over to sleep with the peace of a baby after the satisfaction of the nipple—every so often releasing a pop of flatulence.

Lloyd listened for a while to his father's regular snoring and fluffing, his mother's shallower but soothing respiration, and he began to be aware of faint strains of music. The sadness he felt at losing Hattie—the need to know where she was and if she was all right—would not let him alone. And then, the very moment he experienced any reprieve from his pain, some wriggling other anxiety sneaked in—like music he did not want to hear.

At first he had a bizarre fear that the music boxes in the next room had opened of their own accord, but then he realized that the melody he was hearing came from outside, somewhere down the mud-and-plank streets, and was familiar to him. He picked out a banjo, a fiddle . . . and a squeezebox . . . folks singing. He recognized the song "The Pesky Sarpent" and then "Rosin, the Beau." He crept out of the coffin and tiptoed to the window to listen.

A tall hatted figure passed outside, then a thin white cat. In the starlit space between two buildings across the street, he glimpsed the reflected shadows made by a small fire. He was seized with curiosity to explore the night town—as much to escape the stultifying atmosphere of the coffin room and the lingering smell of supper as anything—but he had trepidations about the safety of venturing out alone in the dark without a lantern or any definite idea of who might be abroad. He would have resigned himself back to a stiff attempt at sleep in the wooden box, when he heard a song that made his hair needle up on his neck.

> There's a place I know
> Where I always go
> There to dream of you
> And hope that you'll be true
> And someday I pray
> That you'll find your way
> Back to the secret place
> Within my heart.

It was a female voice coming in on a cooling night breeze, which even through the plate glass carried with it the odors of charred wood and burned beans—but it was not, his keen ears told him, the voice of Viola Mercy. The poignancy of the melody made his head swim, though, wondering where the chanteuse might be. Louisville? Memphis? New Orleans? And what of St. Ives, his first business partner? Or the professor, the partner he had lied to and cheated? Or proud, scarred Hattie, his partner in a deeper way. His mind and soul reached out to them all, and through them to the phantom at the far edge of his field of inner vision: His sister, Lodema. Stillborn in Ohio and still being born inside himself.

No, it was not the steamboat entertainer he heard singing in the storm-rinsed, clearing Missouri night. Still, it seemed an omen that he could not ignore, and so he unlatched and un-bolted the shop front door, unsure why anyone would break into an undertaker and coffinmaker's place of business, anyway (unless, of course, it had something to do with the music boxes). He stepped lightly out into the gloom, leaving his parents breathing in their open coffins.

He glanced up and down the hog trough of the dark street. The moon was almost full and cast a spectral glaze over the town and the skeletons of buildings in the works. Most of the

folk sheltered within the limits of Independence were either already abed or struggling by lantern and hearth light to repair
ruptures, rips, and leaks, pluck weevils from biscuit flour, air
out sodden fabric, comfort squalling infants, pack tobacco in a
pipe, or take another slug from a fired earth jug. The church
believers, the diligent, the indigent, the exhausted, and anyone
whose guts were clogged with beans and salt pork had called it
a night. But others, and there are always those, had different
ideas. It was to these sounds and shadows that Lloyd was
drawn.

Silhouettes fluttered over plank walls, and in the distance a
hound howled, which made Lloyd think again of poor Tip,
buried back in Zanesville along with their old life. Lodema.

He stepped between the ruts and puddles, moving in the direction of the music, remembering the evil that had befallen
him in that laneway in St. Louis at the hands of the man with
the harelip. Hattie had cured him of the shame, but the anger
remained. And the wariness.

Squishing through the mud, which his mother would no
doubt be angry about, he reached the shelter of a buckboard
leaning down on its hitch across the street. Then in between
the buildings. Somewhere he could hear horses jostling and
whinnying in a stable.

The music, however, proved to be elusive. Where he had
thought to find people gathered around a fire with their instruments, a couple of wagons and oil lanterns propped on casks,
there was but an empty lot and the skeletal frame of a building
going up. The camp where the music was coming from, and
now beginning to die out, lay farther on, behind a row of
makeshift sheds and a cluster of willow trees. The shadows he
had seen earlier must have been made by other people and had
melted away. Yet there were still some lights. The nearest and
brightest came from a crude brick storehouse on the other side
of a drenched pea patch. Someone had taken a spade and dug
several runoff trenches to direct the water into the lumpy gar-

den, and he had to mind his step. The light in the storehouse grew dimmer as he approached, as if the building were beginning to doze.

Now that the notion of investigating the source of the music had passed from his mind, Lloyd was without a plan of action and had half a mind to return to the Clutters' and try to go to sleep, but there did not seem any harm in at least having a peek in the storehouse to see what was going on. Picking his way through the pea patch he became more intrigued, as from its exterior the storehouse appeared to be abandoned, and he had not seen buildings that were not being used in the town. Something was going on inside, though.

He crept up close to the yawning, empty window frame, which, with the softness of the mud underfoot, was infuriatingly just a little too high for him to see into. There was no choice but to stand on tiptoe and hold on to the ledge. By hoisting himself up just a few inches, he would be able to peer inside. Of course, his fingers might be visible from within, but there was no other way, short of trying to sneak in the heavy barn-width door, which might well have been barred anyway.

As quietly as he could, he reached up and grabbed hold of the rough-troweled masonry and dragged himself into the square of light cast from inside the storehouse. In the blend of moonlight and diffused gleam from within, he could see that the chinks in the slapdash brickwork had been patched with mortar and mud, and were flecked with old desiccated wasp nests and cobwebs. He tried to brace his boots against the chinks without making a scraping sound. What he saw at first surprised him as much as the sight that had greeted his eyes when the Vardogers' music box had opened.

It was the Quists, all gathered together in a circle around a group of tallow candles arranged in a Star of David pattern atop a cross, which from his point of view was upside down. There were perhaps twenty or thirty adults, with a couple of older kids and a few mother-cradled infants. Everyone, even the babes in their mothers' arms, were swathed in red turbans and staring with rapt attention as a man straddling the candle flames rising from the sod floor passed around what looked to Lloyd like pieces of sun-dried tree bark with funny markings etched into them. He struggled to maintain his hold on the ledge and to strain up a bit higher to get a better look.

The man who held sway in the center of the group was none other than Increase McGitney, lately arrived in Independence under cover of darkness with an armed escort, to lead his people west and south to a promised land they knew they would recognize when they came to it. The surviving Quists had congregated in this unusually derelict building at a late hour in a ritual of renewal, hoping to find the strength and focus to lead them forward, beyond the reach of their persecutors, to some green valley that lay on the other side of the wolf-roaming plains and scorching deserts. They had turned back to the sacred scriptures upon which their beliefs were founded, not the Book of Buford but the very Headstones that Kendrick Quist himself had uncovered on his way home from the fateful horse gelding in Indiana.

The sections of petrified wood were produced from a strongbox that McGitney's guards carried, but, unlike the relics and holy texts of other less democratically minded faiths, they were not hoarded away as they had been back in the days of Buford's prophetic leadership. Truth be known, McGitney had many personal reservations about the Book of Buford, and was privately of (the arguably heretical) opinion that the Headstones held a deeper mystery than either the great Kendrick or his relative had fathomed. In any case, ever since his inadvertent moment of courageous abandon, McGitney had grasped an often overlooked element of effective leadership: the sharing of authority whilst never shirking from responsibility. And so, at this crucial juncture in his people's journey, he had deemed it appropriate to renew their collective sense of awe and devotion.

It was a risky move, for at first nothing could have seemed

plainer or humbler than the old bits of engraved bark that came out of the box. Lloyd gripped like a cat to the ledge, eyes probing through the glassless space—not, of course, knowing what it was he was witnessing but perceiving, in the quality of attention in the shining eyes of the turbaned group, that it was something important.

Then, very gradually, the effect McGitney had counted on began to manifest itself. What before—at least, at the distance from which Lloyd was viewing them—had looked like the vehement gnawings of insects or the scratchings of some demented child in the ancient bark now began to glow. Over the course of a minute, the glow deepened and brightened as if magnetizing the moonlight. The unexplained phenomenon caused the desired stir around the circle of the Quists and set Lloyd wriggling to gain a clearer view. There was an inexplicable aura of bioluminescence about the markings now, as if they had come to life in the candlelight and indeed outshone the tapers with a weird green phosphorescence that revealed a new level of detail in the figures. To Lloyd's amazement, he found that he recognized the radiant markings as the unmistakable likenesses of the hierograms of the Martian Ambassadors! The shock sent him tumbling to earth outside the window.

"Wait!" called Increase McGitney, becoming hypertense. "Go see what that was!" he instructed the guards, who bolted out between the candles. Trouble had followed the Quists wherever they had gone and they were prepared for more before they made their departure across the prairie. Three burly men in red turbans stormed out of the storehouse, one carrying a torch, the other two cudgels. Before Lloyd could scramble to his feet, they were upon him.

CHAPTER 2

The Blinking of an Eye

MCGITNEY'S GUARDS PLUCKED LLOYD FROM THE MOON-SOAKED mud and hauled him inside the storehouse like a sack of spuds. For all his fearsome intellect, the boy was powerless in their hands. When he recovered from his shock, he was standing, forcibly propped between two turbaned men on the perimeter of the candles that he had been observing moments earlier, with the face, or rather the dense red beard and glittering eyes, of Increase McGitney poking down at him.

"Who are ya, boy?" the Quist headman demanded.

"He's a spy!" a woman cried out.

"I'm Lloyd Meadhorn Sitturd," the boy answered, and shook the big hands off his shoulders with an authority or an arrogance that made McGitney pause.

"Am I to know that name?" McGitney asked, hoping to raise a chuckle among his agitated congregation.

Lloyd instantly regretted proffering his name, but as he could not retract it he let the statement stand and sent his eyes out around the group.

"What brings a lad like you out so late, then?" the Quist leader tried, concerned about this disruption in their ceremony but not afraid. He doubted that any terror gang would send so young a child to scout them.

Lloyd ignored the question, in part because he did not want to have to explain about trying to sleep in a coffin. Instead, he reached out with his hand for the nearest of the thin wooden tablets.

The gray-bearded man who held it pulled back in alarm, but not quite fast enough. As the boy's hand brushed the bark, the luminous glyphs pulsed with brightness.

"I know those markings," Lloyd announced. "I've seen the likes of them before."

"Are you . . . a Quist, then?" McGitney sputtered. "Because naught but the Quists has ever laid eyes on the sacred Headstones."

Lloyd again refused to answer—he was too enthralled by the shimmering writings. He reached out his hand again toward the bark section the bearded man held close to his chest, and this time the fluorescence illuminated the whole of the man's face, as if he were clasping a lidded lantern from which the light wanted to escape.

"My Lord!" a woman on the other side of the storehouse cried. "Look!"

One of the other tablets started pulsing more intently, too. Then another. Murmurs and moans spread throughout the storehouse. McGitney sensed some impending crisis of authority in the presence of this boy and the uncanny effect he seemed to have on the Headstones. But he was curious, too.

"Take out the others," he directed his assistants.

The remaining Headstones were produced from the strongbox and all were now beaming brilliantly, casting their runic mysteries upon the faces and the walls like magic-lantern pictures. The Quists let out a collective gasp and then turned their frightened, composite scrutiny on the boy.

The Book of Buford had promised that there would be another prophet—a true messianic figure to lead the tribe forward into the light of the future and their destiny as spiritual pilgrims and prosperous citizens in the new America that was to

come. It was one of the crucial points of the revealed doctrine
that McGitney had unquestioning belief in. He knew in his
heart that he was but a chieftain of the moment—a trailblazer
to spur them westward. He had no private delusions (or "affin-
ity with divinity," as he called it), however shrewdly he played
upon his role to achieve the ends he deemed best for his flock.
Now here was an undeniable call from beyond, in the sect's
own terms. It could not be brushed aside.

"How are you doing this, lad?" he asked, in as calm a voice
as he could muster. He was relieved at Lloyd's reply.

"I don't know that I am doing it—or doing anything. I just
know I've seen these kinds of markings before."

The Headstones sparkled in response, as if emphatically
agreeing, triggering more exclamations and whispers.

"Where?" McGitney demanded. The Quists' claim to be a
chosen people hinged on the uniqueness of the Headstones.
And yet, had not he, their own leader, always harbored the belief that there was more to the glyphic codes than the Book of
Buford had disclosed? Was not the very hope upon which the
Quist religion was founded—their fundamental tenet of faith—
that revelation was not just real but continuing? The ancient
wisdom embodied in the Headstones was alive. That was what
the Book of Buford and all the Quists believed. The illumination of the tablets was proof of this.

"Are you some kind of proph-et?" one of the black men on
the other side of the circle asked with a tremor in his voice.

Lloyd was not sure how to answer this question, and so repeated what he had said before. "I am Lloyd Meadhorn Sitturd.
I have seen these markings before. These things you have are
not the only examples."

"Order!" McGitney called, as the commotion this assertion
caused threatened to upset the entire proceeding, not to mention draw unwelcome attention.

"Well, young Lloyd Meadhorn Sitturd. My name is Increase
McGitney, and the people you see gathered around you are my

devoted compatriots in a holy mission of discovery and fulfillment. We call ourselves Quists. You may have heard of our
trials—or have even been warned away from us. That is, provided you are not a spy. Are you a spy, young Lloyd?"

Lloyd shook his head violently. It occurred to him that if he
were a spy he was not a very adept one. Hattie would have been
dark with him.

"And where have you seen these writings, Lloyd? In a
dream?"

"No," the boy answered.

"Then where? Where are you from?"

"Zanesville, Ohio."

"And is that where you saw them?" McGitney pestered. Even
if by some fluke the boy was speaking the truth, if another example of the Headstones lay at a distance, perhaps lost, his
claim could not be proved. Perhaps the effect the boy seemed
to have on the tablets could be explained away and they could
return to their ceremony.

Still, he could not get around his own intuition that the
boy's appearance was somehow fated. A defining moment in
Quistory.

Lloyd hesitated. He had become so intrigued by the sight of
markings like the Ambassadors'—and by their unexplained
luminescence—that he had forgotten for a moment about his
precarious situation. Surrounded by strangers with strange beliefs, late at night in a foreign frontier town—his parents not
knowing where he was—he knew that his goal should have
been to get back to the Clutters' in one piece and get to bed
without his parents knowing that he had been gone. He realized that he was always endangering their safety, and re-
proached himself for it. But he could not curb his curiosity—or
his need to show these head-wrapped wayfarers the error of
their ways.

"I have it with me," he replied at last, which set the Quists
chattering and speculating, while the light from the Head-

stones held in various hands around the circle bloomed brighter. "A short distance from here," he added, as McGitney held up his hands for quiet.

"Then you must fetch it," the Quist patriarch commanded. "Drucker and Soames, go with him. We must prove the truth of this claim here and now."

"No," Lloyd insisted. "I will not let you take it from me. It was given to me."

"Who by, lad?"

"That is not for me to say to you," Lloyd fired back. "But I will not fetch it for you to steal."

The circle of faces erupted in discord.

"Hush!" McGitney demanded. "Lad, whoever you are, and wherever you are from, know this: the Quists are not thieves. More honest, law-abiding folk you would be hard pressed to find, wherever laws are fair and allow for freedom of faith. We are merely humble believers in the revealed truth the great Saint Kendrick bestowed upon us. We mean you no harm, as we hope to have none done to us. But see here. You have made a bald, bold claim that strikes at the heart of what we have risked and lost good lives to defend and protect. If what you speak is the truth, then something of your destiny is entwined with ours—whether the genuine nature of this can be fathomed by any of us gathered at this crossroads or not. I say to you—I give our word—you will not be harmed. Your property will not be appropriated. And if you are in the shadow of any danger, as we are, perhaps we may even be of help to you. And yours. You have family, I take it? Unless you just rose out of the ground to haunt us. Or did you fall from the sky?"

This last query had a noticeable effect on Lloyd, for he could not help seeing and hearing the pitiful Ambassadors as they were swept away into the cruel blue above the Mississippi. He had repaid their hermetic trust with betrayal, abandonment, and almost certain execution, unless Hattie's theory held some hope. In any case, all that remained of them now seemed to be the box he had been given with their cryptic language engraved on it. His head churned with questions and doubts—yet he could not shake free his desire to know if the markings on the box he carried were also capable of coming to phosphorescent life like the Headstones, and he recalled the singular line of speculation that had been triggered by Hattie. He had to know more.

He felt that the Quist leader had spoken correctly when he suggested that his fate was somehow linked to theirs. He did not know how that particular machine worked, but the coincidence could not be ignored. That was what had drawn him to the storehouse. He could not turn his back on the mystery now. He owed it to the monstrous twins. He owed it to the Quists—and to himself. While there was fear and skepticism in their faces, he sensed no ill will toward him. These people were not Spirosians or Vardogers, of that he was sure, and both St. Ives and Hattie had advised him to rely on his instincts in a pinch.

"All right," he agreed. "But a curse on you all if you do not keep your word and try to abscond with what is not your own!"

He threw in this last pronouncement for theatrical flourish, remembering the professor—reasoning that such a ritually inclined people, so fervent in their devotion to things they obviously did not comprehend, might in the absence of any physical force he could offer be checked by superstition. His threat had the desired result. He could see it in the eyes around the circle, a response enhanced by a chance gust of wind that unnerved the candles and yet left the sheen of the Headstones unchanged.

"Go with haste and with care," McGitney said, pointing to the heavy door. "We will keep our word, while you put your truth to the test. A boy your age alone at night in a place like this—you took risks of your own accord far greater than you face at our hands. But hurry now. For we *know* we are at risk.

There are folk about right now who want us gone—and others that would like to see us dead. It is not my intention to draw you into our tribulations. Go forth and return with speed."

The two men McGitney had singled out to take charge of Lloyd donned trail-weary dust coats and escorted him outside with the aid of a small lantern. The night was mad with starlight, a buckshot blast of crystal, like some celestial analog of all the scattered souls and dreams below, the moon a distant glass globe full of cold white flame. Lloyd directed them back the way he had come. The going was easier this time, with the extra light and the knowledge of where he was going, but his heart beat faster, flanked as he was by two large unknown men (who had removed their turbans once outside). He wished Hattie were there to give him courage, but that would just have put her more in harm's way.

There were low hints of mouth-organ music in the distance, and every so often the growling of dogs or the whine of tomcats, but other than that the town appeared to have folded in on itself at last. Lloyd led the men to the Clutters' darkened place of dark business and whispered to them to wait while he went inside. The two Quists remained silent, and whether they trusted him or not they did not prevent him from entering the building on his own.

Everything was as he had left it. His parents were both sound asleep in their open coffins—his mother breathing deeply, his father snoring and farting, keeping alive the memory of their supper. It was hard to see, and with so many boxes and stuff to run into, it was a miracle he did not create a crashing confusion to wake the whole establishment. But he knew what he was looking for—his bag burrowed down on the other side of the container he had been assigned. By feel alone he probably would have been able to find it, but he was assisted by a telltale glow from within the bag. The sight drew his breath short. The Ambassadors' box was indeed aglimmer just like the

Headstones! He removed it from the bag and held it aloft, marveling at how it seemed to project its carved message into the room. The aura it cast reminded him of countless visions he had had just upon falling asleep. The sight surprised him, for he had begun to form the view that the Headstones' illumination may have been some kind of trick that McGitney had devised to wow his followers—although he could not account for it, or explain the surges in brightness that he seemed to stimulate.

Nevertheless, without having been able to examine the tablets himself, Lloyd had remained skeptical of any magical power. Now, with his own familiar box in hand and the same phenomenon manifest, he had to concede that there was indeed some force at work, a kind of energy he had never encountered before—save perhaps that night when he met Mother Tongue. It was the one thing he could liken this demonstration to—and it turned his mind back to his bag, where the other eye, the mate of the gift he had given Hattie, nestled in its protective rags. To his even greater astonishment, he now found that the eye had changed, too. Where before it had always felt cool if not cold to the touch, and was always dark unless he held it up to the light (which he had stopped doing because of the unsettling memories it provoked), it was this time quite definitely warm to the touch and lit from within, as if answering some call from the markings on the box.

Lloyd felt a deep, inner need to take the eye in hand. To fondle it. When he did, he found that it had gained in weight and was growing warmer. He wondered how it would react in the immediate presence of the Headstones. For the first time since he had given the other one to Hattie, he stared at it, as if he had never seen it before. Embedded deep inside the iris now, there appeared to be depth upon depth of shimmering layers, like a small golden-green tornado or some almost living mechanism—a minuscule self-illuminating creature, or a cap-

tured strand of lightning. Lloyd could not be sure what it
looked like, only that it seemed to look back at him, filling his
head with a sublime radiance. He was suddenly intensely glad
that he had given the mate to Hattie. His mate.

He might have stood there staring at the eye for quite a while
longer, but Hephaestus gave out a grunt in his sleep and then
there came a furtive tap on the glass of the window. The Quists
were summoning him.

He slipped the eye into his pocket, feeling its cold-hot heat
against his leg. For some reason, he felt he must keep it with
him—that he needed it. Hattie's skull fetish he tucked back
into its protective rags with the precious communication from
his uncle, which had set them out on their perilous flight in the
first place. The box he wrapped in a piece of cloth from his bag
and then he slipped out the door, restoring the darkness to his
sleeping parents in their coffins.

He found that the men called Drucker and Soames were
both wound very tight. They interrogated him by gesture when
he emerged, and when he assented that he had what he had
gone to get they set out again at a nervous pace. As silent as the
two had been before, they were even more so now, listening
with their whole bodies, as if something sinister had transpired
while he was inside. He would have asked them what had happened to put them so on edge, but he felt certain they would
just shush him up and hurry him along. Maybe there really
were people out to get them, he thought, as they pigeon-
stepped through the mud past the wagon lying on its hitch. It
reminded him again that there may have been people out to get
him, too. He did not know what to believe on that score, but
the possibility niggled at him. The one called Soames appeared
to flinch. Then Lloyd felt it, too. A sudden twinge of emergency.
Footsteps—and some other sound. Then, from behind one of
the buildings they had to walk between, a sharp bolt of lantern
light stabbed out at them, creating a sudden infestation of
shadows.

"Allo there, fine citizens!" a muffled man's voice accosted them, and before they knew it as many as eight other men had stepped out from behind the other building. Some of them wore gunnysacks with eye slits cut into them pulled over their heads, which made them look particularly menacing in the moonfall. Others had dirty hats tugged down low with bandannas to hide their faces.

The man with the lantern, who sported two large dueling pistols in his belt, had on the kind of netted hat Lloyd had seen on beekeepers, which seemed especially malignant. He was tall, and his clothes were cleaner and more expensive than the others'. All the other ruffians were armed in some way: hickory ax handles, fence pickets, crowbars. One very large man in the back stood poised with a hay tine. A short, stinking torch was lit from the lantern, the spookish light wavering over the timbers of the wall.

Drucker and Soames stepped forward, putting themselves between Lloyd and the men, but the tall one in the beekeeper's hat just laughed. What would Hattie have said? What would she do now? Captain of dark crossroads. She might have fled—but, like St. Ives, she was a game one with a bluff, too. Despite the acid burning in his stomach and his heart thumping against his rib cage, he could feel Mother Tongue's eye in his pocket becoming both hotter and colder all at once. He sneaked his hand into his britches, gripping the orb for comfort.

"Stand aside," Soames instructed the assembled host.

"Peace, citizens!" the netted hat replied, in a voice that reminded Lloyd of a rat in a gutter full of leaves. "We mean no harm. I swear it! Unless, of course, by some chance you happen to be religious fanatics bent on preaching your degenerate ways . . . fouling the waters of our fair community and taking liberties with our laws that the one true God will not tolerate. You wouldn't be such vermin as that, would you?"

"Let us pass," Drucker demanded, balling up a butcher-size fist in spite of his common sense and the hopeless mismatch.

"Oh, yes, boys!" joked the man in the netted hat to his brethren. "We'll let them pass, all right! Won't we?"

Despicable hoots of amusement rose from the shadowed figures beside him. The torch swooshed in the air, leaving an angry tattoo in the dark for a second.

"We'll let you pass from this point right here into the pit of hell, you swine. We know who you are. Meddling in matters that don't concern you, infecting communities wherever you go!"

Drucker and Soames now both pulled cudgels from beneath their dust coats. Lloyd grew truly frightened. It made no difference that he was not a Quist—he was in their company, this was his fight, too. And they were faced with overwhelming odds, from the lanky sneering coward in the beekeeper's hat to the giant in the rear with the long hayfork. For a moment, Lloyd considered making a run for it. Just leave the Quist men to their fate and flee back to the Clutters'. With any luck, he would not be pursued. Hopefully, no one would see through which door he vanished. He would make it hard for any of these villains to recognize him again. By morning the horror would be over—one way or another. But his blood boiled at the thought of what that might mean. Somehow they had to get word to the others. They had to warn the Quists of the impending assault. He could not be party to any more loss of life if he could help it.

"I'll tell you what," the beekeeper mused. "I see you have a boy with you. No doubt you don't want him hurt. What say you give us McGitney—take us to the others and we'll let you go. I swear on the real Bible. You will go free."

Drucker spat in the mud. "You'll need a lot more than this ragtag posse a yourn."

"Oh, we have more coming," the vigilante leader replied. "Rest assured. Give up the others and you can save yourselves—and the boy."

"No!" Lloyd cried, and pushed forward holding the Ambas-

sadors' box before him like a charm, his other hand still
plunged inside his pocket, grasping the artificial eye. These
men confronting them now were not Vardogers or Spirosians.
They were just brutal, and perhaps as stupid as they looked.

The sight of the box with the luminous engravings startled
them, but not as much as Lloyd had hoped, even when the
etched symbols seemed to project out across their bodies and
covered faces. Deftly, he spun the box around, making the figures whirl about like subtle, intelligent fire. The torch that one
of the hooded men held seemed so primitive and clumsy by
comparison.

"Eh, what's this now? Some trick?" one of the sack-hooded
men growled.

"Keep back!" Drucker yelled, hoisting his cudgel.

"We'll take that bauble," the beekeeper drawled. "Then you'll
take us to the others. They're not far from here, we know. You
can't save them, but you can save yourselves. There's tar and
feathers and a nice oak tree on the edge of town otherwise. Or
maybe we'll burn 'em out!"

The gang cheered at this, and Lloyd thought the noise might
draw some assistance. Then he realized that it was quite possible that these men were not mere outlaws and oafs but prominent local residents, ashamed or afraid in some way, yes,
otherwise they would not be hiding their faces, but nevertheless doing the dirty work of the community by some after-
midnight agreement.

Shades of Zanesville. Mob scenes from across America. The
stories St. Ives and Hattie had told him of lynchings and castra-
tions. The oppression he himself had felt too many times before. Scenes of every intimidation and assault he had ever
endured flashed through his mind, swelling the impotent rage
within him as he gripped the false eye of Mother Tongue ever
tighter. He felt it burning now, so hot had his hand become—
surely that was it. But why did it seem to throb, pulsing in time
with the juice that slopped in the pit of his stomach and the

276 | KRIS SAKNUSSEMM

white-hot hatred that scorched his forehead? He glanced down
at his pocket and saw to his disbelief that the eye was shining
through his hand, through the cloth, radiating up his arm as if
the light and heat could not be contained.

"You'll get naught out of us, you cur!" Soames snarled,
plunging forward to strike the first blow.

The diabolical beekeeper drew one of his pistols and pointed
it at Soames's chest.

"Stop!" Lloyd shouted, and held above his head what was no
longer an eye but the Eye. The Eye of his Storm.

The vigilantes gasped, for the brightness was so intense.
Hotter and harsher than Greek fire or the silver rush of Chinese rockets. The Ambassadors' box burned with a pale-green
surrounding haze—but Mother Tongue's Eye could not be
looked at, it was so fiercely alight. Some of the men in the gang
tried to cover their faces, as the baffled beekeeper man cocked
and fired his pistol at Soames, but wide. Drucker ducked,
shielding himself from the light the boy had produced from his
pocket and trying to skirt the shot from the gun barrel. Soames
dived forward, seeking to cudgel the hand that held the firearm,
and lost his footing in the mud. Lloyd stood firm, one hand
clutching the Ambassadors' box, the other the Eye, whose rippling green electric flame he could feel racing through his
nerves and then out into the dark like a jetted breath of deadly
starlight.

The pistol exploded in the gang leader's grip. The men beside
him dropped their weapons and slapped their hands to their
heads—their eyes. As one single cornered animal, they clam-
ored in horrible unison and then collapsed, wriggling in the
sloshy ground like worms. Only their leader did not fall to the
ground. He was too busy dancing. A dreadful dance of unbear-
able pain that sent a wave of sickening fulfillment through
Lloyd as he lowered the Eye and closed his fist around it, finding it cool once more.

The netted hat of the vigilante captain had ignited like a

tumbleweed, encasing his face in a blue-green cage of flames, so that not even the stench of burning beard and skin escaped. He darted and weaved for a moment like some crazed new kind of pyrotechnic toy—the image of which might have made children laugh and clap, had the body below been some clever machine, and not a flesh-and-blood man, that could not be rebuilt in time for the next performance. Then he crashed into a wheel-rut puddle. The bloody shattered bone of his pistol hand lay outstretched, the fried black mass of what had been his head half submerged in the narrow ditch of rain, all skull and cobweb now, too hideous to look at.

Which his compatriots would never have to do. To a man, their sight had been seared shut like slits of blank slate—except for the colossus with the pitchfork, whose eyeballs had turned to scalding jelly and had leaked out of their sockets, staining his face and coat like offal flicked with a slotted spoon.

CHAPTER 3

The Quest and Questions of the Quists

WHETHER THE INHABITANTS OF INDEPENDENCE WERE SLEEPING
very soundly that night, or whether such trouble had been anticipated in official quarters, after the blinding firestorm that
had been released from the Eye, the dark of stars and the dim
reflections of the moon in pools and rivulets returned, afterimages dwindling away like fiery leaves turned to ash. A lone stable dog howled at the other end of town, answered by the cry of
coyotes or a wild pack in the distance. Soon the morning light
would come creeping across the sky, the aroma of breakfasts
would begin to rise—steel-cut oats bubbling and freshly laid
eggs cracked and popping on buttered grills. Another steamboat would bring wagons and carriageloads of newcomers—
barrels and crates of goods, workhorses dragging fresh timber,
the smell of smoke, sweat, and the river clinging to their thickening coats. But all was still now, except for the mess of depraved and wounded humanity before them.

"Come quick," urged Lloyd, pocketing his treasures and trying to raise Soames back up. Drucker kept blinking and batting
the air, but it was clear that he had not been permanently debilitated. Both men could see all right again after a few moments, but neither could believe what he had seen. With the
exception of the charred leader, the vigilantes lay sprawled on

the mushy ground groaning, limbs tangled, fumbling for one another—for help, for answers to what had happened to them. Lloyd took charge and led the two Quist guards between the bodies and back toward the storehouse as fast as they could move, given their stunned, disoriented condition. After his miraculous performance, Soames and Drucker seemed more than willing to be led, boy though he was.

That Lloyd had no idea what sort of power had been unleashed or how he had unleashed it, he vowed he would not reveal. His one objective now was to return his bewildered new comrades to their families and fellows and deliver the warning about reprisals or further action against them.

Once back at the storehouse, Soames and Drucker poured forth a tale that made the Quists tremble and ululate. Even McGitney, practical man of decision that he had become, was distraught—flapping his arms for order and calling for more details all at once. Lloyd let the hoo-ha run its course and then reemphasized the admonition he had offered the moment they returned through the heavy door.

"You must leave town," he told them. "By the fastest, straightest way you can. Those that waylaid us will not harm anyone again, but they have friends and other fools ready to do the same that they tried. Every moment you stay in this town you run the risk of being hunted down and—"

"We know, lad." McGitney nodded. "We know too well the trials and risks we face. We have faced and suffered them before. That's what brings us here and on the path before us. Our plan was always to leave this burg at first light. It was, in fact, your unexpected arrival that has delayed us. And, as fate or divine will would have it, has saved us, too. This is a night we will muddle over in times to come. But what of you and your family? Are you not at risk from these same marauders, too, now?"

"I don't reckon this boy is at risk from anyone," Drucker pronounced. "He is the next prophet—the one that Saint Kendrick foresaw. The box he carries is a match to the Headstones, and he can draw lightning down from a clear sky and make it do his bidding."

This statement, presented so forcibly, offered a concise and unavoidable distillation of his and Soames's initial attempt at a report. Lloyd dutifully presented Urim and Thummin's box for inspection by McGitney and the others, and squawks of recognition and befuddlement filled the storehouse. The Eye he would not present, and as neither Drucker nor Soames had seen it clearly or grasped what role it had played in their deliverance, he was not about to stir up more chaos and inquiry now. What was more, of course, he had no idea what made the Eye work. It had been but an interesting if grotesque piece of jewelry minutes before—a souvenir of a lost part of his life that he was both afraid and hopeful of finding again. The real value he had placed on it had to do with Hattie LaCroix. The Eyes were a pair that might one day be reunited. That was his dream. That was why he had given her the other one.

McGitney tried with great patience to maintain order and take in the facts presented to him. It would not be long before the blinded vigilantes were found by their co-conspirators and, come the dawn, the tribe of Quists needed to be on the move. But they could not leave without knowing what their night visitor-savior had to tell them.

"Lloyd, are you who we think you are?"

The boy shook his head. "I'm not a prophet or your holy one. But you should listen to me just the same."

"Because of your power?"

Lloyd dodged this. "Because I speak the truth."

McGitney opened his arms to the group, as if calling for their opinion.

"You spoke the truth about the sacred markings. You helped save two of our own. I think you are the one Saint Kendrick foresaw. I know I speak for all the Quists when I say we want you to join us, to lead us to the promised land we know awaits us beyond the wilderness."

Lloyd thought of his parents asleep in their coffins and shook his head. If he could not join the ranks of the Spirosians or the Vardogers, he certainly could not take up with the Quists—and he felt a great weight upon his shoulders when he thought of what he had to tell them, before any more of them were hurt or killed at the hands of night riders.

"I am not your messiah," he said again. "And your faith . . . your theology—"

He was trying to think if that was the right word. To him, religion was what people who lacked magic and science had to fall back on.

"Go on," McGitney encouraged. "We trust you, Lloyd. We would follow you if you would lead us."

"Well, first I think you should stop this following business," Lloyd began (which perhaps showed that, in spite of his prodigious mental faculties, his grasp of human nature was still weak or at least self-deceiving, for he himself was an avid follower—the only problem was that he was devoted to a phantom). "Not all can lead, but no one necessarily must follow."

"What would you have us do?" a pretty young woman, who nestled a sleeping baby to her breast, implored. "Flounder blind like those men Brother Drucker says you left yonder?"

"Those men accosted us—and their blindness is a punishment," Lloyd replied, not mentioning that he had no idea how that particular form of punishment had been inflicted. "The kind of blindness you mean is just not knowing. Uncertainty. Doubt. If you are not able to face *that* and keep on seeking, you will never find anything worth trusting."

He thought of the Clutters, seeing a riddle in the simple, albeit esoteric instruction on the bottom of the Vardogers' music box.

"You will build a church of meaning and procedure upon a mystery you have mistaken. Your church, even if it is a cathedral, will be a house of cards, and the genuine mystery will be missed."

McGitney scratched his red beard. If this boy was not the Enlightened One that had been promised, he sure sounded like him.

"All right," he said. "Supposing you are not he whom we have been expecting. Nevertheless you say you have a truth to tell us about the sacred markings and what we believe. Tell us your truth."

"I'm afraid you won't like it," Lloyd answered, shuffling his feet on the sod floor to wipe off the mud he had accumulated.

"It is written that the truth will set you free. This must be why you have found us tonight. There can be no other explanation. And if, as you say, there are things about the Headstones that exceed your understanding, too, then perhaps there is a larger truth at work than any of us knows—or can ever know. But tell us the truth you came to tell, whoever you really are, wherever you really come from. It must be important. After all that has happened tonight, that much is clear."

Lloyd looked McGitney in the eye, then scanned the faces around the room. Then he held up the box the professor had given him, in what seemed another life.

"The markings on this box, which you can all see are exactly like the markings on the strips of wood you carry, were not made thousands or even a hundred years ago. They were made in recent times by twin brothers. Wild, sad creatures. Freaks of nature, you would call them. From Indiana."

A great choral sigh was released around the storehouse.

"The twins were deformed and disabled. A man who ran a medicine show had found them and taken them in, intending to exhibit them for profit, although I think he had too much heart to exploit them. Maybe because of their monstrous appearance they seemed to have grown up in their own world, never a part of the life that we know—though alert enough and smart in their own way. At least they were not imbeciles. But they could not speak English. Instead, they spoke a language all their own, which was every bit as odd to hear as these markings

are to look at. The pitchman thought their speech was just animal chatter, but I *know* that it had a pattern and a depth—and
a variety at least as great as English, perhaps much greater. I
was given this box with their written language carved into it,
because I hoped to study it and understand its meaning. I first
believed it was something they invented, although both the
writing and their speech had a—I'm not sure of the right
word—an *authority* that some made-up code is not likely to
have. But if they were specimens or representatives of some
bigger group or a people whose language this is, I don't know
where to look for them."

Lloyd paused, and McGitney tugged at his beard.

"You're saying these writings are the creation of idiots from
Indiana, and only a few years old?"

"I did not say they were idiots," Lloyd answered. "It appears
they were from Indiana, but there is no actual proof of that."

"But why do the characters and symbols spring to life? Why
do they glow?"

"That I do not know—yet," Lloyd responded. "I agree with
you that it's wondrous strange, but you have assumed that the
illumination is somehow inherent in the symbols—that they
have a life of their own. Maybe the cause lies rather in how the
symbols have been made. I have seen luminous fungi in caves.
There are water creatures with strange properties, and any
number of minerals with unusual characteristics. I cannot account for the capacity just now, but I propose to you that the
mystery of the gleaming could be reconciled and the secret of
the symbols still remain unsolved."

"But your contention is that the sacred markings are not old
and do not tell of the grand historic legacy that we, the Quists,
have come to know and worship through the Book of Buford?"

"The sheets of bark are old," Lloyd replied. "Clearly. The
markings on them may or may not be. But I saw the wild twins
making such symbols and figures with my own eyes not long
ago. They would use any surface that was made available to

them, and a range of implements from charcoal stick and quill to awl or sharpened bone. You will note that all the illuminated examples we have here are carved, which allows for the indentations to have been treated with some unknown material or by some undetermined process after creation. Sadly, we lack any examples of their writing system produced by pen or chalk on paper or parchment. It would be very interesting to see if such specimens would also demonstrate the same luminosity now. If they did, that would suggest that there is something, however difficult to understand, about the symbols themselves. If not, it would support the theory that the figures have somehow been treated. I myself have never observed the glowing of the writing on my box. In any case, I can see that all this is hard for you to follow, because you did not know other examples of the writing existed. Believing these bark fragments to be unique, you have therefore attributed special significance to them, which by definition they do not have—although they may very well have other kinds."

"But you say this is not a message to us? That these are not a whole that tell a story. A lost book of revelation and prophecy?" asked a man with a large wart on his forehead that his turban was trying to hide.

Lloyd pursed his lips and then replied, "It seems the one thing that is certain in this matter is that none of us know for certain what these markings mean. The showman who was looking after the brothers thought it was just scribbling. We here all agree that there is a beauty and an order to the markings that lie far beyond any aimless scrawling. Far! This is a language—a true, full, rich language, however indecipherable it may seem. It may even be that it opens an unknown door on the nature of all languages. The characters, their shapes and repetitions, are the most intriguing and hypnotic things to look upon I have ever seen. But why the brothers would need to communicate to each other in writing is unclear. And if they were writing for someone else to read, who did they have in mind?"

"So, you maintain," Soames piped up (his eyes still smarting), "that the Book of Buford is not based on an interpretation of these symbols?"

"I know nothing of your Buford," Lloyd said, shrugging. "I gather from what you have said that you think these writings make up some lost book of the Bible, and that you trace some connection with the people you think it describes. I say again, I do not know what this secret writing means, but I doubt very much that it has anything to do with the Bible—unless it is some interpretation made by the twin brothers, which from what I know of them seems unlikely."

"What about the woodpecker?" a sleepy knock-kneed lad called out.

"What woodpecker?" Lloyd puzzled. As distinctive as the story behind the Ambassadors' language was, these people had even more peculiar ideas of their own.

"All right, then," McGitney said in his summing-up voice. "The truth you have to tell us is that our theology is based upon a lie."

"A misunderstanding," Lloyd interjected.

"Kendrick Quist and his relative Buford were frauds."

"They may honestly have believed what they said and taught."

"In that case, dupes. They may have duped themselves, but they certainly have duped us—and we have endured persecution and exile because of it!"

"So it would seem," Lloyd was forced to agree.

"The real source of the sacred writings is a couple of mooncalves from Indiana, where Quist was from. He may even have known them. Do you know anything more about them?" McGitney asked, as members of the group frowned and whispered.

Lloyd considered recounting the brothers' experience with the tornado, but decided against it. The Quists had had enough miracles and unexplained phenomena. He shook his head.

"And what became of these weird brothers?" McGitney queried. "Where are they now?"

"They disappeared," Lloyd answered. "I believe they are dead now. A tragic accident."

"Hmm," McGitney said, pondering. "If we are to believe you, then the true authors of our sacred texts are gone from this earth—and, with them, any hope of penetrating what it seems that you would call the real mystery."

"I would not say *any* hope," Lloyd replied. "The problem is having enough of their writing to examine. I have had but the symbols on this box and little time or privacy for study. Your so-called Headstones are much more extensive samples. There is also the vital matter of the glowing. If my box has never done this before but does so now, it suggests some association or intercourse between the pieces."

"The markings change!" a young horse-faced girl sang out.

Lloyd took this comment as a reiteration of his point and continued. "Proximity may influence the luminosity. Cause unknown."

"What about you—when you touch them?" asked a man with a mustache that curled in a way that reminded Lloyd of the "f" hole in a violin.

"There may be several other factors at work, which we do not comprehend as yet," he answered.

"Fools, fools, fools we are!" an old dark woman gibbered.

"I would not say that," Lloyd barked (somewhat surprised at himself). "The Headstones are not what you thought them to be. But while they may not be sacred in the way that you have believed, they are worthy of great interest and perhaps much more than that, if their secret were fully understood."

Lloyd had intended his comments to be consoling, but, coming after all that had transpired, they were more than the

Quists could bear. A woman in a sunflower calico dress and a knitted shawl thrust her googling baby into her husband's arms and began unwinding her turban. Several others started to do the same.

"Ah," McGitney lamented, remembering his moment of cowardice in the barn back in Illinois and his mad dash through the laundry line. He felt once again on the run, his vision clouded. Could he emerge to advantage once again?

"Dark night of the soul!" he mourned. "A messiah comes to us at last, who says he is not our messiah and yet calls the lightning down to aid our members. Then he tells us that our faith is based on false teachings—that our prophetic forebearers are in fact lunatics or lusus naturae suitable for naught but display alongside the sawdust and hogskin mermaid, and the two-headed calf at a village fair!"

There followed much grumbling and argument and more than a little weeping and wailing. Lloyd could find nothing to say that he had not already said and, in being there to witness the unraveling of the Quist theology, regretted the effect his knowledge had imposed, although he was canny enough to realize that without his performance with the Eye they might well have talked their way around his words. Truly, faith is a kind of blindness, he told himself. But, then again, so is being too sure of what you see. The first pale light of dawn began seeping into the storehouse. It was time for him to get back to his coffin, and for the Quists to mobilize.

"I must go," he told them. "And so must you. Whether you take off your head wraps or not, you will not so easily lose your reputation."

McGitney, who had been comforting one of his wives, turned to Lloyd.

"You are right again, young warrior. We must carry on and come to terms with this new revelation at a safe distance."

"Why? What's the point?" one of the young people hollered.

"I'm a-goin' back to Indy-anna!" an old codger croaked.

"What say you, Brother McGitney? What in God's name do we do now?"

"Who said he's leader now?" A scraggly man choked and started snuffing the candles with a square-toed boot.

"Silence!" McGitney bellowed, recalling that moment of exhilarated surprise when the contents of the clothesline were removed from his head and he had found himself a hero. "Here is what I say. We must try to see the blessing in what has happened here. We are all still alive and unhurt, and if our pride and our faith have been challenged, perhaps in another way it has been renewed. If we are to put stock in what this boy has said—and it seems that we do—then we must remember that we have in our possession these things that have no less meaning than we supposed, just different. Perhaps we are more pioneers and pilgrims than we supposed. I say that we forge on as a family, as a clan and as a community, committed to freedom, industry, and the search for the significance of these tablets— an endeavor we can all participate in without the need for prophets or messiahs. It strikes me that I myself have never looked more closely at the symbols than tonight because I had some inkling, I believe, of what they represented. The Book of Buford was a kind of curtain, not an exegesis. I say that what we leave behind in this meeting place is our arrogance of special providence, not our loyalty to each other or our fascination and reverence for these enchanted characters. It was them that brought us all together—that made us risk life, limb, and old ties. That is powerful significance indeed, worthy of many lifetimes of devotion and study. Other beliefs and sects have but copies or imagined texts, relics and articles of faith. We at least have originals, whose meaning is as undiscovered and untapped as the wilderness waiting for us outside that door. I say we should wipe our eyes and gird up our loins and be grateful. For tonight we have been saved. We have been released and we have been refreshed. From the dark night of despair, we have been given a new dawn!"

Lloyd considered McGitney's speech an example of both sod-level wisdom and true poise under pressure, worthy of both Hattie and St. Ives. If nothing else, the Quists had chosen the right leader, he was sure—a fact that contrasted sharply with the mesh-hatted bigot who had been incinerated. Perhaps an even brighter future lay ahead for the Quists than the one they had envisioned. He hoped so, for all their sakes.

McGitney had much to do now, holding the flock together, repairing breaches in trust and confidence, and trying to organize the group off to their hidden horses and wagons—to reassemble and disperse, or to bid farewell to those insistent members who had lost faith forever and were now determined to return East to their old lives or to team up with other settlers headed West. But still, he made sure that Lloyd was sent off with, if not consensual thanks, then at least an acknowledgment of respect.

"Young Lloyd," McGitney said. "I know you would seek to have these tablets to assist your own inquiry. But these we must keep, because for better or worse they have been entrusted to us. You have your box, and in some way that we may yet decipher, our fates have been connected and may remain so. Go forth with what new blessings we have to give. You will not be soon forgotten."

Soames and Drucker together gave Lloyd a deep bow, which he returned. Then he stowed the box under his garments and stepped out through the door into the ghostly morning, taking a longer, more circumspect route back to the Clutters'. After his earlier performance with the vigilantes, it was deemed that he needed no escort. He thought Hattie would have been proud of the Li'l Skunk.

He glimpsed many shapes and shadows along the way, and smelled the smoke of early cooking fires, the salivatory tang of bacon, and the glug of grits but garnered not a hint of any particular malice or intent toward himself or anything relating to either the vigilantes or the Quists. By the time he reached the undertaker and coffinmaker's establishment and had scraped the mud from his boots, the sky was streaked with bloody color. Softly, he cracked the door, relatched, and bolted it—and had just snuggled back down into his coffin to think of Hattie when his father rose, stretched and farted simultaneously, which almost set him giggling. Hattie could change pitch! Moments later, Rapture squirmed awake.

"Yeh all fine?" she cooed to her husband.

"Lord, I feel like the risen dead!" Hephaestus exclaimed. "I have a crook in my back that will need a poultice. Or, better still, a knee and a yank. But we need to be shoving on. I'm hankering to be gone now. On our way."

"I be there," his wife promised, swallowing a yawn. "How's Lloyd?"

"Ah, just look!" Hephaestus gestured. "A-peace like a suckling. You'd think there were no troubles a'tall in the world. He probably hasn't changed position the whole night. Leave the rousting to me. We have tracks to make."

CHAPTER 4

I Show You Plenty Ghosts

WE HAVE ALL HAD THE EXPERIENCE OF FALLING ASLEEP FOR A minute and then having what seems like an entire night of dreams. Often, these dreams act as a solvent to our day-to-day consciousness—a disbursing, confronting carnival of images and incidents that take us out of our familiar being and into fantastic new (or suddenly remembered) realms. Other times, we find ourselves not swept away from what we had been focused on before falling asleep but drawn closer, so that we seem to pass straight through the matter that was on our mind, merging with it. Such was the experience Lloyd had in the few short minutes of refuge and release that overcame him when he slipped back into his coffin as his parents were rising.

His mind was so aroused by what had transpired with the Quists and the vigilantes, the secret writing of the Ambassadors, and the lethal force of the Spirosian Eye (all of which, of course, had come close on the heels of the time-distorting effect of the Vardogers' music box and the questions raised by the accelerated decomposition of the cannibal dog), that even though he was drained of physical energy, his thoughts ran back over his night episode. The conundrum of the Eye seemed momentarily impenetrable, so he ended up sifting through the things he had said to the Quists—the idea that the twins' symbol system may have been treated by some process to create the illuminated effect. This, at first, had seemed to be the most logical explanation. He had even offered suppositions about what type of materials might be involved. Then he heard again in his sleep the remark made by the equine-countenanced girl: *"The markings change!"*

At the time, he had been aware of some taut string of conjecture her words had stroked in him, but there had been too much happening to address it. Now, in the serial stream of hypnologic clarity, this assertion began to resonate more explicitly. He realized that her remark was like the instruction on the Vardogers' music box. Initially, he had thought it said one obvious thing—referring to the glowing effect of the writings. But it may have meant something both more literal and miraculous. Since he had first come into possession of the box, a vague thought had passed back and forth in his mind—*that the symbols and characters seemed to move or shift with different examinations.* Without the technology to duplicate the markings, it was impossible to decide the matter objectively. All he had was a foggy but needling impression that he had so far not had the energy, leisure, or privacy to explore.

The Quist girl had called his attention to it again, and now, in the twilight morning of half-sleep, he was able to at least contemplate the notion without prejudice. The idea of markings carved on a box, which were able to be altered—or to somehow alter themselves—was on the surface absurd. But suppose one had the suspicion that they did. What if this idea lingered and no matter how many times the writing was consulted one could not with absolute certainty feel as if the suspicion had been dispelled? This alone said something important about the symbol system, Lloyd felt. This was, in fact, a fundamental part of its uniqueness—that every time you confronted it, it seemed new and all the more indecipherable.

Yet if it were just a matter of impressions one could argue that the sense of change and movement was due to the foreignness of the markings. The whole world was like this. Birds arrange themselves like musical notes on the rope between trees where you hang washing. Are they the same birds you saw yesterday? Are they *all* the same? Do all humans appear as undifferentiated and interchangeable to other undomesticated species? This question sent him down a long corridor of speculation, and at the end of the corridor was a painting.

The impression one had that the Ambassadors' writing underwent some kind of alteration (perhaps continuously, perhaps not) struck him as no more extraordinary than a painting that seems to change color and mood depending on the light, which brought to mind again the story that St. Ives had told about the paintings in Junius Rutherford's possession. These apparently innocuous works of art, when observed over time, possessed very odd properties. It was not the effects their surface created that changed but the deeper structure, the very subject matter—or so his friend with the mechanical prosthesis had insisted.

As outrageous as the things the gambler had told him were, Lloyd acknowledged that there was a kind of consistency to them—and consistency, whatever form it takes, is always the hallmark of something one should pay attention to.

To Lloyd, the "painting phenomenon" was a transformation analogous to what he imagined occurring with the twins' secret writing—and what the horse-faced girl may have been alluding to. The amount of space, the frame for each, did not change, but what happened within the frame did, over time. Time was the crucial element. Time and the observer, of course. Without someone to observe the changes, would they occur?

His mind had often spun around this perennial question of philosophy and perception. But now he saw that there was another aspect. There was the much more subtle yet still intensely practical issue of *how* the presence of a perceiver changed the event or object viewed. If, for instance, one was willing to grant some occult instability to the twins' writing, what was it that triggered the changing? People, when they know they are being watched, behave differently from when they think they are alone and unseen. They perform. Could it be that in some way the markings were *performing,* and that the increase in their luminosity was influenced by the number of people and the intensity of attention paid? This would suggest that there was something important about his own particular participation, for the markings had shone brighter when he made physical contact.

This chain of thought brought to mind a comment his mother had made years before, when the husband of one of her herbal-remedy patients had asked with mock seriousness if she honestly believed ghosts were "truly real" or if she was just being colorful and folksy and thought that they were "creatures in the mind." To Lloyd's surprise, Rapture dropped the usual white accent she used in public and replied, "Show me now where yer mine true ends and de worl' begins, I show you plenny ghosts."

Something about ghosts. And time.

Ghosts and time were intimately related, and yet profoundly disconnected. For what were ghosts but people who had stepped out of time—who were now immune to time—watching from outside, interacting with the world but no longer of it?

What would the world look like outside time? Lloyd wondered in his sleep. What would human culture look like—or sound like—outside language?

Time was change. The glyphs of the Ambassadors seemed to be constantly changing, except for the spiral symbol that looked like a tornado. So their language had something to do with time.

But was not a written language always about time? A fixing and freezing of a spoken language? In his dream state it occurred to him that he had assumed that the markings and carvings were transcriptions of the alien tongue the twins seemed to share. Their behavior had suggested that they understood each other's sounds. Because the one was so bizarre, he had made the link to their markings; it was not surprising that a method of transcription would appear alien, too. What had puzzled him was why they needed to write. If no one else could understand their language, what was the point of writing? They could speak to each other.

Looking at these assumptions now, he saw that people often write things down for their private benefit. (He did.) To make things clearer for themselves. To prioritize. To remember. Or for other as yet unknown people to find and read. To teach. What were most books? Messages written in the hope of being found and decoded. Perhaps the brothers were trying to teach people their language, only it was hard to find a suitable student.

Something about ghosts. And time.

In his trance state, Lloyd slipped through the hierograms and the phenomenon of their luminosity for a moment, back to the Martian Ambassadors' speech and the question of what things would not just look like but sound like outside or in some new relation to time. Yes, there was something about ghosts and time when it came to the twins. And tornadoes—or at least the tornado that they had dropped out of.

He spiraled around and around, trying to cut through the shame and guilt he felt about his actions toward them, to hear their voices again, to visualize the changes he had imagined in their hierograms. Why was it that the one symbol that seemed the most representative of dynamism—the spiral icon—was the one element that he was certain remained constant?

It was not a letter like *A* or *Z*. It was not even a unit of meaning, he thought. It was . . .

It was a kind of system unto itself. A value system for interpreting all the other symbols and their relationship to each other. Was that it?

He could not grasp onto the mechanism. All his young life

he had sought out with instinctive acuity the essential elements of machine operations and physical processes. He was a born engineer, with a pathological curiosity. Now he was seeing a whole new world open before his dreaming eyes—the possibility that behind and inherent in language were mechanisms equally as real as the physics of a slingshot or the chemistry of a beer vat, but far more mysterious and perhaps much more powerful.

If one could connect the mechanisms of language with ballistics and pharmacology, optics, harmonics, hydraulics and medicine, mathematics and music. If one could master the secrets of symbols and syphons, surgeries and solar energy. If one knew the exact point where the mind ended and the world began, and could render it . . .

Who would need projectiles if they had mastered that enigmatic science?

He glimpsed then, for just a flutter, a symbol so potent that it was beyond all representation of other things and ideas, but alive unto itself. Inclusive and yet apart. Because it was the Whole—simultaneously inside and outside itself. Not the word made flesh but *the word made time—and the ghosts made flesh.*

That was what the spiral of the twins was, perhaps. That was what he had caught a flicker of that night with his beloved Hattie.

A key and a keyhole, too. And if one could pass through the spiral one could look back and see and hear the secret language unified and clear. He fixed his mind on this and sent himself outward, imaginatively trying to enter the spiral, to gain the other side. And then . . .

Swirling strings and flowering fractals of ideograms and morphemes exploded before his eyes, as if the dusty leather-bound tomes he had pored over in Schelling's bookshop had opened all at once inside his head. He saw Egyptian hieroglyphs, lush brush-stroked Chinese characters on long, unwinding scrolls. Arabic poems tiled into mosaics. Greek and

Hebrew letters hammered in stone. Alchemical and astrological symbols. The tracks of animals in tar pits—the silhouettes of bison and ibex on cave walls—musical notes, tattoos, hand signals, constellations. Complicated chains of numbers twined into lattices that in turn formed the skeletons of fabulous beasts like gryphons and unicorns, whose emerging flesh and scales then took on the mesmerizing puzzle patterns of still more figures—radiant angels and ghastly demons, horned-bone shaman masks and polished metal armor made of tinier masks made of geometric shapes that were the visual representation of still other numbers, coalescing to build vast temples and coliseums of notation that grew and glistened like sentient crystal systems. On and on the symbols rained at him, blossoming into jungles of unknown significance—metamorphosing into monsters and monoliths, titans, totems, face cards, and pieces in forgotten games.

But through all the pictograms and treble clefs repeatedly appearing amid the empires of equations and alphabets was the insignia of the Vardogers' clawed candle, and the tornado emblem of the teratoid twins—a spiral choreography suggestive of conceptual aggregates and psychological associations—which was something entirely different. As different as the momentary flare of a firefly in a bean row from the electric haunted hieroglyph you would see if you could follow its whole life—every single pulse and drift of wing—and hold it in your mind as easily as that one blink. It was as different as the bending of the youngest blade of grass in a fifty-acre field from . . . the wind.

The wind made him think of his ghost sister, Lodema, and he recalled where he had got the notion of building shrines to her that summoned and revealed the subtlety and power of the unseen breeze. It was because of the old Wyandot man back in Zanesville, King Billy.

King Billy made moonshine and talked to himself, but he knew the tracks of every animal, from a field mouse to a fox. He knew when to fish with hellgrammites and when to use night crawlers. He could tell you the time of night by smell. He read the world with his whole body, his being so embedded within it that he was always on the page that was being written. All around his shack he had rigged up nets of tinkling beads and spoons. King Billy called them "ghost traps."

Lloyd saw them again in his dream, feathered, jagged—warning, intriguing—sometimes invisible, depending on the light. They kept away bad spirits and busybodies. They defined Billy's property, reflected his view of the world, and provided decoration. Insects and animals interacted with them, like the shadows and the seasons. Lloyd saw them again now as like the symbols of the Ambassadors. A living web of meanings that marked where the World becomes Mind. Where the Word becomes Time. Where the Ghosts become Flesh.

CHAPTER 5

Looking Alive

LLOYD WAS PRODDED AWAKE BY HIS FATHER, HIS HEAD FILLED TO bursting with ideas and afterimages from his dreams. The awkwardness of extricating themselves from the coffins, the dreary atmosphere of the Clutters' business, and the necessity of packing away what belongings they still retained in a safe place so as not to disrupt the activities of the older couple made all three of the Zanesvilleans concur that they would be wise to get organized and on their way to Texas as fast as possible. For Lloyd, of course, the incentive was all the sharper, given that there could be some backlash from the friends and families of the vigilantes.

There were also the claws of the Vardogers to consider. The presence of the insidious music box under the very same roof was a potent reminder of their ingenuity and long reach. It was hard to believe that it was just chance. Not knowing only increased the threat. He thought it essential to keep his prized possessions with him at all times until they found some reliable haven, and so, with great care, he nestled Hattie's skull and the fearsome Eye into the box of the Martian Ambassadors and tucked it inside his coat, along with the mystery letter from Micah.

As much as the fugitives from Ohio craved company, normalcy, and being settled, it was obvious that they were not going to find such things in Independence. Their hosts provided still greater, albeit inadvertent, encouragement to get on the trail, as both seemed even more dithery than they had been the day before, to the point where boiling a kettle for coffee was quite beyond Egalantine and the completion of a sentence even with the other's assistance was out of the question for them both. Rapture took over in what passed for the Clutters' kitchen, which was still a tad too redolent of the previous night's supper to promote much of an appetite in anyone but Hephaestus (who had started to regain some healthy color and to put a bit of meat back on his pickled bones). After several false starts, she managed to make them all flapjacks and strong black coffee, as Hephaestus commenced working out a list of the supplies they would need, and Lloyd kept a surreptitious eye on the undertaker-coffinmaker and his wife.

He had a suspicion that there was some dispute that the couple was trying to stifle. Then he noticed Othimiel return one of the music boxes to its place on one of the shelves. It was the Vardogers' box. Perhaps the Clutters had had another listen unbeknownst to his parents. It occurred to Lloyd that their disorientation and woolgathering might have something to do with further exposure to the beguiling music, and he recalled a remark from the night before that had struck him as queer at the time but which he had dismissed as just another example of their eccentricity. Egalantine had commented on the "choir" she had heard in the music. Lloyd was certain he had heard no voices, and at this point unclear how the impression of human voices could be mechanically achieved (at least with requisite precision).

Everyone had been so taken and distracted by the music, there had been no actual discussion of what they had heard—and the assumption had been that they had all heard the same piece. Now, in his sleepy, wondering post-Quist way, Lloyd asked himself the question What if they had each heard different music? How would that be possible, and what would it mean?

It was too big a puzzle to resolve without further study (and, ostensibly, more risky investigation of the music box, which he was reluctant to do), but in any case one would have thought that both of the Clutters were suffering the aftereffects of a laudanum binge or some kind of neurological trauma. And the matter worsened over breakfast, with Egalantine dribbling from her chin and making what passed for lewd gestures at her husband, while Othimiel rose from the table and returned a moment later wearing what was, fortunately, an empty chamber pot on his head.

Hephaestus, having done plenty of questionable things himself when soused, tried to be as tolerant and respectful as possible. (His hope was that the Clutters were showing themselves to be habitual tipplers and had been hitting the jug hard and early.) It helped explain their disjointed way of communicating, and the sorry, haphazard state of their business. However, he was stumped as to why they did not smell of alcohol.

Rapture, once she had convinced herself that they were not playing a perverse joke, became concerned for them, and earnestly wished that, whatever the affliction, it was not contagious. "Like the rapid onset of senility," Lloyd remarked to himself, as his mother helped put the couple back to bed after cleaning up the breakfast dishes. Maybe a bit more rest would bring them back to themselves, as fuzzy and intermittent as that had been.

"I think we need to look alive this morning," Hephaestus proclaimed as the Sitturds made their way past the coffins and out into the street. "Another couple of nights with those folks— and in this place—I may not get out of the box!"

"Time egen ta tek 'e foot een 'e han," Rapture agreed. "Firss, we grub nuts an' prospah liken a squirrel."

"I think we need to look alive this morning," Hephaestus repeated, and began whistling.

Lloyd did not like that his mother had dropped her plain white diction and was intermixing more Gullah phrases than he thought prudent, even with the Clutters. What was worse, his father seemed befuddled, and the discordant tune he began to whistle got on the boy's nerves. Lloyd now had no doubt that the Vardogers were real—and therefore the Spirosians, too. Even though the Sitturds had escaped from St. Louis, he could see that they were in the midst of a broader, deeper, and darker mystery than even the one Mother Tongue had intimated back in the grotto. The Martian Ambassadors, whoever they were, were somehow involved. Amazing technologies. Deviant desires. He longed to rise above the details even for just a moment—to get some coherent view—but the thought of ascending, even metaphorically, brought back memories of the courthouse, the black man crying for the Angel of the Lord . . . and the lost brothers blown over the water and into the wall of Illinois timber.

"I think we need to look alive this morning!" Hephaestus announced.

"Farruh, stop saying that," Lloyd pleaded. "You sound like the Clutters. Where's our list?"

Hephaestus froze in his tracks and slapped his forehead. "Jimminy!" he barked. "I left it back at the bone tailor's. After all that!"

"Well, we're not going back," Lloyd insisted. "C'mon. We'll all try to think of things as we go. It'll clear our—your heads."

The last remark conjured a new specter of doubt in his mind. What if he had also been affected by the music box? And why would he not have been? The reasoning was inescapable, which raised the issue of how much of what had happened the night before had been influenced by whatever it was he had heard. His thoughts seemed sharp and clear to him, but perhaps the Clutters' did to them, too. He had had nightmares in the past, but they had always had the aura of an external experience enveloping him for a time and then disintegrating when he awoke.

This new unease was more intimate and, if less fanciful in its effects, far more disquieting. "I am going to have to keep my eyes wide, wide open," Lloyd told himself. "For anything—anything that might suggest that what I am perceiving is not right, not real."

He half wished they would run into some of the Quists. Then he could confirm, at least intuitively, the events of last night. But this, of course, was folly. He would give himself away in front of his parents and perhaps to others who might be watching. And the Quists would just put themselves more in danger's path. If his memory was at all correct, he could only wonder at the impact of the night crisis on their future plans. And he would have to stay wondering—and watching.

The stark open sky of sunup had begun to show signs of clouding over, and the hint of more rain later in the day invigorated the flow of traffic along the streets and boardwalks. Even the stragglers appeared to be loafing and straggling with vehemence. Horses and carts clattered and squished through the mud, saws ripped and shimmied, hammers pounded nails and clanging horseshoes, stick fires brought cauldrons of laundry to a dirty boil. But in between the heat of cooking and cleaning, and the clash of metal and wood, there was a noticeable edge to the air, as if the softness of the Indian summer had turned overnight, reminding the Sitturds of perhaps the biggest and most pressing problem they faced: the lateness of the season.

All of the westbound settlers who had any chance of surviving and reaching their intended destination had long since headed out—most at the first signs of spring growth on the prairie, the vital food source for their oxen and horses. As the Sitturds plunked across the planks or dodged the mud puddles, hundreds of other families who had arrived out West marveled at the Columbia River, the austere forests, or the clashing of the waves of the Pacific. Some people had died along the way, and many had left precious belongings behind when the going got tough. Many other groups had paused out in the desert or on semi-fertile mesas and made provisional camps, with the goal of hunting and foraging, and making it through the winter, to assault the fortress of giant mountains come the next spring. Some had run afoul of bandits or Indian war parties, or drowned in streams. Others had buried children and grandparents owing to influenza or grievous injury. The Sitturds were out of step with all of them, running late and not headed west at all but south, into the brewing turmoil of the conflict with Mexico over the fate of Texas, the forced migration of angry displaced Indian tribes, and the persistent rumors of unheard-of diseases and rum occurrences. Spirits. Unknown beasts. No wonder we feel unsettled, Lloyd thought. We are.

"I think we better look—why do I keep saying that?" Hephaestus groused.

His son's face brightened somewhat at this. Whatever it was that had fogged his father's mind, it appeared to be lifting. It either had a trigger release or a set duration of influence. His mother, too, seemed to be recovering her wits and usual good sense, which was a profound relief to him, given all the wagging tongues and peering faces.

All the local news seemed to be ominous. A farming family outside town had been found dead of unknown causes (a poisoned well, the word went). Another cholera scare had been reported, and the "moaning frenzy" somewhere upriver. But as the Sitturds puttered about the town the hottest gossip concerned the divine retribution meted out to Deacon Bushrod and the loose confederacy of standover men and bedroom raiders that had become known as Bushrod's Rangers. Naturally, Lloyd's mind lit up at the first hint of this intelligence, but it took several stops and inquiries before the matter could be laid out sufficiently to fully comprehend.

The men in question were without doubt his assailants from the night before, and the boy had been correct in identifying the rogue in the beekeeper's hat as a man of some substance and education. Called the Deacon, the fiend had had some affiliation of his own creation with the local religious communities and had at one time been what passed for a circuit judge. His true orientation, however, was as a rabid anti-Mason and Mormon hater. (Lloyd supposed it was only a logical extension for such a figure to despise a group such as the Quists.) The word on the streets of Independence was that Bushrod and his gang had either crossed paths and swords with one of the powerful Masonic militias who operated in semi-secret across America or with a Mormon guard. Alternatively, God Almighty himself had struck them down because of their wickedness. Most of the understandable information on the subject came from a porcine butcher with fingers like his own sausages, and a drab pinch-faced woman in the dry-goods "emporium," who referred to herself in the third person, as in "Well, what Dot Cribbage thinks . . ."

Hephaestus and Rapture, with their now clearing heads, thought Lloyd's fascination with the incident was unhealthy if not scandalous, but the boy was intent on ferreting out whatever facts or received fictions he could. Those "in the know," as Dot Cribbage put it, seemed to be divided on the possible parties responsible: independent Masonic reprisal, some dirty deed done by them on behalf of the Quists (recall the curious hermetic connection between the Masons and the Mormons), a Quist or Mormon strong-arm brigade acting in self-defense . . . or an "answer by fire" from on high.

What was not in dispute was that eight men had lost their sight, as if hot pokers had been thrust into their eyeballs, and Deacon Bushrod's body had turned to dust and ashes, as if cursed. Those leaning toward a Masonic, Mormon, or Quist death squad as the culprit posited the application of acid or lye to the corpse, which explained its quick deterioration. (It looked as though Othimiel's handiwork would once again not be required.)

The theistically inclined felt their explanation was even stronger because of the accelerated decomposition, and were busy hoisting Bibles and even bottles, early in the day though it was. The upshot was that eight local men had suddenly and simultaneously lost their sight and were not talking, and a civic leader of dubious reputation had inexplicably disintegrated. Lloyd, of course, thought of the ravenous little black dog of the day before.

The awful miracle set the town alight with accusations, speculations, prayer-saying, and rosary-clutching. To Lloyd, it seemed he could hear all the private fears that underlay the public mood more truly than the banging of tools or the snorting of the horseflesh. Then out of the ruckus there rose another sound, cool and pure and out of place, a new church bell giving forth its first trial toll—not in honor of the dead and blinded, it was true, but perhaps as some kind of fumbling community lament for all the terrors and wonders growing wild on people's doorsteps.

Not knowing anything about his nocturnal exploits, Lloyd's parents tried to dismiss the gossip and tall tales as just another symptom of life in this crossroads town. They had a wagon and oxen to locate, food to buy, little money to bargain with relative to their needs, and any number of miscellaneous supplies to source. So it was not surprising that they took little notice of the man with the wooden leg hobbling down the plankings tacking up posters. But Lloyd did.

He had a bad feeling about the posters even at a distance, and when they passed one up close his heart leaped into his throat. In big, brash letters were the words:

RUNAWAY NEGRO GIRL—$500 REWARD

Beneath the lettering was a hand drawn picture that captured the unmistakable likeness of Hattie in a rebellious mood. There were more details in finer print underneath, but he did not need to read these, although he caught a glimpse of the phrase "Answers to the names of . . . ," as if she were a dog missing from a farm.

It sickened and infuriated him, and he recalled the numinous fever that had overcome him during the Bushrod ambush. This place was even worse than Zanesville. Even with all the people about, he was sorely tempted to reach for the Eye and set the crippled money-grubber alight—to see if he could again strike his enemy down. That he would offer money, or be the means of that offer, to hunt Hattie down! Captain of dark loving. The memory of the blistering current of power rushed through Lloyd's veins and nerves, so that he thought that he could smell his own hair singeing, but no one else seemed to take any notice. Had he wielded the Eye, or had it acted on its own authority and impulses?

He wondered if Hattie's orb had the same power, and wished for her sake that it did and that he could tell her about it—that he could hold her, help her—glad though he was that she was away. Hopefully, far enough now so that no bounty hunter would pursue her.

If only the Eye were like an eye that he could see her through. But then he would convulse to see her in danger—to witness her sufferings at a distance and not be able to come to her aid. Or for her to observe his predicaments when she had so many more crises of her own. It was a silly notion, he thought. And yet he recalled that moment in the dark, with Soames and Drucker waiting for him outside—the trance he had fallen into briefly, staring into the sphere. There was no denying that he had felt watched then—seen by something or someone—but by what or by whom he could not say. Mother Tongue, that refined hag hiding from the world on her moss-festooned steamboat? Perhaps. Maybe that was her reason for giving him the Eyes—to keep a watch on him, by whatever witch-crazed science she had at her disposal. Then again, there was always the possibility that the Eyes held powers that were beyond her knowledge and understanding, too—like the spook lights in the cavern, a lost technology or magic for which she was seeking the key, or an engineer of subtlety to master its secrets.

Lloyd made a note of where the wooden-legged goblin put up the posters, vowing that he would sneak out that night, follow the route, and take them down. Every last one. He would scour the stinking village if he had to. If only Hattie were safe . . .

His thoughts were interrupted by a cry of chagrin from his father.

"By God!" Hephaestus shouted. "I'm supposed to be at work at the smithy's!"

Rapture's face sank at this recollection, as did Lloyd's. With all that had been going on, the matter of casual employment for Hephaestus and some much needed extra money for their provisioning had completely slipped their minds. His parents were quick to explain the oversight in terms of the incredible news and the distress that permeated the town. Lloyd could not accept this. This disruption of their memories and concentration had a dark association with the Vardogers' music box. He had no doubt that it had done something unwholesome to the Clutters.

Hephaestus limped off to Petrie's blacksmith shed at the other end of town, leaving Rapture and Lloyd to try to make what arrangements they could. He honestly believed Lloyd might be more capable than himself when it came to locating, selecting, and negotiating for the proper equipment, plus there was always a chance that Petrie might know where to find what they needed—that is, if he was not too angry to speak.

Although Rapture had got used to doing many things for herself and her son since the breakdown in St. Louis, she did not feel the slightest bit comfortable scrounging around Independence without her husband. She did not like the looks they received, and Lloyd's cocky, protective attitude, instead of cheering her up, upset her further, for it brought back memories of what was to her the still obscure disaster that had forced their hasty and, to her, frightening departure from the river city.

As it turned out, the crisis had been a good thing in certain ways, getting them back on their way to Micah's property and back together again as a family. They had ended up with means they had not had before, and a new focus on their goal, just when everything was coming apart at the seams. Yet the thought of the man with the humped back and his associates spooked her. She wanted to believe that any threat they posed, or the veiled threats they had referred to, had been left behind down the Missouri River, but she could not bring herself to query her son any more than she had in those first few desperate hours when Hephaestus slept like the dead from the drug the humped dandy had administered, and then thrashed in delirium when he came to. Lloyd had slipped off into a cloud of blank indifference and denial at the first hint of her interrogation then, and she did not want to risk another psychic retreat now. If she had known that the boy carried with him the device that had laid the Bushrod Rangers down, she would have been horrified. And if she suspected, as he did, that they had all been exposed to an equally potent and puzzling kind of weapon in the mechanical music, she might well have lost her bearings entirely. But she did not have this information or trepidation to hand and so turned her attention to the task that she and Lloyd had been assigned.

CHAPTER 6

Justice Street

HEPHAESTUS LOCATED PETRIE'S BLACKSMITH SHED AGAIN WITH-
out much difficulty, and found to his relief that Petrie was too
busy to be mad at his late arrival—and too perplexed. As it
turned out, his chief hand, Rawknor, had been one of the
Bushrod Rangers who was struck blind. Petrie had no truck
whatsoever with vigilantes, but he had benefited from Rawknor's skill and was now ashamed of himself for not speaking out
about his suspicions regarding his employee's private activities.
A bit of counsel at the right moment might have been all it took
to turn the fellow back to the path of honesty and tolerance.
Now it might well be too late. News, or rather rumors, about
the incident had swept through the town, and, being more cen-
trally located than the Clutters, Petrie had learned about the
unheard-of occurrence just after breakfast. In fact, he had
heard about it while astride the privy, his bowels greased with
grits, and in his consternation had almost forgotten to hitch up
his pants. Now blackened and sweating in his heavy apron, all
he wanted was to put the matter out of mind in a banging
frenzy of work, and he was just happy to have another set of
hands to help him. Unlike the Clutters, Petrie ran a thriving enterprise.

Out of practice with his old trade, the lame Ohioan was hard-pressed to keep pace with his Missouri benefactor and to shake himself from the happenings, not to mention the difficult circumstances the family was continually having to adjust to, and the hopes and expectations regarding his brother's legacy, which were beginning to reemerge with intensifying urgency as a consequence of his sobriety. But he and Petrie's apprentice, a beefy, silent lad named Badger, set to with bellows, tongs, and hammers, and soon the familiar smells and sounds swept Hephaestus away from his and the family's troubles. The best tonic for psychological tension is exacting physical work, and the clubfooted former inventor and drunkard found his body, if not his whole being, remembering the tasks, the touch, and the satisfaction in the exertion, as if he had stepped back into his old life again, like a worn, comfortable set of clothes. He figured if anyone knew the best way to locate a wagon and animals in Independence it would be Petrie, and so he set out to impress his employer with gusto for the job.

Meanwhile, Rapture and Lloyd, who had been entrusted with the family funds, turned their attention to the kinds of nonperishable foodstuffs and basic utensils they would need. Not surprisingly, everything seemed overpriced or of suspect quality. But they had been through so much already that this did not deter them. For mother and son, what had started off as an intimidating and alienating exercise turned into a bonding excursion. The economy of the town ran on a haggling/bartering basis, which worked to the Zanesvilleans' advantage, for with her wits now cleared, Rapture had an arsenal of negotiating resources to draw upon, and with Lloyd's shrewd eyes and his unexpected acuity, the two of them worked well as a team, managing to at least identify and reconnoiter the price of the bulk of what they would require. Shifting into her whitest diction and demeanor, Rapture confused many of the merchants and shopkeepers, as well as the wily street traders. Others, like the Indians and the Spaniards, cared nothing about her ancestry or her plans—they had seen all sorts of people pass through and were concerned only for their own advantage.

Most of their purchases the Sitturds set aside to pick up later and some they arranged to have delivered to the Clutters' doorstep, hoping to time their arrival back at the undertaker's accordingly. Others they garnered some advance intelligence about, with the intention of returning to bargain more force-fully once they had a wagon and were ready to depart. The recognition that they had made it this far bolstered them both in their own ways, and the thrill and doubts about what lay ahead for them on the trail to Texas, and the possibilities of Micah's property and a new life, filled both their heads with a new immediacy—a condition that was reflected in the weather, for the air was rich with the scent of rain.

Their conspiratorial sense of achievement was interrupted (at about the same time that Petrie was offering Hephaestus a cold-meat snack and proposing a price for a wagon and two draft horses that he himself owned) by an altercation in the main street. Mother and son had just dined on a pig-knuckle-and-collards revitalization purchased from an old cook wagon, when their attention was drawn to a row brewing between what looked like a heavyset young miscreant and a hardscrabble muleteer of indeterminate age.

On closer inspection, the muleteer proved to be female, but she had the posture and bearing of a man, and she appeared to have been interrupted in the midst of the same sort of supply-gathering errand they were on. Her hair was cut short under a flat storm-worn felt hat the color of dried blood. She wore the same kind of coat Lloyd had seen on the mail rider who passed through town earlier that morning, but with a store-bought shirt and pipe-leg trousers that contrasted sharply with her mud-flecked boots. There was a perceptible bulge under her coat, and, notwithstanding the straightness of her back, her hips seemed to lean as when a door needs a hinge tightened, so that even just standing she gave the impression of a swagger. Lloyd had never seen a woman with such a masculine aura. Rapture, sensing trouble they did not want to be a part of, pulled her son aside. But she, too, was curious, for the frontierish-garbed woman seemed to show no signs of concern, even as the young ruffian was joined by a foursome of shady comrades, one of whom cradled a bullwhip with a menacing gentleness.

"Hey there, sugar gal," the meaty yokel gibed. "You want some help drinkin' that?" He gave a phlegmy spit in the mud and laughed.

The woman dressed in man's clothing had just added a small crate of what looked like whiskey bottles onto a horse-drawn cart loaded with sacks of rice, flour, and beans. She seemed to be ticking off items against a list in her head, not paying the question any mind. Her face was lined but expressionless, her thin, pointed jaw set, mouth tight-lipped, with a long sprig of chin hair brazenly jutting out. Both the Sitturds gathered that the hulking pupstart had been following her for a while, making increasingly unwanted overtures. There was a feeling of slow-burning animosity to the scene, and the other folk nearby either stopped to gawk or shuffled on faster, heads cast down.

"I need no help, sonny boy, as I've told you. Now get along and go do a man's work."

"Bet you know 'bout that," the boor bellowed. "Look like you piss standin' up!"

His fellows joined in his unsavory mirth. Rapture cringed, feeling a sympathetic twinge of female loyalty and fear. Lloyd wondered where the woman's menfolk were, and why none of the other people around showed any signs of standing up for her. The woman herself showed no sign of alarm—just like Hattie. Only growing annoyance.

"At least I don't need help when I do," the woman replied, and finished stowing and securing the cart without so much as a glance at her provoker.

The Sitturds' stomachs turned at this, for they saw that the men all stepped closer as a ripple of jeers spread around the ring they formed.

"Hey, Josh. I think this bearded lady is sassin' you!" the one with the bullwhip said, chuckling.

"Lady? Shit. Gimme that," the big one called Josh murmured, hawking up another glob of spit, and reaching out for the bullwhip. "I'm Joshua Breed, you trouser-wearer. Do you know who ma pappy is?"

"No," the woman said without a change of expression. "And I'm not surprised that you don't. Your mama probably doesn't, either."

Hoots of malicious cackles and curses stirred around the circle as the onlookers cleared off, and the galumph who had identified himself as Joshua Breed stood fuming—a thick vein in his forehead beginning to throb, as he clutched the whip handle and smoothed out the length in his other hand.

The others were all ribbing him now and egging him on. The Sitturds flinched back against a plank wall. Rapture, who was by nature a feisty woman herself, dared not take a stand without Hephaestus against a group of men such as these. She would just put herself at risk and endanger Lloyd by doing so— but she could not bring herself to turn away, for Lloyd's feet were rooted in place, his young green eyes wide open. Inside his coat, he reached for the Ambassadors' box. A fury was building up inside him—at the cowardice of the other townsfolk, the stupid lugs before him. Why would no one step up to help? From the corner of his eye, he saw that the Ambassadors' carved box was beginning to glimmer.

He could see that there was something about this woman that angered and scared not just the bruisers but the so-called respectable people, too. It was like the resentment and loathing the Quists aroused. He did not understand it, but having been a victim of prejudice and violence himself, he identified with it, and with her.

Against his better judgment about calling attention to himself and his mother, he would step forward to stick up for her. Somehow, he felt as if he were defending his ghost sister—and his beloved Hattie. And Miss Viola. He felt the Eye reaching out to him just as he was reaching for it. Would it work again?

What would happen if he torched the stooges in their tracks right there in the main street? He was torn between putting himself and his mother at risk and doing—at least trying to do—right by this stranger. His joints seemed to lock, and yet he felt his hand open the box, seeking the summoning heat of the cool green sphere—like a crystal of electric judgment. He felt a need to demonstrate the power. A glorious, gluttonous need. It was only this that made him hesitate, a fear of the Eye—a fear that the weapon wanted to use him, or that he wanted to use it for the wrong reason. The terror of all that energy surging through him. What if he ignited himself? How could he summon forth what he did not understand? Perhaps the Eye had rules, secrets. He stifled his grasp, his little boots scuffing at the dried mud where they stood. The box shimmered softly beneath his coat, as if speaking to him in a language he did not comprehend yet which reflected his inner thoughts.

"I saw you ooglin' the dance girl at the Two Dollar the other night," Joshua Breed growled. "We know what kind you are. An' we don't like it."

He raised the whip over his head and then levered down his arm with a jerk, so that the tongue of leather thong lashed out and cracked at the caked mud of a wagon rut beside the hair-chinned woman's feet.

"Stop it!" Lloyd cried, bursting out of his mother's grasp. "Leave her be!"

Rapture was both horrified and proud of her son's boldness, but these emotions gave way to sheer fright. As smart as her son was, he was still an impetuous boy—all too capable of thrusting them into hot water on a sudden impulse. She braced herself for a collision with ugliness.

Lloyd, meanwhile, had secured the box inside his coat, opting not to bring forth the Eye unless forced to. The life experience he had gained away from his parents' attention stood him in better stead than his mother knew. The sight of a small boy, unarmed, standing up to a bunch of grown men, who were well known for such shenanigans, had a galvanizing effect on the other bystanders. Another man, in suspenders and a heavy woolen shirt, picked up a small spade that had been leaning against a keg. He said nothing, but his intention was suggestive. Of course, if anyone had known the power that Lloyd had at his disposal, if he was again able to channel it, there would not have been a person left in the street. But no one knew that and so assumed that the boy was acting out of raw courage.

The surprise at this eruption from a mere child stalled the gang and might have bluffed the others, but for the one called Josh the matter had already gone too far. He gave the impression of every movement being a complicated negotiation between his limbs and his brain, and looked to be the kind of saloon brawler who throws huge haymakers that land only if an opponent happens to be drunker than he is. His face had all the telltale nicks and scars of a lifetime of petty combat, and, like a dog too stupid to stop chasing wagons, he wasn't going to stop now.

He did, however, know how to handle the bullwhip, and he let it fly and smack at Lloyd's feet. The boy saw it coming, as if in a dream, and reached for the box. The death rage was upon him now, a hot green madness, as if the threat of the violence had shut down his reason. The barking snake of leather retreated and the oaf's frame swiveled, whether to strike again in his direction or to attack the woman it was impossible just then to say. It did not matter, for faster than anyone could see, the woman flipped back her coat and whipped from a holster around her waist a Colt revolver. A shot blasted from the long barrel and took the whip clean out of Breed's grasp. He yelped and grabbed his bloodied hand with his other, sagging to his knees. Everyone else stood startled by the weapon. Colt revolvers had been heard about by many but were still rare in those days, and although this had the same lines as the ones that some of the rubberneckers, including Breed and his gang, had seen before, it was also different—some advanced new model. It looked heavy, scientific, and deadly—and the ease with which the rail-post woman wielded it caused a communal stir in the street.

Breed tried to yank something from his own pocket, but the woman nailed him cleanly in the other hand, so that he screamed and pressed the wounded paw between his arm and his ribs in agony and astonishment. Horses bucked and stray dogs ducked under the boardwalk.

"Now, that's just a shame," the woman said without any intonation. "With both hands hurt, you're going to have to get one of your friends to wipe your ass."

One of the men picked up a piece of timber. She shot it in half, one section whacking the man in the temple and knocking him cold. One of the others bolted like a jackrabbit. Another stepped back toward where a group of horses were tethered. He pulled a rifle from a saddle scabbard. As he stood in profile, a shot whizzed past and plucked his belt buckle clean off, dropping his pants to his ankles.

"Know what I'm going to shoot off next?" the woman asked. She pulled a well-chewed cheroot from a breast pocket and popped it in her mouth, savoring it like a fresh stem of grass. Shit-scared, the man dropped his gun and dragged up his pants.

Some people in the street were laughing now, many chuckling and whispering. What was happening to Breed and his boys was something a lot of folks had longed to see. Others had run for cover or were bustling away to either call for help or seek refuge in one of the stores. Lloyd stood still in the same spot where the whip had struck, with his hand on the box under his arm, Rapture frozen in place a few feet away against the wall. Joshua Breed wheezed with hurt and humiliation and regained his feet, his eyes a mix of terror and hatred. He turned, and the Colt cracked again. Now it was his pants that fell, and a round of applause went up from those still in position. Then, flustered and off balance, he tumbled down into the rutted mud, clutching at his guts to make sure they were still in place. The fourth gang member made a move as if to charge, but the woman stood her ground and produced another revolver from beneath her coat, and leveled it at the man's chest, all the time sucking on the old cheroot.

"All right, boys. Who's going to wipe your friend's ass? His hands will be a while healing. I reckon he'll need to have many a squat before then. Or would you like another question? Like who wants to die first?"

This inquiry took everyone off guard. Whether it was the woman's unruffled demeanor or the comical effects she had achieved, up to that moment the thought of a homicidal act had seemed unlikely, despite the lethal force at hand. Of course, there was the potential for something nasty to happen, but she seemed too in control for such a thing. Now her dispassionate mastery sent out a chill in the crowd. Only Lloyd was immune. He in fact felt an obscure kinship with it. Hattie was like that, in her own way.

Breed wriggled on his knees, trying to stand up, his tattered dirty long johns showing, flesh wounds and broken fingers in both hands. There was a rascally, doomed look in his face. All his bluster had been cowed. He more than half believed the woman would shoot him. And a part of him wanted it. To see the glee in some of the surrounding eyes was a fate more horrible than he could have imagined. To have to live with the memory and the constant reminders was more than he thought he could endure. And what would his father say? Portion Breed, reclusive leader of the local renegades—extortionist, horse thief, and reputed murderer, who holed up somewhere along the river and sent his riders venturing out (the old villain himself had not been seen in years) to pilfer the town when need be, plague the settlers, cheat the Indians and Spaniards, and bleed the neighboring country for whatever they could get, appearing in town only in groups of four or more to get drunk, molest the dance girls, and then scoot back to their hiding places until the next foray—oh, to think what his father would say if he saw him now. Josh Breed would have preferred a headshot. But something worse was in store.

"Lad," the woman called, turning her head just enough to address Lloyd. "You're more of a man and a gentleman than anyone else I can see here. And I reckon you've got a score to settle with this dolly dumpling yourself for trying to horsewhip you. Go over to my cart. Down between the groceries you'll find my trusty old cane."

Lloyd darted a glance at his mother, but turned when Rapture hissed at him. He did not think it wise to ignore the woman with the revolvers, and he was curious about the request. He went to her pony cart and rummaged about until he did indeed find a cane, of a kind that reminded him of the insufferable schoolhouse back in Zanesville.

Breed's remaining mates held their ground, one still stretched out in a stupor, the other two trembling in their boots, too afraid to run because the woman was such an accurate shot. No one else had the nerve to say a thing, and the crowd that had re-formed was too amorphous a creature to have any spine, and so gave in to prurience. Just what did this unnatural woman have in mind?

"Is this what you mean?" Lloyd asked, and to everyone watching he seemed much smaller and younger than he really was, sidling between the horse cart and the rough-hewn figure holding the fancy guns without a single quaver in her arms. Where had she come by such novel weapons, and how in blazes had she learned to use them so well? That was the question on everyone's lips. (It would have been phrased rather more caustically by Josh Breed, but the essence was the same.) The poor fool struggled to his feet at last, straining to raise his britches, when the woman squeezed one of the triggers again and clipped a clod in front of him, which sprayed muck on him and sent him sprawling down in a collapse of cursing.

"That's just right." She nodded to Lloyd. "Now, none of you boys have had the stones to answer my question, which surprises me not one bit. You there, Joshua you called yourself? As if I should know or care. Well, my name is Fanny Ockleman—Fast Fanny to you. But once upon a time I used to be a schoolteacher. A terror, they called me when it came to discipline. Do you know what I did with unruly boys? Boys who showed no respect and thought they could bullyrag others?"

The whole street was silent. Even the animals seemed to be listening.

"I caned them, Joshua. I caned their hides for all to see."

Hoots and catcalls went up around the gathering, and various children and stragglers dashed down the planks to spread the word. Joshua Breed had lost his pants and his wits and was going to get a whuppin' by a gun-totin' woman with a good start on a beard. Oh, this was too sweet to miss!

But the woman who called herself Fanny Ockleman did not take the cane switch from Lloyd, but instead directed him over toward the hapless Breed, who groveled in the mud. The trail buddy farthest away hightailed it off like a bleating goat. The other one, who had dropped the rifle, made a lunge for it, and had it shot from his grasp, so that the butt splintered and cut his face. He groped for his trousers and pivoted to flee in one motion—but the next shot forced him to dive for a horse trough, which he splashed into like a sack of corn heaved from a wagon, producing a roar of laughter from the spectators.

The news had reached the attention of what passed for the law in town, but, still reeling from the events of the previous night, with one of his deputies having been among the blinded vigilantes, and no love for the Breeds, who more or less ruled the vicinity, the so-called sheriff was not quick to try to assert authority now. Josh Breed knew that, with his friends on the run or incapacitated, he could not count on any help that would come in time. He peered up through bloodshot eyes and saw the little boy he had threatened with the whip striding toward him with the cane.

"Son," Fanny intoned, lowering her guns. "I want you to give that blowhard a good licking. Five of the finest you can deliver. And one more for good measure."

"You bitch!" Breed screamed, clawing at the mud with bullet-grazed mitts—desperate to scramble upright and grab for Lloyd all at once. He wanted to bite that blasted woman's throat out. But he did not even manage to make it up to his haunches before Fanny had grazed his shin with another bullet, just as she had meant to do. Breed plopped forward, facedown in the street, his long-johnned rear end exposed now to Lloyd and the upraised cane.

"You know what to do," Fanny called to Lloyd across the street, and expertly spat a full three feet without losing her cheroot. "Five of the best you can give, and one more to make the memory sore."

While all this had been happening, Rapture had been beside herself with worry for Lloyd, and now to see him actively engaged gave her a rushing sense of disorientation, not unlike what she had experienced when the odd music box was opened back at the Clutters'. She saw him once again as utterly remote from her. He seemed to fit into the scene before her like a piece of puzzle slotted into position, and the thought filled her heart with dread. There was something monstrous in him that she could not accept as having come from inside herself. Truly, he seemed more the child of this man-witch, who had brought the beasts of the frontier village under her spell with an eerily composed violence of the kind that is not learned easily and was somehow invested with an authority far beyond the ken of the shopkeepers and malingerers there to witness it. The sky had gone jet-black over half the town, a harsh religious flare of sun striking a gunmetal edge along the running sheet of storm cloud. Rapture prayed that the lightning would come and disperse the gathering. But it did not come quite in time.

Lloyd stood above the prostrate figure of Joshua Breed, wounded, humbled, defenseless now. The boy saw in his mind the way the tough had directed the whip at him. One pass to scare, the next to smart. Every taunt and insult he had ever been subject to came back to him. The harassers of Zanesville. The robbers along the road. The devil in the lane in St. Louis.

He felt again those meat-slab hands on his slender hips. The excruciating agony of the penetration . . . the reaming . . . like an auger in a summer melon. The boar-heavy grunting . . . and the high-pitched laughter. The stench of the dung cart. And the smack of the spittle the beast let loose on the granite cobblestone when he was done with his desecration. It all came back. Everyone who had ever angered or abused him. The brats who had sabotaged his shrine to his sister, the pig who had tortured his beloved Hattie. He would repay all the evil debts, and he slashed down through the air with the cane, slicing across the filthy long johns with a fiendish sense of release and power. Again and again he struck, as the creature before him howled and squirmed. The force he felt in his little arm was like unto the wave of energy that had radiated through him from the Eye. His sense of time and the street scene around him blurred. There was just the thrashing joy of his vengeance, intoxicating him like a drug. Where before he had always had to outsmart his enemies—or use the Eye—to unleash some demonic force that had amazed him as much as his victims, here he was enjoying the animal truth of physical aggression and he gorged on it, whaling on the vulnerable idiot without mercy. He did not hear the call of Fanny Ockleman or his mother. He did not hear the thunder rumbling like a hundred laden wagons. He did not hear the cries of Joshua Breed, who had soiled his underwear at the second shot and was now bleeding across his exposed buttocks.

It was not the rain that came in bullet-size drops which finally awakened him again to himself and his actions. Nor was it that he had felt himself becoming erect upon raising the cane the second time—the blood-hot thrill of revenge firing through his whole body, seeking outlet in his loins, while the whine of the sturdy strand and the sharp bite on the exposed ass was the ultimate sign of surrender and an invitation to torture. No.

It was something else. Something other.

They appeared on the periphery of his vision, standing in a line in the street, which no one else seemed to take any notice of. He in fact did not notice them visually at first at all. He was animally aware of them before sighting them. Even then, he did not feel that he saw them, but more that they allowed him to become aware of them where others were not.

There were six women—or so he thought—all dressed in pristine white ruffled dresses. They were as clear as anything could be, and yet somehow seemed veiled, remote. At first, he would have said they reminded him of Mother Tongue. But their dresses were stark and formal, and seemed not to be *worn* by them, exactly, but more by parts of them—as if they were inside some sort of armor, wedded to it the way St. Ives was joined with his hand.

Beyond the inexplicable cleanliness of their attire, given the environment, there was about them a summoning grimness that called to mind the gossiping biddies who had so plagued his and the family's life back in Zanesville—the sharp-tongued shrews who hid behind hoopskirts, complaining shawls, and what passed for women's stovepipe hats in those days, matronly old skullcaps tied with ribbons under the chin, only frilly and without color. The instant he was conscious of them, they filled him with a new kind of malice and unease. Abhorrence. Aversion.

No ensemble could have been less intimidating at a glance, not relative to the night thugs he had faced off against with the Eye. But that was not what his instinct told him. It screamed out to him a very contrary message.

These were ones who did not fear the Eye. These were one.

They stood not just in a line but in a plane of vision, or at least perception. There was a dimensionality to them that both seeped forward toward him and receded backward, making it seem that the very depth of field of reality—the essential fabric and framework of the street—had been fundamentally altered.

The second he thought that—as he looked closer—he saw to his unspeakable and unreasonable, shrinking apprehension that they all had the exact same face. It was not a mask, in any sense of abstraction or caricature, but it was not eccentric, individual, and animate, either. It was a face like none he had seen before, even on the nags of Zanesville—repeated, separate yet combined. Blurred. Merged.

Yes, that was what the impression was like. Six figures sharing a single face, so that it was impossible to determine if there were six figures or one.

But he heard a multiplicity of voices. Not, just six—oh, no.

They did not move—they did not have to. He heard them calling to him inside his own head. *Beat him,* they called. *Beat him! Release your hatred . . .*

"That's enough!" Fanny cried, and fired one of the revolvers into the air, as the storm broke and people scattered.

Lloyd dropped the cane, leaving Joshua Breed groveling in the mud, bleeding and soiled, whimpering like the dog the day before.

The six white women with the single face were gone, dissolved in the downpour as if they had never been.

CHAPTER 7
Something in Between

THE SIGHT OF LLOYD MERCILESSLY WHIPPING THE WOUNDED rouster at last spurred Rapture to action. She raised her skirt hem and dashed through the deluge to wrench her son out of his trance. The few items they had purchased she left behind in the streaming rain, dragging the boy along the mud-strewn boardwalk in a huffing flurry of anger and alarm until they reached the relative safety of the Clutters' once more.

She did not look behind her to see the gun-toting Fanny Ockleman shaking her head at the boy's performance. She did not see the sharpshooter stow her revolvers, adjust her hat, and stride over to retrieve the cane as if the sun were shining brightly and the most extraordinary event that had transpired had been the boy's vented fury. Rapture was too busy trying to master the shame and chagrin that had replaced her pride and concern when her son stepped forward.

Lloyd, meanwhile, was beside himself with fascination and embarrassment. The excitation that had arisen inside him was like no other he had ever experienced—a sickening, insatiable lust and release beyond any he had known before. The entire world had been eclipsed in the heat of it. There was only his hunger, his will being fulfilled to the grotesque exclusion of all other senses. And the disquietude of the six watchers.

Were these what the Vardogers looked like? Or had it been a projection of their insidious science?

I wonder if I saw what I did because they wanted me to see it or because of how I felt? he thought.

Strangely enough, the very brutality of his performance drew a very different response from what his mother had anticipated. Racing back to the Clutters' soaking wet, struggling with what she could carry and still mind Lloyd, Rapture assumed that all the items they had abandoned would either be stolen or spoiled by the rain. Not so. What she had not counted on was that the Breed gang, and slobbish Josh in particular, had long been a source of fear and local hatred. While the Bushrod Rangers comprised members who were respected at least in quarters of the community, no one would have spoken in favor of Portion Breed and his son's confederates if they could avoid it, and for once it seemed they could. Perhaps things were going to change for the better around Independence.

So what if little Lloyd had whacked the tar out of Josh? The younger Breed had had it coming since he was that size and then some. The target that had apparently been chosen by chance gave the Sitturd whelp a line of credit to draw upon, and, ironically, the same child and his family who had been hounded out of Zanesville for using the native powers of his brain was now applauded and even lionized by the townsfolk of this Missouri outpost for unleashing some inner force of al- most meditative violence. Rapture could only shake her head in wonder as, one by one, the items she had cast behind them re- turned, supplemented with more store-bought things, hand- made items, food stocks, and provisions of all kinds. No one asked any questions about where the family was headed; it was just assumed somewhere west. People gave in the way that no tithing box had ever known, and when Hephaestus hobbled home after his first partial but still honest day's work in as long as he could remember, he was startled to find his young son a hero again, his wife speechless, and the coffin-crowded shop front of the lackluster carpenter and rather keen embalmer Othimiel Clutter and his wife overflowing with things that the Sitturds would desperately need to reach their destination.

It was several minutes before Rapture could find the words to suggest more than explain what had transpired, and even then her limping husband limped far behind in his comprehension. The rain had cleared off again, the sun was near set, and the hint of a slow damp that would later rise from the ground could be smelled like distant cookstoves and the still prevalent atmosphere of the previous night's questionable repast. With all the purchased and donated booty, they went inside the residential part of the shop front to reunite with their idiosyncratic and previously debilitated hosts—and then had an even greater shock.

Rapture, when she had been able to get past the family's trials of the day, had thought it not out of the question that the older couple might remain in bed all day, and that perhaps their behavior of the morning had its explanation not in inebriation but in some illness, perhaps even some emerging disease of the mind—a mutual senility, for that was what it had so resembled.

When she courteously knocked on the humble door that separated the shop front and business premises from the living area in the rear of the building, it gave her a queasy reminder of Mr. Clutter manically tapping on his coffin lids. There was still the strong presence of last night's dinner oozing under the door, but there was something else, too. A scent of premonition. When she got no response, she eventually opened the door—and then the horror was there for all the family to see.

The kitchen, which Rapture had left so neat and tidy, was a shambles of destruction, as if raccoons had broken in and torn the place apart. Pots and pans had been flung everywhere, the hearth piled with smashed crockery. What was more, every single music box had not just been swept from its resting place on the shelves but slammed to the floor and cracked open, their inner workings gouged out. The Sitturds croaked as one—and then discovered the couple.

"Dear God!" Hephaestus cried.

Mr. and Mrs. Clutter had indeed managed to rise from bed, and apparently had done much more. Inside what passed for their little bedroom, the bed had been demolished, their simple nightstands collapsed, candles snapped, pillows ripped to shreds. The devastation could not have been more complete, except for one old stick-back chair, which the couple still occupied. Both bodies were naked and entwined together in an obscene contortion. Any fear the Sitturds had that the couple had been the victims of some intruder's violence was incontrovertibly dispelled by the fact that the Clutters—still sexually connected, or so it seemed—both had their teeth and jaws locked deep in the blood-soaked throat of the other. The frozen expression on their dead, stained faces was beyond all words.

The Sitturd adults were so stricken with sickness and terror that they forgot to try to cover Lloyd's eyes. It was just as well, for Lloyd alone remained cool enough to examine the scene. That was what Hattie would have done.

Hephaestus, as hardened as he was to normal farm life and the facts of death that presented themselves in slaughtering and butchering, felt the food that Petrie had offered him earlier in the day roar up his pipes and onto the floor. Rapture, meanwhile, was certain the room was rife with evil "sperits" and flittered about like a wounded animal.

Lloyd, on the other hand, as revolted as he was, and as agitated as he was, was also enlivened, his senses brought to full attention. *Beat him, beat him. Release your hatred.*

There was something very important about this scene, he knew. Although the natural first thought was to shudder and look if not run away, his instincts told him to look more deeply, to savor and consider every detail that presented itself. There was a meaning to all this, and perhaps he was the only one to discover it.

The obvious fact that the Clutters had been the cause of each other's death suggested that there had not been any dread invasion. There were no signs of forced entry. The back door remained secure. The front shop was undisturbed and all the Sitturds' possessions were unmolested. Whatever had happened, it seemed, had been confined to the back area of the premises and had, at least to the eye, involved the old people alone. Who else had been present, if no one else had arrived?

While his parents comforted each other and tried to regain control of themselves, and rein in their mixed distaste and grief for their hosts and their now runaway panic about what this catastrophe might mean for them, Lloyd circulated through the establishment searching for clues. There was no mud at the entry to the shop, and the place looked as if it had not been open for business all day, which was probably not an unusual occurrence. If the back door was still bolted and all the windows were unopened, he thought it likely that no one else had intervened. And why would someone come to call with such intentions, and arrive in either calm or stealth and then wreak such destruction? Given the dismantled state of the rear interior, it seemed a telling point that the opportunities of exit and entry were still intact.

Then there was the inescapable matter of the two old folk having bitten each other's throat out! Even the most ruthless and bloodthirsty of invaders would not have been able to force the couple into the position in which they were found. What threat could have been used that would have been worse than the result? It was not as if the Clutters had been bludgeoned or even tortured in some conventionally murderous way. On every level, this seemed to him an intimate matter and, however demented and bestial, there was some dark, inner logic at work.

The more he looked around, the more immune to the horror

Lloyd became. Patterns began to form. He saw that the crockery and the kitchenware had not been piled or pounded apart for their own sake. It looked . . .

"It looks like the plates and pots were used . . . as weapons," he said to himself.

That suggested that the Clutters *had* been attacked—whether from without, in some as yet unknown way, or in the form of some delusion that had taken hold of them.

An intruder of the mind had been floating in his thoughts ever since the family returned. After all, the couple had been strongly affected by their exposure to the music box. And the white-dressed women in the street . . .

Lloyd started pawing through the wreckage, searching for the Vardogers' box. It was altogether possible, he granted, that some malevolent presence had chosen this particular moment to return and retrieve this strange treasure. But no, it, too, was on the floor. Alone of all the music boxes, it was unopened and on the surface unharmed. He knew what he had to do.

Very quietly, so that his parents could not hear, he spoke the password and waited, steeled to snap the lid shut before the sinister, enchanting music could start. To his amazement, when the lid opened no music began and he saw that the tiny artificial musicians were all gone. The box was as bare as one of the Clutters' overturned kitchen drawers. He ran his right index finger along the edges and across the floor of it just to make sure there were no tricks—but the box was empty.

It was possible, he reasoned, that some external agent had come in and absconded with the miniature mechanical orchestra, but he felt that anyone who would have known about the contents of the box would not have needed or bothered to violate all the others. And why would they leave the box? Still more curiously, such a robbery—if that was how it could be described—did not explain the barbaric fate the old people had endured. Nothing he could think of did. He had half-formed theories and intuitions, but nothing that would stay fixed.

"We must separate and examine the bodies," he said, more to himself than to his parents.

Hephaestus felt his partially digested food rise into his throat again. It was discomfiting enough to have their young son witness such depravity—there was, of course, no way to keep it from him now—but to have him so rationally investigating the matter was almost more than he could take. Then something in the wayward blacksmith's mind clicked over. It was in the boy's tone of native authority, but it was also an internal conviction of his own. His son knew and understood things he did not. There could be no pretending anymore. All his life since the boy's birth had been in some way spent denying his offspring's special intelligence, fearing it, resenting it, feeling proud about it—or worrying where it would lead. Hephaestus saw that, if nothing else, it had led to this. *This* was where they all were, still together as a family, still alive—and, with any luck, able to extricate themselves from this gruesome predicament and get back on their way. If Lloyd's intellect was a means to that end, then so be it. As peculiar as he was, he was flesh and blood.

The lame blacksmith found a new personal strength with this recognition and, without any sense of humbling himself or taking an order from his own son, he did just as the boy instructed. He rose and respectfully but firmly wrenched the two rigor forms apart, laying them down on the floor beside the chair for further investigation. That pieces of the bodies burst apart at this maneuver was not pleasant to observe, but still he kept his tongue, even as the Clutters lost theirs.

Then something happened that even Lloyd was not prepared for. Portions of flesh peeled away to reveal not only organ and bone—not even organ and bone—but something truly unexpected. The inner anatomy the separation of the corpses revealed was not human. It was not animal. It was not organic. Nor was it mechanical—or like any machine he had ever seen.

If the Sitturds had gasped before, they swooned together

now, for what they beheld was absolutely alien to everything they knew and counted on. The dithery older couple they had met the previous night, who seemed incapable of normal conversation and had such unusual notions about food—who had, in the time the family was gone, undergone such a dramatic transformation, becoming both mindlessly violent and lustful—were not people at all.

Rapture cawed. Hephaestus reached up to seize locks of hair on his head that were fifteen years gone. Even Lloyd's mouth dropped.

"They're . . . some kind of . . ." his father tried.

"They're music boxes," Lloyd replied, after a moment's aching silence. "They looked like people. They acted like people—to a point. But they were really music boxes in disguise."

"Music boxes!" his mother moaned. "How ya bee speaken that?"

"I don't mean like the others." Lloyd waved, indicating the mess of combs and needles pouring forth from the ruptured boxes on the floor. "I mean more like the one that so confused us last night."

"Which one was that?" his father huffed.

Lloyd's right eyebrow rose at this.

"The one it may be fortunate that you don't remember. What I mean is that they were—or are—machines. Not like machines we have ever seen. But not human. See those fibers there? What are they? Glass, spun very fine? And what of that there? That's no organ that we know. It's not quite meat and it's not quite metal. It's something in between. And that's what they were. Something in between."

"But how can it be?" Hephaestus gurgled, clasping his head in his hands for comfort.

"I don't know," Lloyd conceded. "But I am certain these . . . folk . . . were not born. They were made. Made to look like people and pass for people."

"B-but Petrie!" Hephaestus stammered. "They're his kin!"

"He may have had kin. He may think these are still his kin. But they aren't," Lloyd answered. "Unless he's like this, too."

"No!" his father insisted. "I worked with the man all day. He was straight, he was quick. He was—"

"Normal?"

"Y-yes." Hephaestus nodded, working through in his own mind a host of associations and perceptions. "N-normal."

"Then that raises the proposition that he doesn't know about this," Lloyd reasoned. "Which is supported by the fact that he recommended we try to stay here. Did he say anything about them? Anything that might hint at a change in them and their lives?"

Hephaestus had to turn and stroke his chin at this.

"Well, now that you mention it . . . he did let on something. Once he saw I could do a good day's work for him, honest and expert-like, he did say something at the end. What was it? Ah . . . he said he was glad that we were about to keep a fresh eye on them. That's what he said—a fresh eye."

"What did you take that to mean?" Lloyd asked.

"I'm not sure," his father mused. "He'd said earlier that there'd been a change in them—the both of them. But he didn't say how or what."

"Did he say when?"

"Hmm. Not directly. At least I don't think. I was busy working then. I got the impression it was about a year or so ago. I don't know why."

"That would put it sometime around when the man with the music boxes and the child he wanted embalmed came past," Lloyd put forth.

"What that mean ya be speaken now?" his mother demanded.

"I don't know," Lloyd admitted, shaking his young head. "But I know we must leave here as soon as we can. Within the hour. Whatever the Clutters were, they weren't done in by men with masks and cudgels. But they were attacked, whether from without or within." He deeply regretted that there would not be time to circulate through town and remove the reward posters for Hattie.

"But if they were just machines—" His father sighed.

"I don't think we should ever use the word 'just' about machines anymore," Lloyd replied. "They are—or were—not machines we understand, and there were other machines here that are not here now. The two issues must be connected."

"What othern maysheens?" his mother asked, sobbing now.

"Don't trouble about them now," Lloyd consoled her. "We need to be on the move. As you said, Farruh, we need to look alive—to stay alive."

"Is they after you—dem folks from St. Louis?"

This was the first time any such thing had been mentioned in Hephaestus's sober presence, and his faced showed it. Lloyd spoke his mind.

"It may be, and it may not. I think not. If they were to come, whoever they are, I believe there would be no mistaking it—and they would come for me. This is something else. It may be connected by chance, if there is such a thing. But . . ." and then he could not think.

"What yer sperit voice say?" his mother asked at last, putting into her old and often suppressed family speech the same suddenly accepted confidence that Hephaestus had arrived at in his own way.

Lloyd felt the momentousness of the change in the family dynamic and paused to weigh his words in respect for the new weight that had been openly placed upon his young shoulders. His rarefied mind rummaged through the shattered dishware and gaping flesh for some answer that would satisfy his own flesh and blood enough to get them all out of there. Fast.

"We were not the intended victims of this—if it be a crime," he said. "But there is something about our presence here, and our (and he really meant his own) ability to see this as something outside experience, that must be heeded. How, I'm not yet sure. There is something larger happening in this country than we ever imagined back in Zanesville. Whether we can run from it, and truly get away, or come to understand it remains to be seen. But we can't ignore it, and more than ever I feel we must get to our destination in Texas as quickly as we can. Uncle Micah has already warned and inspired us that something out of the ordinary awaits us there. It was our leaving Zanesville and our old lives that set in motion the wheels that have brought us here—to both this place and this new, unlikely world. We can but go forward, and now we have to do so with the greatest haste."

"So you think we are in danger, real danger?" Hephaestus queried.

"I think," Lloyd said, with a face on him that was far too old for his years, "that just as we must put behind us old ideas about machines—even my ideas about machines (and this remark completed the familial acknowledgment of the change that had occurred)—we need to be prepared for danger wherever we look. From now on, danger is always real. Even unreal danger. Especially the unreal."

CHAPTER 8

Dead of Night

HEPHAESTUS HAD NO IDEA WHAT LLOYD WAS SAYING, AND YET HE understood that what was called for now was belief in his son. The failed inventor had sobered up inside himself at the deepest level.

"The Clutters have two horses and a wagon they used as a hearse," he announced. "Petrie told me. I think I heard them out back. They may not get us all the way to Texas, but they'll get us out of here. When any kind of word gets out about this, we'll be in strife. People will think somehow we done this. Whether these be the real Clutters or no, locals will need to make sense of things."

Lloyd nodded.

"These are the Clutters that Petrie knew. And what happened to them may have something to do with our arrival. But we aren't to blame and we won't be burned for it if we keep our heads."

"We takem wib us and give 'em proper beerial," Rapture said.

"That's right," Lloyd agreed. "We take everything with us, we get a head start. Then anyone who wants to know more has got to find us, and they have no proof of anything being wrong."

"Let's load up the coffin first," Hephaestus suggested. "The way these folk lived, we might get a couple of days or even more before they're missed. Even Petrie said he hadn't had a meal or a jaw with them in weeks."

Over the course of the next hour the Sitturd family worked in a frenzy of divided labor. Once Lloyd had indicated that he was finished examining the wreckage in the back area, Rapture set about gathering up all the broken, scattered bits into a neat pile. Hephaestus went out to inspect the wagon and the horses. "These animals have got to be real," he said to himself when he found them and had lit a lantern. "If they were machines, they'd look better." Both animals were desperately skinny, which seemed to fit in with everything the family had learned about the couple. "Perhaps they didn't know any better," Hephaestus reasoned.

While his mother was cleaning up and his father was giving the horses a feed and preparing the hearse, Lloyd completed his analysis of the bodies. In addition to the obvious mortal indignity they appeared to have inflicted on each other, he noted odd puncture wounds and gouges in their feet and legs, as well as on their hands. A couple of samples of their innards, some of which seemed organic and were already decomposing as the black dog in the street had, as well as some pieces of what were clearly manufactured workings of an intricate, complex nature, he placed in a bag that he found in the kitchen. Along with the now empty Vardogers' music box, he tucked all his findings away with the Eye, the Ambassadors' box, Hattie's fetish, and his uncle's map and letter.

Beyond the fatal wounds, the aspect of the corpses that he found most puzzling was discovered only when he pried open their mouths to find shards of comb and bent metal, as if in their delusional fever the couple had taken to eating the contents of the music boxes they snapped open. How very curious, Lloyd thought, remembering the ravenous hunger that had overtaken them all before.

When he combined this phenomenon with the ravaged interior of the living quarters and the position and unmistakable nature of the activity the bodies had been engaged in, he was forced to conclude that the Clutters had undergone some rabid confluence of animal cravings and instinctive behavior. Gluttony, fear, violence, lust, bloodlust. That machines of any kind could experience these states and needs was startling. But all at once? "Perhaps that's just the way it would be," Lloyd mused, not at all sure he knew what he was thinking.

Once Hephaestus had the horses hitched and the wagon ready, he returned to help Rapture and Lloyd load the two bodies and the miscellany of demolished kitchenware, music boxes, and household items into one of the larger coffins. It was only because the bodies were beginning to soften and break apart that they were able to stuff everything that needed to be disposed of in the one box. All three Sitturds helped lug the coffin out back and onto the hearse.

They fed themselves with what decent food they could find and then began hauling the goods they hoped to take with them. It was frustrating that many things would not fit with the coffin in position on the wagon, which, of course, needed to remain easy to unload. They could have managed everything if they had chosen to take the coffin and bury it first and then return to load their things, but no one in the family thought this was a good idea. Better to be seen by as few people as possible. Two trips would increase their vulnerability.

By the time they were ready to depart, it was close to midnight. In one sense this was good, because it meant fewer people would be abroad. However, it would also make their errand more suspicious if they encountered anyone—and, as Lloyd had learned the other night, anyone who was out at that time was far more likely to be a threat. But there was nothing to be done about that now.

Once more the Sitturds found themselves stealing away, hoping to avoid the detection of prying eyes. The difference this time was that all three were united in alertness, the bond of family stronger for the trials they had survived.

ENIGMATIC PILOT | 339

They were on the southwestern side of the town, so extricating themselves from the community was somewhat easier, given that this was the direction they were heading in. Nevertheless, they had intended to leave at first light, with full supplies and the best maps they could acquire. As it was, they had a compass, one of the large-scale maps used by the mail riders, a small duck gun, and a waxing moon swathed in clouds. With any luck, thought Hephaestus, the clouds will hold until we clear town and then break and give us some help.

The road was still muddy, but the Clutters' emaciated horses seemed relieved to have made their escape from the funeral parlor and found an effort their sorry frames would not have indicated they could deliver. Their pace was slow, because the Sitturds wanted to make as little noise as possible without at the same time appearing to be sneaking. Their senses were sharp and their breathing was shallow. They saw a man snoring drunk beside a hogshead, which gave Hephaestus a prick of conscience, because he realized that this was what he must have looked like often in the past.

The dwindling aroma of a savory stew drifted out of a makeshift boardinghouse, so unlike the fare they had been inflicted with at the Clutters'. The whole sordid scene passed through their minds again, but passed through Lloyd's the fastest. He was ruminating on the music box he had plundered. He could not imagine not having taken it—it was too tempting a prize not to want to examine further, even though it was empty. And that was the thing that troubled him, although he could not say why. Did having something of the enemy's—if that was indeed what the Vardogers were—strengthen their position or weaken it? He did not like to think he carried with him something that might endanger his family further.

The frail horses hauling the overloaded wagon squished along in the hardening mud as the clouds thinned and the moon broke through. By the time they were past the edge of the town proper, they had counted just two figures they knew had seen them. One was an Indian smoking a long store-bought pipe, leaning up against his dozing horse as if there were nothing more natural than using your horse as a pillow—as at home as he would have been a hundred miles away in prairie grass.

Lloyd wished that he understood more about the Indians and their ways. He had known things about those closer to home in Zanesville, like King Billy, but in the family's travels since, he seemed to have been cut off from any close contact. He had seen many, but they were more like parts of the landscape. Even by moonlight, it frustrated him not to be able to intuit more about the man. How far away did he live? What was his tribe, his language, the magic he believed in? Lloyd had already come to understand something that eludes or deceives many: everyone believes in a kind of magic, though it may go by other names. "I hope my life has more to do with Indians," he told himself as they creaked past.

The other denizen of Independence to confront them was a dog, which at first made them all wary, because they were afraid it would bark and call notice to them. There was also not far in the back of all their minds the image of the black savage that had shredded the Spaniard's dog in the street. But this dog seemed to be normal. Curious but not vicious. Scruffy, of no particular breed, it began to tag along behind them, tempting Hephaestus to load the duck gun.

Lloyd observed his father's annoyance and said, "It's all right, Farruh. Maybe he needs to leave town, too."

The lame man sent out more energy through his arms into the reins. His son was right again. They had much more to worry about than stray dogs. And what were they if not stray dogs themselves? "You can't blame a critter for wanting company," Hephaestus told himself, his eyes ferreting through the moon shadows, hoping for some sign of the mail track on the outskirts.

They were a long time finding it, and then getting far enough down it to think of veering off—someplace they could get the wagon to so as to bury the remains of the Clutters in as much privacy as they could manage. Along the way they passed a couple of buckboards and simple farm wagons with canvas shells trying to be houses large enough to contain a ragtag of families and animals. It gave them all a little hope that their designs were no more foolish than many folk's, torn between old lives and new. They also passed a large Spanish camp under some chestnuts. Here the fires were still burning—the scent of food and scheming. "Spaniards never seem to sleep," Lloyd said to himself. "Perhaps I should become a Spaniard."

Finally, they found themselves far enough away from Independence to consign the remains of the Clutters to earth and to heaven—if such in-between beings were allowed into heaven. There was a grove of trees off the track, which was becoming less a road and more tall grass with a seam running through. As far into the grove as they dared to venture, and as close in as they could get with the wagon and the now exhausted horses, they set about the strenuous task of digging a grave deep enough to hide the coffin.

All three Sitturds pitched in. The heavy rain that had softened the earth made the back-aching work somewhat easier, but not much. It was a good hour of team excavation before an acceptable depth was achieved. At some point, they each recalled poor old Tip back in Ohio—and the Time Ark. Rapture's heart wandered further back in time to the stillborn body of Lodema, while Lloyd thought of his cove of wind charms and the slave cemetery across the river from St. Louis, where Schelling had taken him to meet Mother Tongue. Hephaestus remembered vague flashes of his drunken sprees in the shantylands, and how he had once passed out in a graveyard, and very well might have remained if not for the grace of chance and the love of his family. It struck them all that every camp is made amid graves. It is just unknown who lies buried.

It was with this welter of woe and anxiety that they at last completed their morbid mission. The horses were refreshed from the respite—slightly. To be able to push on past sunrise seemed hard. That would leave them still too close to Independence for comfort. Not being able to talk above a whisper and share concerns made the anxiety grow. A damp mist was beginning to rise, which was unsettling to see and unpleasant to feel, and the shambling gait of the horses seemed to herald some imminent breakdown, when around a stand of broken trees and heavy bracken they heard a sound that brought their hearts up into their mouths. It was not an animal sound, like a wild pig or a coyote. It was not a human sound, but it made the duck gun they were carrying seem as useful as a feather duster.

"E' Gawd love!" Rapture exclaimed, too loud for the male Sitturds' liking, for out of the patchy mist the beast noise rose as if in response. It was followed by the yelp of a dog—the mutt that had tagged along with them must have slunk out ahead of them, as dogs liked to do, Lloyd reasoned. Now the poor wayfarer had flushed some savage creature out of the underbrush and was about to become a meal. Or was something lying in wait for them?

All their mutual fears forced them to freeze. The moon swam out from behind what was left of the clouds, and the sky above the low road fog sharpened into cold clarity—the intensification of the light revealing the silhouette of something like a man, and something a little too much like a bear for their liking. The thing seemed to recognize its greater visibility and made a gesture that demonstrated a fierce desire both for confrontation and for greater camouflage.

Both inclinations were thwarted in a strangely comic fashion when the creature rushed forward, to be dragged back and to fall with a thump, as if it had run to the end of a length of chain. The next thing, which to Lloyd's and Rapture's minds at least, was the most unexpected of all was that a familiar voice rose out of the darkness. "Hey there, Senator," it said. "Don't fret now. I knew they were comin' for the last half hour."

It was Fast Fanny Ockleman, the gunwoman they had met

on the main street earlier in town. The unmistakable ramrod shadow strode up out of the gloom about ten paces away from where the creature had appeared, and which now had returned to an upright but crouched position, making a low, threatening sound that was somewhere between an ursine growl and some kind of protective chant.

In the moonlight, Lloyd could see that she had one of her newfangled guns drawn, but she approached with no hint of alarm and seemed to step through the thigh-high mist to meet them with the grace of an Indian, just as casually as she had greeted the outnumbered situation with Joshua Breed and his hooligans. I wonder if anything scares her, Lloyd thought, before turning his mind to what she was doing out in the wild, awake and alert, at such a time of night.

"You folks'll have to be right quieter if you expect to get where you're goin', and travelin' at this hour is for those who have to or know how. I take it you have to."

"Who . . . is that?" Hephaestus gasped, almost dropping the reins.

The weary horses had snapped awake at the first hint of the creature's presence. Perhaps if there had been a breeze they would have known about the brute long before. In any case, they were nervous and distraught now.

"Tid be now a long tale tru," Rapture muttered, not wanting even to think about the incident back in town.

"I am the best shadow you'll meet in these parts tonight," Fast Fanny replied. Nearby, Lloyd thought that he could make out a group of shelters tucked away, hidden by both branch and mist.

"We weren't wanting to meet any shadows a'tall," the elder Sitturd replied.

"Best not to venture by moonshine then," the woman answered.

"What's that . . . animal?" Lloyd called, unable to help himself.

"Hush there, boy," Fanny returned. "Other folks are trying to sleep, and you don't want to be stirring up Senator again. I'll be to sunup getting him peaceful and he'll be a sack of possums all day on the trail. Now follow me, with a lid on your questions. I can give you a place to bunk for a bit, and come a brighter hour you can make a better plan than the one you got."

"You know this woman?" Hephaestus demanded.

"Aye that," Rapture assented, not wanting to say more.

"And you trust . . . her?"

"Yes," Lloyd answered decisively, still curious about the teth-ered creature, which was quite obviously of the same mind re-garding them.

Hephaestus took stock. They had just fled civilization, well before their preparations were complete, to embark on the most difficult leg of their entire journey, having witnessed some kind of nightmare magic that had beset their hosts, then buried the evidence of the atrocity in an unmarked grave on the edge of what was to them real wilderness, with the possible charge of murder hanging over their heads, and maybe even more serious trouble awaiting them if anything like what his son had hinted about was true. In this mix of moonlight and mist, the idea of following a total stranger—a woman who looked like a man and who wielded a kind of gun that he had never seen before, and had some kind of monster animal, no less—seemed if not rea-sonable to him, then at least possible and maybe even advis-able.

Fanny led them around the stand of trees to two wagons, one of them large and of odd design, and several improvised struc-tures, which Lloyd recognized as Indian-style tepees made of animal hides supported by wooden frames. The rest of the camp, whoever they were, seemed to be asleep, except for a short, stocky man who had been leaning against a wagon wheel with a large cudgel on his knees. He got to his feet when Fanny gave a tight whistle.

"Who's this now?" he whispered.

"At first light," Fanny replied, as if to say no more would be said until then.

She ushered the Ohioans into a squat tepee pitched in the lee of the larger wagon and ducked her head in when the family had straggled through the slit.

"I'll unhitch your horses and give them some feed. We don't have much for our own, let alone yourn. But they'll get some rest. We rise early and we'll be on the trudge earlier than usual. I reckon you should do the same. But take a load off now. Whatever called you out on the move at such an hour won't have an easy time making worry for you for a few hours at least. Now, no questions till birdsong. Get as much shut-eye as you can."

Suddenly, the hardened woman was gone, and the Sitturds were left in deeper bewonderment than ever, but more than a little grateful not to have been attacked by the beast or waylaid by dark men with even darker designs. All three were bone-fagged and brain-sore, and still coming to terms with the crazed events of the day. Lloyd felt particularly bleary, since he had not slept more than an hour the previous night owing to his encounter with the Quists and the Bushrod Rangers.

Something in the performance with the Eye had drained him, he felt, and perhaps had also energized him in some new way, which he considered might account for the spell that had overcome him when caning Josh Breed. He had no explanation for the women in white. Then the shock of finding the Clutters, and all the questions their grisly situation called forth! It was all such a jumble, and yet he sensed that just to the edge of his mind's sight was an explanation that brought it all together. The hint of it toyed with him for a while, as he lay clutching his bag of precious items on the hard bedroll in the skin-smelling tepee that kept the night damp at bay.

For a few moments he listened to his parents' emphatic whispering, trying to clear his head—trying to feel the protective presence of Lodema and to imagine where his beloved Hat-

tie was, hoping she was out of danger and knowing that almost
certainly she was not. It was in this anxious, exhausted, wondering state that a dream began to enfold him.

He had the idea that he was hunting for Hattie, trapped inside a giant music box. The inside of the box was like an empty
theater he had peered into in St. Louis. Hattie was hidden
somewhere within, but he could not find her; she was being
held prisoner by a man like Junius Rutherford with mechanical
crab-claw hands. Then into the darkness of the empty seats
there came a weird wind that brought with it a cloud of what
looked like fireflies, luminous tiny insects that were so beautiful to behold that he wanted to reach out and touch them. But
when he did they burned his hand like cinders. He swatted at
them, trying to escape, and when he readjusted his eyes he saw
that on every empty chair there now burned a sleek candle with
even flames rising from them like the voting hands of some dire
and unanimous congress. A door opened, and he saw a figure
he took to be Hattie dragged from the theater and out into the
light. He raced after them, feeling the scorching flecks of the
insects against his face, hearing the hissing of the candles, like
a religious chant.

He knew that he was still inside the music box, but it was
much larger than he had first thought. The door of the theater
opened into the street of a town, a ghost town lit by unknown
means, like the lights he had seen in Mother Tongue's grotto.
Dead people were walking about as if in a trance. Skeletons and
mechanical men and women, like a vast fair of haunted machines. There were folk dressed in historic costumes and all
manner of fantastic creatures from out of fairy tales, while
women in hoopskirts with the same porcelain mask for faces
paraded past in silence.

In the dark of the windows he ran by, he glimpsed things like
torture chambers—people getting their limbs removed, human
bodies with the heads of other animals, pits full of reptiles with

the faces of children. On and on he ran, trying to catch the man who had Hattie—or was it his sister?

Gradually, the light began to change, and he saw that the music box that he thought was a theater and then a town was like another kind of theater yet again. There were living people watching, pointing, ogling the sights—as if the entire maze he was lost in was but one huge medicine show. The people were in costumes of a type he had never seen before. Bright artificial colors, ridiculous shoes. Many of the women were baring obscene amounts of flesh, and everyone seemed obese. The more frantically he explored, the more disgusted he became, for he came to see and smell the overpowering aromas and quantities of the nauseous, tempting food they were devouring. Gorging like maniacs.

In the labyrinth of the automata ghost town, there were islands and lagoons where machine men dressed as pirates fought with swords and fired cannons. Somnolent blank princesses sang to birds and squirrels, whose mouths opened on hinges in perfect time. He saw riverboats like the kind he had ridden on, filled with talking dolls. All the living people were laughing at these distractions, stuffing food into their mouths as if they had never eaten before. The horror of it almost made him forget why he was there, what he was chasing—for in some unspoken way he understood that it was the mechanical creatures and the fantasies unfolding all around that were driving the living people mad with gluttony. Everywhere he turned, there were more frightening visions.

The giant music-box theater, which had turned out to be inside a town, which was really a bigger theater, revealed itself to be a city, swirling and swarming with bloated people in insane colors with masks like clock faces. Hunkered in doorways, like beggars, were rodent forms and filthy derelicts with the tails of lizards. There were trains that whisked by as if they ran on light, and carriages without horses or oxen that looked like eggs or beetles. In the sky overhead were flying machines like those he had envisaged, but inside them were just more people eating and drinking. The women wore next to nothing, and yet street-corner preachers set fire to random passersby. Bodies and baubles hung from the street lanterns—a murder and a sale of some kind were transacted on every corner. And, all the time, Lloyd told himself, "The oddest thing of all is that I know I am still inside the music box."

Still, knowing this did not help him find Hattie. Then he peered out beyond the festering false-face emporia and saw something that held his eye. It was, in fact, something like the Eye. Only in the shape of an enormous building, like a cathedral. Limestone and metallic green, it towered in the distance. Until he saw that it was not a citadel of some kind, nor was it human-made. It trembled rhythmically, like some deep music. It was laced with lightning and rainbows as dark as the skin of the fish he remembered catching in the Licking River back in his other life. Hovering on the horizon like an omen and a promise, he saw in its inverted pyramid shape the complexity of the Ambassadors' master symbol. It was a tornado—heaped and spiraling chaos that somehow retained its form. And at the base, in the gorgeous crisis that anchored it to the earth, was a door—and in the doorway was a girl. *Then the shadow of a jeweled claw reached out to him.* He turned to run and headed for one of the riverboats, for they were most familiar to him. He chose the one that seemed most authentic—and to his astonishment he found himself confronted by his old comrade, St. Ives. The gambler appeared lost in reverie, smoking a cigar and staring down at the water.

CHAPTER 9

A Bend in Another River

EVERYTHING WAS JUST AS BEFORE—THE NIGHT ST. IVES TOLD HIM the story about the hand. "You wonder about it, don't you, boy?" St. Ives asked, and tapped an ash. "How I came by the hand— and how I came to lose my own."

"Y-yes," Lloyd found himself saying. "There's no hiding there's a story behind it." Yet there was something different about this scene. *Indefinably different.* Was the boat moving?

"Well put, lad." The gambler nodded. "And well spoken. Like a gentleman. But I fear if I tell you the truth you will think me mad. Still, you have been an excellent partner. I believe you deserve my trust and may reward me with your discretion." St. Ives lowered his voice and glanced around to see if any other passengers or crew were within earshot. He had not been wearing a hat the night before, but now he was—and a very stylish hat, too.

"A little over ten years ago I used to be the secretary to a very rich man in the East. He valued my memory and my head for calculations. That may be hard for you to imagine, given your skills, but I took the bait. Phronesis Larkshead, or so he called himself then. But that was not his real name, I am sure. Owner of the Enigma Formulary and Gun Works in Delaware. An inventor, a wire-puller. A formidable figure.

"He had the tinge of some sort of acid burn on his face and wore a flat-brimmed hat pulled down low, with a veil, which he claimed offered protection from all his 'substances.' He always kept his skin covered as much as possible in a dark suit without buttons. I used to fancy that his body was riddled with unnatural signs and scars. My initial belief was that one of his experiments had backfired on him. He was forever fiddling with new combinations of chemicals—schemes for weaponry. And other things. Weirder things. He was far, far ahead of his time, was Mr. Larkshead. He had designed and built a mechanical manservant. A sort of butler named Zadoc. What it was powered by I do not know, he would not reveal it—but it was not steam. The device had an almost blank, bland face, but I suspected he had other faces baking. How the thing could see or navigate I have no idea. This was the first of many things I wish I had not discovered, but my fascination got the better of me. His estate was like nothing you can imagine. He called it the Villa of the Enigmas."

"Go on . . ." Lloyd said, feeling the hairs on his neck rise. This was like what had happened before—but not the same. Not the same.

"Well . . . I know this will sound like utter flapdoodle, but he had a colony of live ants from the jungles of South America in a great glass nest. I could not guess why or how he came by them, but I know that he spent a good deal of money keeping them alive in the northern climate . . . and that, as outrageous as it sounds, he had some notion of communicating with them. I could see that he was at work on a grand scheme. There was a whole wing of the estate I was never allowed to enter—and, frankly, I had no wish to, given what was in evidence around me."

"How did you *really* come to work for someone such as that?" Lloyd asked. "Such a person would need no hired head for figures." He had not thought to say that before. But it struck him now.

"Indeed," the gambler smirked. "I wanted to think then that it was because of my abilities. Now I know I was a fool. I believe I was one of his test subjects, without knowing it."

"Test subjects?" the boy queried.

"Aye. I believe I was lured to the estate with the offer of employment, but I think I was given drugs—some kind of powerful narcotic that did not disrupt all perception but yet was responsible for visions. I cannot explain the things I saw elsewise. I witnessed a meeting. Whatever they were, or are, I suspect it is the real force behind his company and his wealth—behind a great deal of other things, too. Things we would do well not to know about."

"That sounds like something far better to know about than not," Lloyd replied.

"Just the kind of young-headed notion that got me into the mess," St. Ives lamented. "What I saw was a group . . . of people, if you like. Who all looked like him. I can't explain it. There were twelve of them in total! Yet they did not seem like individuals. They seemed as one. They had a kind of diagram they conjured out of the air—a mosaic-like puzzle—and they were engaged in some type of ceremony or strategy-planning session. I swear I have never told anyone else this!"

"Where were you hiding while you were watching?" Lloyd wanted to know.

"Well, this may be the most miraculous part!" the gambler whispered. "I saw the whole thing through a bewitched glass cube I found in the library. I had seen the cube before, but it had always been clear and empty. I had assumed it was just some type of mirror made into an art object. There were so many peculiar artifacts about the place, I gave it no special thought, until that day when it came alive. As the scene unfolded, I could not but conclude that Larkshead and the others were assembled in the forbidden wing of the mansion and that I was somehow eavesdropping on them. The images could not have been *inside* the cube. It was some kind of window."

"An interesting deduction," Lloyd said, his mind churning like the river, which was flowing now. "What did you witness?"

"Oh, my young friend . . . I hesitate to tell you. They took off their hats and veils. They were not men—or women, either. They were . . . I know not what. Creatures. Ghosts. Their apparent bodies were but masks, camouflage. Their true forms were hideous and impalpable. As absurd as they appeared, there was a malevolence about them . . . as if their forms were punishment. I felt that malignance radiated through the cube. Their resentment, their envy. Their relentless hunger for other shapes. But I felt that they were still somehow human. Not demons, not inhabitants from some distant star. They were—"

"Shadows of the mind . . . from out of time," Lloyd said, as a nightjar sounded in the distance. "Please tell me all that happened next—and I must know *everything* that happened."

The gambler dropped his smoldering cigar into the river but had regained his composure when he stared at the boy again in the pale light.

"I grew . . . so hypnotized by what I was observing . . . I did not hear that repugnant Zadoc sneak up behind me. The machine subdued me with some kind of sedative delivered by a needle . . . and I was brought before that unholy tribunal . . . awake but unable to resist or escape. Oh, Lord . . ."

"As painful as it is to recall," Lloyd said, squeezing the mechanical hand, "you must tell me everything that transpired. Please."

"They reinstated their body cloaking," the gambler answered, staring down at his boots. "I could not stand to look at them without it, and they seemed to understand this. I could not understand their words, but I gathered that my witnessing their congregation had not been intended. It was some mistake. The cube was fetched. Zadoc was disabled. Things beyond my reckoning were transpiring in that secluded wing of the mansion."

"Be as precise as you can," the boy pleaded.

"I could not look upon their mosaic puzzle and see it clear and whole, but it was certain they could. It wavered and vibrated like something that was alive. It was like a cyclone . . . a labyrinth."

"What happened then? What were you allowed to see—and why?" Lloyd asked with growing impatience.

"*What* I saw was like some jumble of alchemist's dens, a brewery and an insane asylum. I do not know how to put the rest . . . machines I have never known. I have the frightening idea—"

"You think they were making people—or what resembled people," the boy filled in. "You believe you saw a man, with multiples of himself, who was not a man but not female, either, for those gathered were revolting jelly-like forms that you nonetheless regard as human, who were nurturing the growth of some kind of tissue as both a means of concealing themselves to normal eyes and cultivating others—beings who would be taken for people if you passed them in the street but that were not people the way we like to think of them."

"Exactly!" St. Ives exclaimed, catching himself. "This is the strangest thing of all! That you should know! How is it possible? Have you—"

"No," Lloyd answered. "We have seen some of the same magic-lantern pictures. But it was no magic-lantern image that took your hand."

At this the gambler broke down weeping, although he made an effort to stifle himself. "Too right, my young friend! I was experimented on like a dumb animal! I was made to . . . to . . . oh!"

"Tell me," Lloyd commanded.

"I . . . was introduced to a . . . woman . . . an auburn-haired beauty with eyes like sapphires. She was lovely. They wanted me to . . . to mate with her. They wanted to watch. It was so unthinkable! Because I knew—that they had *made* her. Why I was chosen I have no idea."

"That may be the most hopeful thing so far," Lloyd remarked.

"Hopeful! Of what?" the gambler moaned.

"Their technology of survival lags behind their technology of manipulation," the boy replied, gazing out over the flattening water. "If they have to employ animal methods of reproduction, and yet can project images by stealth over distances, that shows they have vulnerabilities. Somehow they need to maintain form, human flesh. It's not sufficient to their purposes to influence and direct—they need to manufacture new vehicles, and any manufacturing process is a continual one. They have not perfected theirs. As monstrous as they may seem to you, they are engineers—and that is something I understand. They still have problems to solve, whatever their religion. That is the hope."

"You scare me, Lloyd. Not like they do—but still . . . the student has become the teacher," the gambler gasped.

"We teach each other," the boy responded. "And some fears are good if they lead to the truth. Now finish your story."

"I was allowed to enjoy the beauty . . . and then . . . they seized me," the gambler said, wincing. "Their forms were flesh and blood enough for that. I felt them searching my mind. They wanted to know what they looked like to me in their other guise. Then they performed surgeries, Lloyd . . . they took my hand . . . and gave me this artificial claw."

"How did you escape?" the boy asked.

"The most unthinkable part of the whole story!" St. Ives coughed. "Zadoc, the mechanical thing, reactivated. He—it—released me while they were in another chamber one afternoon . . . perhaps vivisecting some other poor victim, like a rabbit. I was torn. I was bandaged. But I fled, as fast and as far as I could in that state. I owe my life to the mercy of a machine!"

"Machines that have mercy are hard to think of as machines," Lloyd replied. "The question is, did you escape or were you allowed to escape?"

"I have wondered that myself ever since," St. Ives rasped, still blinking. "But . . . are you not horrified by all that I have told you?"

"I see hope in what you have said—as well as horror," Lloyd replied. "It may be that what happened to you had been planned. Still, it somehow sounds that it did not go quite according to their plan. If things can go against their desires in the heart of their control, that reassures me. And I think it a very encouraging sign that they are worried about physical survival."

"You, young sir"—the gambler shrugged, and then could not control a crest of emotion—"are the son I've never had. Always raising the ante. And then some."

"You taught me what an ante was," Lloyd replied.

"Friends always?" St. Ives said, offering up his mechanical hand once more.

"Partners," Lloyd answered, squeezing down on the metal digits. "This is the biggest mystery of all. Why do you think they gave it to you?"

"Who can say?" the gambler grumbled, a storm of anger and grief filling his eyes. "I would not rule out pure cruelty as their motive. I sensed it in them. Some conspiracy of hatred. A mania. What does your intuition say?"

Lloyd frowned and then stared out across the river to a stand of cottonwoods. "I feel that they are one . . . a different kind of creature than we are familiar with. Of one mind. I sense this being or beast is some holdover from long ago . . . and I feel some shadowy sympathy with all that you have related, which raises the question whether I am in fact who I believe myself to be—or as young as I appear."

"But you are just a child! A boy!"

"Am I? I know how many syllables you have spoken in the last minute. Give me the materials and a bit of time, and I could make this hand. But that is not all. Do you see the dog I am thinking of? Boomer. That was my old dog, buried back in Zanesville. Smell his ragged blanket."

"Oh . . ." The gambler shivered, seeing in his mind . . . smelling . . . "How did you do that?"

"I cannot say," Lloyd answered. "It has something to do with the rapport we have. This is one of the reasons we have done so well at the tables. Seeing the others' cards through my eyes. It is a species of communication like unto the cube you discovered, but the mechanisms that underlie it are obscure to me. I'm now thinking of a number between one and one thousand. What is it?"

"What?" the gambler squawked caught off guard. "Uh, seventy-three."

"Correct," Lloyd replied. "The odds are *very* long against you getting that right. I suspect you may have hidden talents, Mr. St. Ives, which is why we work so well. That may have something to do with why you were chosen. And it may provide some hint as to their larger purpose. You said you could not see the gathering's mosaic diagram whole and clear, yet they or it can. Perhaps the adversary is working to a plan we cannot perceive . . . and we are a part of that plan. The hunger for human form may be part of the struggle to endure so as to fulfill that plan. What I find puzzling is that your hand is a baser technology than what you described in the female you were offered. If they can cultivate a fully fleshed human, real enough for you to find attractive, why bother with these metal joints and hinges?"

"Well, the hand is useful." The gambler shrugged. "For years I hid it in a glove and loathed it. Resented the sensation of being able to direct it. I have no idea how I am able to make it work. It is a part of me, though."

"To graft nerves onto raw metal is no small feat," the boy agreed. "But this may be another hopeful sign—that they have had to become more mechanically ingenious because of some other lack. In any case, you have not finished your story. I can see that the oppression did not leave you when you fled."

Rage gripped the gambler's face. "Too true," he said, sighing. "I went to Boston and into hiding. Two weeks later, I read that an enormous conflagration had swept through the estate. Whether it was an accident or a strategic retreat I cannot say. And what would provoke the need for retreat? It seems like an extravagant price to pay to withdraw, but who knows what resources such an organization or entity has at its disposal?

"Not long after, I learned that the Enigma Formulary and Gun Works had been acquired by a European consortium based in London calling itself the Behemoth Innovation Company. They have empty offices in several American cities, but there is no information about *any* of their directors. I poked and sniffed around a bit—made inquiries and checked records—but there were so many bank ledgers and writs and decrees, deeds and lawyer's gobbledygook, there was no way to find the end of the knot. I withdrew and took up banal bookkeeping for the most colorless mercantiler I could find in Boston, where no one knew me, and I kept the hand concealed as much as I could. In time I came out of hiding enough to migrate West, using what wits I still had left to pursue the trade you found me in. I came to make peace with the hand, though it is an abomination and a constant reminder of the brutality. But it has often saved me from harm, as you have seen, and so it may be an unexpected and unintentional gift."

"Up to now," Lloyd answered. "Get as far away as fast as you can. Somehow I sense I am a lightning rod for these people, this other creature—whatever."

"Say it is not so, Lloyd, please!"

"You may have gotten lucky before, although I understand you may not think so. But your luck may run out at the next encounter. Go far."

"What about you?" the gambler garbled, the hand opening and retracting.

"I am destined for some confrontation of my own. Sooner rather than later, I believe. If you are my friend, you will take my advice and keep the hand hidden."

"I know not what to say," the gambler replied after a moment's pause. "You have shed light brighter than any moon or candle. And you have cast shadows darker and more supple than I have imagined. What should we do if this . . . thing . . . is among us?"

"There is no 'if,' " Lloyd answered. "You told me at the start there was a time to cut and run. That time has found you. It's possible that there are many people throughout the world who have stories similar to yours. Our insane asylums, prisons, and military hospitals may be full of them. But there are chinks . . . like the need to find human form. And they, or it, have some mission of destiny—a master stratagem. That is a strength and weakness, too. Great plans usually fail. On that we can perhaps hang our hats in hope."

"Here's to that then," said the gambler, and tossed his fine brim into the river. "Good night, my friend, however old you are. Tomorrow we will play our last hand, and this hand will be kept under wraps. Perhaps when I reach my new destination I will find someone with the skill and discretion to remove it, as was my first inclination years ago. Sleep well, and may the dreams that find you be your own."

The gambler headed for his stateroom. Lloyd remained on deck, watching the hat floating away in the moonlight. He had forgotten all about the music boxes—he was taken by the vividness of the hat bobbing along on top of the water. It was the vividness of the hat in the river that finally caused him to wake.

I waited for a moment to summon him outside the tepee—into the light of the deeper horror. He felt my call, even groggy and disjointed as he was. At first he imagined it was the creature somehow escaped from its chain and prowling about the camp, sniffing out the new arrivals.

As remarkable as he may have found that specimen, I knew that he would be more surprised to see me. Vague intuitions had flashed like ripples of star-strewn river through his dreams, but this would be absolutely different and decisive. It could cause untold rents in the spiral schema, but I had no choice.

He was a long silent moment longer gathering the concentration and the courage commensurate with his curiosity. Then he appeared—and the image was almost as shocking to me.

To discover yourself standing in the moonlight in waiting is not an easy thing. His jaw cracked, and my green eyes shone back at me.

"What are they? Who—?"

"I think you know too well," I said as simply as I could. "You are not who you think you are. Or where—or when, either."

"But!"

"Shh," I said. "I cannot help the intrusion. And I cannot remain master of the spiral if you resist."

"I'm still dreaming!" he gasped, for what other explanation could there be? Except for—

"You are in a different kind of wilderness than you imagine," I said. "And now I must take your place, because I need a deeper hiding place, and to lay a snare."

"Who?" he hissed, and I could tell that the trauma was already accommodating itself to some terrible new acceptance of the larger hellequinade.

"The Vardogers? The Spirosians?"

I let him gather his wits. Or try to.

"You must go through the door," I said.

"What door?" he demanded. Just as I would.

"One I have made," I answered. "The bridges I will have to build now from inside. You will find it right behind me. And you will understand."

"Are . . . are you a ghost?" he queried, trying to make sense of what was beyond his grasp.

"I would not put it so."

"Am . . . am I . . . a ghost?"

"Say, rather, a hope. A strategy. A necessity. A casualty of war."

"But you can't be real!"

"Real enough."

360 | KRIS SAKNUSSEMM

"But then what am I?"

Who does not seek the answer to that question?

"A desperate measure in a desperate contest. No more can I say that you could fathom."

"What if I refuse?"

"You will not. The truth has come for you, and as difficult as it is to accept, you recognize it, as you do me."

"You're some kind of will-o'-the-wisp!"

I flung one of the stones I had picked up instinctively.

"Ow!" he whined. "Damn thing hit me."

"I have more," I said. "Everything is some kind of will-o'-the-wisp."

"You're a Vardoger trick! I've been trapped!"

"No, it is I who am in the trap. But they will not anticipate me *hiding* in the trap."

He rubbed his eyes, trying to make me go away. An illusion of moonlight, a specter of the mind, a lucid dream. If only the technology were so simple. If only I understood fully how to use it.

At last a hint of a tear escaped from the brilliant green eyes, which was more than a little moving and disconcerting for me to witness.

"Am I going to die?" he asked.

"If life and dreaming are not what you have taken them to be, then how can death be, either?" I replied. "Think what Hattie would do."

"What will become of her?" he asked. And I saw for myself how much he had grown.

"I can say no more about that than you can, now that I am here. I inherit all your uncertainties—save one."

"Is this because of the slave, and the Ambassadors—a punishment?"

"I take responsibility for Mule Christian," I said. "You are released. As to those you call the Ambassadors, they are more an enigma to me than to you. I take responsibility for what happened to them, too, although I suspect I have even less to say about them and their fate than you did in the kite. But now you must face another trial. Remember your teachers—the gambler and the runaway girl. Honor them, even as you doubt me."

Then he did just as I would have done. He rebelled, with all the force of the meaning I had conceived. For that is the wondrous and diabolical nature of the technology. The coming to life. The independence of tactics and vision.

He charged at me, thinking to wrestle me into the oblivion from which he believed I had emerged to supplant him, not seeing that it was more a change of rider. He had no idea that I was the door of which I spoke—and the instant that he touched me he stepped through, fluorescing in a puzzle of hierograms, like fireflies and lost symbols swept into the cyclone.

I crept into the tepee as the last of the luminous hierograms spiraled into vanishing. I was as sorry to see him fade as he was to have seen the twins blown over the river—and not to have said goodbye to Hattie. *Folks like us.*

And now the trial was upon me.

The scent of the interior was a moment in hitting—and when it did it hit hard. Astounding. The depth and the texture.

I straggled into the bedding where the talismanic objects lay secret in their bag. Hephaestus turned from his rumpled sack of sleep and mumbled, then wiped his face and stared straight at me without the slightest hint of the unfamiliar. It was an eye-opening sensation, to say the least.

"You all right, son? You scared?"

Talk about the child being father to the man.

"Indeed I am, Farruh," I said. And indeed I was.

Out in the moon-mad dark of this Enigmerica, I heard the cry of things I knew so well—and the call of things more obscure to me than to all others. My own unknown. So many "squeschuns," as they say in Gullah.

The next day would bring more lightning . . . and thunder. The primordial answer to the lightning's question—the original enigma that set the cyclone swirling. I lay down and closed my eyes, trying to master, for at least a few moments of illusory peace, the alien mechanics of this new sleep.

Rapture rolled over in her blanket. "De preechuh put on 'e shroud whin we beeried Boomer," she said, sighing.

"It's all right, Murruh," I said. "It was just a dream." The last time I would ever say those words.

Boomer.

Poor old Tip. You see the need to be ever mindful? To be mindful of the details? Sometimes it is wise to count the trees before they become a forest. Because if you see a tree clearly enough, others will see it, too. Stampedes start one hoof in the mind at a time. But learn to see the thunder . . . then you can call the lightning down.

Powerful though they were, they had taken the bait. As wasps are drawn to raw meat they had come, and would come closer still. That is the one true trick there will ever really be in time. *Change the boundaries.* Everything genuinely dangerous is afraid of itself, and so cannot resist a mirror.

ABOUT THE AUTHOR

KRIS SAKNUSSEMM is the author of the critically acclaimed novels *Zanesville* and *Private Midnight,* which became a bestseller in Europe, and a collection of short stories entitled *Sinister Miniatures.* His latest works, *Reverend America* and *Eat Jellied Eels and Think Distant Thoughts* will be appearing internationally in 2012. A book of his paintings called *The Colors of Compulsion* is being published in France and Denmark.